follow the Sun;

become the Moon

(novel memoir

of a 1970s "Moonie")

by

A. R. T. Byrd

Artwork and cover by Merri Rose Fink

to Mama Sue

(my true parent)

ISBN 10: 0-9724101-5-5
ISBN 13: 978-0-9724101-5-1

For sales and distribution information contact:

New Hope Press

e-mail: cronkitesue@gmail.com
phone: (850) 653-6965 (leave voicemail)

How did the Rose
ever open its
Heart
& give to the world
all its beauty?
It felt the encouragement of
Light
against its being.
Otherwise,
we all remain
too frightened

Hafiz

Preface

Late summer of 2012 (the year the Mayan calendar ended) I got a phone call from my daughter, followed by a call from her father. The Reverend Sun Myung Moon, a messianic evangelist from Korea, had died on Monday, August 27, at the age of 92. There was no talk of a resurrection (no mysterious disappearance of the body). The news did not report sightings of him by disciples, claims that he had returned to take a walk with them, share a conversation, a meal. He had never said that he would return in the flesh (like Jesus in the gospel stories). The media had often described Sun M. Moon as a "self-proclaimed messiah". However, I had followed him for nearly three years (as a teen and young adult) and never heard him overtly make that claim. He talked about "the coming of the Lord of the Second Advent" sometimes, as if prophesying a future event, or maybe referring to himself in the third person (as Jesus did when he spoke of "the Son of Man"). At other times, when Rev Moon spoke of his mission and message, offering "hope for the future", it was clear to me that he was offering himself (his teaching, his path) as that "hope".

The 1970s were turbulent and magical. Those of us who followed Rev. Moon assumed we were living in "the last days" of biblical prophecy. We believed we were following the messiah of the new age, the Age-of-Aquarius, and we were God's chosen ones. In our own hearts and minds and lives, we were the hard-working, self-sacrificing, symbolic unifiers of all humanity. Unificationists. The media called us "Moonies".

When I heard of Rev. Moon's death, forty years later, I was working fulltime and had little chance to reflect. The *New York Times* published a story the following Sunday, with Rev. and Mrs. Moon's picture on the front page, in the white robes and golden crowns they had worn when conducting mass-weddings. Marriages were arranged, often by Moon, sometimes pairing people from backgrounds so diverse that they would never have met if they had not been swept up by the Unification movement. The official organization was The Holy Spirit Association for the Unification of World Christianity, or simply, the Unification Church (which still exists under various official titles, and in some independent branches, at this writing). I met my children's father in a sub-group, the International One World Crusade. In the

United States (as well as South Korea, Japan, Europe, etc.) during the 1970s, we pounded the streets in droves, selling flowers, candles, etc. and handing out literature. We invited people to our church "Centers", where fulltime members lived communally. There we shared meals with, along with songs and prayers, and taught Rev. Moon's "Divine Principle" on portable, old-style school chalkboards.

"I'm sorry," my 29-year-old daughter said, respectfully (as if Rev. Moon was a friend or family member). She was sorry for my loss, a loss that I had been grieving since before she was born but had barely acknowledged. Maybe she knew something I didn't, sensed something I had buried. This book is my way of acknowledging and sharing that experience (and some of what I gained and lost from it). Though her father and I were "ex-Moonies" before we married, and before our children were born, he and I would not likely have met without the lifelong efforts of Sun M. Moon.

I have been writing about both the positive and negative aspects of my experience, off and on, ever since I joined the Unification Church in 1972. Some of the journal entries I made during the two-and-a-half years that I was a member are included here. Also, my mother, Sue Riddle Cronkite (a novelist who was a newspaper writer and editor during the 1970s), wrote a personal account from which some excerpts are shared. She could have sold her book, "How I got my daughter out of the Moonies", in the mid-'70s, if she had been willing to condense and sensationalize it to suit a popular magazine editor. I have chosen, with my mother's permission, the excerpts used here (and left them unchanged, as I have the name, Sue Cronkite, which she wrote under during that time). Some personalities and events in this book are historically significant and accurate. (This is not overall, however, a documentary.)

Sun Myung Moon and the Unification Church were very controversial, around the time that I left the organization. Published stories of disillusionment abounded (one about me coming home, in my local paper, having been no exception). However, everything that I read or heard fell short of conveying the heart of that experience. I have long felt compelled to share something more authentically representative of the very young, idealistic Unificationists that I knew, for whom this was primarily a calling of the heart. So I have put my heart into this work, cherishing memories of the friends that I called "brothers and sisters".

This is not intended to deny problems inherent in "cult" experiences, communicated by many. I have written openly about my own issues here, and how I work through them. The early Unification Church in America was not a way of life that carried well into adulthood in our society. For some, however, it was a training ground.

I have changed most names and left out some details, etc. (out of respect for the privacy of those who mostly went back to living more ordinary lives after this extraordinary experience). A mind-boggling number of people, and stories, comprised this journey. For readability, some characters are fictionalized composites (that any number of my old friends, Unificationists, or ex-Moonies may identify with or think they see themselves in). When my brother read an early draft, he said he wished I had used his real name (for the character who is my character's brother). Some others may think they recognize themselves here and may have the same, or an opposite, reaction. Ironically, I have found that some fictionalizing (writing in third person at times, for example) has helped me to be more honest and open (less self-conscious or concerned with what others might think). I am not the same personality that I was in the 1970s. Others could say the same. Regardless of past conflicts, I have ended up feeling mostly love, compassion, and forgiveness (where needed) for those who inspired these stories and the characters that are reincarnated here.

So much of what is available, about Sun M. Moon and his church, is negative. "Bad press" written from an angle to arouse, excite, and sell. My book is sensational at times, but not sensationalistic in orientation. I am not offering the adrenaline rush of a cult thriller. Nor do I intend to promote any particular religion. I am sharing my experience. Though the stories of others may intersect with mine, this is not exactly anybody else's story. (For me, that is what makes writing and reading worthwhile.)

This may be categorized as "fiction" or "non-fiction". It is both historical fiction and creative memoir. I do not expect it to be considered a literary work of art. I have used literary tools when they served to help me tell my story, but it does not fit a prescribed literary form throughout. Although I studied English and journalism and have worked as a copy editor and proofreader, there were rules I simply chose to break. The writing was done on-and off for decades, so that I brought different styles to the typewriter (and journal, and finally the computer) at different times.

So, what I am offering here is like a patchwork quilt, with cherished scraps of memories saved over a lifetime, pieced together, and embroidered, in my golden years. It is a coming-of-age story, a heroic adventure, a love story (or two, or three...), a bittersweet slice of historical pie, and a shared journey toward healing, wholeness and maturity. Enjoy!

milieu

While I had been growing up, the 1960s had ushered in new levels of freedom for women and other minorities, via the civil rights movement, the rise of feminism, and the changes in attitudes and popular culture brought about by "the peace movement". Folk singers, such as the young Bob Dylan, had expressed it with words like "The times they are a-changing" in a song that warned parents that "your sons and your daughters are beyond your command". A few years later, with the start of the 1970s, the times had changed. Another popular songwriter, Carole King, was singing "I feel the earth move under my feet". People were still rocking and reeling from the aftershocks of the '60s.

Though my friends were on my mind far more than the politics of the day, 1972 was an election year. Richard Nixon, a Republican, was president and running for re-election. American involvement in the Viet Nam war (Nixon's war, according to some at this point) was winding down, and Nixon was making more promises that he would get the U.S. out of the war completely. I would turn eighteen one month before the November election, when 18-year-olds would be allowed to vote for the first time (formerly a right given only to those twenty-one and older). "Old enough to fight; old enough to vote!" was the slogan.

Most young people had been leaning to the left ever since the obligatory military draft, and the uprisings against the war. My "hippy" friends were planning to vote for McGovern, a liberal Democrat who had long positioned himself against the war. My mother, Sue Cronkite, who was Assistant State Editor for a major, metropolitan newspaper in the deep South, said the paper was endorsing Nixon and she would most likely vote for him. I respected my mother, but I had not yet decided who to vote for. Nixon (not a beloved personality, but popular amongst conservatives for his anti-communist stance) had gained some respect from liberals in recent times for uncharacteristic moves, such as legalizing the youth vote and talking to China. Nixon even started the Environmental Protection Agency. He also signed Title IX (against gender discrimination in federal funding of educational institutions). And Nixon changed economic policies midstream, allowing for more government spending to ease inflation.

So, some liberals were no longer sure their conservative president was all that bad. No other American president had ever smiled into the slanted eyes of a Chinese dictator, much less extended his hand so personally on that far eastern shore. "Yes! World Peace! Right on, man! Go Nixon!" were some of the phrases uttered by unlikely allies, including my friends (who would be more likely to vote for Nixon, come November, than they would yet admit).

Only a few weeks into the summer of 1972, however, the president would slowly-but-surely start earning the nickname "Tricky Dicky", with a criminal act that would not be linked to him soon enough to stop him from being re-elected in the fall. The ugliness of the war would start to be replaced by the ugliness of the Watergate era, with a break-in at the building where the Democratic National Committee had its campaign headquarters in Washington, D.C. Then the mistrust of the leaders of the greatest democratic nation in the history of the world would go on for years, until many of Nixon's cohorts had been indicted for "covert operations" and he had resigned to avoid the impeachment that angry Americans wanted. People were tired of dishonesty, hypocrisy.

Meanwhile, two weeks before the Watergate break-in, with summer holding all the promises of a sunrise for students on their summer breaks, the whole American scene was already in flux from the cultural revolution of the 1960s. In the sunny summer of '72, every American institution (the traditional family not being the least of these) stood on shaky ground.

People were searching. Another still-popular '60s hit was a Dylan song saying, "The answer my friend is blowing in the wind," which inspired people to open up and listen. There was, indeed, something in the air. Freedom had taken on a new freshness for Americans, and it felt good to be alive during that time. People were exploring, trying to "find" themselves. However, as the fresh winds of freedom blew, some found life's choices overwhelming. The music alone was energizing but offered larger-than-life questions along with few and sometimes simplistic answers. John Lennon, a former Beatle, created a whole new world in his song "Imagine", which offered radical ideas (no countries or religions to divide humanity) but offered no concrete solutions as to how his imagined utopia could come about. George Harrison, another former Beatle, had joined the Hare Krishnas and had a hit song entitled "My Sweet Lord", which was as puzzling to the traditional Western world (whose "Lord" was Judeo-Christian) as it was inspiring to the younger generation. Some young Americans who had joined the Hare Krishnas were starting to be a more common sight, selling incense on street corners, with shaved heads and traditional Hindu dress. On the same street corners stood long-haired "Jesus freaks", handing out tracts with dire warnings and cartoonish drawings of hell-fire and end-times, along with "easy steps to salvation". Some "Children of God" seemed more intent on looking like Jesus than acting like Him.

"What next?" people were wondering.

The younger generation had already tried to take over the country (if not the world), half-a-decade earlier, when "The Summer of Love" happened in San Francisco and beyond, essentially generating a cultural revolution. By the early 1970s it seemed that the sentiments from the sixties had worked their way into popular culture to such an extent that what had been important ideals, to some revolutionaries, had become little more than the jingle-jangle of radio ads and TV commercials. (A soft-drink commercial had a diverse group of people singing, "I'd like to teach the world to sing in perfect harmony.") The newspapers printed Peter Max's colorful psychedelic artwork, with pop-poetry captions, in their cartoon sections.

An eighteen-year-old college student, home for the summer of 1972, I struggled to make my leftover flower-child dreams come true. (The prayer that follows was written in one of my early journals the previous summer, when I was seventeen, before I went away to college and before I had ever heard of the Unification Church and Reverend Sun Myung Moon.)

Dear Heavenly Father...
As I sit in the midst of tall grass and scattered flowers,
I stare at a slow-moving stream
and I feel the dew of twilight
cleansing my soul.
As I gaze in awesome wonder at
the splendor of Your creation,
I am filled with Your spirit
and I have a sudden inner peace
that makes me think...
You gave us a wonderful world,
a world of beauty and love,
but You also gave us individuality:
You gave us the choice
of how to live our own lives.
We can cherish and respect Your creation
by enjoying the natural & beautiful
things that You have given us;
Or we can take them for granted,
polluting our air and waters
& littering their sandy shores
with the products of our stupidity.
We can love our fellow man,
Each and every One,
without seeing first
his color,
his social class,
the length of his hair,

or the difference of his beliefs
from our own.
 Or we can hate
anyone who does not choose
to live just as we do;
And still claim to believe in Freedom.
You sent Your son
as an everlasting example
of how our lives
should be lived…
A life lived for others,
a life ruled by Love.
Dear Father,
You have taught us through Your son
that Love is the only answer
to the problems
that humans face
in this life.
My prayer is
that Your holy spirit
will keep this Love
constant in my soul,
And that somehow
my life can be a contribution
to the peace and contentment
of our world.
Amen
A.R.T. 1971

BOOK I

Follow the Sun

Part I

Moonstruck

It was the highest of highs, the lowest of lows, the summer of '72. Arti Rose Riddle was a long-necked white bird of a girl. Seen at water's edge, one might have been startled at her beauty and delicate grace. So solitary. So slow-moving and careful. Surely, she would get whatever she was seeking, even as her long legs tread out deeper than most. Yet one who looked long and hard enough might notice something slightly awry, askew, in the way that her head was cocked, and she held one wing higher than the other (as if tense for flight, or maybe broken). A predator might take a chance at her but would most likely be surprised by her sudden flight, large-winged and magnificent.

.

"on our way home . . ."

A summer breeze blows, fresh and new as a June bride, scattering wildflower seeds down an Appalachian hillside and across a campus lawn. Arti Rose's roommate Vera Montgomery, alias "Sunshine", pulls her yellow Volkswagen Bug up to the entryway of the brownstone dormitory that has been their home for the past nine months, puts it in park, and gets out. Sunshine's unbound breasts bounce off her tall, lean, t-shirt and blue-jean covered frame as she walks around to unlock the trunk. Arti Rose stands at the top of the wide, steep steps. She is wearing a homemade cotton sundress with a deep blue background, smattered with little red flowers, tiny white dots at their centers. Arti Rose tosses thick and wavy, dark auburn-brown locks back, behind fair shoulders that look too narrow to carry as many bags and bundles as her slender arms can manage to lift or drag from their pile on the curved portico. The stately old brownstone dorm has been her first home, on this earth, outside the womb and the various houses around the Southeastern United States that her mother has raised her in.

The home Arti Rose is about to travel to won't be an old Southern Victorian fixer-upper in a historic district this time. It won't even be a ranch-style brick-and-stucco in the suburbs, like the one they were living in when she graduated from high school the previous year. Her mother, recently divorced, has rented an apartment on the outskirts of the same suburban area (so that Arti Rose's younger siblings are at least in schools with some of their old friends from church).

Mama is in The News

The petite and feisty 39-year-old redhead, busy at her desk in the newsroom, is barely aware that her daughter is on her way home (though instinctively, subconsciously Sue Cronkite knows, as she has been distracted by thoughts of her family, especially her eldest child, all day). Sue did manage to get Arti Rose to answer the phone (in the hallway of her dorm) not too long ago. She knows her daughter will be coming home one day this week but isn't sure which day.

Meanwhile, Mr. Walters, Editor of the big-city newspaper where Sue works, is making the rounds in the expansive newsroom, like some ruler surveying his kingdom. Sue pretends not to notice her boss, looking down at an article the new reporter, Patrick McMulligan, just handed her. The new horn-rimmed reading glasses propped on the end of her nose (first pair she's really needed, instead of just wearing glasses to look older and smarter like she did with her first newspaper jobs) magnify a multitude of mistakes that Sue, the Assistant State Editor, will need to correct before she can turn the article in to the copy desk.

"What's that, Cronkite? Something from the new guy?" Mr. Walters takes the piece of typing paper from her hand and gives it a glance.

"Not ready yet, Mr. Walters."

"I can see that." The old gentleman peers at the paper through thick spectacles. "It's full of errors. Interesting story, though. Well, make it snappy. The paper won't wait past the next sunrise for young Mick over there to say what he's got to say. Right Mick?"

"It's Patrick. Sir." a young man at a nearby desk pipes up.

"Patrick McSomething, isn't it?"

"McMulligan. Sir."

"See? I knew it was some Micky-Mac name. Okay, Patrick. I'll give you a mulligan, if you catch my drift. Undoubtedly Ms. Cronkite can clean your story up proper for our fine newspaper. But you may want to start putting your dictionary to work."

"Yes Sir," Patrick says, his fingers perched on the typewriter keys in front of him.

Sue gets to work with a red pen, dotting Patrick's I's and crossing his T's. But her emotions keep welling up, keeping the back of her brain busy with thoughts of her eldest daughter, her family, their history, their future and how she might manage that (or try).

Just for today, Sue thinks as her boss walks away. *If Arti Rose shows up at the apartment...*

Sue's other two kids are out of school for the summer, so somebody will be at the apartment to let Arti Rose in. If not, Sissy will likely be in the pool with her friends, and Arti Rose will have to walk past the pool to get to the open stairwell that goes up to their second-floor apartment. Sissy leaves the key under the mat, but she's supposed to keep the door locked and not have any visitors in while Sue is at work. Sue trusts Sissy, maybe too much, but she's not sure she trusts her teeny-bopper friends. Some of them are a little older than Sissy and trying to grow up too fast. One girl is so wound up every time she comes over, that Sue suspects she is on drugs. Her Daddy shot himself, and Sissy said "he was a speed freak". Sue can't bring herself to be unkind to the girl but tries to set boundaries for Sissy. Sue's sixteen-year-old son, David, has gotten a job. So, Sue is glad Arti Rose will be home soon; she can keep an eye on Sissy.

She must get this story cleaned up by deadline, and she has piles of other copy on her desk to be edited. That boyish-looking new reporter is sharp as a tack (and Sue struggles to keep her eyes, and her mind, off him), but she wishes he could spell. And his grammar is far from conventional. It's like Patrick has invented his own language, and Sue is his interpreter and translator. She glances up at his wavy brown hair and compact, muscular back, tensed as he pounds the keys of his typewriter only a few desks away from her in the large, open, busy newsroom. Despite his immaturity, Patrick seems a nice person. Maybe if she had found one like that when she was young, Sue daydreams. Maybe she'll find the right one yet; she's not *too* old.

Sue looks around the newsroom. Mr. Walters has returned to the editorial offices, to a closed-door area (located just past the managing editor's office which is surrounded by a big glass wall of windows clouded with cigar smoke). Mr. Walters is the Editor of editors, a cut-above. Sue won't let him down. He gave her the best editorial position he could when she came back to the city recently, after her divorce.

Sue wonders if she might be farther up the ladder in the newsroom by now, if she hadn't allowed Dick (her recently exed husband) to side-track her with his attempt at semi-retirement in rural Florida last summer. How she ever thought she could work with that control-freak in a crossroads store in the sticks, she can barely fathom (even if it was in the beloved county where she grew up).

Being a single mother is not easy. It is hard to survive living in a continual state of not having quite enough money. Taking another sip of coffee, Sue gratefully re-focuses on her work. At least she is back with the well-established, respected, big-city newspaper. Maybe she'll get a raise or promotion if another editorial position opens up.

The mother Arti Rose is going home to (the mother who *is* her home) grew up in a backwoods (and sometimes socially backwards) area of the Florida panhandle ("a hop, skip, and a jump" from the state line). Her origins were humble, but Sue was proud, a cut above, the leader of the pack. She was a cheerleader who read every book she could get her hands on and got out of the rural farming community as fast as she could.

As soon as she graduated from high school, Sue had escaped with a handsome young man, seven years older than her. Charlie had come home after WWII and some time in the army stateside, but he had not been satisfied to work in the cotton mill for long (just long enough to meet Sue's widowed, working mother, who'd introduced the future couple). Charlie had found a better-paying, unionized job in a Northern factory. Sue had followed him there, started college, and married him. However, Sue (depressed by the long, freezing winter, and joking that she did not want to have a "Yankee baby") had soon come home (to the deep South where her Mama was) to give birth to Arti Rose. Charlie's mother and sisters were there too. There would be plenty of open arms. Sue would have to quit college, but maybe she could still write the novels she imagined (while voraciously consuming every book she could get her hands on).

First, they moved into the "cotton-mill village" with Charlie's parents. The bungalow was clean and tidy, but very small. There were only two bedrooms, and Charlie's youngest sister still lived at home. They slept in a room back of the kitchen that was supposed to be a dining-room. The dining room table went into the shed in the back yard and came out on special occasions. There was a table in the kitchen anyway, and a picnic table out back. However humble, their first room together as a family was sunny and pleasant, with flowered curtains and the love of extended family flowing through (and cousins dropping down to play, as Arti Rose began to crawl and toddle).

Charlie did not want to work in the low-paying non-unionized, deep-Southern mills, like his parents (who had once considered it a move up, from being share-croppers). Charlie had a winning smile and a firm handshake, which got him hired here and there. But he hopped from job-to-job, torn between laboring jobs and sales. He was not especially good at sales, but he liked dressing nicely. He loved cars and was a natural mechanic but hated to get greasy. His mother had always taken pride in him as her best-looking child and dressed him accordingly. ("A dirt-road sport" was the term.) Even in the army Charlie had been assigned to jobs that allowed him to show off his good looks. He had guarded the Tomb of the Unknown Soldier and modeled for U.S. Army recruiting posters. He was flattered but ashamed about not fighting. Then they had assigned him to help deliver dead soldiers home. Charlie knew it was an important job that took guts, and he was honored to do it. Not that he would ever brag about such a thing, but he could feel personally proud about having been chosen to serve in that way. Most of the folks he helped take those dead boys home to were common people, like himself. Charlie shared their seemingly contradictory characteristics of pride and humility. He held his small frame with the bearing of a prince and had the dark and handsome look of the most romantic actors of the day. But Charlie's ears were almost too big, he talked with a twang, and sometimes found himself at a loss for words. Still, he was a charmer. He had a winning smile and a country-boy way of keeping things light. So, Charlie easily got sales jobs, but he did not have the cunning or verbal savvy to close many deals.

Sue never found herself at a loss for words. For as long as she could remember, Sue had always intended to write books (and would eventually get around to that). She had tried scribbling in notebooks when her new baby napped. But when Arti Rose's daddy started hanging out in the back room of the local Veterans Hall (instead of going to work) and gambled away the money they had saved to buy a house, Sue got a job. First with the telephone company and then with the local newspaper. Later, when Arti Rose was starting kindergarten, Sue bought and ran a small-town newspaper in the Florida panhandle.

20

Sue kept that post for several years before divorcing Charlie. A year after that she moved south of The South with her second husband, Dick (an older, widowed man from the cool, blue North, that she had met while covering a national convention which he was presiding over).

Sitting at her big-city news desk now, amidst the brains and bodies of mostly men and all the revulsions and attractions they engender in her (tensions mostly released in the humor their verbal skills help them to harvest and translate into banter that makes the job fun, and sublimates their sexuality), Sue feels a twinge of her deep-seated Baptist guilt. Divorce had been against her religion. Now she's done it twice. She doesn't regret her recent divorce, but she sometimes regrets the first one.

Maybe it was a mistake, Sue thinks, *taking Arti Rose from her father at the tender age of ten.*

Sue remembers being in love with her own "Daddy" at that age, before being a teenager. On some level, Sue still carries fear that she will eventually have hell-to-pay for ripping Charlie's girl away. The kid clashed with Sue's second husband. But, otherwise, so-far-so-good (and knock-on-wood). Arti Rose has yet to be a problem-child.

Looking around the newsroom now, thinking about how unpredictable males can be, Sue quickly talks herself out of the Baptist guilt. Her intelligent, "Scotch-Irish" father had taught her to take all those church rules with a grain of salt. "They mean well," he had said. Craving the sense of community, Sue had never stopped going to church for long; but her spirituality was private. Her beliefs were her own. Now she has children to raise, and work to do. She cannot let the funk of guilt get her down for long. That would be succumbing to the brainwashing that has historically kept women and poor people down. Sue is a natural and early feminist, daughter of a mother who had to go to work to pay the land taxes when Sue's older, WWI veteran and gentleman-farmer father had died.

Sue's marriages had happened in the 1950s and early '60s, an era of change for women. Neither one of her husbands had wanted Sue to work outside the home. It was a matter of pride then, for men to provide for their families, and a source of shame if it appeared that they could not. Sue loved the domestic arts as much as any woman of her generation, but she could never confine herself to the nest for long.

Something would always tip the scales in that balance of power with the male who tried to rule the roost. Young or old, male egos ripening or rotting on the vine, the ones she had picked just turned sour when they had too much power (or too little). And Sue had her own pride to deal with. Her children did too; so there had been drama in their family life. They were all fighters, and Sue was tired of it. "Love and Peace" was the popular slogan of the day, and Sue intended to make it the theme of her home life with her children.

Both of her husbands had spurred Sue's independent nature, and she always ended up back in the news business. At work she dealt with another set of "male chauvinist pigs" (the 1960s term for the syndrome), though she rarely referred to her coworkers that way except in jest. Sue took her share of their overbearing ways. She worked on the "Women's Page" when she first got her own desk at a major, metropolitan newspaper. After having been Editor-in-Chief of her own weekly, Sue learned what it felt like to be one of the token females on the staff of a daily, segregated in a section of the paper not considered important by the newsmen.

Now it is 1972. Sue is surrounded by males in the newsroom, and in charge of many of them. She is doing what used to be considered a man's job, and they still pay her less. But that is okay for now (a battle she'll put off). She can pay her own rent, and she is looking for a house, a real home for she and her children.

They are enough of a family. Sue's children do not need some man lording over them. Her son should be free to wear his hair as long as he likes. Her daughters should not have to fight for every ounce of respect, for their rights to speak out against arbitrary and restrictive rules. They are like she was, when her father died and her mother went to work in the cotton mill and the shirt factory and Sue had to grow up fast.

They are smart and conscientious and independent, Sue thinks as she edits copy at her newsroom desk, reassuring herself that her kids are fine.

Sue's Arti Rose

"You raised yourself," Mama Sue would tell Arti Rose years later.

That was partly true. There had been the grandmothers and aunts in the earliest years. Then there had been a few "maids" who kept house and served as nannies while Sue worked. Later there were the older stepsisters that came with Sue's second marriage. For the most part, however, from the time Arti Rose excelled at reading, writing, and arithmetic in her early school years, Sue had largely left the girl to her own devices. Working full-time, with long hours and the cross-town commutes to the suburbs in Arti Rose's middle and high school years, Mama Sue didn't have much choice. In both marriages, she had ended up the primary breadwinner. Sue never meant it to be that way. It was just survival-of-the-fittist, and she was the fittist. Like a walking stick of dynamite, she was a red-headed blow to some struggling male egos.

Now Sue worries sometimes. Thoughts flow through her mind like the wind, changing directions, sometimes colliding, stirring up storms. *Maybe I should never have left Charlie; children need their father. But I'd had enough. He was irresponsible. And he would never have left me alone if I hadn't married Dick. I thought Dick was more of a grown-up. At his peak. I didn't see his midlife crisis looming on the horizon. Maybe I should have left him sooner. So many blow-ups may have taken their toll.*

Mama Sue had always been proud of her children. It had hurt to have Dick belittle them, when he was at his worst. She had always tried to build them up. If she could fix anything about Arti Rose, Mama Sue would have her be more proud, less shy. But even painful shyness was a beautiful trait when worn by Arti Rose, her head bent gracefully as a flower under the weight of beauty. Sue had tried, for a while in the early years, to shape Arti Rose up a bit, get her to stand up straight and carry herself proudly. It didn't seem to matter, however, how many times Sue gently guided her little daughter to stand against a wall or closed door, tenderly pressing her head against the surface and turning her tiny, rounded shoulders back until they touched what was behind them. Even with words of encouragement, Arti Rose would walk away with her shoulders turned forward, ducking her head, blushing shyly.

Yet the girl would say her piece in most any argument, the blush of shyness turning to red-faced passion or righteous anger.

Sue had confidence in her eldest child, though Arti Rose was not exactly the alpha she-wolf, leader-of-the-pack sort that Sue had always been. Arti Rose had spent hours doing cheers with her neighborhood friends, just for fun. But she had never been able to do the cartwheels or other gymnastics required to try out for the squad. Those clarinet and baton lessons had not served to make her a majorette in the marching band either. But Mama Sue had never made a big deal about any of that. Arti Rose always seemed to hold her own, in her own way.

Sue and Charlie had won contests, doing all the gymnastics that went with dancing to big-band music, and later the "jitter-bug". The clarinet had been a popular instrument then. A decade later, Sue had picked one out for Arti Rose's tenth birthday, when the school offered band as an elective. Sue had picked the girl's backyard birthday party as a time to introduce Dick to her eldest. She had even wrapped a red hat for her daughter, with his name on it (which did not fool the girl). Then, when Arti Rose (who had already been playing a recorder in music class) put the clarinet together and started to try playing a simple tune for her friends, just for fun. Mid-performance, Dick took the instrument from her, turned the mouthpiece around backwards, and started instructing Arti Rose. She never liked Dick after that. Arti Rose also hated her band teacher (another male midlife-crisis case) who picked on her and kept her after school, seeming to relish her contentiousness.

Of course, Mama Sue had cheered for Arti Rose at that first performance, and every one that followed. The clarinet squeaked and squealed when the girl practiced, for several years. But when they moved during her first year of high school, Arti Rose was excited that her new school had sewing as an elective. She'd dropped band class and put the clarinet away for good (to the relief of the tired ears of grumpy old "Daddy Dick", and the family dog).

Arti Rose had always been a music-lover though, and that never ceased. She sang and danced around the house, choreographing little skits for her siblings and the neighborhood kids to perform for their parents around holidays. Sue sometimes felt that there was some talent she should have helped her daughter develop more, though she'd hardly had time to think about it...Maybe Arti Rose would have made a pianist, if they had stayed in one place long enough to own one. They'd had a piano in the farmhouse Sue grew up in, and during visits "home" in the early years, Arti Rose had entertained herself playing "Chop-sticks" over and over (and "Heart & Soul" when someone would join her on the piano bench).

The piano bench, with a lid that lifted, had stored sheet music that Sue's father had used for her music lessons. But even the most cheerful tunes had taken on sour notes when young Sue's originally gentle "Daddy" went crazy and stayed up nights with his headaches, playing like a madman. The autopsy had said it was a brain tumor, probably from the mustard gas her father (twenty years older than Sue's mother) had been exposed to in WWI. With all the piano lessons from her Daddy, along with his encouragement of his little "prodigy", the only songs Sue could remember as an adult were Chopsticks and Farther Along ("we'll know all about it; farther along we'll understand why").

Arti Rose had begged her mother to play those songs when they visited the old farmhouse (where Sue's mother continued to live until she remarried in 1960). Sue would play a few songs standing but never lingered for long, never sat on the bench where Arti Rose spent hours whenever they traveled to the farmhouse that Sue had called "home" (now burned down from a fireplace accident that, fortunately, had not taken any lives, only memories, good and bad, of a different time and way of life).

Anyway, even if Sue could hardly bear a piano, she had intended to buy one for Arti Rose. At least the girl had sung alto in the church youth-choir. Her voice was not powerful, and she didn't have much of a range. But Sue had learned, singing harmony in the car with her daughter during the trips back home, that Arti Rose had a careful ear. Her sweet voice blended in just fine, and Arti Rose had looked lovely standing with the second row of the choir.

Maybe Arti Rose will sing in the church choir again, Sue Cronkite thinks, sitting at her desk at The News, with her daughter on her way home. *If that is something she wants to do.*

Sue wants her children to be who they are and do what they

want to do, and she thinks encouraging them to make positive choices will be enough. She never liked Dick's way, as he sometimes went from instructing them about what he thought they should do, and how, to criticizing them personally (especially when they did not agree with him). Sue, on the other hand, repects children and fears that words uttered in criticism of a child may become self-fulfilling prophecy. Mama Sue had the "criticize the behavior, not the child" philosophy, before psychologists were touting it.

"Children are people," Sue has often said. She had to say it way too often in her ongoing battle with her recent ex.

Arti Rose had never looked like a fighter, but the girl had risen to the occasion and held her own in some arguments with "Daddy Dick". She had even taken a few licks without making a big deal out of it. Bruises were easily explained by a girl who got out and played ball in the neighborhood, with her brother's rough and tumble friends.

Sue had gone to a lawyer during her lunch hour, the last time her ex hit Arti Rose. In that incident he had not hit her in the usual "spanking" way (which was an acceptable parenting practice at the time) but on her face (which was far from acceptable, to Sue). The blossoming teen had confronted Dick when he had yelled at her pubescent brother while they were all getting ready for church. Arti Rose had gone in Davie's room to check on him after she'd heard Dick yell. Her little brother, ever the sufferer of growing-pains, was crying while trying to force his growing feet into the "Sunday shoes" he'd gotten months earlier, for Easter. Last time Davie had complained, Sue had said he could wear his tennis shoes. But Dick (who insisted the boy dress like him, and wear a military-style haircut) had disagreed. Arti Rose was tired of the torture and could more easily take it herself than to have her younger siblings mistreated. The girl had charged, red-faced, into their bedroom, where Dick was tying his tie.

Arti Rose came close in the small, modern bedroom of the ranch-style rental, which was crowded with antique furniture. She stepped between Dick and the full-length mirror where he had been checking his tie. Arti Rose was a skinny little thing but tall for her age, and she had yelled right in her stepfather's face, as loudly as she had heard him shouting at her younger brother.

"YOU should buy Davie a new pair of shoes instead of yelling at him!" she said.

The way Arti Rose said it was too commanding a tone, too accusatory and challenging for the domineering old male to take without reacting. He had hit her quick, without thinking. Sue, in her slip, had been choosing a dress from the closet when she had seen Arti Rose suddenly come flying and tumbling across the bed. She'd moved quickly between her daughter and her husband, so that he would have had to hit her if he got carried away. Dick knew better than to hit Sue, but he might as well have. The damage was done.

Sue had intended to leave him, and she let Dick know that in no uncertain terms. But while she was talking with the lawyer, Dick was talking with the kids, apologizing and getting their sympathy. By the time Sue got home from work, he had them under his spell. Ironically, Arti Rose had talked her out of divorcing him then. He used to say Arti Rose was "a glutton for punishment". Dick had a whole collection of old sayings like that. Sue had originally hoped Dick would be a more responsible, mature mate than Arti Rose's father had been. At least Dick had a good career when Sue married him, but that had quickly peaked and declined (wounding his ego and making him meaner).

"He's just sad, Mom," Arti Rose had said. The 14-year-old had covered the bruise on her face artfully, with make-up she had learned to apply at a department store Charm School she and her best-friend had attended on Saturdays. "Look at him. He's getting old. Where would he go? Anyway, he said he was sorry."

Ironically, Arti Rose's attitude of forgiveness did not feel masochistic or weak in any way. Somehow, though Sue could still see the bruise under the teenager's make-up, she saw no aura of woundedness. It was Dick who appeared broken. They had stood up to him.

Dick seemed easier to live with after that. So, Sue had let it go for three more years. She couldn't really afford to go back to the lawyer anyhow. But while Arti Rose was away at college, Dick went too far. Lording over the kids had been bad enough, but he started trying to lord over Sue. He put her through another move, derailing her career. Then, at the country crossroads store and gas-station he had bought from her own mother and stepfather, Dick tried to be Sue's boss.

That was worse than when her first husband had tried working for her at the small-town weekly Sue had owned in her mid-twenties.

Charlie had been such a lousy employee (incapable of operating the clunky, metal line-o'-type printer, and untrustworthy as a too-handsome door-to-door subscription salesman). Sue had to fire her own husband (the father of her children). This time, a decade later, nobody fired anybody. Sue quit the job, and the marriage to Dick.

So, Sue was a "divorcee", for the second time in her life, starting over as a 39-year-old single mother, working as Assistant State Editor on the professional ladder she had left briefly. Life was harder, financially, without a second income from an adult partner. It had been worth it though, finally beating Dick (after all the beatings, more often psychological than physical, that Sue and her children had taken from him).

Sue was just glad the paper took her back, even if it meant less pay. Now someone else would likely get the Managing Editor's post she had hoped might finally be filled by a woman. She thought Mr. Walters believed women should receive equal pay for equal work and dreamed of herself being lifted above the proverbial glass ceiling. Meanwhile Sue had a stimulating profession. Her sixteen-year-old son had a part-time job, and Arti Rose could get a summer job.

Arti Rose was different, but she was smart enough and pretty enough, maybe even feisty enough to do just fine, her mother had long reasoned (focusing increasingly on her work, her friends, her own life outside the series of homes she had raised her children in). That sweetness, kindness the girl possessed endeared her to most and was even an odd sort of defense against bullying. Young Sue, as a child, would more likely have socked a bully in the eye, somewhere along the dirt road between school and her rural home. Bullies, not seeing any sort of threat or challenge in the girl's mild demeanor, loved Arti Rose. Half converted, talked down from their temper fits, bullies had followed Arti Rose home since she had insisted on walking home from school in the first grade. Being kind and sympathetic, and a bit of a misfit herself, the girl had always attracted an odd assortment of misfit friends that seemed to look out for each other. And generally, Arti Rose could be trusted to look after her younger siblings. Sue had let herself quit worrying too much about Arti Rose a long time ago.

1972 is something else though. Sue seemed to be worrying about her children more than ever lately. Arti Rose turned eighteen in

'71, so legally she is not a child anymore. Some of her freaky friends had begun to startle Sue Cronkite a bit, getting her attention. But Arti Rose had a right to choose her own friends.

It will be years, however, before Mama Sue will admit to herself, and say to her daughter, "You raised yourself." Sue is still under the impression that she is raising Arti Rose. She brags about her daughter all the time, shows her co-workers at *The News* the wallet-sized, studio senior-portrait of the photogenic young lady, tells them Arti Rose writes for the college paper at State U. She also painfully but proudly writes the checks for tuition, room and board, books, and a meal ticket. But Arti Rose's grades have come down; she even made a few Fs (for the first time ever). And some of her friends look like dirty hippies, smell like pot, and say the F-word way too casually for Sue Cronkite's taste. She tries not to let her ruffled feathers show. After all, she is the cool Mom, not exactly a hipster but certainly far less conservative than most suburban, Southern mothers.

If Sue could rename herself (which she has a few times, in those earliest and yet-unpublished autobiographical novels), Pride would be her name. Pride motivated her to divorce both of her husbands. Pride motivates her to do positive things as well. She is driven by pride. Pride is her strength, and her weakness. Her oldest daughter is one source of the pride that defines her (though Sue barely realizes this because it has not yet been significantly challenged). Pride has carried Sue forward for a long time, with that ever-growing list of accomplishments, credentials. From the time she started reading the local weekly that her father subscribed to, Sue has been mentally writing her obituary. (*Sue Cronkite spent the 1960s and '70s as a sort of pioneer, working her way up in the newspaper business, a historically male-dominated industry…She won many awards for her stories and photographs as well as her editorial merits. She also vowed to break the glass ceiling, or at least crack it trying…*).

Sue Cronkite would still have to work several more years as an assistant state-editor before becoming one of the first American women, in the 1970s, to be an editorial-page writer for a major newspaper.

Meanwhile, with her eldest daughter coming home from college for the summer, the working single-mother is as much a personal casualty of "women's lib" as she is a success. Still reeling from a second divorce, Sue has moved into a two-bedroom apartment with Arti Rose's sixteen-year-old brother and eleven-year-old sister. She no longer has an adult financial partner, or anyone to help supervise her kids. And her romantic life is out-of-control. Sue is pretending not to be dating a "friend" who is a rookie reporter from *The News* while she officially goes out with a car salesman about her age who just sold her the cheapest new car on the market (some pseudo-sporty thing called a "Duster", shaped like a muscle car with the insides of a wind-up toy).

Sue Cronkite has too much on her mind to make any real plans for her daughter's homecoming. Sue cherishes her eldest daughter, like some rare jewel, a family heirloom tucked away in a beaded purse in the bottom drawer of her brain. She cannot imagine her most mature child being anything but lovely and sweet and bright ("Professor" was a nickname bestowed on Arti Rose in early childhood, when an uncle noticed how she stood out among her cousins). *She's bright enough to take care of herself,* Sue thinks, trying to let go of worrying about Arti Rose's grades and to bring her mind back to the work on her desk. The top drawer of Sue's brain is so full and wide open every day that she barely gets it closed at night before the alarm goes off and she has to open it again.

Sue knows her 18-year-old is coming home for the summer but has not thought much about how that will change either of their lives. She is almost afraid to think about it now; anyone in touch with the news knows that the youth of today are a troubled and a troublesome lot. And any mother knows that these days the kids get into trouble, a lot; there is plenty of trouble for them to get into. Her daughter needs to get a summer job; that much Mama Sue does know. (Maybe if she buys her own college books in the fall, Arti Rose will do a better job of reading them.)

Distracted by thoughts of her daughter, Sue looks up from the copy she has been editing, neatening her desk and sipping the coffee that got cold while she was cleaning up an article that had to be in by deadline. Good thing Patrick is a talented writer. With so much about her family on her mind, Sue has not done much thinking about the cub reporter's story. (With an eye like a tenured English teacher, Sue notices every typo or misspelled word, every grammatical error and run-on sentence. Mistakes stand out as if they were highlighted by some magical part of her brain, even when Sue is on autopilot.) She pauses to move a few personal items from a corner of her desktop to her purse, including a summer schedule for the local junior college.

Maybe Arti Rose will take a few classes to make up for the ones she failed at State U. Sue does not mind making sacrifices to pay for her daughter's education, but she resents the partying and the pot smoking that she suspects Arti Rose has been doing with her friends when she should have been studying. As brilliant as Sue knows her daughter to be, since the divorces (first from her father when the girl was ten, now from her stepfather recently) Arti Rose has not been the sort of front-row student that she started out to be or even the get-by average student that she became. Now she appears to be failing. She never failed a grade or even a single class during her twelve years of public school. But her college report card looks like a mistake, like it belongs to someone else, someone Sue doesn't even know. Arti Rose made high grades in her electives but failed half of the requirements, putting her on academic probation. She also got in trouble with the women's dean for climbing out of her dorm window after curfew.

With that picture in mind, Sue holds back a chuckle and takes another sip of her coffee, trying to lighten up. Climbing in and out of a window after hours sounds like fun, like something Sue might have done if she had not been married when she went to college. She figures her daughter has just been temporarily distracted by the newness of living on a college campus. Hopefully she will be more well-adjusted when she goes back to State U in the fall. But Sue wonders (glancing across the newsroom to look at the new reporter's back as he pounds the keys on his typewriter) to what extent her daughter's life has been complicated by young men. (If you could call that last one Sue met "young". She had gone up to visit her daughter and been invited to lunch at the rented, off-campus house of a veteran of the ongoing war in Viet Nam. He had cooked out on the patio, but when Sue went in to use the restroom the place smelled like pot. And she hadn't seen any furniture, just a mattress on the floor inside and some crates that they ate on outside. Hadn't seen an awful lot of books either. The guy said he wanted to be a lawyer. Maybe he'd been in trouble with the law. "He's too old for you," she had told Arti Rose later, with no sense that her daughter was really listening. Nothing unusual about teenagers not listening though.)

31

Looking back, until her senior year of high school it did not seem to be the boys that distracted Arti Rose; she was too shy for that. During her middle and high school years, Arti Rose had surrounded herself with a bevy of young beauties, busy with slumber parties and charm school and clubs and church functions. (And the sewing it took them both to outfit Arti Rose for all of that.) The family moved a few times, and it seemed like surviving socially was more important to the struggling adolescent than surviving academically. When it came to her studies, Arti Rose had managed to pass while barely cracking a book here and there. At a younger age she had loved reading books like Heidi and other classics, Nancy Drew mysteries, and books about horses and heroic dogs. In her teens, however, the girl was more interested in subscribing to "Seventeen" magazine and studying the Sears-Roebuck and J.C. Penney catalogues that came in the mail (especially the sections selling "Mod" fashions from the "British invasion"). As much as she would have preferred to have her daughter reading good literature (instead of using "Cliff Notes", summaries and "crips" to get by), Sue had always read for pleasure and could not bring herself to force the issue. She didn't feel like tutoring kids after work anyway. Their schoolwork was their own. And their pastimes were their choices, within reason.

During her high school years, Arti Rose was more sincerely a student of fashion than anything else. She even took sewing at school, as a home-economics elective. At the time, Sue was content to have her daughter interested in something and wanted to encourage her to excel at whatever she liked. Sue enjoyed helping Arti Rose make her own clothes.

When Sue was growing up, in a rural area, her mother had worked as a seamstress at a shirt factory in a cotton-mill town just over the state line. Sue knew how to sew and taught Arti Rose. If Arti Rose did not have a club fundraiser (such as a carwash or bake-sale) to participate in on a Saturday morning, she did household chores, earned an allowance, and took the money to the fabric store for patterns, material, and notions. By Sunday, many weekends, Arti Rose had a new dress for the morning church service, or a fashionable skirt or pants suit for Youth Fellowship that evening. It was usually a team effort, but Sue gave her daughter all the credit. Sewing was a good hobby, and it saved the family money.

Other than that, Arti Rose had a few part-time jobs and helped with the housework and the younger kids, but she had mostly worked at being pretty. Sometimes she hogged the bathroom for hours. Now, when she made the trip home from college for holidays, she usually wore her latest boyfriend's faded jeans and smelly t-shirts and never rolled her long hair on big rollers (at one time she had used frozen orange-juice cans, held to her head by big bobby-pins). And she rarely wore make-up anymore, though there had been a time when the girl wouldn't walk out to the mailbox without mascara. (Heaven forbid if she hadn't been prepared to bat her eyelashes at the shyer-than-she boy-next-door.)

Arti Rose was pretty enough without working at it, but nobody could have convinced the girl of that. In fact, when the family had moved, and Arti Rose was "the new girl" in the middle of her sophomore year, several popular boys had tried to show an interest in her. The attention only served to embarrass Arti Rose, who feared that they might have been making fun of her. She had just shied away, never really dating much until her senior year, and never getting too serious about any one boy for long. The boys she dated seemed more like friends than lovers and were not particularly handsome (though plenty of kissing went on when they were left alone in the den). She went out with one high-school athlete but did not take him seriously. The boys Arti Rose liked best were oddballs, poets. It was an age of poets, a cultural renaissance when songwriters and poets were as widely popular as athletic stars (and athletes were sometimes derided as "jocks"). Two young men that Arti Rose dated seemed to be competing with their poetry, which made for some family fun.

When one of the boys, a friend from church, sensed that Arti Rose's interest was leaning more heavily toward his rival, he had walked miles to leave a poetic note on their doorstep, which Mama Sue had found.

"You are only a single teardrop in the ocean of my life," he had written.

Sue had found it heartening and humorous. When the other kids playfully picked on her eldest daughter, Mama Sue defended her teasingly. "Don't knock Arti Rose; she is a teardrop in the ocean of somebody's life!"

Arti Rose liked writing poems herself, and had started filling up journals in high school. More recently she wrote for her college newspaper, had a front-page byline for a historically important story (the first time a black student was elected president of student government at her college...).

So maybe Sue's Arti Rose has the right stuff. She might end up with a good career. Hopefully she will get back on track with her studies, get an education, improve her grades. Sue got into the news business with only a year of college, but these days the well-paying papers are mostly hiring college graduates. Getting her daughter to go to college had been easy, but getting her to graduate might be a challenge. Maybe she spent her freshman year at the wrong school. Maybe she got in with the wrong crowd, Mama Sue worries.

Arti Rose's college roommate, "Sunshine", who used to be called Vera, was a quiet, well-groomed and well-dressed wallflower in the early years of high school, with mild manners and short, neat, straightened hair. Hurt somehow, deep-down angry, maybe jealous of her older sister's popularity, Vera did not shine until her sister graduated. Then she went a different way, joining the more bohemian crowd in the high school Drama Club. Still, she was a backstage type, supporting cast. Who could have predicted what she would be like at State U.? Arti Rose learned soon enough. Mama Sue, however, still has no idea to what extent her daughter's roommate flaunted her rebel image and braved a path into every hippy haunt the college town offered (no matter how hidden, even forbidden). Sue can't imagine to what extent "Sunshine" manipulated Arti Rose into scary situations that became less scary and more dangerous, on various levels, as the girls grew less wary.

Mama Sue could not begin to fathom the fact that it is a good thing Arti Rose *can* come home. Instead of just ending up on academic probation, she could have ended up the school year in jail.

Sitting at her desk at work, Sue Cronkite does not want to think about where her daughter may have been, off-campus, in that college-town where she has lived for the past nine months. But Mama Sue does have an uneasy feeling she keeps trying to drown with coffee while she sits struggling to concentrate at her desk (with her daughter now in Sunshine's VW, on her way home).

Sue does know that Vera ("Sunshine") is now a wild-haired, brash and brazen, braless, blue-jean wearing, pot-smoking hippy. Not that Arti Rose isn't the quintessential poetry-writing flowerchild herself, but she was not a pot-smoker when she went away to college. Sue figures her daughter's roommate has been a bad influence. Still, she knows Arti Rose is too deep-down good to be more than superficially and temporarily corrupted. Sue thinks whatever her daughter is going through that made her fail some of her classes is just a phase, and she is a bit concerned but not overly worried about Arti Rose.

Anyway, Sue Cronkite has deadlines to focus on and more dates than her weekends can handle. Not to mention a sixteen-year-old son, who is a recently born-again Christian (thank you Jesus), and an eleven-year-old daughter who insists on hanging out with the wildest kids at the apartment complex. Sue has to believe that her eighteen-year-old daughter can take care of herself and work out her own problems (hopefully helping to take care of her younger sister, for the summer, as well). Besides, Sue's editor-in-chief is peering over his spectacles at her, like he wants that article she is supposed to be editing (never mind the one in her typewriter, that she is supposed have written by tomorrow's editorial board meeting). Sue tosses back her coffee cup, swallows the last sip of bitter-sweet liquid, and empties her brain of those worrisome thoughts about her daughter as the copyboy approaches her desk.

"Nothing now, Joe. I'll have that copy for the news desk soon. Maybe if you get me another cup of joe, Joe?" Sues says, handing her empty cup to the college student who runs errands devised to keep reporters and junior editors at their desks, focused on work.

"The joke is getting old," the copyboy says, smiling at the assistant-editor he has a secret crush on. "Don't forget about deadlines," he adds, feeling a rush of power beyond his station as he takes her empty cup.

"Bring me a grilled cheese too."

"You got it," he says, strutting away in his too-tight jeans.

Too big for his britches, in more ways than one, Sue thinks to herself, as she starts punching keys on her typewriter almost faster than she can think.

"…We're going home"

The Beatles song is playing in Arti Rose's head as she moves lightly, brightly between the dorm room and the lobby, and up and down dozens of stone steps to and from the little yellow car parked in front.

"How-the-hell am I supposed to get us home? This car is thirsty, sitting on E," Sunshine complains as they load suitcases and duffle bags into the trunk of the VW "bug".

"Didn't your dad send you gas money?" Arti asks, just as a matter of inquiry, trying not to take on that same complaining tone. Arti Rose often tries to offset Sunshine's brash and blunt-edged outbursts, especially lately, since Sunshine seems to have lost interest in and patience with everyone at State. Besides, Arti really has no solution, no donation to the cause of getting them home. Arti Rose's mother seems to have mostly forgotten her, since the day she dropped her off nine months earlier. Not that it has caused any misery (though misery has not been left out of the whole experience). To be forgotten by the parents has meant *freedom* for Arti and friends.

Sunshine and Arti Rose came to this haven in the hills as shy, high school goody-goodies turned hippy wannabes. Sunshine, formerly known as Vera Montgomery, had started her transformation senior year. Nicknamed "Sunshine" by a dark, creepy long-haired boy she met in Drama Club, Vera shocked her social-climbing older sister, her conservative parents, and everyone else who thought they knew her. The wild mane her mother had always tried to tame became her trademark, along with her new name. And Sunshine had paired herself up with hippy geek-freaks, from band and chorus and theater.

Arti Rose's changes were subtle during high school, but her college experience had changed her drastically. Riding home after her freshman year, with the convertible top down and too much wind to talk, she remembers the girl she was before. She wonders if any of her old friends will look her up this summer. Arti Rose's high-school "sorority sisters" would barely recognize her now (well, maybe today they would, since it was hot and she had put on a sundress she'd made for her old "Alpha Girls" club trip to the Gulf after graduation). These days she mostly wore her first semester boyfriend's throwaway, threadbare jeans and t-shirt, with no make-up at all, not even a lip gloss. But her old friends had seen the changes coming. The high school friends who had dubbed her "Sweetest" junior year gave her the title "Club Hippy" senior year. It wasn't just the clothes she was starting to choose; it was the way Arti Rose carried that journal around, doodling with colored pens and writing poems about love-and-peace, interrupting conversations about boys with her "deep" thoughts.

In 1971 the public -school dress code, in the Southern city where Arti Rose lived, did not allow girls to wear jeans or pants of any kind other than pant-suits (which had to match and have long tunic tops). The girls' club Arti Rose belonged to, a high school "sorority" called "Alpha Girls", had "tea" at a different club member's house every week. Tea was at Arti Rose's house the first day she wore her new jeans; so, she had a chance to change from her school clothes. The new jeans were white sailcloth, with red and blue stripes, which could have been a summer sailor look or a radical anti-American flag-burning/flag-wearing look, in that era when social unrest had a uniform that was beginning to infiltrate mainstream fashion. The bell-bottoms, ordered from a Sears department-store catalogue, were not a perfect fit. They were supposed to touch the top of the foot but fell a little short for Arti's long legs, stopping just above her ankles. The short length gave her a slightly nerdy look (as bell-bottomed capris were not a style that had even yet been imagined), but her shyness had already branded Arti Rose a bit awkward around the edges long before she chose to wear the wrong pants to "tea". The renegade jeans buttoned instead of zipping at the crotch, crossing the line toward too army/navy, too closely bordering on "hippy" in the eyes of her conservative (practicing to "pledge" at real college sororities, where they intend to find eligible conservative husbands) "sorority sisters". Admittedly, however, the fact that they were hip huggers made Arti Rose's red, white, and blue jeans look almost sexy enough (since she almost had hips) to make up for the fact that they were too short. Still, no matter how almost-groovy the new jeans looked on Arti Rose, the room full of mostly A-line dresses (hemmed just above the knee) had buzzed with the butter-cookie and sweet iced-tea laced whisper, repeated like a chorus; "She's changing."

Arti Rose was always writing in journals and notebooks, and

when she was elected secretary of the club senior year, she started reading poetry to the group sometimes, as a kind of meditative moment, before reading "the minutes from the last meeting". It wasn't really poetry like in English class, just her thoughts about friendship and stuff, or war and peace, social justice, the beauty of nature, love, whatever she had written in the notebook lately and considered inspirational enough to share. A few times she even read a poetic kind of prayer she had written. It was weird but sweet, in a way. That's how all the sorority "sisters" thought of Arti Rose, as weird but sweet. She was sweet to everybody and helped everybody get along with each other. Her first year in the club, when she was voted "Sweetest", her trophy was a giant rainbow-colored lollipop. Arti Rose was a natural flower child, a born love-and-peacenik. So being voted "Club Hippy" was not a long shot, even though Arti Rose had never smoked (or seen or smelled or touched or tasted) the illegal plant that had become essential to counter-culture rituals. Toward the end of senior year, when Arti Rose announced that she was going to State U and rooming with "Sunshine", instead of joining the ranks of sorority sisters pledging at a larger, football-oriented University, Arti Rose's friends were worried.

"Watch out for her; she's weird, honey" was the word about Vera Montgomery, who had only been rushed for one sorority (her freshman year, when everybody thought she would be more like her older sister) but showed little interest in it and seemed to have contempt for most popular kids. They all figured "Sunshine" was at least smoking pot. "Don't let her talk you into anything," they had warned.

Sunshine had said they were a bunch of goody-goody hypocrites; their Alpha Girl rules would soon be forgotten, and they would all be drinking alcohol at the first frat parties they got invited to at the jock-worshiping football capitals of the South. This brainwashing, against Arti Rose's previous membership in polite society, had started when Sunshine first had Arti Rose to herself at campus "Orientation" weekend.

They had been in the bathroom of the girl's dorm, late that first night of Orientation weekend, when Sunshine had removed her make-up to reveal a strawberry birthmark that Arti Rose had never seen. Propped against a row of sinks, in front of a row of mirrors, Sunshine had released her childhood pain like so much psychological vomit. A sympathetic listener, Arti Rose- the shy but pretty "new girl" who had somehow snuck into the second most popular sorority at their high school sophomore year- suddenly, at college orientation became the scapegoat or sacrificial lamb, the sin-eater for the cruelty that little Vera had endured.

Leaning against the sink next to the one where Arti Rose was washing her face with Noxzema, Vera confronted her new roommate with the fact that the "popular" kids, who had proceeded to climb to the heights of the social structure in high school, had been, in many cases, the same bullies who had pulled Vera's unmanageable curls and made fun of her birthmark. If Arti Rose wanted to be Vera's roommate, she was not to be rushing or pledging or having anything to do with a college sorority—the new Vera Montgomery would make sure of that. Arti Rose, not knowing any other girls at State U, did not argue. (It's not like she was an "alpha" girl, in the top-dog sense of the word, anyway. That had been her younger neighbor, who had wanted her as a "best friend" and gotten her in.) Arti Rose had started to identify with the creative side of the counterculture anyway. So, she mostly sympathized and agreed with "Sunshine", while brushing her teeth that first night.

Subsequently Vera, as "Sunshine", proceeded to push, shove, and prod Arti Rose into every door she smelled pot smoke oozing out of as soon as the girls had settled into their dorm room and started exploring their new surroundings together. Besides the beauty of the campus and the little college-town (in the foothills of the Appalachian Mountains), and along with the blissful sense of newfound freedom the two girls had, there was a darker side to that experience for Arti Rose. Again, she was a "new girl" in a strange place, at the mercy of her peers for acceptance. And, with a new "best friend" aggressively "rushing" her into a new (though informally organized) group, sometimes it felt worse that being a high school sorority "pledge" again. Worse than "H-week", like some frightening and embarrassing initiation rite that had to be done to join the club of "cool people" at State U.

The first hippy hovel Arti Rose was led into (via a character called "Fat Al" that Sunshine had brazenly approached) was so dark and smoke-filled that it was impossible to see the faces of the dozen or so students who sat on the floor, passing a bong pipe around. The only lights in the room were a red lava-lamp and a black light hanging over a Grateful Dead poster of roses growing out of a skull. Arti Rose just passed the frightening object along when it came her way (Sunshine commenting later that it hadn't made the bubbling sound when Arti Rose had it). The initiation had at least begun. Also, Sunshine said they needed to go to a protest rally or something "far-out" like that. Unfortunately they found little to protest, on this too-far-from-Berkley (or Columbia, or Kent State...) campus a few years past the infamous late-'60s.

Still, both girls in their own way wanted something different to belong to (some sub-culture with more meaning than football and social-climbing sororities). And so, they identified as hippies. Arti Rose drew posters, with colorful ink on typing paper, promoting "Sunshine" (Vera Montgomery) as dorm rep to Student Council. She won. Arti Rose went with her to meetings, took notes, wrote for the college paper (got a byline when a black guy won President of the group). But they weren't really revolutionaries. And they were only social pot-smokers, toking off joints passed around by others. Only once did they splurge on a "dime bag" of pot for themselves (spent a "nickel"-$5.00- each) and smoked it in the unused upper floor of the old dorm.

There was one protest rally, on the cafeteria steps the first week at State U, against mandatory meal-tickets. Sunshine and Arti Rose had fun screaming against "the establishment" and meeting long-haired boys. The event was ultimately ironic, however. Since Mama Sue was broke from going through a divorce, and almost never sent her any cash, Arti Rose would not have survived without that "mandatory" meal ticket (included in the cost of tuition) for campus cafeteria food. For the most part, it was the same government-cheesy, wheat and potato stretched food they had consumed in public school cafeterias. A lot of ground beef, a little chicken, and fish-sticks on Fridays. There were simple salads, with anemic-looking iceberg lettuce and pink, tasteless tomatoes. There were vegetables from cans, and Jell-O salads with fruit (also from cans) suspended in brightly colored gelatinous squares. There were endless mountains of white rolls, sometimes warm and soft as a mother's breast. Sometimes there was fresh fruit (an apple or an orange or a banana to take back to the dorm for later). They had not known hunger.

"I spent the last cash my dad sent on that bag of herb we smoked the day you were supposed to do your final for Speech class, remember?" Sunshine hisses.

"Yeah; it was supposed to make me brave," Arti says, somewhat regretfully.

"More like silly-as-shit and paranoid-as-hell," Sunshine retorts, half laughing.

"Oh, don't remind me. And stop cussing," Arti Rose pleads, as she heads back up the steps of their beloved old brownstone dorm to get some more of their stuff.

"Fuck!" Sunshine yells when she opens the trunk.

Sunshine is rearranging what she has already put in the trunk, when Arti gets back down the steps. "We have got to make room for somebody else," Sunshine explains. "That's the only way we're gonna get gas money. Who do you know that needs a ride?"

"I'll call Rob; he can ask around his dorm," Arti Rose yells from the top of the steps, not stopping at their pile of things on the porch but walking through the big stone-arched doorway one last time, to use the phone in the lobby. She stops to say goodbye to a few friends who are on their way out, offering greetings and hugs. Then she dials and waits as the phone rings in the hall outside Rob's dorm room. A guy finally answers and goes to get Rob.

"Know anybody who needs a ride?" Arti Rose asks her second semester friend-turned-boyfriend (from the Speech class she just failed by not showing up for the final).

"I was hoping you would ask," Rob replies before Arti Rose can finish a complete sentence. "My parents want me to fly home, but I told them I would rather stay down here for the summer, especially since you and I are planning to get married and rent a place off-campus this fall. (Rob is the only one planning, but Arti Rose has not been able to break it to him). My roommate thinks I'm going home with him, but I would rather go home with you. All my friends are down here anyway. Just because my dad got transferred back to upstate New York doesn't mean I should have to stay where they are. It's time for me to make my own life; ya know?"

Arti Rose is quiet, for the few seconds Rob gives her. She has only told him that Sunshine needs another passenger who can buy gas.

She wasn't necessarily talking about him; she thought maybe he would know somebody who needed a ride. Sure, on some level she might want to spend more time with him, see if they can work things out. They are connected, in love maybe, but something is missing. Maybe they are just friends who worked together for the school paper, dated, tried sleeping together (which was not what Arti Rose had ever expected that to be like, but then nothing so far had been…). Anyway, about bringing him home with her…She has not thought that through. Now he seems to be asking if he can stay with Arti Rose for the summer. She hasn't even talked with her mother. Rob is putting her on the spot. He does not seem to require much of a response. He moves faster than her (thinks faster, talks faster), and he has gotten in the habit of taking her pauses for acquiescence.

Rob was always making plans, making lists, budgeting, figuring. When Arti Rose wanted to make love, Rob wanted to make plans. When he gave her a few seconds to pause, to listen to her insides, her inner voice offered no response to his plans. She felt no enthusiasm for his plans; she felt no resistance to his plans. He was a stream running fast and clear, something out of the cool, blue North, heading for Niagara Falls. Lately she just made a habit of going-with-the-flow, but her undercurrents were as muddy as a lazy river (full of life down deep).

Arti Rose needed to go fishing. She needed to stop living the crazy college coed life for a while, if she could just manage to get back "home". Home wasn't even where her mother lived, in the city; home was where her mother's mother lived, on a red clay road by a spring-fed creek. That's where Arti Rose was born and where she had spent every summer of her growing-up years, where her tap root had grown down deep enough to drink from the purest springs. A part of her just wanted to tell all her mixed-up friends that she would see them next school year; it was summer, and she always spent summers in the country with her "Mema". But a part of her knew that she would have to get a summer job and the jobs were in the city, not the country.

Arti Rose had taken Rob to Holmes County once, during spring break. Rob was polite enough, but he could not stomach the grits her Mema served for breakfast. And, back in the dorm, Rob had made fun of the way her Pepaw had said, "Thank-ye fer the grits please, y'all," when they were sitting around the big table and the old man wanted someone to pass him another helping. Rob happened to be in the proximity of the big bowl of coarsely ground white corn with a pool of melted yellow butter floating at the center. The old man's words sounded like a foreign language to Rob, and Arti Rose had to translate before the passing of the grits took place. Rob's circle of buddies from Huntsville, Alabama (way up near Tennessee, where the Space Center had attracted Yankee engineers and their families), all had a good laugh about Pepaw's way of asking for the grits.

Rob's misfit Yankee buddies hung on his every word and laughed at all his jokes. Arti Rose didn't really think Rob's jokes were all that funny, but she tried not to hold it against him. They had other things in common, like being on the college newspaper staff. They enjoyed some of the same music too, like Neil Young. Rob liked Elton John more than Arti did, but she liked when Rob played "Blue-jean Baby" on the piano in the empty chapel and sang for her while she danced.

Arti Rose had picked Rob out because he was the smartest and most articulate guy in her speech class. He made a case for the legalization of marijuana even though he was not a pot smoker and considered himself a political conservative. He did not look conservative however, which Arti was glad about because she liked his shoulder length dark hair that sort-of matched hers except his was more walnut than chestnut and straighter than hers, silky as corn-silk. He had a sexy way of tossing his head to sling his hair back, away from his big, brown eyes (framed with dark eyebrows that gave him a serious expression).

Arti had told another girl in Speech that she thought Rob would make a good husband, and the other girl told Rob. Not long after that Rob asked her to the Ted Nugent concert on campus. Arti Rose preferred acoustic to electric guitar, but she went and swung her long hair wildly to the music, the way hippy girls did. They went for a long walk and talked after the concert. Rob told her on that first date that he thought she would make the perfect wife. He liked saying the word "perfect" in reference to her, even though one of his buddies advised him against it (right in front of Arti Rose).

"She's perfect," Rob said to his sidekick since high school, who visited him most weekends and joined them on their first date.

"Don't say that; it'll go to her head, man," Rob's buddy said.

The next time they went out it was date night in Rob's dorm, and they had sex on his bunk. Arti Rose didn't think the sex was the way sex was supposed to be, but she thought maybe Rob was just nervous. She didn't feel much, and it did not last long. Maybe they hadn't really had intercourse. Not knowing much about what that felt like, Arti Rose was not sure she had really lost her virginity this school year (as much as Sunshine and the other girls in the dorm had insisted that she should "do it", even making fun of her for being the last one to hold out). Maybe she was lying when she told the other girls she and Rob were "doing it". Truth-be-known, though Rob liked to cuddle, he had confessed, early on, that he was "already burned-out on sex" because of his high school girlfriend. "All she wanted to do was fuck," he had said.

Anyway, everybody knew Arti Rose-and-Rob were a couple. A photo of them together had appeared on the front page of the campus paper, sitting on the lawn of the main courtyard, holding hands and looking soulfully into each other's eyes. If there had been a sunset behind them it would have been the perfect picture for one of those posters from the sixties and seventies, with words of wisdom printed underneath. "If you love someone, let them go. If they come back to you, they are yours; if they don't, they never were." But Arti Rose and Rob were hanging tight at that point.

Rob's dorm is newer, more modern, a sky-rise honeycomb. The rules are more modern too; girls are allowed in for visitation at certain regular, designated times. Rob is waiting out front with a few duffle bags.

"Is this *all* of your shit?" Sunshine asks, unlocking the trunk of the yellow VW.

"Actually? Yes. The stereo system and black-light posters were my roommate's."

"Did you hear that, Art?" Sunshine yells as Arti Rose gets out of the bug. "Your boyfriend is not as cool as we thought. None of that stuff in his room was his," Sunshine says, laughing a little, trying to tease Rob, who she actually likes better than most people.

"Sunshine; cool stuff is not what makes a person cool. Rob is cool on the inside; aren't you baby?" Arti Rose pulls the back of her seat forward and gives Rob a peck on the lips before he bends to get into the back seat, swinging his silky brown hair away from his serious, dark eyes and smoothing it alongside his face with his right hand as he settles in behind the girls, leaning forward between them.

"Hey, I know somebody else that needs a ride," Rob says with his little bowed lips. "She doesn't have much stuff either. Said her parents came and moved shit out of her dorm-room over the weekend, except for one duffle bag and some books. She came to our dorm during visitation hours and ended up staying with us all week."

"You're kidding; I'd bet I know who you're talking about. That bleached-blonde bitch, Felicia. They call her "Leash" for short, get it? Like a dog...She's always on some guy's leash, or they're on hers..."

"Sun! Leash is the middle syllable of her name! What else you gonna call her for short? Fu or yuh? 'Leash' has nothing to do with a dawg; it's just her nickname!"

"Okay ART! Since you know her so well, *you* can baby-sit her!"

"I don't know her that well. She was just in my English class, but she was no dumb blonde. She read *everything*. Sat on the front row and talked to the professor..."

"A man, right? See? You tell her, Rob. Leash slept with your roommate for an entire week and didn't get caught!" Sunshine says, almost sounding jealous. Sunshine had managed to spend a weekend at boys'-dorm, but never a week. Visiting hours were only supposed to be Friday and Saturday evenings until midnight (and the high-rise was the only dorm on campus with regular visiting hours, open to the opposite sex).

"She only went out to take a few exams last week," Rob explains. "She wore Hank's big hoodie and took the side stairwell,"

"I guess that flat-chested bitch could pass for a guy if she covered up her big ass," Sunshine says, hesitating, putting the beetle back in park but leaving the engine on. "I can't stand her, but if she's got cash and you can tolerate her speed-freak rattling mouth, I guess she can have what's left of the back seat."

"Felicia does speed?" Rob asks. "I guess that's why she hardly ate the food Hank brought her. I ended up eating most of it myself, and I didn't need it," Rob said, rubbing the Poo-bear tummy he had grown second semester.

"Her middle initial is RJS," Sunshine goes on. "It's printed right on those pills she pops. Yeah, she's got cash. She was visiting our dorm, making the rounds, selling the shit the day before finals. Told the housemother it had something to do with her sorority. Hell, I bought some black beauties myself. That Felicia girl is in love with them. You'd better tell your roommate he's got a rival, and it ain't Jesus, no matter how much she talks about Jesus… Geee-zus, does she talk!" Sunshine says, clearly not looking forward to the added passenger but resigned to get the cash back that she, in fact, gave Felicia for some speed before finals. "Go get the bitch, man."

Arti Rose gets out, lets Rob out, and waits outside with the front passenger seat forward.

Sunshine gets out too. "We'd better put the top down, Art. I can't stand that perfume Leash wears. I'm gonna need plenty of air to stomach her." They fumble with the convertible top.

"Let me help," Rob says eagerly, running down the steps of the dorm, ahead of the well-camouflaged Felicia.

It is a bit warm for a hoodie, and Felicia strips it off as soon as she gets to the car, revealing a skimpy little top (her nothing-but-nipples showing through), tossing her obviously bleached and straightened hair back over her shoulders as she and her duffle bag get in behind the folded-forward seat, before Rob.

"What's happenin' Leash? Did the sorority sisters find out you were a freak and kick you out of New Dorm?" Sunshine says, getting in, cranking the car and turning the radio on before the new passenger has time to answer. Nobody really wants to get Sunshine started about sororities anyway. There is enough tension in the air.

As soon as Sunshine pulls out of the nearest gas station, Felicia and Rob, with the duffle-bags between them serving as pillows, crash in the cramped backseat, despite the sun and the wind and the radio.

Sunshine turns the radio up so loud that there is little conversation between her and Arti Rose on the way home. Just John Lennon and Janis Joplin and The Doors and Cat Stevens and Led Zeppelin and George Harrison and The Moody Blues and Joni Mitchell and Yes and Elton John and Pink Floyd and James Taylor and The Who.

"Who are you? Who, Who, Who, Who?"

Home?

Once they are on the outskirts of the city, Sunshine is not interested in chauffeuring the whole lot of them wherever they need to go; so she dumps the three off at Arti Rose's mother's apartment complex in the northeast suburbs. Sue Cronkite is working downtown at the newspaper office, as usual, and Arti Rose's younger brother and sister are fending for themselves. Dave is sixteen and has a job, helping one of Arti Rose's old high-school boyfriends put antennas on roofs for his father's TV sales and service company. Sissy is sitting at an umbrella table by the pool with her wild bunch of pubescent pals, all left at home for the summer by their single working-mothers.

"Hey Sis; you got the key?"

"It's unlocked," Sissy yells back from her freckled and bespectacled face, her underdeveloped body scantily clad in the same sexy style of crocheted string-bikini her more well-developed friends are wearing. "Hey Art; don't let Scotty out unless you put him on a leash," the kid yells, an air of responsibility, even territoriality, lacing her tone. "He's due for a walk!" the sassy tween adds, increasing her volume and depth of tone as she verges on delegating one of her chores to a potential subordinate (or subordinates, considering Arti's boyfriend Rob and some blonde chick are following Arti Rose into the apartment little Sissy is used to being in-charge of weekdays).

Arti Rose opens the door and lets her friends into the living room of the two-bedroom apartment, where they immediately make themselves comfortable on the long, secondhand modern earth-tone sofa that lines one wall. She puts one of her favorite albums on the all-in-one radio, eight-track tape and record-player that sits on its own wire rack next to the TV on the opposite wall. Arti has not been listening to Dylan much lately, and she is secretly excited that the old boyfriend who turned-her-on to the hipster folk-artist in high school will soon be bringing her brother home from work. It is not the same house Arti Rose left, when she went off to college, but the family and friends she left behind will be there for her. Only the strict old stepfather who made her feel stifled and afraid is gone. Arti Rose is glad to be back with her true family.

Before Dylan finishes singing "If dogs run free, why can't we?" Arti Rose's brother Dave and his buddy William (who Arti had dated off-and-on senior year, even though he was in love with her then-best-friend who has since married the young coach she had a crush on) come in from work, sweaty and wild-haired as cavemen.

Opening his arms wide, Arti Rose's younger brother is hugging her before he can finish saying, "Hey Art."

"Wow; your hair has gotten long Bro."

William doesn't open his arms, but his face cannot hide the joy he feels, seeing his old romantic friend and poetic pen-pal.

"Big Art!" Will exclaims, prefixing her nickname with the title Davie sometimes gives his "big sister" and her friends.

Arti Rose immediately introduces them to her new friends, who make room on the couch.

"Sit down William," Arti Rose says, blushing just a little as she lowers herself to a cushion on the floor by the antique-style wooden coffee table that has always been a center piece in her mother's various residences.

William is blushing too, not only because of Arti but because of the blonde on the couch and because Arti Rose told him to sit down there, which means his sweaty body will be next to the sexy-looking blonde. Thankfully, Felicia moves over, not so much as to make him feel rejected but just enough to make him comfortable.

"I'm a b-bit sweaty," William (who has a slight speech impediment, aggravated by excitability) stammers apologetically as he tosses his head back a bit to move the wild mass of curls that frame his face and fall over his slender, t-shirt covered shoulders. He does as Arti Rose suggested, lowering his bony butt and lanky white legs to the couch.

"Anybody else need a glass of ice water?" Dave yells from the kitchen, which is not far from where they are seated, separated only by a wide, low bookcase, painted bright yellow and serving as a room divider, and a green wrought-iron garden table that nearly fills the small dining area.

Dave brings a few extra glasses and places them in cork-centered coasters, lined with geometric bright orange plastic and scattered around the coffee table. Reaching for a glass, it is impossible to look at the antique coffee table without noticing something even more dramatic than the modern-art coasters. Besides Mama Sue's latest issue of Southern Living magazine, the Smithsonian, and the Atlantic

Monthly, there are some rather cartoon-y Christian pamphlets scattered about. Knowing they would not be to her mother's taste or representative of her style of Christianity, Arti Rose assumes that Dave or William would have placed the pamphlets.

"Did you guys put this here?" Arti Rose asks, picking up something entitled 4-Easy-Steps-to-Salvation. "I heard you two are into the Jesus movement now."

"Yeah...Hey; Big Art. Your little brother finally got saved; I even got baptized," Dave brags, bubbling with his usual excitement about whatever he does in life. "And Big Will; he's a real Jesus freak, man. He's back-to-the-Greek."

"The Greek?"

"The B-bible," William starts to explain. Embarrassed by his stuttering, he pauses, takes a breath. "It's far out man," Will says, tossing his tangled mud-brown hair again, somewhat self-consciously, as if to remind Arti Rose that he is still the beatnik-hippy poet she once fell in love with. Church has not changed that.

"Wow; you really let your hair grow out, William," Arti Rose says. "But you were the long-hair type, before your hair was long anyway..."

"Greek. That sounds interesting," Felicia says, practically interrupting, batting her made-up eyelashes at William (for some strange reason).

"Felicia is quite the scholar. Some nights she was the only person on campus up studying," Arti Rose offers, thinking maybe she should warn Will later, but not mentioning, now, that Felicia was so high on speed she couldn't have slept if she had wanted to.

"Far out," Will responds, nodding encouragingly at the bleach-blonde scholar.

Arti Rose has a history of feeling sorry for her old boyfriends and matching them up with her friends. But she would not have predicted this one, since Felicia usually goes for hunkier bods. William is like a giraffe minus the natural grace, plus the spotty complexion (be it freckles or pimples or various combinations of the two, according to hormonal and/or actual weather conditions). Maybe it's the hair, Arti thinks, a bit puzzled by Felicia's flirtatious vibe in Will's direction. (But Sunshine is the one who flirts with every guy who has long hair; Leash, they say, goes for anything in pants).

Maybe Felicia also senses Arti's underlying historical attraction to William and figures there must be a reason for it. He does have gorgeous baby blues and a great, almost perpetual smile. And he does wear pants, but who doesn't wear pants these days. When William dressed like his parents wanted him to, he wore nice, expensive pants, which made him a good date for sorority dress-up parties in high school (where he stood out as being tall enough for a tallish girl). The hippy style does not make William look his best, but Arti Rose never really fell in love with him until he started wearing jeans and quoting Bob Dylan and writing free-style romantic poetry to her, if you could call it poetry. William was the first guy Arti ever knew who wrote poetry. But it seems like everybody writes that stuff these days. Anyway, William stopped sending his poems to Arti Rose not long after she went to State, and he went to Ole Miss; so, who cares. Felicia can have him. Rob is a cooler guy; he has a better head, inside and out. Minus the zits, Arti tells herself, mentally squashing little jealous bugs that are trying to crawl up her spine.

Arti Rose turns her attention to her brother, who seems to have adopted "Will". Or William has taken the fatherless, brother-less adolescent under his wing. Or both. Dave is still standing, smiling, talking about nothing with enough excitement to make you think it is something. Arti Rose's brother is a much more attractive guy than William, with a way hunkier "bod", but a few years younger and somewhat immature. Dave is super-lovable, irresistible, and always animated, like the pup that can't decide whether it wants to sit on the sofa or play on the floor or try to sneak out the door when Sissy comes in to use the restroom. Where Arti Rose and most of her closest friends were not the most popular kids in school, usually because of shyness related to some physical quirk, like extremely curly hair when the style was silky straight locks, or fair skin and freckles when the style was tan, her brother Dave never had those kinds of problems. He never stuttered like William or blushed like Arti Rose. Nearly seventeen and somehow unspoiled by adolescence, Dave is as unselfconscious and natural as he was in childhood.

In the middle of the living room now, serving ice water to Arti Rose's new friends, Dave's cool, confident frame is comfortable as the center of attention. Everything about him is regular, except for the length of his hair. He stands at medium height and build with shoulder-length, slightly wavy brown hair and natural golden highlights that draw attention to his blue eyes and classic handsome-guy features, like the square jaw, full lips, and animated smile. But it is really his lack of awareness of his physical attractiveness that makes Dave so universally appealing. In what seems to be an increasingly narcissistic culture, Dave looks like a model for the cover of a romantic novel, but he is not wrapped up in himself. All of Dave's senses are focused outward, on whatever delights Mother Nature is offering in the present, including the people around him. And he does not discriminate; almost anybody who is blessed enough to be in his proximity at any given time, is loved. To Arti Rose's collection of oddball, misfit friends and downright rebels, Dave's friendliness symbolizes acceptance by the norm. He bubbles over with a contagious sort-of "I'm OK; You're OK" vibe (as opposed to the I'm-IT-and-you're-NOT message all too common from members of the high school *in* crowd). David Riddle, Mr. "Best-All-Around", adds high school pep to any scene. Having Dave as a kid-brother type sidekick, helper in the family business, buddy (especially buddy) is big for William, who stutters less when Dave is in his aura (or when he is in Dave's aura). William can actually move on a sexy bleached blonde, scooting a little closer to Felicia on the couch, after making his entrance with his buddy.

"I wish they would let us wear cut-offs in the pool here," Dave says, drawing attention to the only garment covering his healthy-looking suntanned body. "I need a dip," he says, putting his empty water glass down on the coffee table and walking toward his room.

"Got an extra suit, man?" Rob raises his voice in Dave's direction.

Arti wonders if Rob really wants to swim or if he just doesn't want to hear William try to impress Felicia with his knowledge of the "B-Bible". At this point Will has opened "Good News for Modern Man", a modern, illustrated paperback of the gospels that graces the coffee table. William is explaining to Felicia why this version, (one that Mama Sue likes), is not as good as "the Greek". Felicia has moved closer to Will on the couch, presumably to see a passage he is examining. Arti is still sitting on a floor cushion opposite them, but she seems to be interested in the religious conversation. Actually, she is wondering how William could be reading Greek when he failed

French. She glances at Rob, who is exiting with Dave. Rob is a relatively optimistic, up-beat kind of guy, but when it comes to religion, he is a cynical agnostic. He and his Bible-belt born sweetheart have had enough arguments about God for him to shy away from the subject, especially in front of her Bible-thumping former boyfriend.

Rob follows Dave into his room. Arti takes his cue, gets up, and digs through the pile of duffle bags in the corner by the front door until she finds her bathing suit. Soon they are all out in the pool except for Will and Leash, who manage to make the transition from talking about the Bible to making out on the couch, via Felicia's wiles. Dave gets into a game of Marco Polo in the pool, with his kid sister and friends. Rob and Arti Rose come back into the apartment and walk past the couch to Dave's room, figuring they should be making out if anybody else is. They lock the door and Rob says something self-conscious as he takes off Dave's Hawaiian-print surfer-style swimsuit, which he never would have been able to wear if it had not been drawstring-style. Rob is developing a bit of a beer belly at this point. With all the partying going on at State, Rob has been drinking a lot of beer and worries out loud that he might be alcoholic like his mom. None of his insecure talk turns Arti Rose on, not to mention the blooming belly, but she locks the door and pulls Rob down on top of her on her brother's bed anyway. Rob is on and off of her so quick that she is not sure anything happened, as usual. After nine months away from home, with no parental supervision, sex is still a mystery and Arti Rose wonders what all the hype is about. She feels so frustrated she'd like to scream, but she starts a pillow fight with Rob instead.

"Hey, what's going on in there?" William yells from the next room when things get noisy.

"C'mon; let's get something to eat," Arti Rose says, stepping her lean but subtly curvy body into loosely fitting jeans, which are really (and almost always, since she left home and the sewing machine and the Sears-Roebuck catalogue) a borrowed pair of her boyfriend's army-navy style button-up, bell-bottomed and gradually fading deep blues. Luckily, she and Rob are about the same height, and he didn't mind giving her a pair he sort of outgrew. Her brother's clothes fit her okay too. She glances around the room and grabs one of Dave's surf-shop Hawaiian silk-screened t-shirts, red with deep red flowers across the chest (conveniently giving her enough coverage without a bra).

Always her mother's best helper in the kitchen, it doesn't take Arti Rose long to figure out that the next meal is supposed to be spaghetti, which doesn't take long to make either. She feeds everybody with some left for Mama Sue when she finally gets home. There is a salad, too, which is nice. But Sue has to wonder, with the pile of duffle bags by the door, if all of these young people are planning to stay in her already cramped apartment for the summer. Will offers to take Leash home, which brings a sigh of relief to the lady of the house.

Sue never flinches or bats an eye or raises her voice the least bit when her daughter mentions that Rob might be staying for the summer because they are planning to get married anyway and will probably rent a place together at State in the fall instead of living in dorms.

"I hope you guys can find summer jobs in walking distance of the complex," Mama Sue says in her sweet iced-tea tone of voice.

As cool as her mother sounds, Arti Rose knows she is expected to get a job pronto. So, she and Rob start out the next day looking.

They walk to the neighborhood shopping center and all the fast-food places and storefronts in walking distance and fill out applications. Arti Rose dons her favorite hippy dress, which is a fashionable "granny dress" she made from a simple, new pattern. The dresses these days tend to be extreme in length, either mini or maxi. This one is ankle-length, with an empire waistline and short, puffed sleeves. The fabric Arti Rose chose is soft, comfortable cotton with big flowers and leaves printed in various shades of pink and green. She looks like the quintessential "flower child", ready for "the Summer-of-Love" (which happened sometime in the past decade, in San Francisco, California). She wears no jewelry and no make-up, with her long hair down her back and flat, leather "Jesus sandals" on her feet. With this dress on Arti Rose feels beautiful inside and out and can only imagine that the world will eagerly embrace her (as if she was at the Woodstock music festival, instead of a shopping center in the deep South). Rob wears his newest pair of un-faded blue-jeans and a black t-shirt, which gives him a slimmed-down appearance. Arti Rose feels confident that the record store will hire them, because they are so cool-looking and smart and knowledgeable about music. Rob wrote the music reviews for the college paper at State.

There is a clean-cut tech guy working in the Radio Shack part of the store. Rob strikes up a conversation with him, tells him he wrote the music reviews for the college paper and could probably sell a lot of albums. But the guy says they don't need anybody. Arti Rose buys an album with the cash she borrowed from her mom to buy lunch with. It is George Harrison with that new song "My Sweet Lord", which Rob does not like because it is religion again, but at least it's Hare Krishna instead of some Bible-thumping Jesus-freak song.

Rob doesn't understand why hippies have gone from being political to being religious. He doesn't think he is really a hippy anymore, if he ever was, and maybe somebody would hire him if he got a haircut. They argue about this when they say goodbye to the short-haired shopkeeper and walk along the sidewalk of the boring shopping center, only stopping at one more place to fill out applications. Arti Rose cannot imagine Rob without that long, silky dark hair framing his face and drawing attention to his honest brown eyes and noble brow. She can't imagine being nearly as attracted to him if he cuts his hair. She does not say this, but she does steer him away from the barber shop. He can't afford a haircut anyway; he is dependent on her (or her mother, actually) for his next meal. And when he talks to his parents on the phone, they say the only thing they will send him is a plane ticket.

The next day Arti Rose puts on one of her mother's dresses and talks Sunshine into giving her a ride to a temp agency to take a typing test. Rob doesn't even bother going. He doesn't like being in the yellow VW convertible, cramped in the back seat, with Sunshine in the driver's seat, shifting gears and cursing about the clutch. Arti Rose has offered to let him sit in front, but Rob is too much of a gentleman. If Sunshine would let him drive, Rob would go with them. But he doesn't ask. He is thinking about getting a manual labor job anyway; so he won't have to cut his hair. But he stops Arti Rose at the door and looks her up and down. She is wearing a sleeveless yellow polyester shirtwaist dress, with little pockets over the breasts and top-stitching and various details, including a wide white patent leather belt. It is supposed to be knee length but looks like a mini-dress on her because she is taller than her mother and the dress is a petite size. Her long hair is pulled back in a ponytail, revealing white plastic hoop earrings, which also belong to Sue. And she is wearing a pair of Sue's shoes, white dress-sandals with sensible heels and an adjustable back strap (which Arti Rose does have to adjust, since her feet are longer).

"I hope nobody notices my shoes are almost too small," she says.

"You look great," Rob says, with his already big-enough brown eyes widened to cow size, which kind-of bothers her.

Maybe he wants her to be somebody else, she worries, somebody like her mother. Sometimes Arti Rose likes it when her friends idolize her mother, but sometimes it bothers her. They don't really know what it's like, having a workaholic, social butterfly, man-addict for a mother. Though Arti's friends have adopted her mother and given her a nickname, Mama Sue is not the attentive mother idolized in the American black-and-white TV sit-coms of their earlier, formative years. Arti Rose's friends are just sick of their leftover from-the-fifties, fat and frustrated, alcohol and valium-using, nagging and busy-body stay-at-home moms. Too many old-fashioned mothers try to live through their kids, not bothering to have their own lives. Sue is cool, because she is her own person and she lets the kids be themselves, within reason. As long as the kids respect her, Mama Sue respects them and gives them their space. That attitude has Rob, and the rest of them, charmed. In fact, it is not unusual for Arti Rose to sense that one or more of her friends has a crush on Sue.

"Don't get used to me looking like my mom," Arti Rose says, adjusting the ill-fitting shoes on her way out the door. "If I get a job, I'm buying my own clothes."

"Does that mean I can have my jeans back?" he hollers down the stairs, half kidding.

"Forget it," she hollers back up to the balcony, before getting into the passenger side of Sunshine's yellow convertible. "They won't fit over your beer-belly anyway!"

"Gee-zus. Are you two fighting again?" Sunshine says.

"Hey Sun. Why don't you have the top down?" Arti asks.

"Na. That would *not* be cool today," Sunshine says, moving an oversized, multicolored, jewel-toned fabric bag from the passenger seat to the back floorboard as Arti Rose gets in.

Sunshine is not her sunniest self. Whitney left her tapestry bag in the car, and it has dope in it. Whitney is the freaky girl Sunshine started hanging around with senior year, when she got in with the theater group at the high school. All they do is smoke dope. Sunshine and Arti Rose got high sometimes, when they were partying with the hippy crowd at State, but not every day like Sunshine and Whitney.

"Not now," Arti says at a red light, when Sunshine lights up and tries to pass the joint to her. "I'm going to a job interview!" Arti Rose feels a surge of power, saying No to Sunshine. Maybe Arti's head has started to clear after a few days away from the hostage-like situation of being Sunshine's roommate for nine months.

Sunshine, glad to be out of the house, is taking a winding back road to the temp agency. "Well, I wouldn't know about that; I've never had a job, remember?" Sunshine says, taking another drag. "Daddy doesn't want his girls working. He is just hoping I will find an educated husband who can earn a good living and take care of me."

"So, how are your parents, Sun?"

"You know you can call me for a ride anytime you need one, Art," Sunshine says. "My mom drives me crazy; she won't stay out of my room. She still comes in and cleans it. *God.* I wish she was more like Mama Sue."

"Yeah. That's what everybody says." Arti Rose fidgets with her mother's dress.

"That get-up actually looks pretty good on you," Sunshine says as she is letting out a toke. "Love those plastic earrings. But you should have worn white go-go boots instead of the sandals." Sunshine laughs, coughing a little.

Arti Rose thinks Sunshine is smoking a lot because she is depressed, from breaking up with Kirby. Sunshine would deny that, of course. But she gets real edgy when they drive past Kirby on the same windy road, near where Kirby's folks live, on their way back to Mama Sue's apartment later. Kirby waves and honks the funky sounding horn on his blue-grey VW bug.

"Why don't you come in?" Arti says, opening the passenger door of Sunshine's car back at the apartment.

Sunshine can't come in because she knows Whitney must be freaking out after leaving her tapestry bag with the dope in the VW. Sunshine needs to take the dope to Whitney, ASAP. Besides, Kirby might stop by if she hangs out with Arti, and she doesn't want to see Kirby. It is too soon. No, when she sees Kirby again Sunshine wants to be completely cool so that he *knows* she is over him. Sunshine doesn't say any of this to Arti Rose, except the part about needing to take the bag to Whitney. But Arti Rose knows what her best friend is thinking.

"Kirby hasn't been over but once since I got back home, Sun. He's not into the Jesus-freak thing that Dave and Will are into. And he doesn't like Rob that much, remember?" (Arti Rose and Sunshine had cooked a special dinner and invited Kirby when Rob came home with Arti on break, months earlier. The girls had been sure that since they were both smart their young men would like each other, but all Rob and Kirby had done was argue. And they both seemed offended that the girls were so sure they would "like each other").

"Yeah, I didn't get that. Something political, maybe. But I didn't get half of what Kirby was talking about...ever. Oh well. I gotta go Art," Sunshine says, shifting gears, sounding edgy, paranoid like she has been lately.

Getting out of Sunshine's car, Arti Rose misses her already, misses their friendship the way it was first semester, before they got too mixed up with guys. And now it is another girl; Sunshine has even said that Whitney might be coming to State next year and wants to be roommates with her. Arti Rose wonders if she really will be in an apartment with Rob by then. So maybe Sunshine will be happier if Whitney rooms with her. Sunshine has not seemed truly happy, to Arti, since she and Kirby broke up. And sometimes Arti wonders if Sunshine blames her for getting them together in the first place. Not that Arti played matchmaker on purpose, but it might have seemed that way at the time.

Kirby, a quietly but energetically outgoing scholarly leader type, voted "Most Likely to Succeed" senior year, was Arti's old friend from the Methodist Youth Fellowship. They were in church together so often during the last few years of high school that Kirby became like family to Arti Rose. They were usually dating different people, especially Kirby who had a steady girlfriend, an early-blooming, similarly outgoing dishwater blonde nerd who (looking to marry as soon as she graduated from high school) shifted her bespectacled seductions in the direction of the new, fresh-out-of-college "youth minister", toward the end of senior year. By then Arti Rose and William were "going steady". So, the friendship between Arti and Kirby seldom took on romantic overtones (despite the undertones) for long. But Arti Rose and family never knew when Kirby was going to drop by, even after the divorce and the move. He and William both wrote poetry and were into Bob Dylan at the time.

Sunshine and Kirby had not been acquainted in high school, but over the Christmas holidays they met when both were hanging out with Arti Rose and the gang. In no time they were getting it on. There was no stopping them. It wasn't like anybody had to play matchmaker. Sunshine and Kirby must have felt like they were looking in mirrors when they first laid eyes on each other; people used to say they looked like twins.

At a Methodist college where Kirby went on scholarship, he had started to let his curly brown hair go past his dad's designated "time to see the barber". In fact, by Christmas holidays, Kirby was working on a bit of an Afro. Since high school one of Kirby's favorite songs had been "Almost cut my hair" on Crosby, Stills, Nash, and Young's "Four Way Street" album. And when he saw Sunshine, he knew it was time to let it grow, time to forget about any particular style and just let it go, "let it all hang out", let his "freak flag fly" (no matter how much that got on his dad's nerves). It was fun to flaunt a popular style, especially after feeling left-out when the thing had been long, straight hair and silky Beatle-bangs that would swing with a toss of the head (impossible for those with tight curls).

Sunshine gave Kirby the courage to be as wild as he had wanted to be for some time. And Kirby gave Sunshine sex. They gave each other sex, without guilt, without inhibition or reservations. Sunshine and Kirby were so all-over-each-other, for a while, that it was difficult to distinguish one from the other. They always seemed to be tangled up, on the couch or the floor or the ground or in a chair or in a car or anywhere, anytime, in their same-sized shared blue-jeans and ivory long-underwear shirts with their similar-looking wild, dirty-blonde hair and creamy skin. But when they separated their lusty flesh long enough to see their differences, the mirrors broke. They were just too different. For example, Kirby, the Eagle Scout, loved camping, and Sunshine, (dragged along on too many of his adventures and misadventures) hated sleeping in the creepy, crawly woods. Kirby needed camping to balance himself out, shut down his mind for a while. But Sunshine was not an intellectual; she considered herself "A Natural Woman" (and had the same, all-important "look" as Carol King on the "Tapestry" album). Sunshine was a natural-looking city girl, but she would only go so far with that image. When Kirby threw her Cover Girl compact (with mirror) into the woods when they were camping, Sunshine broke up with him. He wanted her to be somebody else, and too much of their time together was wasted on a battle of wills.

When they were going together, at least Kirby had the patience to teach Sunshine to drive his blue-grey VW beetle-bug car, with the manual transmission. Then her daddy had bought her a used VW convertible for Christmas. It was painted sunshine yellow (not to be confused with "yellow sunshine", an LSD pill Arti and Sunshine had broken in half and popped in their mouths during a hike up the mountain with friends at State. To Sunshine, LSD was just another party drug, though it had helped to give her that nickname amongst her new hippy friends first semester. *For Arti Rose, the experience had forever changed how she saw the world, though she could only express what she had seen in a few words: "Everything is everything is everything...").*

Like sunshine and rain, those two, Arti is thinking, still excited about having seen Kirby on the road in passing. Arti Rose misses them as a pair and wonders if she will ever get to hang out with both Sunshine and Kirby, at the same time, this summer. "Bye Sun; thanks for the ride," she says, as Sunshine drives away alone.

Rob answers the apartment door with a smile. "Good news, baby. Woolco called you today. They want you to come to work tomorrow."

"You're kidding! Wow! I got a job already. It's a good thing 'cause I did lousy on that typing test."

"Sit down," he says. "I've got some sort o' bad news too, but I think it will be good for us in the long run...I talked to my folks today, and I am going to fly home like they want. My dad knows a guy who owns a gas station in Binghamton, and he needs somebody to pump gas this summer. If I work full time, I can save enough money for school next year and we will be able to get a place off-campus. My mom will feed me better than I need to be fed; so I'll be able to save about everything I make."

Tears start to brim up around her eyes. By the time they are dry, Rob is gone.

The next day Arti Rose feels a little sad but more relieved than she would have expected. With Rob gone, her mom at work, her brother at work, and her sister out in the pool, Arti Rose has a little time to herself before she goes to work. She puts George Harrison's new album on the stereo and dances to "My Sweet Lord", like a Hare Krishna devotee. (Rob would have rolled his eyes, mildly disapproving. If he had written a review, he would have said the music was Ok- at least it was a Beatle).

Woolco is right across the road from the complex; so Arti can walk. It's a giant new department store with a lot of cheap stuff. Like maybe Woolworth's old 5 & 10-cent store had sex with K-mart and Woolco is their brand-new baby. They put Arti Rose in "The Red Grill", making hot dogs and filling waxy cardboard cups with soda and wiping off tables. Nobody leaves tips. It is a miserable job, for the most part. Of course they had snatched up Arti Rose because she had prior experience at Burger King. And she looked cute in their uniform. Dark haired girls look good in red, which was Arti Rose's favorite color. But Arti Rose is not excited about working at Woolco. All their clothes are polyester, and hippies are supposed to wear natural fabrics. Woolco is a plastic place.

Sue takes her daughter to the community college after work one day that first week the girl is home. She gets her registered for a few night classes. One is Painting and the other is Sociology. Arti thinks sociology will be a hippy class about changing the status quo, but it is not. It's mostly about mean, median, and mode. Stuff like that. Statistics, charts and graphs. It is just factual reading, boring lectures by some bland looking not young and not old lady, and easy multiple-choice tests. But the painting class is a real challenge.

First, they must cut and stretch their own canvas from some old boy-scout tents that the eccentric-looking old-lady teacher brings to class. Then, they have to paint, right there in front of other people who actually know how to paint. Because it is a night class, most of the students are older, actual adults, and seem to be there as an outlet for their already well-practiced hobby. Arti Rose is a pencil and pen doodler, but she has never put paint to canvas. She is a nervous wreck. There is a large bouquet, a loosely arranged variety of bright, blooming flowers in a glass vase on an artificially lit table in the classroom, with some synthetic wood-paneling behind it. Arti Rose loves flowers, but she is not inspired by the scene. She feels out-of-place somehow and has made the mistake of sitting next to the only other teenager in the class, a girl who is even younger than Arti and soon shows herself to be a prodigy. In no time at all, while Arti Rose struggles to pencil sketch an outline for the image, the confident and bubbly girl next to her (who talks effusively to the teacher while she works, as if they are old pals, co-conspirators in some underground world of real artists) paints larger-than-life, brightly colored flowers all over her canvas. By the end of class, the girl has produced a large, acrylic painting that could be put in a store for sale. Woolco.

Arti Rose has not spoken a word to anyone during the entire class. She has only worked on the background, which she tried to imagine as natural wood, rough-hewn and raw, washed with light from a cottage window. After class she asks the teacher if she can take the canvas home and paint some flowers there. The teacher says yes, but it must be a still-life of real flowers since that is the assignment.

There are some plants in the apartment, but none of them are flowering. Arti Rose picks a bunch of yellow wildflowers near a tree by the swing-set behind the complex, which is her favorite spot to be alone (especially some evenings, when the kids have gone in for supper and the moon comes out full enough for her to see the face and talk to, like a friend who really listens), The wildflowers she picks are deeper than yellow, gold without the shine, and the petals are scarlet around the center. She puts them in a ceramic vase in the front window of the apartment and props the canvas there, on the floor. She works on the painting off and on, sitting cross-legged or kneeling on the carpeted floor, with newspapers spread out under and around the canvas.

Arti Rose never goes back to that class except for once, when they are scheduled to do sunsets from the top of the building. She has no problem painting sunsets, even in front of the girl who is a confident painter. But there is a syllabus which says that she must turn in one realistic still life of flowers. It also says she must turn in a landscape, which they are allowed to do at home. There is no inspiring landscape outside her window at home. She tries to paint the overgrown shrub that grows green against the blue sky outside the second-floor apartment window, gracing it with black wrought-iron railing. But Arti

Rose gets bogged down in the overwhelming blob of shapeless tree, lost in infinite details as she attempts the sort of realism the class is geared toward. She intends to go to the painting class regularly when she gets a little farther along with the still-life of the flowers.

So, the unfinished canvases sit on the floor of the apartment all summer (where Arti Rose writes poetry and draws and eventually paints other stuff, just for fun, while listening to The Moody Blues and Pink Floyd and Yes, when she is home alone). Sometimes she makes herself work on the tiny yellow wildflowers which don't look very wild at all. The real flowers, in a vase on the windowsill, wilt before she has finished one timid little blossom with all its careful details. Consequently, with no more live flowers to look at, she patterns the ones that follow after the original. The rest are practically uniform, perfectly formed and wide open, facing the viewer as some plants might face the sun. Not wanting to take the shy little bright-faced soldiers to the class where the other girl's flowers look so free, she focuses on shading the vase, with dark umbers added to her favorite true red on one side and white added to the same red on the other side, along with subtle graduations in-between. Although she plans to turn it in as an example of realism, the actual vase that the wildflowers have already died in is one that she made in high school, when her favorite color was blue. This makes her feel like a rebel, changing the color of the vase. She does not understand why the teacher insists on realism anyway. Her aunt gave her an extensive art history book when she was only six, and she has always liked the impressionistic paintings better. She will end up with an "F" in the class for the same reason she got a few other Fs freshman year at State. There is just something about the teacher and the assignments and the situation that makes her uncomfortable, too uncomfortable to go to class. She doesn't even know how to drop a class and has never been to a school office voluntarily or asked to talk to a counselor unless she has been summoned. The office is where kids have to go when they get in trouble, and Arti Rose has not yet learned the difference between high school and college. She did not make the decision to go to these classes. It was her mother's idea, and her mother is paying for it. Sue makes sure her daughter gets to the sociology class but believes the bullshit about it being okay for Arti to do all her painting work outside class. Sue sees the paintings and knows Arti Rose is doing something constructive, which is what matters. Sue does not even realize that some of the better work her daughter is doing is not for the class (which the girl is, in fact, failing).

To offset the frustration from trying to paint the wildflowers, Arti Rose does produce some satisfactory work of her own, outside the realm of the syllabus. She buys a smaller canvas, half the size of the canvas the flowers are on and paints a brightly colored geometric spatial abstract to hang in the dining area of the apartment, over a wooden filing cabinet that Sue previously painted yellow. Sue likes the abstract and tries to encourage her daughter, never complaining about the messy newspapers on the floor, under the unfinished painting, even though the Scotty-dog makes a bigger mess of the papers at times.

A week or two after Rob leaves, Arti Rose gets a call from Tex, a guy she had a thing with before she met Rob. He had to leave campus suddenly and has been staying with his grandparents in Texas. She never heard from Tex after he left, even though he was the first person Arti Rose ever had sexual intercourse with, that one time (she thinks). Anyway, they were pretty stoned, and she did sleep with him all night that time. She never told him she was a virgin, and it was another one of those sexual experiences that she didn't think had been what it was supposed to be. But she was pretty sure he did go inside her, for a second, before he passed out. There wasn't any blood on his mattress the next day. And they didn't say anything, just went on about their day.

At least Tex had been cool about it. Not all weird like her first semester boyfriend who didn't want to take Arti Rose's virginity and went home to marry the girl he had been fucking since they were fourteen. Not all weird like Rob, second semester, either. Rob thought planning their budget for a future off-campus married life was a form of after-play (when Arti was not done, in fact had barely begun to feel what Rob seemed satisfied to call sex).

Not like Arti Rose had considered Tex to be the-one, either. Just more grown-up than the boys in the dorm. Sort-of. Too into drugs though, like most off-campus guys Arti Rose had met, wandering around the outskirts on weekends, with Sunshine leading the way.

Arti Rose had been somewhat relieved when Tex had vacated their college town. She had not intended to get involved with him again, but his call takes her off guard. She must have told him about her mom, whose name is printed clearly with the list of editors on the newspaper every day and listed in the phone book as well. In the days before answering machines and personal cellphones, the phone rings and whoever is home picks it up. Answers.

"Where did you go?" Arti asks.

"Texas!" Tex says. He goes into a story about his grandparents being really old, like they might have needed him to be there for health reasons. Arti Rose doesn't think that's why Tex left, because the house where he was staying got raided right after that and some of the kids went to jail, including a sweet girl named Suzy who was dating his evil junkie roommate. But she can't think about that right now because Tex is asking her out to dinner, and she needs to think about whether it would be right to go out with someone else when Rob is gone.

Well, Rob did write the words to that song in his last letter. ("Walk along the beach with someone new; have yourself a summer fling or two; just remember I'm in love with you, and save your heart for me…")

"Okay. I can go out, but just for dinner."

Arti Rose feels kind-of depressed when she is shopping for a dress at Woolco. She has not shopped for a dress since her sorority days. Everything is polyester, which she hates. If she had time and transportation of her own, she would go to Pier I at the mall and get something in cotton or silk; or better yet she would sew. She buys a long dress in a cheap, shiny fabric (a lightweight satiny-looking polyester, but at least it's not the heavy polyester knit that everything else on the rack is made of) with a solid black fitted bodice and a dark blue skirt with light-blue moons and silver stars. It reminds her of a pretty Halloween costume, but nothing else on the rack looks remotely hippy and dressy at the same time. Tex had long hair and wore a full beard the last time Arti saw him.

Turns out Tex, by way of a trip to the neighborhood mall, has traded his '60s look for a '70s look (to a certain extent). His long blonde hair has been cut to chin length and he has shaved his beard, except for big sideburns. Arti Rose actually liked him better with that totally wild Johnny Appleseed look he had when she met him, but she doesn't say so. He still has the tan and the big sun-bleached blonde mustache. He is wearing a stylishly wide tie, loosened a bit at the neck, and a dress shirt with an oversized collar that doesn't button down, tucked into the same old well-worn faded blue bell-bottoms that always cover his long, lanky legs and touch the tops of his brown leather boots. She has never seen him at-all dressed-up in anything like a dress-shirt and tie and thinks he must have wanted to impress her mother, the newspaper lady who isn't home (as usual) anyway. The shirt looks new and is light blue, which brings out his eyes. Arti Rose blushes and goes speechless at the sight of him.

"I like your dress Kid; you should dress up more often," he says.

Tex is twenty-four and has been calling her "Kid" since the night he met her at the hippy house with the big porch and the sunset murals where he lived off-campus at State. Arti Rose thinks Tex is already somewhat stoned when he picks her up. He talks slow anyway, with a sort-of affected drawl that doesn't really sound Southern because the words are carefully enunciated, like in Austin, Texas where the coeds are known for being artistic and articulate. Not that Tex is all that articulate, just that he enunciates well, however limited his vocabulary. When he can't think of the right word, he just says shit or fuck, but he doesn't like to hear Arti Rose say those words because they don't suit her. Tex tries not to cuss too much around her. His roommate at State had been in Viet Nam with him, where he had been given the nickname "Tex".

Arti Rose is glad her mom is out with the car salesman. She thinks Mama Sue would be able to tell that Tex is stoned, and Sue has been on a campaign against marijuana ever since she caught Sis smoking with a thirteen-year-old boy on the balcony one night recently.

Tex picks her up in the rusty old white work van his dad handed down to him when Tex got back from Nam. It needs a paint job and has no air-conditioning, but Tex opens the passenger door for Arti Rose, in the manner of a gentleman. She lifts the hem of her long dress and steps up in her leather sandals, as gracefully as Cinderella getting into the magic coach. He takes her to a nice restaurant attached to a hotel. There is a piano player. They dance to a Carpenter's song, "Close-to-You," which was Arti Rose's favorite song before she was a hippy, when she was in high school dating William, and he didn't even have long hair yet. Arti is relieved that Tex does not suggest they get a room because her conscience is bothering her a bit (not because the song reminds her of a date that she had with William in high school but because she is supposed to be saving her heart for Rob, and she feels like she might be sort-of falling in love with Tex again already).

Tex was so slow and easy with her at State. And that's the way it feels now, like she can have however much of him she wants, if she wants, whenever she wants, with no pressure. She feels a little guilty with him, sinful, like maybe she is waltzing on the wild side, dancing into the darkness with her witchy-woman dress. With Tex, she imagines there will be sex, and she knows there will be drugs. During the drive home, she takes a toke off his joint and starts to feel paranoid. She decides not to ever wear that dress again unless it is Halloween. Jimmy Hendrix is playing his electric guitar on the radio, and for some reason she is thinking about heroin, a drug she has never done, a drug that killed Hendrix. Maybe the fear she is feeling is about Tex, but he is being so gentlemanly tonight. She is quiet all the way home.

Tex actually takes her straight home, all polite, walks her upstairs to the second-floor door, gives her a sweet little kiss, and says "G'-night Kid". Then, before he turns and walks away, he touches the freckle on the end of her nose and makes a little clicking sound with his tongue like he thinks she has a cute nose, which she never thought she had because it is longish, with nostrils that flare out sometimes.

A few days later he calls and asks if she would like to see "A Clockwork Orange." She is thrilled because all the hippies love the director, Stanley Kubrick, and it will be the cool thing to do this weekend. The movie is opening downtown.

It is a Saturday afternoon matinee and there is a line stretching a couple of city blocks. People are passing joints around, and by the time they get in they are too stoned to concentrate on the movie. Afterwards, most will have at least some vague memory of the scene in the futuristic druggy milk bar, but few will talk about whether, or not, they think violent people should be chemically controlled in the future. Most will walk out baffled, oblivious to the questions Kubrick was trying to raise. But when people ask them what they thought, they will say it was "far-out, man" (even if whoever they are talking to is not a man). Then they'll just start talking about how stoned they are, how they've got the munchies.

Arti Rose has never been quite so stoned when she wasn't

tripping on acid, which she only did once when a friend at State gave her half-a-hit of yellow sunshine before the group hiked up to the fire-tower to watch the sunset. She wanted to be a bird then (but at least she didn't really think she was a bird, like some crazy people she has heard about who have killed themselves on LSD by jumping out of windows and such, apparently trying to fly- but maybe that was propaganda). After the movie, Arti thinks something she and Tex took a toke of while they were standing in line must have been treated, laced with something more powerful than pot she has smoked before. She doesn't want to go back to the apartment until she is sure her mother will be asleep.

Tex takes her to his room, through the back entrance at his dad's house (a somewhat rundown ranch-style home in an old suburb behind the mall). His parents are divorced and his father, a longtime maintenance worker for the city, is out anyway. Tex's room is an add-on where a sunroom used to be (but it looks like he is trying to block out the sun rather than let it in). There isn't much in Tex's room but a bed and a stereo, a black light and a popular black-light poster of the Garden of Eden (with Adam and Eve naked, a waterfall, and various animals peeking out from amongst a jungle of tropical plants). He plays some music that Arti Rose has never heard on the radio, something dreamy (the *Genesis* band maybe, like singing from the first garden into forever). Her body feels heavy. She sits down on the edge of the bed, but soon feels the urge to stretch out. When Tex comes back from using the restroom, he lies down beside her.

At State she had slept next to him several times before he touched her. To Tex, Arti Rose was just a kid who was hanging out at the off-campus house he and his old buddy from Nam rented. They had gotten government grants and intended to go to school, but neither of them was really college material. They were from working-class families who had watched TV all the time. There weren't any books in their houses. They had gotten through high school copying "Cliff Notes" when they'd had to do book reports. And it wouldn't have mattered if they hadn't been drafted; their dads had been after them, since puberty, to join the military ASAP. Then they had shamed their fathers by returning with "Dishonorable Discharge" for possession of "drugs" (which had actually been plants that grew naturally there, and some soldiers had found to be tools for their survival in physically and psychologically harsh conditions). But their peers back home, protesting an unwanted war, had already labeled their service "dishonorable". Getting free government money to go to college felt like a way to fit in again, but it really wasn't. They were too old for the dorms, and the house they rented just became the druggy partying alternative to the alcoholic frat-houses.

A lot of kids hung out there, too many really. That was the real reason Tex had left; the place was hot, out of control. Arti Rose had liked the great stereo system Tex had set up in the den there, with shag carpeting and cushions all around so people could sit in a circle on the floor. But it had started to scare Tex to see so many kids casually wander up to the big, welcoming front porch of the old, rented house. At first, he had enjoyed being master of his element, his created environment. But he was not prepared to handle such a following. Because he was older, he seemed more sure-of-himself than the wayward students who wandered in and out. Tex just sat and smoked and listened to the music quietly, like a Buddha or a king, holding court. And the most courageous (or maybe the craziest) kids trickled in off the porch. Sometimes the door the music came from was locked, and they just hung out in the big, empty front room with the sunrise (or sunset) mural painted on the widest wall. Sometimes Tex shared his wealth, passing the bong around his little den. Students who ventured in knew immediately what they were supposed to do. Even the most boisterous went suddenly quiet and lowered themselves to the floor, losing themselves in the smoke and the music, the aura Tex created. It was nearly impossible to talk, with King Crimson being played so loudly, or Procol Harem mesmerizing with "A Whiter Shade of Pale". With Tex not saying much, it was easy to imagine him being as cosmic as the music he played and as wildly wondrous as he looked.

Arti Rose had stared at him most of the whole first night she came over with some other girls from her dorm. The only time she wasn't staring at him was when Eric Clapton was on the stereo, playing "Layla"; then she closed her eyes and swayed her head back and forth slowly, feeling as if the music itself was moving her and had her completely under its control. Looking at her then, with her eyes closed (though he had been trying to avoid looking directly at her all night) Tex could not help wanting her but felt almost guilty about that, with her looking so innocent, like some kid who had no idea where she was or what she was getting herself into by being there. Before she went back to the dorm that night, she asked Tex, (real wide-eyed, despite all the dope she had smoked every time the bong was passed around), "Did anybody ever tell you that you look like Johnny Apple-seed?"

She didn't even cringe when he laughed, even though people had been telling Tex lately that he was developing a weird laugh, like a madman. He looked in the mirror for the first time in quite a while, after she left that night, to see what Johnny Apple-seed might have looked like. His long, baby-blonde hair and beard and mustache had sort of blended, like a halo all around his head and somewhat weathered, suntanned face. He brushed it for the first time in a long time, wondering if he should get a trim. Maybe it was cool though, to look like some wild man who wandered around the wilderness, planting seeds. Talk about "getting back to nature"! He had to laugh at himself, looking in the mirror, holding back somewhat to check the maniacal edge of his laughter, as it echoed back from the high ceiling of the old house. Maybe Johnny Apple-seed should plant some seeds in that little chickadee; no, maybe not, probably shouldn't. She was just a kid, but she kept coming back.

She was different from the other chicks though, like she wasn't just coming back for the dope. Most of the time, when she walked over from her dorm, she stayed out on the big front porch, which she said was like her grandmother's porch. Or she hung out in the front room, where one of the chicks had painted sunset murals and peace symbols and other flower-power shit on the walls, which was cool. Arti Rose didn't like coming in the den, where everybody got high, unless she was *sure* Tex's loud, insensitive roommate and/or that skinny guy with the sunken-in eyes were *not* in there.

Arti Rose was taking a pottery class and she used to bring her clay over. She would be working with the clay, on the porch or wherever, and she wouldn't talk to anyone. It was like she was alone, with loads of people walking in and out. People would say, "Who's that weird chick with the clay?" Once, while observing the various "freaks" who came and went, Arti Rose fashioned a head from the clay, with sunken-in eyes and a tongue sticking out from a mouth that appeared to be screaming. It looked like a clay version of artwork on a King Crimson album. She said it was the soul of the super-skinny, speed-freak guy that hung out at the house, pushing the black-beauties students bought to "cram" for exams (though most ended up talking like space-cadets all night instead of studying, after they'd popped the pills). The guy didn't like it too much when word got around that Arti Rose had immortalized him in a weird sculpture. He gave Arti Rose the evil eye. She felt justified in giving him a hard look as well. (But, for some reason, she never gave Tex a hard look.)

At Tex's house off-campus, it was like Arti Rose was in-the-place but not of-the- place. She was out-of-place. In spite of the fact that she looked like a fashionable freak, Arti Rose was a different class of hippy. She was looking for the revolution, not the drugs. People would be getting high, trying to chill-out, and this chick would start talking about wanting to make a difference, to *do* something, to change the world. People at Tex's house were into the vibe of the music, the physical feeling that happened when drugs and music mixed. Arti Rose was into that too, to a certain extent; but the chick really paid attention to the words. When Crosby, Stills, Nash, and Young sang *"We can change the world, rearrange the world,"* Arti Rose believed it and looked around in frustration. Sometimes she came right out and asked whoever was hanging out, "Why don't we *do* something."

Tex had lost all idealism since Nam. He agreed with what Arti Rose was saying sometimes, but even the war did not seem worth protesting to Tex anymore. He liked Arti Rose's spirit though. He just had no idea what it was she thought the local redneck hippies (at what was basically a "party school" for average students) should *do,* besides get high. "Tune in; turn on; and drop out" was the word he had heard some Harvard psychology professor was spreading, after experimenting with LSD. "Timothy Leary"; that was his name. Tex had heard it in a Moody Blues song. And the professor he had worked with changed his name to Ram Dass and wrote a book called "Be Here Now". Tex figured he got their message without reading any of the shit they wrote. ("Shit" being the word, there were plenty of cow pastures just outside of town. And being a "Feed your Head" forager- Grace Slick screaming the song in his brain- Tex had eaten his share of silly-'shrooms.)

High as he was most of the time, Tex tried to keep an eye on Arti Rose, to look after her a bit. Not sure what to make of her, when she did not leave by midnight (meaning she would not be able to get into her dorm for the night) Tex would let her crash in his room, on the other half of his mattress-on-the-floor. Arti Rose had crawled into bed next to Tex several times before he finally got on top of her and tried to go inside her, for a second. He got no response, so it hadn't really seemed worth the effort. Maybe she was just too stoned. Maybe he was.

"You were terrible," he says now, when they start kissing in the summer of '72, in his room at his dad's house in the city. "That one time I made love to you; you were stiff as a board under me. If we ever do that again, you are going to be on top."

"That was my first time," she says.

"You're kidding," he says, not sure he believes her. She is eighteen and good-looking.

"No. It's true," she says, not looking happy, looking utterly miserable about the fact.

He is thinking that she should be proud of herself, that she is special; even his fat, ugly sister had done it by the time she was sixteen, if not before. But he does not say that. He suddenly feels overwhelmed by a feeling of compassion for her. Like maybe she needs his help growing up.

"Come here, kid," is all he says. Then he proceeds to put her on top of him and straddles her legs on either side of him. Ever so slowly he instructs her, but somehow makes her feel that she is in charge.

After that there is no holding her back. They have sex every chance they get, with wild abandon. One lazy weekend afternoon they have been doing the "69" thing he taught her, and when he goes inside her they both have orgasms at the same time. She has been giving herself orgasms since she was ten, but nobody else has ever gone that far with her. She feels some part of herself surrendering to him, maybe forever. It feels good in a way but uncomfortable in a way, when she thinks about it afterwards.

They stay in each other's arms for a while, listening to the Emerson, Lake, and Palmer album Tex bought especially for Arti Rose (after he took her to a Black Sabbath concert, and she preferred the more soothing, ethereal opening act. "Like heaven before hell" she'd said, after she walked out early). When he gets up to turn the album over, Arti Rose notices how slack his muscles look in the afternoon light (coming in around and through the colorful hand-printed India-import spread he has hanging over his window). Tex is long and lanky and could not be called fat by anyone's standards, but he looks soft for a young man of 24, like he is already getting old. There is something strange about his muscle-tone (or lack thereof). Some people might say he looks like a junky.

Arti Rose gets up too, puts on her jeans and t-shirt. She is thirsty and goes into a part of the house they rarely venture into. Looking for a clean glass and finding none, she starts doing the dishes. There is no woman living in the house; his dad is usually at his woman-friend's house when he is not working. The trash can is full of stinking beer bottles. The sink is full, and the counters are covered; there are roaches. Somehow it makes her feel dirty, having made love in a dirty house where she can't even go to the kitchen for a drink without seeing a bug. So Arti Rose gets up from having her first orgasm with a man and does the dishes. He thinks she is "fucked up", but there is no stopping her until the kitchen is clean. At some point he puts on some clothes, gets a towel and starts drying and putting the dishes away, just to get her to calm down.

When the dishes are done, they go back to bed, smoke some more pot, and have intercourse for longer than she has ever had intercourse before. Arti Rose lets-go and just enjoys herself, thinking she is finally finding out what sex is supposed to be like. She does not have an orgasm this time, but they make a lot of noise, with the headboard banging against the wall and her moaning (not too loudly, but more than she has ever moaned before).

They hear his father come in the front door. She has abandoned all self-consciousness and ignores the distant intrusion (which barely registers anyway, as her nervous system is overloaded with pleasurable sensations). But Tex stops and says something about his dad being in the house. She has only met his father once, in passing, and has never heard her boyfriend acknowledge the man with any special consideration or respect. Anyway, the sex stops, with every nerve in her body tingling. Arti Rose puts her head on Tex's shoulder and struggles to quiet her body, breathing as hard, for a while, as if she has been running uphill. Resting against his body, she pretends contentment but cannot stop thinking how odd it is that Tex has never curbed any of his own appetites before, in that room he occupies inside one back corner of his father's house. So why the sudden consideration for the man when she was finally letting go enough to quench her own appetite, for the first time in her young womanly life? Did Tex stop for another reason? Was he somehow threatened by her wild abandon? Maybe he had liked the virgin better.

It is not as she had thought it would be, Arti Rose decides, resting quietly on his shoulder, containing herself. Her thoughts are strangely driven to separate herself from him as their sweaty bodies lie merged in warm liquids, like two bodies of water that have swelled and flowed into each other after a summer rain. Maybe they feel close at the moment, but she is compelled to hold back something of herself emotionally, even as he embraces her and falls asleep in her arms. Her body cannot have all it wants of this man, if it wants, when it wants. Though there may be the occasional orgasm, (and she does not yet realize how rare, the mutual orgasm), the man's flesh will always be his, and her flesh will be hers. It won't be the stuff of Emily Barrett Browning's poems and Karen Carpenter's love songs; the dreams of love that she favored in her virginal, budding years. And although she still believes in the Bible (not that she has read the whole thing), she has to wonder about the part, at the beginning, that says man and woman will be of one flesh. Talking herself down, mentally, while Tex sleeps, Arti Rose begins to feel more comfortable with her disillusionment about sexual love, less threatened, but lonely again, always lonely. Resting on his shoulder, her body is so close to his, her mind light-years away it seems.

There might be some-kind-of mental or spiritual oneness that could be achieved with another person, she is thinking later when they smoke another joint and he puts on a Yes album. But it probably will not happen with this man, even though they both appreciate the fine, classical rock sound of a group like "Yes". Deep inside, yes and no have come to a balance in the part of Arti Rose's virginal psyche that this man entered for a moment.

Arti Rose begins to open her eyes to the fact that there is a mental and physical laziness about Tex. He will probably never care to do much of anything with his life, never have a real sense of purpose worth sharing with a partner. He has good taste in music but his responses to the songs seem to be purely sensual; she never gets anywhere with him when she tries to discuss the ideas, the visions in the poetry of the songs. And as far as his life goes, she does not believe that he has any real interest in getting a college education, much less in being a lawyer like he said he was going to be when she first met him in that hippy house off-campus. He may have gone to State U on some sort of grant, but she never saw him crack a book or go to a single class. There were a few books in his room at State, but that house was so wide-open, so communal that the books could have belonged to anyone. Maybe he had lied to her about being a student. Maybe he was in that town strictly to party and deal dope. There is not a single book in his room at his dad's house. And at twenty-four-years-old, he is content to work for the city parks department, riding around getting stoned in the back of a truck that picks up fallen tree limbs and other natural debris from the parks (a summer job he got through some connection of his father's). At least Tex has a job that does no harm, but Arti Rose wants more than that. She wants to help her generation change the world, and she wants a working partner who shares that vision. Tex will probably never be anybody Arti Rose can bring herself to marry. But she cannot imagine breaking up with him right now. It might break his heart.

So Arti Rose settles into her summer routine, going to work at Woolco when she is scheduled to be there, going to the Sociology class two nights a week, doing a little painting at the apartment window, giving her little sister a glance over the balcony as the kid swims with her crazy, under supervised teeny-bopper friends in the pool below. Davie and William are in and out, but they have a work routine too. Sunshine calls and stops by occasionally. Kirby comes over once with some weird poetry he wants Arti Rose to read, something about "breathing and drowning alone". Arti Rose never feels like she has enough time alone; so, she doesn't really get it. She wonders if he had some swimming accident, maybe as a child. Kirby's poetry has always been harder to understand than William's, and Arti Rose does not want Kirby to think she is dumb. So she doesn't ask what it means.

"Beautiful," is all she says after ready Kirby's poetry. Her face radiates sincerity, because Arti Rose thinks Kirby is beautiful. She knows Kirby misses his friends, but he does not want to get back with Sunshine. (Sunshine is a trip. And she's mostly been hanging out with

Whitney lately anyway.)

Tex calls and makes weekend plans before Arti Rose can even think about what she might want to do. Not like she has her own vehicle anyway, and she can't keep up with her mother and brother. One thing for sure, they will have dates Saturday night. And Sissy will probably spend the night with that crazy new friend of hers whose speed-freak dad shot himself with her in the house (before the kid's now-single mom moved them to the apartments). Arti Rose hates leaving them alone, but she can't stand the little bleach-blonde punk's vibe (and can't help wondering if the kid confiscated whatever pills her dad left behind, when he checked-out).

"Whatever that kid is on," Arti Rose tells Sissy, "Please stay off it!" Arti Rose is somewhat concerned, but she does not feel the full weight of it. The weight of it belongs to her working mother, who cannot control (or even allow herself to be fully conscious of) a situation that she cannot attend full-time.

Going out with Tex, ending up in his room with the music and the pot and the sex, is a somewhat welcome escape. However, Arti Rose knows she cannot commit to the relationship, which is disheartening. She knows she is still growing, and she sees Tex as someone stuck. Tex is a disillusioned war veteran who came home to a broken family.

Arti Rose tries to talk with Tex, to get him thinking, help him snap out of it. All Tex wants to say about Viet Nam, in most random conversations when people bring it up, is that he got his nickname over there, and there was a lot of dope. Once, in a more intimate moment, he opens up to Arti Rose about Viet Nam just slightly for a minute. He says the only way to avoid the pure misery of the jungle and the fear and the random, exploding violence and the sudden, shocking maiming and death of his friends (who became like the brothers he'd never had) was to do as much dope as he could get away with and to help his nerve-wracked buddies do the same. He goes so far as to confess to Arti Rose that he had been sent home on a "dishonorable discharge". After that they rarely mention Viet Nam to each other again.

When Arti Rose really starts to see Tex, she realizes he must feel the same about life in America as he felt about life in the jungles of Viet Nam, because he is still doing as much dope as he can get away with and sharing it with his friends as if it was love, medicine. The people he takes her to visit (or pick up pot from, truth be known) when they are out on dates, are always wasted. If there is anything worth caring about in Tex's life, it is probably Arti Rose. She feels like she should at least keep dating him for the summer, until she goes back to State. Then it might be easier to break things off without him getting hurt. Tex knows she is just a college kid. He even calls her "Kid", waking up from his nap, looking at her sweet young face on the pillow next to him.

"Hi Kid," he says softly, tenderly, gazing into her eyes and stroking the hair around her face.

Tex is Arti Rose's first man. Maybe he doesn't live on his own yet, but he seems more like a man than any of her other boyfriends have been. Her earlier boyfriends have only been to school and worked part-time jobs in their communities. Tex has seen the harshest reality the real world has to offer. And he has been sweet to Arti Rose. They have been sweet together. Maybe Tex was right about stopping the sex when he did that time. Maybe they should have more respect for his father. Tex's mother and sister left, and his father kept the house Tex had grown up in, for his son to come home to.

"I hope your dad is happy about the dishes being done," Arti Rose says, having made it a regular routine when she visits.

They leave out the back door without seeing Tex's father, as usual. For the first time, Arti Rose thinks about how lonely Tex's father must be, how lonely they both must be, the two men living completely separate lives while sleeping in separate areas of the same house, never even meeting in the kitchen to cook or clean up together, living on fast-food and leaving the wrappers everywhere (beer cans too, in his dad's case). It must have been different before Tex went to Viet Nam, when Tex's mother and sister lived there. It is not a bad house, not a bad neighborhood. In fact, it's not far from the neighborhood Arti Rose's family lived in before… Arti Rose is thinking about all of this while Tex is driving her home with the radio blaring "Riders on the Storm" by the Doors. "Into this house we're born…"

When Tex walks her to the door of the apartment, he gives Arti Rose a French kiss, then takes a "joint" (a hand-rolled marijuana cigarette) out of his pocket, hands it to her, and says, "G' night, Kid".

The next day it occurs to Arti Rose that Tex has facilitated yet another first for her. She has never had a joint of her own that she can smoke by herself alone if she so desires. She decides to save it for painting or writing poetry. But she comes home from working at Woolco with a headache and lights it up in the bathroom with the exhaust fan on. It does not make the headache go away.

Dope Re-thunk

In the summer of '72, Sue comes in from work earlier than usual and immediately smells pot. She thinks Sis has let that thirteen-year-old boy inside the apartment against strictest orders. When she opens the bathroom door and it is Arti Rose, she loses it. "I don't get up before the crack of dawn and go to work to pay the rent so my grown daughter can smoke pot in my bathroom," she says.

"I've got a fucking headache," Arti yells. "I was hoping the pot would get rid of it."

"Don't say the f-word in my house, Arti Rose. What is WRONG with you?" Sue draws her hand up uncharacteristically, like she wants to slap her daughter, who is taller than her but about the same weight. Sue catches herself, pulls her hand back; she does not believe in hitting her children. Instead, she yells so loud that Arti Rose feels kind-of afraid, but not that much, not like if it had been Daddy Dick because he really would have hit her. "I have HAD-IT!" Sue yells.

Arti Rose is trapped in the smoky bathroom with her petite, "Scotch-Irish" mother standing at the door yelling. Sue's angry face was about as red as her hair. "You NEVER used to say CUSS words like THAT! I don't even know WHO YOU ARE anymore!" Sue yells, starting to back away from the bathroom door. "I am NOT going to argue with you. It is bad enough that I have to argue with your little sister about the pot these PUNKS that live around here smoke. YOU are eighteen years old! I should not have to argue with YOU!" she says, standing in the hallway outside the bathroom. "There will be NO MORE POT SMOKING here; is that UNDERSTOOD?"

"O.K., O.K.; I AM SORRY!" Arti Rose yells back from the bathroom where she stands with a towel around her naked body, her long, dark hair dripping water on the tile floor.

"I am going to bed!" Sue says, retreating to her bedroom (the bedroom that she shares with both of her daughters). "I'm *tired*."

It is not even dark yet, but Sue has been up since before dawn. On Mondays she cleans up the copy that comes in over the wire on weekends when nobody is there to edit it. It has been a long-enough day. Sue goes straight to bed without even bothering to use the smoke-filled bathroom she was trying to enter when the whole ugly scene started.

Her bathroom, HER apartment, Arti keeps thinking, feeling unwanted and out-of-place in her mother's space. She sleeps on the couch that night and decides not to sleep in her mother's room ever again. The twin bed next to Sue's double bed is supposed to be Sissy's anyway. Sis has been sleeping with Mama Sue since Arti Rose came home. Dave is the only one with his own room. There isn't a single piece of furniture in this apartment that belongs to Arti, nothing. Not that the furniture in the old room she shared with Sis was that great. It was just used stuff, not the canopy bed Mama Sue used to say she was going to buy Arti Rose before Daddy Dick took over. But at least her old twin bed and dresser were hers; or so she thought. When Sue had to downsize after the divorce, she got rid of nearly everything from the old house.

Arti Rose starts spending more time than ever with Tex, mostly in his room. When she's not working or in class, she is usually with Tex. She doesn't get why it makes any difference to her family and friends, because she was almost always alone in her mother's apartment before. Now everybody is trying to spend time with Arti Rose. Sunshine appears at The Red Grill in Woolco and wants to go shopping at Pier I with Arti Rose when she gets off work. Mama Sue wants her to go to the Wednesday night spaghetti supper at their old church, even though they both feel uncomfortable there now. Dave wants to take her camping down on the Gulf of Mexico and says she can bring all her friends; he knows a great place and Will has a tent and some extra sleeping bags. Sis does the dishes and cleans the apartment and says she wants to go to the beach too. Mama Sue says they can all go to the Gulf this weekend if they will help clean the apartment and go with her to Wednesday night supper at the church.

Daddy Dick was big on church. When he was ruler of the house, they all had to go every time the church doors were open to the congregation. He also insisted they sit up front and be engaged and involved. Arti Rose sang in the youth choir and once she was appointed president of the youth fellowship because she was the only one who was always there besides Kirby (and he had been president the year before). She was extremely shy and embarrassed about having to stand up in front of the group; so all she ever did was lead them in the pledge and sit down. Then the adult youth directors had to take over. Another embarrassing thing that happened was when Daddy Dick volunteered to teach her Sunday School class. Arti Rose's friend Kirby actually liked Daddy Dick and always got into big discussions with him that Arti Rose tuned out. Arti Rose had to listen to enough of his lectures at home; no way was she going to listen to that old man at church.

Dave and Sis manage to worm their way out of the Wednesday night spaghetti supper, but Arti Rose makes a special point of going because she has not really spent any quality time with her mother since their fight about the pot. Arti Rose is still feeling defensive about that; especially since she smokes pot with Tex a lot (and goes out to the picnic area by the swing-set behind the apartment to smoke when he gives her joints to save for later). Arti Rose likes smoking alone, and if there are kids on the swings or anyone around the picnic table, she wanders into a wooded area. She finds a tree with a large, low branch, climbs up and props herself there. Smoking helps her to be still and just daydream until she feels like a part of nature.

Lately she has been reading a book entitled "Marijuana Reconsidered". While they are standing in line at the church spaghetti supper, Arti Rose is telling her mother about the book. Sue feels self-conscious about the subject of conversation, with so many people around, but does not want to discourage her daughter from talking about whatever she needs to talk about. She tries to be positive and open-minded while Arti Rose argues for this drug as if it has some redeeming value.

When Arti Rose was active in the youth group at this relatively liberal church, they were always discussing controversial social issues, like the war and sex and drugs. She is not trying to embarrass her mother, just talking about what is on her mind and the information she is getting from the book she is reading. The church fellowship hall is not a situation where Sue wants to get into an argument with her daughter; so, she keeps smiling a polite little smile, no matter what her daughter says while they are standing in line and later when they are seated at a long table with a lot of other people around.

Mama Sue was hoping that Arti Rose would see some of her old friends from the youth group, but it seems that they have all grown up and gone somewhere else, except for one significantly overweight young woman who is an older sister of a boy who was in Arti Rose's class. The girl is sitting with her significantly overweight mother and looks like a younger version of the same, even mimicking her mother's outdated hairstyle and general fashion sense. Arti Rose and the other young lady say "Hi" and Arti asks about her brother, but that is as far as the conversation goes.

Sue does not have that many friends at church anymore either. There is no such thing as a "singles class" yet. And when Sue has tried going into her old group, the women act like they think the petite redhead is flirting with their husbands. She even tried teaching a youth class, that way nobody expected her to go to the class she went to with her ex-husband before they divorced. He lives in another state now, but things do not seem to be any less awkward. Sue tries not to let this awkwardness show. She is stubborn and thinks she and her children need the stability and continuity of attending the same United Methodist Church where they have been members for years. But her attendance has dropped, and she has let someone else teach the youth class.

A few more people say "Hi" to them in passing, but nobody goes out of their way, or saves them a seat; so, they sit at a table where nobody they are too familiar with is sitting. Arti Rose keeps talking about the book she is reading, and by the time they leave, she has the mistaken impression that her mom has "reconsidered" marijuana.

Sue only knows that she is concerned about her daughter and does not want to make the mistake of losing patience with her and alienating her. She has decided that the best approach is just to listen and learn all she can. Like Bob Dylan says in that song on the radio, "Don't criticize what you can't understand. Your sons and your daughters are beyond your command...The times, they are a changing."

Sue tells Arti Rose she will read the book, "Marijuana Reconsidered". She will try to keep an open mind she says, but deep-down she can't help feeling that her daughter is in trouble. Obviously, their old church is not going to be a solution. Maybe Arti Rose will find another church group, like the one Dave and Will go to, where the kids don't smoke pot. Too bad their literature is so weird though. Arti Rose has already said she does not like the cartoonish, simple-minded stuff they put on the coffee table, and Sue would have to agree with that. Sue does not throw away the tracts her son puts on the coffee table though, not wanting to be guilty of censorship. A free exchange of ideas is the best avenue to the truth, she thinks.

In Sue's way of thinking, God is one thing and religion is quite another. Faith is just faith, a blessing all its own and apart from explanations. And sometimes Sue does not know what to do for her children other than to pray. She prays about the pot issue and lets it go for now. Hopefully she has said enough about her position on having drugs in her home, to her own children at least. But next time Tex comes to her door to pick up Arti Rose, Sue will look him hard in the eyes. She will tell him that she does not allow marijuana in her apartment, that it is illegal, and he is not to be giving it to her daughter.

When this occasion comes to pass, Sue is matter of fact, cut-and-dried with her words. She does not raise her voice when speaking to Tex, but Sue is red-faced, obviously mad.

"Yes Ma'am," is all Tex utters.

"Arti Rose! Your boyfriend is here!" Mama Sue yells afterwards, turning from the door.

Arti Rose feels the tension as she walks through the living room and out the door, where Tex is still standing on the breezeway.

"Why didn't you come in?" Arti Rose asks as they walk down the stairwell.

"Your mom didn't *invite* me in," Tex tells Arti Rose on the way to the van.

"That's not like her," Arti Rose says, getting into the passenger side of the van.

"Guess she wanted to put the fear-of-God in me," Tex said. "About dope."

(Surfer)

Up before the sleeping sun
his dreams were drifting on waves
as high as the sky.
There was a song in his soul
that sang with
the rhythm of the sea.
As we reached the sandy shore
the stars kissed us goodbye,
and the orange sun
turned the summer sky
into swirls of pink and blue.
He stood patiently
in the glassy green ocean.
Time was not on his mind,
neither was his Wendy,
slumbering on the sand.
There was only the dream,
as he stared longingly
at the sea and the rising sun,
that the next wave
would lift him gently
& give his balancing body
a portion of
its wild and free-flowing spirit.

(A.R.T. 1971)

Gulf

A caravan of young people drives down toward the aqua and emerald waters and sugar-white sand, to camp in the dunes under a million stars, somewhere between Destin and Fort Walton where few folks in the world go for fun yet. None of them have any money to spend on motels or amusement park rides in Panama City anyway (where they would have gone last year, before they were hippies). All of them are game to "turn-on, tune-in, and drop-out" of the rat-race rush to the rollercoasters. It's high time to appreciate what Mother Nature has to offer.

Davie is the leader of the pack because for him heading south toward the panhandle is going home, where he was born and spent every summer of his childhood (not to mention recently doing a stint there with his stepdad). Now that he has his license and a van, it's nothing for him to take off for the four-hour drive to his grandparents' place at Lake Victor, FL. Plus there are aunts and uncles for pit-stops heading down. Then it's only a few more hours from Mema's Bait & Tackle to his destination on the Gulf of Mexico.

This time, with his sister Arti Rose home from college, and some of her hippy friends tagging along, they run into trouble on the way down.

Outside a small town near the Florida line, Davie pulls his van over at one of his daddy's sister's houses. Will parks his mom's wood-trimmed station-wagon behind him along the shoulder of the road and waits for Davie to come to his window and explain why he stopped. Tex, and Davie's cousin Cole (visiting from California with his musician dad, who is Mama Sue's younger brother) follow Davie out of the van.

"Wha's happenin', man?" Will asks from inside his car's driver-side window.

"Pit stop, dude. My aunt and uncle's place. I always stop here," Davie says.

"Cool," Will says, getting out without bothering to wake his sleeping passengers.

"These guys are dying, taking turns with the back of the van," Davie explains as Will greets groggy-looking Tex and Cole.

"It is hot," Will agrees. "They're all crashed-out in the woody".

Davie is thinking about Aunt May as he walks up the driveway. His daddy's younger sister was his first babysitter when Mama Sue went to work, so she has always felt like a second mother. Remembering the open-armed embrace Aunt May usually greets him with, Davie smiles and walks lightly up the long, pine-straw covered driveway, barely thinking about the entourage following him. The brick ranch-style house sits way back behind a stand of stately pines. Will picks up his pace and flanks Davie.

"Dude, you look like a wild-man," Davie says, laughing a little. "I hope you don't scare my aunt." Davie looks like a classic young surfer, his hair sunlit and silky. Will and Tex have been letting their beards grow out some, but Davie doesn't have noticeable hair on his face yet.

"I've got the wind-blown frizzies, man," Will says, proudly tossing his plain-brown mane (the only thing that has ever stood out about him, except the height he carries on his lanky frame). "But, hey; I don't look as wild as those dudes behind us."

Davie glances back without slowing down. He lets out another little Davie laugh, as his eyes catch sight of his groggy California cousin and the Johnny-Appleseed looking wild-man beside him. Tex and Cole have been smoking weed the whole way down. Tex said that's what he did in Nam to tolerate the jungle heat. And Cole is a rock-&-roller. His dad has been passing him a guitar and a joint since puberty. Cole is a year younger than Davie, but his frame is more like a wrestler than a surfer. Davie has bowed, muscular legs, and Cole has wide shoulders. And Cole wears beads and bracelets and anklets and feathers and leather-like tattoos, like things he couldn't take off if he wanted to. Otherwise none of them are wearing much in this heat. Cut-offs. T-shirts (cut and torn, soaked with sweat) or no shirt at all, and flip-flops or bare feet.

Aunt May has always been as sweet as the iced tea she often serves up quick, without asking. Uncle Earl is just as quick with his shot gun, and any game he goes after hasn't got a chance. With a hunter for a husband, Aunt May is as likely to offer leftover quail as fried chicken. And Davie is used to hearing his cousins out back doing target practice with their 22-rifles. What Davie has never seen before is the barrel of Uncle Earl's gun pointed at *him* as he walks up the driveway. But then he's never walked up that drive with Will and Tex and

California Cole.

Of course, if they were in California, Cole would be closer to the norm. Even in Atlanta or Birmingham, his flamboyant hippy garb wouldn't startle people too much these days. And the other guys would not scare many city folks with their shoulder-length hair. They look like typical city laborers, which they are (with Will and Davie putting up antennas and Tex cleaning up city parks). But Southern country people are a different breed. In the early 1970s they still shave their boys' heads in summer to keep the lice off and to remind them that they are not girls. And hippies raise the hair on their necks like Indians used to do. Uncle Earl has not forgotten what his grandfather taught him, so he greets these wild-looking young men with the sound of his gun cocking.

Davie and his pals are innocently shocked, oblivious despite the "Billy Jack" movies they have seen. All Davie had done was mentioned his Aunt May's sweet tea one minute, and the next minute he'd had enough followers to look like representatives of a warring tribe heading toward Uncle Earl's house through the pines. Iced-tea predators.

The girls are still asleep in Will's woody, but Kirby is wide awake. He'd had sense enough not to go charging up to some redneck's house. *Rednecks don't like long-haired hippies*; Kirby was thinking but did not say anything before the guys were on their way up the long drive. Now he suddenly sounds his alarm, waking up Arti Rose, disturbing her with a wild look in his baby blues and his golden curls bouncing as his head shakes in a belated "No". She looks out the window from where they are pulled over by the side of the road. Her Uncle Earl is standing in his driveway, pointing his shotgun at the guys (who have stopped in their tracks).

"You boys better get on up the road!" Uncle Earl is saying at high volume, after his gun made that clicking noise (a bullet falling into place, ready to fire).

The guys are back in a flash, stunned. They burn rubber heading out of there.

Davie tries to laugh it off, like everything else. But nobody else really laughs.

"Jesus had long hair," Arti Rose says, fuming with righteous anger and bursting into tears when they get to her grandmother's place on Lake Victor. "And He taught us to love all kinds of people."

"Shore did, Sugar," Mema says from behind the cash register at the Bait & Tackle, where everyone is digging in the big, red Coca-Cola cooler for their favorite frosty drinks.

Arti Rose is overheated and boiling over, like the radiator in Will's woody outside. She grabs a napkin from the metal dispenser on the counter, and wipes tears that keep coming.

"You don't pay your Uncle Earl no mind now Shug," her Mema says. "Some folks just don't know nothin' 'bout the Word of Love."

When they got there, Davie had told everybody his Mema don't care who comes in the Bait & Tackle, long as they buy a cold drink. Besides, Cole is the scariest looking of the bunch, and he is one of her own.

Mema gives Cole a big, fat hug. She's just glad to have him home and wishes he had brought his daddy. Her boy was always wild as an Indian, even before he took off for Nashville with his guitar, then went to Texas and California. Hasn't been home in a month of Sundays.

"Daddy'd be here, if he hadn't had a gig," Cole says as he hugs his Mema.

They all hang around the lakeside for a bit, giving Will's car a chance to cool down (along with their flared-up tempers). Then they go a few more hours south before sunset so they can set up camp by the Gulf in daylight.

Davie learned to surf as a chubby pubescent, when the family lived in Jacksonville, Florida (on the Atlantic side). His enthusiasm for surfing is so great that he has all of the guys trying it, in spite of the Gulf of Mexico's small waves. As challenging as it is, trying to ride waves that are barely there, Dave's confident form makes it look as easy as skateboarding on a parking lot. He particularly likes the "tubes" (waves that curl long and smooth, like blown glass). Davie's blue eyes and bright smile radiate over the whole beach, warming everything like the sun. With his long sun-bleached hair, compact body, and slightly bowed, muscular legs, Dave is a classic surfer dude, in his element.

Davie's girlfriend Wendy is a soft-spoken, petite blonde who was Arti Rose's "little sister" in their high school sorority, the Alpha

Girls (which Wendy is still a member of, since she has not yet graduated). Wendy picks up Dave's board when he and the other guys put theirs down. Wendy's long hair blows in the breeze, and she gets a dreamy, faraway look, like she might have the soul of a surfer too. She starts a game of riding the board down dunes, and the girls join in, taking turns, balancing as they slide down the sandy white hills (which are much higher than the waves).

The guys set up a couple of tents in the dunes. The girls claim one, putting their personal things inside. Arti Rose knows that she has been entrusted with the younger girls, Wendy and Sis. Mama Sue was not sure she wanted Sis to come, but Sissy had begged and Arti Rose had reassured their mother. Wendy's parents had only asked if Arti Rose was going. Wendy's mother thought she knew Arti Rose well, from when the girls had been high school "sorority sisters". The "Alpha Girls" had gone down to Panama City, Florida for a week after Arti Rose's senior year, and Wendy's mother had gone as a chaperone. Arti Rose had been a club officer, setting a good example by following strict rules against drinking. Sex and drugs were not even an issue then; it was understood that they were not those kinds of girls. Little do Wendy's parents know now; Arti Rose has taken more than one forbidden fruit, and Wendy has lost some of her innocence as well. But Arti Rose is careful to see that Wendy and Sis have settled in the tent with Sunshine, where all three of her female cohorts are on their way to dreamland before she sneaks out and slips into Tex's sleeping bag with him. (They make love and fall asleep under the great, wide sky full of stars.)

The second night Arti Rose is too sunburned to be touched; so she shares the tent with the girls. Kirby (who was Arti's friend from church, and those Kumbaya-around-the-campfire nights at church camp, long before he and Sunshine hooked up, then broke up) plays the Eagle Scout role as usual, chivalrously building a fire outside the girls' tent. Cole puts his sleeping bag next to Tex's, and Tex talks himself to sleep, staring up at the stars and telling Cole what Nam was like, advising him to stay out of the military if he doesn't get drafted. Davie and Will had spent most of the day in the water with their boards, wishing the waves were bigger. Sunburned and exhausted, Will and Kirby crash in the boys' tent. Davie pulls his sleeping bag out under the stars. And that second night, Wendy is the one who sneaks out of the girls' tent. It is too hot and crowded in there anyway. She crawls into Davie's sleeping bag with him.

The wind has changed direction, and a discomforting breeze blows the heat inside the girls' tent, from the fire Kirby built. They are too tired to change their situation and have fallen asleep with their skin burning, Sunshine cursing Kirby for this and other (more personal) offenses as they drift into dreamland. The next day their skin is burning worse than ever. So, heaven has turned to hell, and the girls are ready to go home. The boys don't argue.

Davie and Cole take the van back to Mema's so Cole can spend some more time with her and Pepa before he goes back to California. When the others cram into Will's old wood-trimmed station wagon, with Will's surfboard tied to the top, the conversation goes cosmic. Maybe they have burned their bodies out, and they are in out-of-body mode. Arti Rose starts talking about God and stuff. The recently born-again Christians, Will and Wendy, are on the front bench-seat. They turn the radio up and try to stay out of it after reasserting their simple solution to the problems of the world.

"Admit you are a sinner, accept Jesus into your heart, and follow the Word…He will save you…And when Jesus returns, as He promised, He will save the world."

Arti Rose says she just cannot see Jesus of Nazareth coming back on the clouds with trumpets blowing and a band of angels to fix the mess men have created on planet Earth. She has a feeling the job belongs to regular people like her, but she doesn't know what she is supposed to do. Arti Rose is just trying to throw ideas around as part of her personal search. If she is supposed to help save the world, Arti Rose thinks it might help to know why the world is so messed up, what is wrong with people, and what she can do to help fix this mess, so the people and the planet don't have to suffer so much.

The sunburned passengers are all tired and cranky, but there is energy in cosmic questions, and Arti Rose is reaching for it, partly as a way of getting high. The ones who smoke already smoked all the pot Tex brought anyway. Now they need some other form of stimulation. But it is hard to get anywhere in a deep discussion with Will in the driver's seat. As soon as the conversation starts to flow in the back seat, Will hears some little bit of it (over the volume of the radio) and interrupts with a biblical quote. The radio is playing Led Zeppelin's

"Stairway to Heaven" and Will sings the "dear lady can you hear the wind blow" part, obviously trying to compare Arti Rose with the lady in the song, which makes no sense to Arti. William seems to understand the symbolism in songs, and he used to write some okay poetry back when Arti Rose was going out with him. In fact, that was what she liked about him. He was never as cute as some of the other boys she'd had crushes on in high school, but Will was smart. Now his intellect has lost its appeal. He makes no sense to Arti Rose. Ironically, after displaying a love for symbolism in his earlier attempts at poetry, William takes the Bible too literally, especially since he is a relatively recent student of a back-to-the-Greek version. And it is really aggravating how her little brother (who used to look up to *her*) now agrees with everything Will says, then Wendy agrees with everything Davie says. The three of them are all parroting Pastor Paul, the "Youth for Christ" minister who has taken them into his flock.

If Davie and Felicia were in the car with them, the hippies in the back would be outnumbered by the Jesus freaks in the front, not to mention the blondes. (What is it with blondes and Jesus anyway, Arti Rose wonders quietly, thinking about Felicia but also thinking about bleached-blonde Southern Baptist ladies in their pretty dresses, stepping out on Sundays in their high heels, attracting insects to all that sweet smelling stuff they wear, with all that make-up and the bee-hive hairdos. Do they think Jesus, having once been a natural man, will like them better if they are all gussied-up? Yes, it is partly a cultural divide that Arti Rose is experiencing. Even though her brother and his friends have joined the new hippy branch, Arti Rose can no longer stomach the whole circus of modern "Christianity". And she certainly had her fill, growing up in the "Bible Belt".)

Wendy is at least a *natural* blonde, parted right down the middle, long and straight. Arti Rose likes Wendy and has a bond with her from their high school sorority days. Arti Rose tries extra hard to listen when Wendy is talking, just to help bring her out because Wendy does not talk much. She thinks her brother Dave has too much control over Wendy. Davie is gentle and affectionate with his girlfriend, but it still comes across as controlling to Arti. They may not look that much younger, but they are not adults. Arti Rose feels somewhat responsible since she set them up for that first date, to the annual sorority dinner-dance last year. It was such a big deal, for everybody to have a date (like some archaic mating ritual, from when it was not uncommon for teenagers to be engaged by senior year and marry right out of high school). Wendy was the new kid in the club, and Arti Rose did not want her to be left out (so she had set Wendy up with her handsome and popular little brother, who was Vice President of their sophomore class then). Arti Rose still tries to look after Wendy to some extent when she has the opportunity. But, with Arti Rose being away at State U, and Mama Sue being so busy, the sixteen-year-olds have sometimes been left unsupervised. (Not that they wouldn't have managed to make-out without Dave's room, since he had gotten his license and his stepdad had helped him buy an old van when he turned sixteen.)

Even now, on this camping trip, Arti Rose wonders; did Wendy's parents think that because she, Arti Rose (Wendy's "big sister" from the goody-goody Alpha Girls) was going, Wendy would be *safe?* Arti Rose figures that by now Dave and Wendy may have done it. She knows Dave has at least done it once, with Sunshine (right after she broke up with Kirby, but they both knew Sunshine was not over Kirby and Dave was in love with Wendy). If it was the old days, like when Mema and Pepa were kids, Dave and Wendy would be okay; they would be right on time to get married at sixteen, right on time to start farming "the back-forty". The neighbors could help them build a cabin, a place to start raising up the young that would be coming up soon, sprouting like freshly sown seeds after a summer rain. But these days they will be expected to go to college, get some knowledge, (the knowledge of good and evil maybe, like from that infamous tree). In the here and now, no matter how much they talk about Jesus, it is difficult for Arti Rose to feel comfortably celebratory about Dave and Wendy's romance. Arti listens hard when Wendy talks, hoping the girl is *thinking*, under that lovely head full of natural blonde hair.

Now William is quoting the Bible from the drivers' seat, and his tone is so arrogant that Arti Rose does not pay much attention to him. But when Wendy has something to say, Arti Rose stretches her imagination in Wendy's direction.

"The problems of the world are all because of the fall, because of Adam and Eve disobeying God," Wendy says, simple as that.

Arti tries to support Wendy's right to an opinion by taking the position, for just a minute, that maybe there was an original set of human parents, call them Adam and Eve or whoever. If they made a big mistake, like in the Bible (but the apple must be symbolic, of course), then it would make sense that we inherited some warp that has made human beings the cancer that we are on the planet. Arti Rose tries to grasp the Biblical point of view, out loud, which suddenly gets on Kirby's nerves. (Kirby is sitting between Sunshine and Arti in the back seat but has been leaning forward, partly to avoid Sunshine's now-forbidden body space and partly to hear what Wendy was trying to say, over the volume of the radio and Will's occasional singing-along). Then nearly everybody starts to argue in a different, louder tone (waking Tex and little Sis, who are in the very back of the wagon, snoozing on the pile of sleeping bags and duffle bags).

Kirby is the toughest nut to crack, because he is scientific and agnostic, and he has actually bothered to read the Bible (while his parents forced him to go to church three times a week his whole life, until he went off to college). He has also read Freud and Nietzsche and a bunch of other writers who have helped him cancel out religion for the natural hedonism his youthful energy prefers. Kirby looks almost like Sunshine's twin, but less dazzling. Impossibly wild curls frame both of their angelic faces, but Kirby is somehow plainer, less cute. And although their features are angelic, their expressions seldom are. Sunshine has an innocent glow about her, a vitality that shines out past her sharp and jagged edges. Kirby has the vitality too, the bounce to the step. But there is something sort of blank about the expression on his face, like he is reserving the judgment he will inevitably impart, taking it all in with a sense of skepticism. Both Kirby and Sunshine are somewhat burdened by an underlying cynicism that developed when they were labeled "different" as young children, but they carry it well most of the time. It is now fashionable to be "freaky", to have impossibly curly hair that seems to spring from untamed brains. Despite their similarities, and this group's tendency to shove them into the same seat, lately they repel each other like oil and water.

Privately, when Sunshine is confiding in Arti Rose, she says Kirby used her hippy image to help him get in with a cool group of kids at Southern City College second semester; then he dumped her to be a hippy playboy. Before he showed her off, (when she started spending weekends with him there and telling her parents she was staying at State), everybody at Southern thought Kirby was just another nerd. Kirby didn't even really let his hair grow out or start smoking pot until Arti Rose introduced him to Sunshine at a bonfire thing they did by the rock quarry over Christmas break (until they were busted for trespassing and taken them to the police station, which was another adventure that bonded them all). Anyway, Kirby was always well-liked (for a nerd) but never considered all-that-cool until he started dating Sunshine and let his hair grow out wild like hers.

Now, Kirby acts like he invented cool, and it is somehow attached to braininess. In fact, Kirby talks as if he has already read *everything* and is an authority on *all* of it, including everything about God, who he says he does not believe in. Not that Jesus didn't exist, ("if He didn't, that would be the greatest hoax ever perpetuated by human history", Kirby says) but that doesn't mean God does (not in the way the Bible describes Him anyhow). And to think Arti Rose met Kirby at church, when they were in the tenth grade and both of them going there three times a week. Kirby cringes when anyone references the Adam and Eve story, for example, which Wendy just did when Arti said something about wondering where all the problems in the world *started*. Kirby considers the Bible to be ancient history and myth with little relevance to the problems of today's world (except for some basic rules made to hold society together, some of which should be questioned).

Kirby says, "Everything is psychological. 'Where it all started', if you are talking about the fucked-up state our world is in today, is not a historical question. It started in a lot of fucked-up individuals. It always starts in early childhood. Kids get fucked-up by their parents and turn into control freaks and try to rule the world. It's all Freudian. Wars and everything, politics, even religion."

Kirby starts going on and on about Freud, who he has evidently been spending a lot of time under the covers with at home, where he has long been in the habit of staying up nights, reading in bed by flashlight because of his parents' "lights-out" rule at "bedtime". Kirby had read the whole Bible to spite his parents, so that he knew more about it than them when they argued. Arti Rose doesn't know much about anything that Kirby seems to know everything about. But she has heard that, with Freud, everything is based in sexuality. So, it doesn't surprise her that's where Kirby's head is. She finds it irritating that, as smart as Kirby is (and he was voted "Most Likely to Succeed" as a high school "senior favorite") he can't come up with any answers that will help their generation save the world. She's not even sure he cares about that anymore, even though he used to turn every spiritual discussion in their church youth-group into a discussion of social issues. And she wishes Kirby wasn't sitting so close to her. He has bad breath, and that's why she never wanted to kiss him when he tried to date her in high school.

Nobody else in the station-wagon has really tried to study Freud yet either, except for William who felt tortured by subjects like psychology and philosophy when he went to Ole Miss. William was a year older than Arti Rose, and recently he had happily rejected all the intellectualism he had formerly used to impress her with. When she was a mere high school senior he had written to her from his dorm room, late nights when he was trying to poetically untangle thoughts that his studies have left dangling from his brain like the tangled head of hair he grew while he was away. He'd kept the head of hair and some of the poetic music that he had turned Arti Rose on to- Bob Dylan and the like. But this was not the same William that Arti Rose had daydreamed and written some of her first poetry about. That William had been a suffering artist. Apparently, life had gotten easier for him, inside and out, since he'd found Jesus and dropped out of college to work for his "D-d-Dad" and live back in his old room at home, with his doting mother doing his laundry and cooking his meals. (Freud indeed, but you wouldn't hear Will agreeing with any of that. He just kept stuttering biblical quotes, etc. from the driver's seat.)

Kirby says, "Jesus was a great moral teacher to a point, but some of the guilt-inducing bullshit was invented by the Roman rulers and the Catholic Church, to control people."

"Hey, don't knock the Ch-ch-church, man. I'm not Catholic anymore, but my mom is. So, let's be cool about the Church here. The Catholic Church may have gotten off track along the way, but Jesus started it, man. It can't be all bad," William says, turning his wooly head slightly from the front seat and raising his voice over the radio, rosary beads and a cross dangling from the rearview of the station-wagon that was originally his mom's.

"I heard the Pope is the Antichrist," Tex chimes up from the back. "But I wish you guys would cool-your-jets."

"Please," Sissy agrees in an irritated tone at high volume. "I need a nap."

Arti Rose can't stand the negative vibe in the station wagon now, the tension, the threat of conflict. It's not the kind of energy she was after when she started the conversation. "It's all about Love anyway," she says. "So what does it matter about religion or philosophy or psychology. Love is bigger than all that, and Love will save the world. And people should be free to believe whatever they want, as long as it doesn't stop them from loving other people."

"So, what does *that* have to do with what I just said?" Kirby says, his face twisting, his hands getting in on the action, turning palms up, arms out, invading the spaces of the girls on either side of him.

Sunshine can't stand to hear Kirby condescend from his academic ivory tower of braininess (especially since he has quit worshiping her body); so she agrees vehemently with anything Arti Rose says. "And what does it *not* have to do with what you said. 'Love is all there is'; like the Beatles said, like Arti Rose said. That about covers it, Kirb; so you can get down off your soap box, your *high* horse. Geeeeeeeeeeez."

"Oh, get real, Sun," Kirby says, shaking his head, catching his breath, catching himself before he gets into it with her. He settles back into his seat, shuts his eyes like he is going to take a nap, folds his arms across his chest, calms himself down by analyzing this unsophisticated bunch, separating himself from them mentally. Kirby thinks Sunshine is a pop-culture fed pseudo-hippy who needs to get real and quit covering her birthmark with make-up all the time (not just when she's too sunburned like now). And although Kirby does not doubt his old friend Arti Rose's heartfelt sincerity, he cannot stomach her emotionally based way of looking at the world. He thinks Arti Rose is a gullible flowerchild who looks at the world through rose-colored glasses. And she is kind of preachy, like she is trying to convince herself and everybody else of something that she is not sure of, something she just wants to believe in so she can feel good and get high on the feelings that come from whatever pretty words she has to say. *Love is All There Is; that's original.* And Sunshine takes up for Arti passionately even though she is not really into existential questions, much less their answers (or lack thereof), except when she is tripping. It does not help much that she takes Arti's side, because Sunshine is being *purely* emotional. So, what is the point in trying to have a conversation with these dumb punks, Kirby is thinking.

Arti Rose quiets down too, looks out the window, but feels upset. There is so much love in this group, love gone awry, confused love, immature love, but love. It bothers Arti that her friends can have fun together, when nobody is thinking or questioning, but cannot seem to communicate very well, much less agree on what seem to her to be important questions in life. And what's worse, lately they don't show much respect for each other's points-of-view.

Sunshine hates it that Arti even cares what Kirby thinks. It obviously bothers Arti Rose a lot, not to have her ideas respected by Kirby. Arti admires Kirby's intelligence and misses the friendship they had when they were in the same church youth group. They used to do fun things, innocently alone together, like going over to Kirby' house after Youth Fellowship and listening to his Crosby, Stills, Nash, and Young Album. Arti Rose also has some repressed romantic feelings for Kirby. In high school he had a nerdy girlfriend that people used to say he was having sex with. When they broke up, Kirby shared some of his poetry with Arti Rose and even wrote one poem to her, walking several miles to put it on her door. He made attempts at courting her for a while toward the end of senior year (under the guise of friendship, since she was already dating William whenever he came home from college). Kirby even got to be friends with William when he visited her while Will was around. It got to be a family joke, when they both showed up with their poetry (brought because Arti Rose was their biggest fan) and sat at either end of the sofa., comparing notes.

"Maybe they like each other more than they like Arti Rose," was the family joke.

Now Arti feels like she missed out on both Will and Kirby, as boyfriends, since she knows more about what it is really like to be lovers (after having lovers while she was away) and not just "date" or get together as friends. But she misses the dating too. Her time with Tex is increasingly spent in his room and talking is never what Tex has in mind. She misses talking with her male friends, one-on-one. Lately, she only sees Will and Kirby when her brother invites them along. It was worse when she only saw Kirby with Sunshine, because they were all over each other the way she and Kirby never got the chance to be (except for the time Kirby tried to kiss her at a weekend church youth retreat in the mountains, but she wouldn't let him because he had bad breath…).

It feels strange, to miss people on an intimate level while being in group situations with them. It's like being too close and not close enough at the same time. There is a tension, a holding back; then there is verbal aggression from the need to release. Arti also misses Rob, who she could talk to easily when he was around but has not been able to open up to when he occasionally calls. Tex (who is waking up in the far back end of the wagon) seems dumb compared with Arti's old boyfriends. But in a way it is relaxing, being with someone who doesn't want to analyze everything.

Will and Arti's brother Dave are not dumb but just decidedly anti-intellectual Jesus-freaks and nature-freaks. They admire Kirby because he is a good Boy Scout, not because he is well read. And maybe Kirby likes them sometimes because they are not impressed with his bookishness, which he needs a break from anyway (no matter how tightly he may be hanging onto all of those ideas inside his head). Anyway, there is just no point trying to throw ideas around with this group for long, because everybody is hanging onto something for dear life. Tex is the only one who does not argue much; he is just trying to hold onto what is left of his dope (which nobody else in this group buys, but nearly everybody tokes at one time or another when it gets passed around).

And Arti Rose, with all her efforts to grasp a hopeful idealism and share it with her friends, is still hanging onto all she really has, which is one big question mark. She doesn't wear one around her neck, like the pewter peace symbol on a leather cord, but the question mark is a symbol of the times. Arti Rose had a poster with a pop-art picture of a question-mark hanging over her bunk in the dorm room at State U, a big question mark with the top part as a mushroom cloud and the dot at the bottom as the earth under the cloud left behind by a nuclear bomb. That was next to the other poster with the beautiful sunrise and the words "Today is the first day of the rest of your life".

A band called "The Who" sings "Talkin' 'bout my generation..." on the radio, as gulfs widen between the growing, changing individuals in this group, on their way home.

Focus

One evening Arti Rose takes Sunshine with her to the painting class she has been skipping all summer. The syllabus that the art teacher handed out during the first class, the only time Arti has physically been, says the class will meet on the roof of the student union building and paint sunsets on small canvases using hand-held palletes. Since the patio on the roof is open to the student body, Arti Rose invites Sunshine (even though Sunshine is not enrolled at the junior college). The teacher doesn't ask any questions about whether Sunshine is a student there. Sunshine looks like a student and an artist; so she just blends right in as an observer. Arti Rose feels much more comfortable, having her friend next to her instead of the overly confident painter girl that was working next to her during the first class. She also finds acrylics easier to work with in the smaller format and wonders why the teacher did not start them out on smaller canvases. Arti Rose paints two sunsets, one in warm colors and another in cool colors, on the little canvases that do not intimidate her. She turns the paintings in, at the end of the class, and tells the teacher she is still working on the large still-life of the flowers at home. The teacher tells her she also needs to do a landscape.

Arti Rose and Sunshine stay on the roof long after all the other students leave. They talk about everything. Arti Rose tells Sunshine she might be pregnant. Her period is late. She already told Tex, and he was happy. If it's a boy, they are going to name him Christopher.

Sunshine does not know whether to be happy or sad. Their friendship will never be the same. But she tries to be happy for Arti. When she opens her arms to hug her friend, Arti Rose starts to cry.

"I love him, but I don't think I can marry him," she says through her tears. "He is such a pothead, and he doesn't make enough money to take care of a family. I don't think he wants a better job either; he'll probably just sell more dope. And I worry that he might do other drugs besides pot. He says he used to, but he doesn't anymore. I know he got a dishonorable discharge from the service too; he never explained exactly why. He just said all the guys in Nam were doing dope. I know his roommate at State that was in Nam with him used to shoot up. I never told you about it, but I opened the wrong door at that house one time. Tex was in there with him, and the other guy was putting a needle in his arm. It looked like Tex was helping him in some way, holding something that was tight around that junkie's arm. But I didn't really get what I was seeing, like I was in shock and denial. I closed that door real quick and quit going over there. I wouldn't even let myself really think about it, much less talk about it. Remember when I used to say I didn't want to talk about Tex, because it gave me a stomachache to think about him?"

"I remember. I couldn't stand that guy. The first time I heard his maniacal laugh, I felt like something evil had gotten hold of my innocent Arti Rose. I was so relieved when I heard he had left town, because I thought he wouldn't have any more power over you."

"I'm just glad I wasn't in that house got raided. I couldn't believe sweet Suzy ended up with her name in the paper next to that junkie roommate of Tex's. And Tex was long gone. I still feel guilty about not telling Suzy what I saw when I opened that closet."

"She probably wouldn't have believed you, or it just wouldn't have registered in her brain, like it didn't register in yours at the time. I think that was the first time Suzy even smoked pot, when we all went to that party where you got infatuated with Tex," Sunshine said, staring off at the dying sun. "It was a cool house, with the sunset murals on the walls. But I never trusted those guys. I couldn't believe it when I heard you were going out with Tex this summer."

I didn't think about it much when he started calling. I guess I was lonely at the time, depressed from working at Woolco and coming home to an apartment where everybody in my family was busy somewhere else. And Tex was being so nice, inviting me out to dinner and the movies. But now it keeps bothering me, especially since I might be pregnant. Sunshine, what if Tex was shooting up too? What if we have a child together and he starts shooting up and I have to leave him and raise the child alone?"

"That guy is such a creep," Sunshine says, sounding disgusted and angry. "I swear, he may come across as a mellow dude, but there is something evil about him, Arti; I can tell by that weird laugh of his. It's unnatural sounding. He probably does shoot up. But, of course, he is *not* going to do it around *you*. That's what's evil about him; he's hiding something. I just do not trust Tex, never have since the first time I went in that house and saw him holding court in his cushy little hippy-den. No sir. Why do you think I kept going back out on the front porch?

That was a cool porch, with all those wooden chairs and rockers. Naturally every hippy in town was going to stop by. But you got sucked in. I hated it that you started sleeping with him. It was like, he *got* you; something evil *got* my sweet best friend."

Sunshine hasn't even referred to her in that endearing term since she started hanging out with Whitney this summer. Arti cries even harder, and Sunshine puts her hands on her friend's shoulders and looks her square in the face. "Do not worry Arti Rose; you have a wonderful family. Your family will help you, and I will help you. We can get an apartment together in one of those old buildings on Southside near a park where the kid can play. We can work and go to school at the University, right here in the city, and take turns watching the kid. I wouldn't mind, Art. It would be fun. You are my best friend ever. I can see it now," Sunshine says, letting go of Arti and staring dreamily at Venus, shining just above the horizon. "Me and you and little Christopher."

"Sunshine, you must be trippin'. But I love you," Arti Rose says.

When they are walking down the stairs and back to the car, Arti Rose says she kind of wishes they could have stayed in their old dorm room at State. Things were crazy there sometimes, but this summer is even crazier. They start being nostalgic about their freshman year and everything they went through together their first time away from their families. Despite some differences, they became family to each other, and they always will be.

But when Arti Rose is alone and thinking to herself later that night, on the swing out behind the apartments, she knows she does not really want to room with Sunshine again this fall. It was fun; but it was too much fun. Sunshine was bossy and domineering at times, especially when it came to partying and following long-haired boys into situations Arti Rose would have shied away from on her own. And the worst of it was how Sunshine and some of the other girls had bullied and made fun of Arti Rose about being the only virgin in the dorm at the end of first semester. They had literally done a survey and threw it in her face late one night when everybody was supposed to be studying for midterms. Now Arti Rose can't help thinking how much easier her life would be if she could have admitted she wasn't ready for the partying and sex that college students seemed to consider ritesof-passage into adulthood. All of that had just messed with her mind, made it impossible to study. What Arti Rose wants now is to get serious, to grow up and do something important with her life. Maybe Tex wants to grow up too and that's why he is happy that she might be pregnant. Anyway, no matter how scary, the idea of a child does seem to bring everything into focus.

Reality

The following weekend Arti Rose gets a dose of reality. Tex says he has to stop off somewhere to get pot before they go out for the evening. Arti Rose usually stays in the car when he does anything like that, but tonight she feels like hanging close with him. They are usually alone or with her family; she has never met any of his friends in the city.

It is dark when they walk into this place. Arti Rose does not notice much about the outside. Inside it reminds her of a cave, darkish and dingy, and the people look like cave people to her. For some reason she thinks there is a dirt floor. But that can't be possible, can it? She lowers herself to a cushion around the oddly shaped coffee-table like everyone else, carefully because she cannot see very well. The only light is a candle burning on the low table, which must have been cut from a cypress tree because there are wooden knees underneath, competing with human knees. There is a big bong pipe in the middle of it. There are cats crawling everywhere, and one climbs into Arti Rose's lap. She pets it and and feels a little calmer and a little more creeped-out at the same time. (Cats are usually more stand-offish, in her experience). Tex takes a big toke off the bong pipe when the guy who lives there passes it to him. He holds the toke in, then turns his head toward Arti Rose and blows a steady stream of smoke toward her face. She inhales a little and turns her head away while he is still blowing; she's trying to cut back. Tex tilts his head down and blows the rest in the direction of the cat's face, and everybody laughs. There are a couple of other guys around the table but Arti Rose is the only female.

Just then a young woman comes out of a back room with two toddlers wearing only diapers, both with long, blonde hair. The woman looks like another cave person, short and thick, tough, not smiling or offering any sort of greeting. The toddlers are sort of tough-looking too, but beautiful. The woman lowers herself to another cushion around the table. The kids play all around the table, with the cats. When their dad has the bong, he grabs the slightly more boyish looking toddler and blows smoke in his face.

"That'll calm him down," he says, laughing gruffly. The other men around the coffee table, including Tex, seem amused by what the young father (assuming he is the child's father) has just done and laugh along with him. Arti Rose notices (or maybe just acknowledges to herself for the first time) that what Sunshine said is true; there is something eerie, almost maniacal about Tex's laugh.

Arti Rose is depressed for the rest of the night. When they leave, she tells Tex why she is sad and he keeps trying to reassure her that he might blow pot smoke in a cat's face but he would never do that to little Christopher.

"Then why do you do it to me?" she asks.

Tex does not give Arti Rose a joint to save for later, when he walks her to the door of her mother's apartment that night and makes that clicking sound with his tongue while he briefly touches the end of her nose with his pointer finger. "G'night kid," he says, in that affectionately drawn-out but not completely Southern accent, the only vowel in the "night" being more short than long (and more i-ee than I-ah) reminding her that Tex has been somewhere else besides here, besides Texas too. He has been to places, done things that she can't even imagine.

Tex turns and walks away, the up-beat sound of his boots on the stairs following him and echoing in Arti Rose's mind for a long time after he is gone.

Inside, Sue is out for the evening, Sis is at a slumber party, and Dave has Wendy in his room.

Neil Young is on the stereo. "Don't let it bring you down. It's only castles burning. Just find someone who's turning, and you will come around."

"Are you OK, Arti?"

Arti Rose starts lifting every heavy thing she can get her hands on. She moves the furniture around in the apartment, then puts it back where it was before her mother gets home from work. And when nobody is looking, she beats on her own belly with her fists. Sunshine does not know this, but she knows enough to be worried about her friend. She wants to take her to Planned Parenthood for a pregnancy test, but Sunshine doesn't say anything about her plan when she talks to Arti Rose. She just meets her at Woolco after work and says, "Let's go somewhere."

Sunshine hates Woolco and walks out of there really fast, her wild hair and braless boobs bouncing as usual. Arti Rose drags behind her, trying to keep up, in a greasy Red Grill apron with her hair pulled back, just feeling miserable and not really wanting to go anywhere except maybe to bed, if she had a bed and a room of her own to be left alone in.

On the sidewalk just outside Woolco, Sunshine stops to wait for Arti and turns her head toward her friend just in time. Everything goes black for Arti Rose and she collapses. But Arti wakes up soon, when Sunshine starts hollering at her with an uncharacteristically concerned whine to her voice, like she is talking to a child. She sees Sunshine's face in her face and feels that Sunshine is barely holding her up off the sidewalk, like she must have caught her.

Sunshine takes her to the apartment, and when Arti Rose goes to the bathroom there is a lot of blood. They are both relieved she got her period.

Arti Rose bleeds more than usual and thinks she is having a miscarriage but does not tell anybody. Only Tex and Sunshine knew she thought she was pregnant anyway. Tex is a little disappointed but says this will give him some time to get his shit together before having a kid.

Arti Rose grieves alone and decides this thing with Tex has to end. She just does not know how or when to break it to him. She doesn't want to take the bounce out of his steps. Arti Rose knows that Tex carries something heavy down deep, even though he is walking light in his boots these days, making that upbeat sound she likes to hear when he comes and goes. She goes with him to see fireworks on the

Fourth of July anyway, but all she thinks about, looking up from the grass where they are stretched out together under all those starbursts, is what Independence Day really means to her and her alone.

New Life

Arti Rose started reading the literature Dave and Will left on the coffee table at the apartment. Maybe if she could possibly stand to go to Pastor Paul's youth rallies she would meet some cool looking Jesus-freak guy who didn't do dope and wouldn't mind waiting until they got married to have sex. Will was already taken by Felicia, for now at least, but there were plenty of other Christian hippies these days. If Arti could just stand the literature, but it was pretty weird. Cartoons about the end of the world and Jesus coming back on the clouds were the worst. But those "4 Easy Steps to Salvation" tracts weren't very intelligently written either, like a recipe for instant something Arti Rose had already tried.

She too had been "saved", but it was like a sugar high, like those cakes her country Mema fed her with Sunday dinners after revivals at Mt. Olive Pentecostal Church. Arti Rose had been to the altar countless times, bowed and cried and rose clean and worthy of love. "Thanks for blessing us, Sugar," an old lady with a big mole on her face had said just last summer, as she took her turn with a dozen or two other congregants who stood in line to hug sweet Arti Rose (flushed again with the Holy Spirit, as in a dozen summers past). There were no propaganda tracts at Mema Etta's church in the piney woods, just those cardboard fans from the funeral home (with pretty pastoral pictures on one side and ads on the other). The fans came in handy when ladies fainted, stricken with the spirit and the lack of air-conditioning.

There was one pamphlet that looked different on Mama Sue's coffee-table one day though. It was yellow with an abstract, funky artistic orange sun and flower that went with the décor in the apartment. Sis had been decorating the bookcase/room-divider with candles she made from a craft kit, green frogs and turtles, and mushrooms painted yellow with bright orangey-red dots, like the ones in the woods on Pine Mountain. There were also Arti Rose's paintings, the bright abstract

103

over the yellow wooden filing cabinet and the timid yellow wildflowers on the floor by the window near the front door. If only she could start over with that painting, Arti Rose thought, she would make the flowers bigger and more abstract like the orange flower on front of the yellow pamphlet on the coffee table. It said "New Life Lecture Series". Arti Rose looked it over, read some of the topics to be discussed. It was very intelligently written, and the topics were some of the same questions she and Kirby and everybody had argued about on the way back from the Gulf. The origin and purpose of life, good and evil, the future of mankind. There was a man's name and phone number on back, with a Southside address and apartment number. What could be cooler? A Southside apartment and a guy named Gabe Dane (probably Gabriel, but he is being informal). No title like Pastor or Rev. Just a guy, in an apartment, talking about these interesting topics. She picked up the phone and dialed.

The young man did not have a southern accent. He called himself "Gabe" and said he was from San Francisco. He asked what would be a good time for her to come to "the Center", and she said Saturday. She figured that would be the easiest day to get a ride to Southside, Sunshine's favorite part of town.

Meanwhile Arti Rose kept thinking about the young man she had talked to on the phone. She had been reading a paperback book entitled *The Strawberry Statement*, about a student uprising at Columbia University in NY. It was written by a young man who had been involved and Arti kept wondering, while she read the book, why she couldn't meet a young revolutionary, someone with above average intelligence and a sense of purpose. Maybe if this guy Gabe was from San Francisco, he might have participated in the peace movement and the "Summer of Love" and the whole cultural revolution that happened big-time in California. Anyway Arti Rose just knew, somehow, that he was a cool guy.

She called Sunshine and told her about him, and Sunshine said that sounded cool because, remember, they were just talking about maybe getting an apartment on Southside instead of going back to State. But she had already promised Whitney they would spend Saturday together; so she might have to bring her too. Arti said that was cool.

"Sounds like a plan, man." (Sunshine was saying "man" all the time, since she'd started hanging out with Whitney. It was a hippy thing.)

"The Principle"

Sunshine picks Arti up in the yellow bug on Saturday, with the convertible top down. Whitney is waiting in the front passenger seat with a joint in that big tapestry bag she carries. Instead of politely getting in the back seat to accommodate the new passenger (as Arti Rose would have done) Whitney moves forward just enough to let Arti Rose climb in behind her.

Arti Rose is oblivious to the cold-shoulder she gets from Ms. Cool. She bubbles over as she sits forward in the middle of the back seat, her head between the two girls in front. "Both of y'all remind me of Carole King's album cover today," Arti says, "Sunshine because of your hair and Whitney because of your tapestry bag. Did y'all know Carole King was the one that wrote 'You've got a Friend' even though James Taylor made it a hit?" Arti Rose asks, trying to make conversation.

Whitney doesn't talk much, but she has a way of just sort of grunting and saying "Yeah-uh," like she is so cool that nobody could possibly tell her anything cool that she doesn't already know.

Arti Rose has about quit smoking, since when she thought she was pregnant and got freaked out about dope; but she takes one little toke when Whitney passes it to her, just to be sociable. Sunshine and Whitney smoke the rest of the joint on the way to Southside. When they get to Southside, Sunshine starts talking about how blown away she is by all the far-out old brick buildings and how neat the red brick streets look winding through the green parks and the big, old trees.

"What a cool old building," Sunshine says when she parks and they get out of the VW beetle near the address on the yellow pamphlet. It is a brick and brownstone building with big steps going up the front and interesting details, like screened-in balcony porches that face a park across the Avenue.

Sunshine is not wearing shoes because Whitney did not wear shoes. Whitney always tries to go the extra mile toward super-coolness by being different in some far-out freaky way, which is why Sunshine started to hang around with her in high school. Sunshine was sick of how the sorority girls and cheerleaders like her older sister always conformed.

Arti Rose is wearing those little leather sandals from India, with the toe straps; she got them at Pier I for small change. They are all wearing their oldest patched jeans, because those are the coolest and this guy is from San Francisco. Arti Rose's patches are the popular store-bought kind: one with a peace-symbol (in the shape of a fisted hand, with the middle and index fingers sticking up) cut from an American flag, and one of a big, green letter "e" (for "ecology").

It is summer and they have on little nothing cotton tops with their bare nipples showing through. They aren't really trying to be any sexier than usual; it's just how they dress (how a lot of young women have been dressing since the bra-burning 'sixties). Arti washed her long, dark-auburn hair with Herbal Essence shampoo; so it wouldn't smell like the hotdogs at the Red Grill. Walking up the steps of the old apartment building, she is enjoying the smell of her own hair as it flows down her back and blows behind her in the breeze. Whitney has a chopped up dirty-dishwater blonde shag she did herself, which won't be a mainstream hairstyle for another decade unless you are John Lennon (or some other avant-garde rock star). They are all three tall as majorettes (which they would never be, because football is so uncool) and lean, with little on their frames except denim and hair and breasts that are barely there. Sunshine has enough to bounce, but her fantastic golden mane draws more attention. Even though they aren't rock stars; the trio would look good on the cover of the Rolling Stone.

Arti Rose has been imagining this apartment, or "Center" as Gabe called it, to be a hippy pad without the dope. Even the church youth fellowship halls have big cushions and bean bags on the floor now, and everybody sits in circles and sometimes they light candles when they have "rap sessions" (encounter groups where people are encouraged to open up and talk) and sing popular folk songs with spiritual messages. Arti thinks that's what it will be like, but a really straight-looking young man answers the door. He is tall and sturdy and has short brown hair and kewpie-doll features that seem to be straining slightly to project a clergyman's seriousness through his wire-rimmed, John Lennon style glasses. He is wearing a white dress shirt and his pants are not jeans, but Arti Rose tries not to stare at his clothes because it seems rude to check him out when he is looking her straight in the eyes and introducing himself. He invites them into the 1940s or '50s pre-modern furnished apartment and seats them at the large dark-wood dining room table where his big green chalkboard stands on an easel at one end. When he stands before them, Arti Rose sees that his tan pants are polyester, a fabric she hates, but they are a new casual design with a wide, relaxed waistband and no belt loops. And he is wearing strap-y leather sandals (with a heel and a toe and a buckle) and white cotton socks. Little John-John Kennedy used to wear those, but Arti Rose has never seen a grown man wearing shoes like that before. They do look comfortable though, airy but sturdy. Despite his somewhat unusual but rather plain, modest style (certainly not "cool-looking" by Sunshine's standards) Arti Rose makes a conscious effort to focus on what Gabe has to say. He does come across as respectable, which lends credibility to his words. However she is somewhat distracted by the fact that his clean-cut image puts him in a new category that her emerging womanly aspect has recently created for itself. He looks like (what her old sorority sisters would call) "husband material".

Arti Rose has spent more time in church than most people she knows, but she has never seen anyone draw yin-yangs on the board. In fact she has only seen the symbol on sterling silver jewelry in "head shops" (boutiques where they sell hippy paraphernalia) and maybe on a few t-shirts and posters. She might have seen a yin-yang on an album cover or maybe on that book <u>Be Here Now</u>, but never in church. However he says this is a Unification Church Center; not that she has ever heard of that, unless it is like Unity or Unitarian. Sunshine has been going with Whitney to the Unitarian, because they can wear whatever they want and believe in whatever they want. But this is not just a discussion of different ideas, like Arti thought it would be; it is a teaching, a very definite set of beliefs.

Gabe said that the *Divine Principle*, "a revelation from God" to a Korean man named Sun Myung Moon, included The Principle of Creation which would be the topic of his first of a series of lectures. "The Principle of Creation", which Gabe outlined on the board and explained for the next hour, began with (a description of) God as "Source Energy". This got Arti Rose's full attention, since she had never heard a description of God presented with such authority. Sure, she had heard various people talk about what God might be; but Gabe was not presenting his ideas that way. This, he was saying as he drew on the board, is what God IS. He went on to say that this source of all the energy in our world also has the loving heart of true parents, the unconditional love of not only a "heavenly father", but also a heavenly *mother*, thus the saying "God is Love".

Several drawings of something called "The Four Position Foundation" used yin-yangs in diagrams of something like atomic structure, with God as nucleus and arrows representing "give and take" of energy between (and within) the several yin-yangs. Positive and negative, male and female, subject and object, mind and body, were some of the terms used. The "Three Blessings" from the book of Genesis in the Bible ("be fruitful, multiply, and have dominion over the creation") were explained and elaborated on while Gabe drew these yin-yangs in atomic-like formations.

"With God as nucleus, man becomes fruitful by having harmony between his mind and body, centering around God," Gabe said, drawing on the board and pointing to his yin-yang atomic drawings while he spoke. "With God at the center of their lives, man and woman form a blessed marriage and multiply their blessings by bringing forth the true children of God. And God-centered families build a God-centered society which has a loving dominion over the creation, thus building a Heavenly Kingdom on the earth. Gabe emphasized responsibility to Earth, mentioning the new "ecology" movement.

Arti Rose could not help letting her mind wander sometimes. She could imagine marrying a cool preacher guy like this and being a mother to futuristic kids (saviors of Earth). But first she would try to understand what he had to say, even if she was just a little bit stoned from that one toke she took on the way over. She managed to hear the important stuff.

"The ultimate purpose of life is Joy," Gabe said. He even wrote it on the board, above all the yin-yangs and "four-position-foundations". JOY.

Gabe got a little personal at the end of his talk and said that what they needed to think about, as young people in a world full of choices, was serving God with their lives and taking responsibility for their own spiritual growth and development as children of God.

"Just as the physical body needs food, the spirit needs love,"

Gabe said. "And just as the physical body needs light, the spirit needs truth, to light the way. Also, just as the physical body needs air, the spirit needs a positive, energizing spiritual atmosphere. If you are not getting those things, you are not growing, spiritually, at the rate that you should be. So, that should give you something to think about," the pleasant young man said, putting his chalk down on the little wooden tray that was built onto the front of the green chalkboard easel, relaxing his stance, turning back to the very young women, who projected a mixture of dazed boredom, distracted (and *attracted)* restlessness, and the bright light of wide-eyed epiphany, according to which one he chose to look at. "Would you all like some lemonade?"

Sue Cronkite's Story

I was the assistant state editor for one of the South's largest daily newspapers. Recently divorced from a much older man, I felt young again, free. I was an independent, "liberated woman". Life was busy and exciting for me. I had never heard of Sun Myung Moon as I walked down "The Green" on my way to the bank, one day in the summer of 1972. Standing on the corner beside a big pot of flowers was a smiling young man. He handed me a leaflet.

"Have a nice weekend," I said pleasantly, and stuck the leaflet in my purse. Later at home, which was a second-floor apartment where I lived with my three children and a Schnauzer named Scottie, I emptied my purse, and left the leaflet on the coffee table in the living room.

The bright yellow leaflet had a modern art design on front, an orange sun and flower, (which matched the coasters on the coffee table). It mentioned "love" and "peace" and called "unity" a "source of joy"...On the back was the young man's address and telephone number.

The pamphlet seemed innocent enough to leave with the mixture of various reading materials on the coffee table. I have never been one for censorship of ideas. I have always thought if I could just keep my children reading, their minds would develop and they would sort things out for themselves, as independent thinkers. We often argued various ideas at home.

My oldest daughter, the most argumentative of us all, found the leaflet...and fell for it, hook, line, and sinker.

The Rap Session

"So where did you get the literature with my number on it?" Gabe asked when the four of them had moved to his living room with their glasses of iced and watered-down lemonade.

"I found it on the coffee table at home," Arti Rose explained, suddenly blushing and feeling awkward in the somewhat stiff and formal antique chair she was seated in. Not that she wouldn't have felt unsure of herself in any situation with such a self-assured young man.

Sunshine and Whitney had taken the wood-trimmed couch. Gabe was also in a stiff-looking chair. As if sensing their discomfort, he brought his long legs up and positioned them cross-legged, as if he were sitting casually on the floor, hippy style. But Gabe Bernard looked more like a well-scrubbed business-man, smiling, glowing almost, like a Buddha, but also like a big kid somehow. One of them, but not.

"Just out of curiosity, which one was it?" he asked. "I've been handing out several different pamphlets around town."

There were some on his coffee table. "The yellow one with the orange sun and flower," Arti Rose said, looking in the direction of one of its duplicates.

"Oh, yes. The 'New Life lecture series'. I handed out a bunch of them downtown. You don't look familiar though," he said, as if he was sure he would have remembered her.

"You must have given it to my mom," Arti Rose concluded. "She works downtown, at *The News*. I thought my brother or one of his friends had put it on our coffee table, because he is always putting Christian literature there."

"Oh, really? What religious background are you?" he asked.

"Me? Oh, um. Well my parents took me to a Baptist church when I was little, but when my mom divorced and remarried we started going to the Methodist Church with my step dad. And I always went with my grandmother to a Pentecostal church when I spent summers with her, which was different because they were holy-rollers."

"That sounds interesting," Gabe said, almost grinning, except that his mouth was too small to manage more than a cute little dimpled smile. He seemed happy to have them there. "I was raised Catholic, which was sort of formal, ritualistic, not very exciting. I was an altar boy though, which was kind of exciting sometimes. So what religious background were you girls?" he asked, still smiling but looking at Sunshine and Whitney.

Sunshine looked at Whitney liked she wished she would go first, but Whitney's face was blank. Sunshine's voice wavered, maybe from shyness or maybe from the pot, or both. "Uhhh. My parents used to make me go to a Methodist Church sometimes because my older sister went there," she said, pausing for a second and taking on a bitter tone to ward off the feeling of vulnerability that was trying to surface. "She was popular and they wanted me to be like her. But we weren't really a religious family. My sister just went to hang out with her friends, but I didn't think they were that cool" she finished, kind of rolling her eyes and looking away from Gabe. Enough said.

When he looked at Whitney, she just said, expressionless, "I go to Unitarian sometimes."

Since none of the girls seemed comfortable talking much, Gabe gladly let them be his audience for a while. He showed them pictures from the center in San Francisco where he had joined the Unification Church and lived communally with other members, even working for a while on an organic farm that the church started in Booneville. Gabe had spent the first Earth Day planting seeds there, in 1970. He was proud of the recent years of his life, which he had spent with the organization, crediting it with his salvation from the streets and his hope of helping save the world.

Gabe's story was that he had been a run-away young hippy from Chicago when a Unification Church "sister" found him wandering around Haight Ashbury in San Francisco (hung-over from the infamous "Summer of Love") and invited him over for dinner and a Divine Principle lecture. He glowed when he talked about that "sister" and also when he talked about "Miss Kim", a middle-aged Korean "missionary" who headed the San Francisco Center and had brought the church to the United States a decade before Gabe showed up. When Gabe talked about Miss Kim his eyes seemed to slant more and he took on a strangely oriental aspect, in his otherwise big-boned

Germanic looking body. Gabe had a persistent glow about him; so did the Asian man in the poster on the wall.

The picture, above an announcement about a speaking tour in several major American cities, was of a beautiful Asian family. The handsome middle-aged man with a glow about his face was wearing a suit and tie, but his lovely wife and two little children, a boy and a girl, were all wearing kimonos. Gabe noticed Arti Rose staring at the poster.

"That is the leader of our church, and his family," Gabe said proudly. "I heard him speak when he came to America, and it was very inspiring. He is supposed to be coming again soon and going to more cities this time, including this one. That's why he sent me here, to get the church started in this state and prepare people to hear his message when he comes." Gabe uncrossed his legs, put them on the floor and sat up straighter in his chair. "I'll talk more about him when you come back for the other lectures," he said, standing suddenly and taking their empty glasses. "You will come back; won't you?" he asked, talking to all of them but mostly to Arti Rose since she seemed to be the only one of the three who was really interested.

"Sure," she said.

"Yeah, maybe," Sunshine said.

Whitney turned her attention to her tapestry bag, as if to get her car keys (but Sunshine had driven them there).

The Real Thing

"Man, that was fuckin' weird," Sunshine said, in a breathy sounding stoned whisper as soon as they were on the sidewalk and walking away from Gabe's apartment (or "Church Center"). "I never should have gotten stoned before I went in there, because I was freakin' out," she went on, getting louder as they got closer to the VW.

Whitney just made a little grunting sound and shook her head from side to side a couple of times.

"I thought it was pretty cool, the teaching and all," Arti Rose said, "especially the yin-yangs and the stuff about love and joy."

"It sounded like a bunch of gobbledygook to me," Sunshine said. "But my mind definitely wandered. He was pretty cute though, for a straight guy," she said, ("straight" meaning conservative, regular, normal, not a hippy or a cool freak like her).

"His wire-rims were cool," Whitney said. She was wearing a nearly identical pair of wire-rimmed glasses herself, like the ones John Lennon (the British rock star and former Beatle) wore on the cover of his album, "Imagine".

"His sandals might have looked cool if not for those socks," Sunshine said, suddenly breaking out into full-blown laughter as they got into the bug and she took the wheel.

"So what," Arti Rose said, feeling suddenly defensive and protective of Gabe, her newfound friend. "Hippies aren't supposed to care about clothes anyway; what matters is on the inside. And I have a feeling this guy is the real thing."

Whitney shook her head again. Sunshine felt really uncomfortable about the whole experience and turned on the radio real loud, just trying to think about something else. Don McLean was singing "Bye-bye Miss American Pie".

Arti Rose looked out the window and thought about Gabe and the "Heavenly Kingdom on Earth".

"Bible Study"

by Sue Cronkite

I didn't notice too closely at first, except it was sort of nice that my eldest daughter had gotten interested in religion again. She was going to Bible Study now, as often as her brother. She talked about the high ideals of the Unification Church.

The Unification Church was going to "unify" the world, and bring peace and cooperation to all God's people, over the face of the earth, my daughter said. It seemed like a pretty big task, but since I was constantly telling my senior high Sunday school class, at the United Methodist Church, that God is as big as you believe He is, it still didn't seem too alien to me at first.

"It's really such a deep ideology that it's difficult to express it," my daughter said, during one conversation, "but I really believe it to be the most great and powerful truth ever revealed to mankind."

"What is the great and powerful truth? What do you mean

'great and powerful truth', " I asked.

"The Divine Principle. It can change our doomed world," she said. She took on a pious, dedicated look. "It has given me hope," she said, "and since man is a universe within himself, what occurs in one man can occur in the entire cosmos, I hope."

"Cosmos?"

"The universe, or even bigger than that. The spiritual and physical worlds."

I did some research and learned that the church, formally known as the Holy Spirit Association for the Unification of World Christianity, was established in the United States in 1959. The self-ordained Sun M. Moon, who says he was inspired at the age of 16 by a vision of Jesus, founded his church in 1954 in South Korea.

My son went to at least one of the lectures. His sister wanted him to hear the whole series, but I remember him saying early on that one was enough. Some of his friends from the evangelical Christian youth group he was involved with went to the lectures, and they ended up saying Moon was the anti-Christ. They were all being overly-emotional for a while, and I didn't know which group was crazier.

I just wished my children would go with me to the Methodist Church we had attended as a family for years, before the divorce. I sometimes required my youngest to attend there, because I wanted to go and did not want to leave her unsupervised. It was also a way of giving her another group of youngsters to socialize with, other than those at the apartment complex.

My father had taught me to ignore the dogma at the Baptist church that was the center of the rural community where I grew up. Daddy did not agree with the rules against dancing and various forms of fun; but he took me to church because he believed in socializing with people who meant well, who were at least trying to be good. However, I was taught not to believe in any form of forced indoctrination.

I always invited all of my children to go to church with me, every time I attended, as long as they were in earshot. However, I would not have felt comfortable insisting that grown children attend my chosen denomination. My former husband had coerced all of us into going to church three times a week. The divorce, less than a year earlier, had finally freed me to practice my own style of parenting, which meant that my children could worship where they pleased, when and if they pleased. We had all lived in a dictatorship for eight years. It was time for some lessons in democracy.

I just hoped this Moon character would not turn out to be another dictator in my daughter's life.

Getting It Together

When Tex called to ask Arti Rose out for the weekend, she said she would rather hang out at the apartment but he was welcome to come over. He thought that was odd, but she explained that she wanted to get her friends together for a change. Except for the time when they went to the Gulf with Dave and Will, they hadn't been together much as a group. Her mom was cool with everybody coming over; Sue was always friendly with anybody who dropped by. And it seemed like there were always a few extra kids hanging out at the apartment lately, whether they were friends of Arti's or Dave's or Sis's. But they were still kind-of like ships passing. Arti had decided to make more of a conscious effort to get everybody together; so she and Dave were going to do a barbeque when he and Will got off work Friday evening. Sunshine was coming, and Dave had invited Wendy. Arti Rose had not called Leash because Felicia has never really been her choice of a friend. But she had told Will he could bring Leash if he wanted to. Kirby had stopped by one day and said he would come over Friday night if everybody was going to be there. And Tex was welcome, of course.

Dave and Will bring some groceries to the apartment with them when they get off work Friday. They are hot, tired, hungry, and sunburned from putting antennas on roofs. Luckily, Sis has already started the grill (a skill the eleven-year-old learned when it was just she and Mama Sue at the apartment, before the divorce was final, when Dave stayed with Daddy Dick for a while and got born-again). Sis likes steak and has learned to cook it for herself so she can have a good meal when Mom goes out to dinner with the car salesman. But the guys didn't buy steaks, which disappoints Sis somewhat. Arti Rose is in the kitchen and starts making hamburger patties from the big package of ground beef they bought. She has already made a salad and some iced tea, and potatoes are boiling on a back burner for her famous chunky mashed potatoes with skins. When Mama Sue gets home, she helps by putting all the fixings and trimmings on the table and setting things up so everybody can serve themselves, buffet-style.

As soon as Sunshine, Wendy, and Kirby arrive they dig in. Some of them sit around the wrought-iron picnic table in the dining area and some sit around the coffee table, on the couch and on the carpeted floor. The "area room" is small enough that they are still close enough to converse with everyone in the group. Scotty-dog keeps pestering everybody in his friendly but hungry-looking way, until Sis puts him out on the back balcony with some scraps.

People are mostly saying "yum" and "wow, this is really good", when Mama Sue makes a joke about Arti Rose's super-buttery, salt and peppery, chunky mashed potatoes with the skins on.

"Arti Rose is just too lazy to peel them, and she doesn't have the muscles to mash them very well," Sue says.

Everybody laughs, including Arti, but the big bowl of "taters" is clean before Tex gets there. He says he had to work overtime, but Arti Rose knows he always buys his dope after work on Fridays. She is just through arranging her life around that fact. He sits down at the table and starts putting his own hamburger together.

Sue puts some ice in a glass and pours Tex some tea. She wants to get to know her daughter's boyfriend better and plans on sitting down at the table with him, but while she is up her date comes to the door. It's the car salesman, and she invites him in. There is no obvious place for him to sit down near the door, which is convenient for him because he never sits down when he comes to pick her up. He is a car salesman, which means he is used to standing. So he stands there and makes a few friendly comments about the weather and stuff while Sue gets her purse.

Arti Rose feels bad about not inviting him and says next time they barbeque he should join them. He says that would be nice, but they both know it probably will not happen. He is just not into hanging around Sue's place and would rather take her to his place as soon as possible. The kids do not care because there is nothing interesting about him anyway. Arti Rose thinks her mama only likes him because her real daddy was a car salesman for a while and had that neat, trim, well-groomed appearance that they like at the better dealerships. But he does not remind Arti Rose of her real daddy in any other way.

Kirby is sitting on the couch across from Arti Rose's favorite floor cushion, and she tells Kirby, between bites of her salad, a little bit about the *Divine Principle* and the guy from San Francisco who is teaching it in an old Southside apartment. He actually thinks it sounds kind-of cool, because of the yin-yangs and the atomic foundation principle she tries to explain. It sounds more like a combination of science and oriental philosophy than religion. Arti tells him she is going to another lecture tomorrow if he wants to come. Kirby says he might come along if he doesn't have anything else to do.

"I feel like I might finally be getting my head together," Arti Rose tells Kirby.

Kirby's face automatically starts to take on that skeptical twist, but for some reason he stops himself and says, "that's cool", real fast, without any emotion and with a hard period at the end which says end-of-subject. "I've written some new poems that you might want to read," he says.

"Yeah, sure. Bring them over if you want to go with me tomorrow."

Kirby picks up a guitar he brought, but he only recently started teaching himself to play. He strums for a while. Dave puts a Neil Young album on and turns it up as loud as Sue's cheap stereo system will go without distorting. ("I wanta live; I wanta give. I been a miner for a heart of gold"). Kirby tries to figure out the chords.

Tex rolls a joint when he is done eating, but Arti says they can't smoke it in the apartment. Tex and Sunshine and Kirby go out by the oak tree and the big swing-set, near the field that borders on the school yard, behind the apartments. Arti and Sis clean up, with a little help from Will. Then Sis goes over to her best friend's apartment to spend the night, which gives Arti some time alone in the kitchen with her old buddy. She tells Will about the guy from San Francisco, calling him a "missionary" because that sounds more Christian. Will says he might go with her to the lecture.

Dave and Wendy have been sitting on the couch listening to Neil Young, but Wendy is upset about something and pulls Dave into his room to talk. When they come out, Arti thinks both of them look like they have been crying. They head outside, with Arti and Will following, but Arti can't get them to talk about what's wrong.

"Nuthin'" is all they say, real blue. They perk up some when they go to the playground.

Outside under the summer moon and as many stars as the edge of the city will allow them to see, everybody plays and swings, forgetting about everything but being young and enjoying the sweet wine of friendship and just having fun, for a while.

God's Stolen Apple Wasn't Ripe

Kirby shows up a couple hours early the next day, because he is anxious to show Arti Rose his new collection of poems. (At least he didn't walk over in the middle of the night and leave them on her door the way he did a few times toward the end of senior year, when she was "only a teardrop in the ocean" of his life). Arti walks out to the swing-set with him. She sits in a swing and reads his poems while he goofs around on the monkey bars.

The poems are in a little spiral stenographer's notebook. Arti doesn't really get what they are about, on any level that would actually move her in any way. But they seem good in the way some of the poems in English class are good but the teacher has to explain them. Arti Rose tries to find something about herself or Sunshine in them, but she can't. One of them is about drowning alone, but it does not seem to be about a literal drowning since there is also breathing involved. Another one is obviously about making love, but it compares the bodies of the lovers with engines. And it could be anybody (which reminds Arti of something Sun said about Kirby and sex recently). Another one is about a family and Arti has to wonder whether it is hers, because it says "your sister in the sweltering sun" (which Sis is most of the time, because of the pool at the complex) and "your father on the floor", which could be something symbolic about Daddy Dick. It could be about Kirby's family too though, because he has a sister. But Arti doesn't know why Kirby's father would be on the floor when he is always sitting in that wing-back chair reading the paper when she visits. She does not ask Kirby whose family this is about. She does not ask him anything. Arti Rose knows these poems are more sophisticated than the ones Kirby wrote in high school. She just tells him he has done some fine work here, and he should keep at it. When she tries to hand him back the notebook, he tells her she can have it.

"Oh, thanks Kirb; I'll treasure them always," Arti Rose says sincerely, clutching the green stenographer's notebook to her breast. Besides feeling happy that Kirby would pick her to share his poems with, Arti actually feels a little bit uncomfortable but is trying not to let it show.

Her old friend needs her for something. Even though she is basically attracted to Kirby, Arti hopes it is just friendship he wants, not sex. Sunshine says he cannot be trusted. She said she heard Kirby has even been participating in orgies and doing it with guys (not to be gay, just to "be an animal", which Kirby actually advocates lately). Maybe Kirby is mixed up and just needs a friend, Arti thinks. If he needs someone to know what is going on inside his head, the poems have not done the trick. But if he needs encouragement with his artistic expression, maybe her interest in Kirby's poetry has done something for him. And if he has been doing crazy, experimental stuff with other students at Southern, he probably does need old friendships from a more innocent time, to balance him out and keep him from going off the deep end. They are all kind-of safe here, with Mama Sue in and out. She has rules, but Mama Sue is cool too, in her own grown-up way.

They walk back to the apartment, because it is time for Arti to call William and see if he still wants to go to Southside for the *Divine Principle* lecture. Kirby has his blue-grey VW (another thing he and Sunshine have in common, image-wise. Kirby taught her to drive his VW, then her dad bought her one). They can fit five people in there, if anybody else wants to go. Sunshine already said she does not care to go this time. Tex didn't show any interest when Arti tried talking to him about it. Will says he has been talking to Leash, and she wants to come. He asks for directions and suggests they meet up at the park on Highland Avenue, across from Gabe's Southside apartment (which is the "Unification Church Center"). Dave rides over with Kirby and Arti, in the blue-grey VW. When they meet up, the five of them throw the Frisbee around in the park until time for the lecture.

Gabe is a bit taken aback when he opens the door, his eyes widening behind the John-Lennon wire-rims.

"So you brought different friends this time," he says to Arti Rose, quickly offering the disarming smile that seems to shrink his could-be overbearing size (not that he is any taller than Will, who stands over six feet, but Gabe's bones are bigger).

"Come in," Gabe says, stopping in the foyer for introductions. "I'm Gabe," he says, offering his hand to Will, then Felicia, then Kirby, then Dave, who return the gesture and say their names.

"You must be Arti Rose's brother," he says to Dave, noticing the resemblance around the eyes and mouth, as well as a kinship of spirit, a shared warmth.

He seats them at the big dining room table and gets started at the chalk board. At the top he has already written the words "The Fall", but he seems a bit hesitant to start the lecture.

"It is best to present the series in order," he says. "This lecture is a bit heavy to start with. The first lecture, 'Principle of Creation', is much lighter and more joyous. I would be happy to work around your schedule if those of you who are here for the first time would come sometime during the week and hear the Principle of Creation. That way you would be on the same page as Arti Rose by this time next Saturday." Gabe, an odd look of concern on his face, seems to be waiting for a response before he continues with the lecture.

"Th-that might be cool, if you don't mind nights," Will says, a bit unsure.

"Yeah, we work weekdays, man," Dave says.

"Nights would be fine. I work at Sears and my schedule varies. But I'm not working Monday night; how about Monday?" Gabe seems determined to hook them into saying they will come back for the first lecture of the series, before he gets started with the second. At this point, they just want him to get on with it, especially Dave who does not normally sit still for more than one sermon per week and is thinking he might have to skip church tomorrow if this preacher takes up any more of his time. He would like to get back out in the park and play some more Frisbee, then maybe go for a swim when he gets back to the apartment.

"O.K. Fine. Sure," they all say, except for Kirby, who is intentionally noncommittal these days and has a quizzical look that Gabe ignores. Three out of four is not bad.

"O.K." Gabe steps back from the table and takes a deep breath. Then he takes another deep breath and closes his eyes for several seconds, like he is praying but he does not say anything out loud. He does this unselfconsciously, like it is the most normal thing in the world.

His hands are folded in front of him. He opens his eyes and looks at the group with a grave seriousness. "I think we would all agree that there is something wrong with this world that we live in," he says. "If we were to discuss the matter, we would probably not agree about exactly what is wrong with human beings and how the world might be saved."

Knowing glances are exchanged between various members of the group who have been known to argue about this subject. Arti Rose thinks about that awful argument with Kirby, on the way home from the Gulf. Sparks fly silently between them. Gabe is energized and glad to see that the group is more awake than the girls who accompanied Arti Rose previously.

"What I am about to present is a modern interpretation of the biblical story of the fall of mankind, originally recorded in the book of Genesis. Whether or not you believe that an original set of human parents actually existed, I think that, upon reflection, you will find this story, and especially this interpretation of it, to be relevant. I have certainly found it to be relevant in my own life."

Gabe picks up the chalk. "In the first lecture I usually explain that God's original commandments, as written in the book of Genesis, were to 'be fruitful, multiply, and have dominion over the earth'. We, of the Unification Church, believe that these commandments, which result in blessings when they are fulfilled by man, have the purpose of ultimately bringing joy to mankind, and to God through mankind. But humankind is not, for the most part, in a blissful state, sharing joy through oneness with God, all of humanity, as well as the heavens and earth. On the contrary, there is much suffering in this world. Today we will talk about why."

Gabe starts drawing those atomic-looking "four-position-foundations" with the yin-yangs on the board. He draws three of them and puts the name of each of the three blessings over them.

"Let's think about the first blessing, 'be fruitful'", Gabe says, facing the group. "When does a tree bear fruit? When we first plant the seed that the tree will grow from, or when it first sprouts and starts putting out leaves, or when it has had some time to grow?"

Gabe pauses for a second and Arti Rose says, in a shy voice,

"When it's had time to grow."

"That's right," Gabe says, turning back to the board. He starts writing words around the yin-yangs in the four-position-foundation that he drew for the "first blessing". The word "God" goes over the yin-yang at the top, the word "mind" goes to the side of the yin-yang on the left, the word "body" goes to the side of the one on the right, and the words "mature individual" go underneath the yin-yang at bottom of the diamond-shaped "four-position-foundation". There are two slightly curved arrows drawn back and forth horizontally, between the "mind" and "body", and similar arrows are drawn vertically between "God" and the "mature person". The drawings look something like scientific illustrations of atomic energy, but with symbols from oriental philosophy and words from Judeo-Christianity.

Arti Rose glances at Kirby, her most scientific friend, who does not seem to be resisting the ideas (as he has resisted every mention of the Bible lately).

"So, we say that to fulfill the first blessing, an individual must unite his or her mind and body, centering around God, to produce, in the fourth position, a spiritually mature person. Only then is true 'fruitfulness' possible.

"The second blessing, to 'multiply', then becomes a worthwhile endeavor," Gabe says, writing around the second set of yin-yangs. He writes the word "God" at top again, "mature man" on the left, "mature woman" on the right, and "blessed children" at bottom.

"Centering around God," Gabe says, pointing to the second diamond shaped diagram and making a circular motion with his hand, "mature man and mature woman multiply to create blessed children of God."

This is food for thought, but not much time for thought is given. Gabe immediately begins writing around the third diagram. He writes "God" at the top again, "True Family" on the left, and "Creation" on the right. At the bottom of this third diagram, he writes "Heavenly Kingdom". Then he points and starts making circular motions where the various arrows are again.

"With give and take, centered around God, spiritually mature individuals and their blessed families have loving 'dominion over the creation' as God commanded in the book of Genesis, thus establishing a heavenly kingdom on earth.

"Are there any questions so far?" Gabe asks, facing the group.

"You use the word 'creation'," Kirby pipes up. "Do you mean, as opposed to evolution?"

"Actually, we don't consider those to be opposing ideas," Gabe says. "Before time, in the human sense of the word, how long was a day to God?"

"Yeah, really," Felicia says.

Arti senses that Leash is attracted to yet another pair of pants, and not blue-jeans this time (beige polyester even).

"According to the Divine Principle, everything goes through three stages of growth: formation, growth, and perfection or maturity," Gabe continues answering Kirby's question. "There is no evidence in creation that God works with the snap of a finger. So we say that the six days in the book of Genesis were actually six time periods or eras. There is a lot of symbolism in the Bible; let me get back to this interpretation of the fall, and we will have time for questions and discussion later," Gabe says, turning back to the board.

Arti glances at Will, wondering if any red flags went up when Gabe mentioned "symbolism", that dirty word to Biblical literalists.

"Let's say that Adam and Eve were the first humans on earth," Gabe continues. "the first of God's creatures here to walk upright and to have an eternal soul, in the image of God. Did they fulfill these three blessings as commanded in the book of Genesis?" Gabe asks, pointing to the diagrams. "Did they reach spiritual maturity, as fruitful individuals, before multiplying and having dominion over the earth? If they did fulfill these blessings, as commanded, wouldn't we have a heavenly kingdom on earth? Obviously, something went wrong here, something bigger than eating a bad apple. So what does the fruit symbolize? And who or what was the serpent, the proverbial worm in the apple or on the tree or wherever?

"It does not make sense that an actual snake would tempt a human being. It would take another human being to tempt a human being. But there were no human beings in the garden other than Adam and Eve. So it must have been a spiritual being, an angel. Angels, throughout history, have been depicted as helpers. So we can assume that the being who tempted Eve, symbolized by the serpent in the story, was an angel who was supposed to be in the garden as a helper to the first human beings. This angel, called "Lucifer", the archangel, is depicted in the Bible as taking the position of enemy to God and, as Satan or the devil, is said to be the spiritual ruler of the fallen kingdom of mankind.

"It may sound far-fetched in a way," Gabe pauses to admit. "But please remember that we are trying to explain things from a spiritual perspective, from God's point of view, which may be difficult for us to comprehend with our limited, earthly set of experiences.

"These first people on earth were God's most precious creation, God's children who were to be the parents, the forbears of all mankind. So in what way did Lucifer seduce Eve? And why do we even use words like tempt and seduce when interpreting this story. Are we in fact talking about a sexual act? Is it possible that this spiritual being, this Lucifer, in some way molested the original female child of God? Well, as far-fetched as it may sound to most of us, there have been a number of written references to acts of sex committed by spiritual beings. In fact, the Bible says that, after the fall, there were angels who came to the earth to engage in sex with women. It is difficult to comprehend what is meant by spiritual sex. But what else, other than sex, would have caused Adam and Eve to become ashamed of their genitals and hide themselves with fig leaves? If eating the wrong food had made them ashamed, wouldn't they have been more inclined to cover their mouths?

"So, we say that the fruit in the story symbolizes Eve's sexual love. If Eve had been allowed to reach spiritual maturity, the natural fruit, so-to-speak, of her maturity would have been her sexual love. She would have shared herself with Adam, her natural mate, at the proper time as designated by God, the Father. Instead, when she had been seduced by Lucifer, Eve immediately went to Adam, trying to set things right, and seduced him into partaking of the same forbidden fruit, so-to-speak, that she had taken without God's blessing.

"So, we say that the spiritual being, placed in the garden by God to be a helper and guide to the first humans, seduced Eve into partaking of, and later sharing with Adam, premature, forbidden, and therefore selfish and Godless, sexual love.

"Of course it was her destiny to share sexual love with Adam. So we can only assume that this was wrong, at the time, because the act had not been blessed by God. This, we say, must have saddened

God deeply, as sexual love, between a mature man and woman, was surely designed to be one of the highest expressions of love on the physical plane.

"Here we refer back to the order of the three blessings," Gabe says, turning to the board and pointing to the first diagram. "Before multiplying, Adam and Eve were to 'be fruitful', which could only be achieved by reaching spiritual maturity. Instead they participated in the act of sex with selfish motives, prematurely, without the blessing of God. And we all suffer as children of spiritually immature parents.

"The whole world suffers from various acts of selfishness by human beings. People wonder how a benevolent God could let the world suffer. Perhaps God needs to work through humans, who are unfortunately separated from God since the fall. The Bible says that God warned Adam and Eve that they would "surely die" if they ate of the forbidden death. And yet they did not physically die. So we must assume that God was talking about spiritual death, which is separation from God. Many people today are depressed, fearful, angry, lost. It is as if we were unplugged from our source of energy, comfort, security, and guidance.

"This will only be remedied when the first blessing is restored, by people who consciously make the decision to center our hearts and minds, our lives around God," he says, pointing to the diagram and waving his hand in a circular motion where the arrows are drawn, "spiritually maturing as individuals before being blessed in marriage and participating in the act of love that brings forth children."

Arti Rose notices that Gabe says "our" lives, including himself in the solution being prescribed, meaning he must be planning to be blessed in marriage someday, whenever he reaches "spiritual maturity". She imagines herself at the altar with him, then looks at Felicia and wonders if she is thinking about the same thing. Leash is looking at Gabe sort-of goo-goo eyed. Arti Rose, not wanting to be just another boy-crazy college girl, looking for a husband, makes herself snap out of the fantasy (at least momentarily).

Gabe stood silent, looking at the group. He took a deep breath, relieved to have finished what was, for him, the most difficult lecture of the series. It made him feel a bit uncomfortable, near-naked, like Adam maybe. He really did not like talking about sex and hoped they would not want too much of a discussion. He often wished he could save this lecture for later, because so many never came back after hearing it. This looked like a fun group, and he really hoped they would come back. He was alone in this town and needed friends as much as he needed members for his church. He knew Sun Myung Moon's interpretation of "the fall" was a lot to put on this group of young people, especially those who were here for the first time. But God had sent him Arti Rose, this he was confident of. He could feel it in his heart. She was a sister. He had to get her through the whole series, in order, as quickly as possible. In the meantime, Satan would surely attack. Gabe braced himself inside but relaxed his expression, to put the very young people (at least several years younger than him, it appeared) at ease.

"So, you're saying the story can't be taken at face value, the way it is written in the Bible?" Will asked. "Because I am into the most literal interpretation I can find, man. In fact, I am back to the Greek," Will said.

"That's interesting. I would love to see that text sometime, if you would bring it with you to another lecture. I hope you will reserve judgment and come back to hear the rest, because this interpretation makes more sense when you see how it progresses through biblical history," Gabe said.

"Oh, is that what the other lectures are about, biblical history?" Will asked.

"For the most part," Gabe said, looking away from Will. "So, would everyone like some lemonade?"

"Sure."

"That would be great."

"Yeah, man, I'm really thirsty."

"Would you like to go out on the balcony? I'll bring the lemonade out there?"

"Cool."

"Far-out, man."

The balcony overlooks the park, and they watch a couple playing Frisbee with their dog. Dave tells Gabe that he has a Frisbee in Kirby's car, and Gabe suggests they all go down to the park. Gabe takes his tie off and rolls his sleeves up. He is very jovial and light-hearted.

Everybody seems to like him, although Kirby is a bit stand-offish. At the park, Gabe behaves like a big, friendly dog: a Great Dane, perhaps. He takes charge of the group, suggesting they do a circle toss with the Frisbee so everybody can participate, including the girls. But later, when Arti and Leash go for a walk, Gabe shows off with the guys, throwing with a steady glide, from a longer distance.

They all agree to come back, some on Monday night for the lecture that they missed. This is mainly because they like Gabe. Nobody really talks about the lecture they just heard, until later.

In the VW, on the way back, Kirby tells Arti that what they just heard is kind-of the opposite of what he has been reading. "Freud blames the evils of the world on sexual repression," he says.

Arti and Dave don't really get what he means by "repression" or how that is the opposite of what they just heard. Arti sort-of wants to ask Kirby what he means but does not want to seem dumb. Dave is in the front seat and turns the radio on. That's cool with Kirby because he hasn't heard that "Bye-bye American Pie" song for a while. It was a big hit toward the end of senior year, when Kirby was trying to date Arti Rose, offering her rides to all their church functions, listening to the radio.

Dave sings the chorus out loud, "Drove my Chevy to the levee, but the levee was dry".

Arti looks out the window and thinks about how she is going to break it to Tex that they cannot have sex anymore. She just knows that neither of them is "spiritually mature".

"Hey Dave; why didn't you bring Wendy today?" Arti asks (thinking about immature people who are having sex).

"She said she's not feeling too good," Dave says. ("And good ole boys were drinking whiskey and rye"…).

"Why was she so upset after the bar-be-que? Y'all aren't breaking up are you?"

"No, I guess not. Not on purpose, but we might have to. I don't want to talk about it," Dave says. ("And singin' this will be the day that I die").

"You should talk to her sometime Art; you could probably help her with what she is going through better than me," Dave says, suddenly deciding to engage in the conversation with his sister. That is, if her parents will even let her talk to you. They would probably let her talk to you, because they remember you from high school when you were such a goody-goody. They think I'm bad. They won't let her talk to me; she is on phone restriction and every other kind of restriction. She managed to sneak over last night, but they are practically holding her prisoner at this point. I wish I could help her, but her folks don't want her seeing me anymore."

"Why?"

"It's not that they don't like me. But they think we're too young. They've got her head all messed up. They're blaming me, but it's them. They've been taking her to a shrink that wants to give her shock treatments to forget about me."

"What? That's crazy."

"Well, there's more to it Art, but I'm not supposed to talk…Wendy made me promise not to…It just hurts so freakin' bad," Dave says, starting to choke up. He looks out the window.

Kirby is stopped at a red light. He looks at Dave like he wants to say something but does not know what to say. "Man, if you ever need to talk about it," Kirby says, "It's not cool to keep shit bottled up."

Dave is obviously crying, but he keeps his head turned, looking out the window. When it is obvious Dave is not going to talk about it anymore, Kirby turns the radio up louder, to give Dave some cover. But it is Joplin now, screaming "cry-eye bay-a-by", which only makes it worse. With Joplin it is always about letting go, letting it all hang out. At least Dave gets some of it out of his system. He is obviously in a lot of emotional pain, and it hurts to see Dave hurting. He is such a fun guy, innocent-hearted as a child; Dave would never hurt anybody on purpose.

After what Arti Rose just went through, thinking she was pregnant with Tex's baby, she can only imagine the worst. Whatever it is, Wendy's parents are probably right. Wendy and Dave are too young, especially if they have been having sex. Arti reaches around the seat in front of her and pats her brother on the shoulder. Then she settles back in her seat and tries not to think about it anymore. With her brother refusing to talk about it, there is nothing she can do. Arti Rose starts daydreaming about Gabe again, looking out the window. Maybe she and Gabe could reach spiritual maturity together and have blessed children, fulfilling the three blessings and the purpose of creation, returning love and *Joy* to God. There must be a way, it seems to Arti Rose, for love to lead to joy.

That night Arti goes out with Tex but tells him she can't go to his room after the movie. He takes her to the apartment complex, and they go out to the swings to talk. She tries to explain about the *Divine Principle* and "The Fall", but he does not understand. He thinks she has found someone else, probably the guy who teaches the lectures. She says he will just have to come and hear the *Divine Principle* for himself, maybe he will get what she is talking about. He is aggravated and frustrated when he leaves her on the swing and gets in his car without even kissing her or touching her on the end of her nose with his pointer finger or saying G'night kid.

A Historical Perspective

Dave is not interested in going to any of the lectures during the following week, and Kirby doesn't go either. But Will and Felicia make-up the first of the series on Monday and join Arti Rose for the third on Wednesday. The third is about how God has been working through select people to restore the original birthright of Adam and Eve. God uses the bloodline of the Jewish people. There are Cain-Abel relationships, repeated throughout history. Indemnity has to be paid through suffering and blood loss. It all leads up to Jesus of Nazareth, who is to be the second Adam, the new beginning.

William likes this part of the *Divine Principle* because it is biblical. Leash likes it because Will likes it. Felicia likes Gabe too. She is not sure which one she likes better, but she has been thinking about what it would be like to be "blessed in marriage" to Gabe. Will hasn't made a move yet, and Leash is getting impatient. Will is quite the tease, kissing her and everything but. That lecture about "the fall" being sexual did not help either, even though Felicia and William have not made up their minds about this "interpretation".

Arti Rose finds the biblical history boring and yawns a lot; so does Tex. He still does not get why Arti thinks it is wrong for them to have sex without God's blessing. And how can they go about getting God's blessing as soon as possible, he wonders. Maybe they can get God's blessing somehow before Saturday night. Tex figures he will do whatever it takes.

Playing Frisbee in the park after the lecture, Tex really shows off. He is obviously competing with Gabe for Arti Rose's attention. Gabe is not surprised, but everyone else is. Tex has always been so low-key, so background, so laid-back. Maybe going a few hours without pot makes him hyper-active, his friends are thinking.

Gabe knows he is in for a challenge, with this one. For one thing, most of the people in this group are kids, under twenty-one. Tex, like himself, is a man of twenty-four. Gabe can smell the drugs on Tex, in him, staining his fingers and seeping out his pores, way more than Arti and her younger friends can imagine. But Gabe has been there, or somewhere near enough to know the signs. Satan will attack through this man, Gabe thinks. He decides to out-party the party animal. With the week-end coming up, Arti Rose and her friends will need to be occupied and pre-occupied.

"Hey, how would you guys like to come over for dinner Friday night and walk to Five-points afterward? They have open-mike at the Cadillac Café; or they might even have a band."

"Sunshine and I have been wanting to go there," Arti pipes up.

"Bring her," Gabe says. "Bring your brother, too."

"Far out."

"Yeah, sure. That would be cool."

Five Points South

When Sunshine hears that there won't be any lecture Friday night, she is thrilled with the idea of going to Five Points South and the Cadillac Café, which have become local hippy hot-spots. Dave goes too, along with Will and Felicia. Kirby ignores the fact that Sunshine is going and decides to join the group anyway. Tex tells Arti he might show up at the Cadillac later, but he has to do his dope deal (or deals, he is thinking, since she is preoccupied, and he will have time to make the rounds).

When they go to Gabe's apartment, "the center", he has a big bowl of fresh fruit on the dining room table and jokes that it is "not forbidden". He gathers them around the table for a prayer and serves the same brown rice, flavored with soy sauce, that he says he lives on, along with the watered-down lemonade that they are used to by now.

"If this doesn't fill you guys up, I know where we can get additional free refreshments," Gabe says, grinning with those little bowed lips that rise way up to show his pearly whites, making him look more like a kid than a man, in the face. "There is a Catholic church on the way, and they have a folk sing-in on Friday nights, a few hours before the music starts up at the Cadillac," Gabe says, serving everyone's plate before he serves his own, sits down, and passes the bowl of fruit around.

The brown rice has bits of onion and celery. It has more crunch to it than the white rice this group is used to, and there are mixed reactions.

"I belong to a Southside food co-op," Gabe explains. "We buy whole grain organic foods in bulk, for way less than grocery store prices," he says, "through the Golden Temple Health Emporium."

"I've been there," Kirby says, "next to the Little Professor bookstore at Five Points".

Arti Rose starts picking up plates and taking them to the kitchen as soon as she notices that some people are done eating. Dave comes in and helps her wash them, which Gabe finds delightful.

Everybody is excited to be on Southside and ready to get out on the brick streets. Nobody minds following Gabe around. He lives there and knows people everywhere they go, speaking to folks on the street and ducking his head into mom-and-pop shops to say "Hi".

Sunshine acts like she is on her way to a rock concert, bouncing along Highland Avenue with her golden curls catching the summer-evening glow, raving about the beautiful stained-glass windows on the old Catholic church, like she cannot wait to get there. Gabe gives her a new nickname, "Sparky", and tries to keep up with her, which turns the rest of the group into their audience. Arti has a suspicion that Sunshine's dramatics have more to do with making Kirby jealous than getting to the church on time. Oddly, Arti finds herself feeling jealous of Gabe's obvious enjoyment of her "Sparky"-ness.

Sunshine pipes down when they are in the singing circle, because she really is too shy to project her voice, no matter how familiar the folk songs. They all are a little shy, except for Gabe, who sings out delightedly, along with a young priest and his handful of youthful adult followers. "How many roads must a man walk down, before you can call him a man? (No wonder Dylan has gone into hiding, incredulous. They are even singing his vagaries in church now, as if he had a clue); the answer my friend is blowin' in the wind." The group doesn't sound too bad when they sing the familiar "come by here, my Lord" of the favorite church camp song *Kumbaya*. And the sweet praises of "Morning has Broken", by Cat Stevens, sound okay. Simon and Garfunkle's "Bridge Over Troubled Waters" needs an orchestra, but they get through it. Only the bravest souls in the circle attempt the highs and lows of a few Joni Mitchell's songs; however, the idea that "we've got to get it back to the Garden" seems quite relevant in light of Gabe's Divine Principle lectures.

The Cadillac Café, at Five Points South, is Peter Max style pop-art, and potted plants, and tiffany lamps, and an antique Cadillac up on the roof of the old brick building (the kind with great big chrome wings). There is an open mike where everybody can read their free-verse attempts at poetry and/or strum a few chords. Kirby borrows a guitar from a scraggly-looking guy who has been at the mike too long. Kirby doesn't sound any better or much worse. Meanwhile, Gabe entertains everybody at their table with his stories about hiking across the country and living in the Grand Canyon, and Sunshine continues to flirt with him shamelessly. Leash sits in Will's lap, and he laughs out loud a lot, feeding into Gabe's stories. Dave gives Kirby a hard time, between his renditions, requesting some Neil Young. Arti wonders about Tex but sort of hopes he doesn't show. Everybody is drinking iced tea except for the priest, who obviously prefers Jesus's choice of drink. If Tex shows, he might get drunk and embarrass Arti Rose. The only person who is embarrassing her right now is Sunshine, who is smoking a cigarette she got from somebody and acting like she is on something way stronger than iced tea. Maybe Sunshine is nipping at the priest's wine when nobody is looking; she has her chair scooted right between the priest and Gabe so that she brushes up against both of them every chance she gets. Gabe calls her "Sparky" all the way back to the center, where Arti has to think twice about getting into Sunshine's VW. Oddly, Sunshine acts perfectly sober once she is behind the wheel. But then, there aren't any guys in the car for her to show off to; they all rode with Kirby. It's just Arti and Sunshine, all the way home.

"You like him, don't you?" Sunshine says, talking loud, over the radio.

"Who?"

"You know. You can't lie to me, Art. You like him a lot. Does Tex know you're in love with him?"

"You're the one who was acting like you were in love with the guy all night," Arti Rose says.

"Yeah, but I'm not," Sunshine says. "I was just having fun teasing his preacher-man ass. And it bothered you, Art. That's why you've got your panties in a wad, all spaced out and blue, lookin' out the window and trying to turn up my radio so you don't have to talk to me. I just hope you know what you're getting' into. I don't trust that Chinese fucker he worships."

"Worships? The guy is Korean, and Gabe does not worship him," Arti defends.

"Oh, Yeah? Who does he pray to, Art?"

"He just says 'Dear Father.'"

"See, he probably calls that Korean guru-guy 'Father'."

"Sunshine, when was the last time you went to church? Jesus said to pray by saying 'our Father who art in Heaven'."

"O.K. I don't want to argue with you. I don't care if you're in love with him. At least he is nicer than Tex. But I hope you don't move in with him."

"What do you care? Whitney wants to room with you at State this year anyway."

"Yeah, but me and you are supposed to end up two old maids in a Southside apartment. So don't go marrying some hippy preacher who dresses like a salesman."

Arti Rose turns the radio up, even though it is some Neil Diamond song neither of them would admit to liking that much. "I am; I said."

The Thwarted Christ

Saturday Tex called earlier than usual, trying to make up for the fact that he never showed up at the Cadillac Café. He even agreed to go hear another lecture later that afternoon.

Will and Felicia said they were going. Dave said he liked Gabe "as a friend", but that one lecture had been enough for him. Arti Rose figured Gabe's references to the Adam and Eve problem made Dave think about his painful issues with Wendy too much; he would rather stay home and hang around the pool with Sis and play with Scotty-dog. But if Gabe and the group decided to go to the Cadillac Café again, they could count him in, Dave told his sister.

Kirby had decided to start being an open-mike regular at the Cadillac Café; so it was convenient for him to go to the center first and see the gang. Plus the lectures were interesting in a way, sort of a weird take on the Judeo-Christian perspective. He had shared some of the ideas with a few of his friends from Southern who were studying theology. Most of them had never heard of the Unification Church or its founder Sun M. Moon or the *Divine Principle*, which gave Kirby the edge.

This lecture turned out to be the most controversial one so far, when it came to getting an argument from the recently "born-again" faction. Gabe dared to say that Jesus did not come to be crucified, that in fact He failed his mission of being "the second Adam" because He was unable to fulfill the Three Blessings. Jesus did, however, fulfill the first blessing, to "be fruitful" (by reaching spiritual maturity, as an individual) and was therefore able to salvage the second blessing, to "multiply", on a spiritual level by forming a trinity with God and the Holy Spirit (a sort-of marriage, with born-again Christians in the fourth position, as spiritual children). And He promised to return and accomplish the third blessing as well, establishing a loving "dominion over creation", a Heavenly Kingdom on earth.

While presenting these theories, Gabe drew more atomic-looking four-position-foundations on the chalk board, with the yin-yangs and the arrows. Under the "first blessing" Gabe put God at the top, "mind" on the left, "body" on the right, and Jesus as the mature person or "perfect man" under the fourth yin-yang (with arrows drawn vertically and horizontally between God and Jesus).

"Jesus was able to fulfill the first blessing," Gabe said, making circular motions where the arrows went back and forth horizontally, "by centering his mind and body around God, subjugating his body to the higher cause and purpose, and surrendering to God's will."

Gabe changed the direction of the circular motions he was making with his chalk, switching to the vertical arrows, drawn between

God, at the top of the diagram, and Jesus, at the bottom of the diamond-shaped four-position-foundation. "Functioning as a spiritually mature individual who could manifest the power and love of God, Jesus was able to bear fruit," Gabe said.

Then Gabe turned to the group and spoke. "On a spiritual level, Jesus became a tree of life. Christians today are an example of the fruitfulness of His mission on earth."

"However," Gabe said, pointing to his diagrams of the second, then the third blessings while turning his face to offer the group a grave expression, "Jesus died without being blessed in marriage or bringing forth the children of God. And He died without establishing the Kingdom of Heaven on earth. So, we say that ultimately, Jesus died without completely fulfilling his earthly mission."

Will, red-faced, stirred like he wanted to say something in protest, like he was about ready to explode.

Gabe turned his back to the group, facing the board, pointing to the diagrams again, as he spoke. "Adam's responsibility was to 'be fruitful, multiply, and have dominion over the earth'. As the son of God, this was also Jesus' responsibility and mission," Gabe said, facing the group again and speaking with a sense of authority that was making Will very uncomfortable.

This was Will's Jesus that Gabe was talking about. Will was taking this personally. Leash sensed Will's rising pulse-rate and stirred with excitement, ready to agree with whatever Will was about to say. Seated next to Will on one side of the table, Leash reached her hand over and placed it on one of Will's legs. He flinched a little and put his hand on her hand.

Gabe had turned his back on the group again, erasing some of the words on the board around the diagram for the second blessing. "Fortunately, Jesus was able to salvage the second blessing on the spiritual level," Gabe concluded, writing new words around the middle diagram. "By forming a trinity with God and the Holy Spirit," Gabe explained (writing Jesus where 'mature man' had been and Holy Spirit where 'mature woman' had been- something new, since modern Christianity does not refer to the Holy Spirit as female), "Jesus was able to assist Christians in being reborn, into the spiritual kingdom of God."

Gabe pointed to the trinity within the diagram, drawing a

triangle in the air over the top part of the four-position-foundation. Then he erased the words "children of God" at bottom and wrote "Christians". He turned to face the group, taking a deep breath and bracing himself for Will's inevitable explosion.

"So, what about the third blessing," Kirby said first, cool and matter-of-fact.

"That's why he promised to return," Gabe said. "That's the next lecture."

"Oh, I get it," Kirby said. "Dominion over the earth, the thousand years of peace and all that. It makes sense. If He didn't fail, why would he have to come back? Right?"

"Right," Gabe said, looking a little worried, reaching for his glass of water and hoping enough has been said.

"H-how c-can you s-say Jesus failed, man. He d-died for our sins, hung on the c-cross, p-prayed 'Father forgive them for they know not what they d-do'," Will said, emotional, sounding like he was near tears. "He was the l-last s-sacrificial lamb, the u-ultimate sacrifice."

Feeling compassion and respect for Will, Gabe takes on a gentler tone but maintains a sense of authority. "If he was the last sacrificial lamb, Will, why do we still have wars? Why don't we have the Heavenly Kingdom on earth, like the prophesies promised before Jesus was born."

"He's c-coming back, man," Will said. "It's all p-part of God's plan. G-god does not make mistakes."

"No, but man does," Gabe said.

"So, you're saying Jesus was just a m-man," Will said.

"Not just a man, He was the son of God," Gabe said.

Will was quiet for a moment. Everybody was quiet.

"I'm g-glad we agree Jesus was the son of God," Will said. "B-but I don't think we see eye to eye on everything, man," Will concluded, trying to calm his emotions, trying to settle into reason. He really liked Gabe; they all did. Will did not want to go home mad.

"The final lecture of the series will clarify my position and hopefully answer any further questions that you may have," Gabe said. "Would everyone like some lemonade? I made it fresh this morning."

"Sure, man. You got any ice? It's pretty hot in here," Tex said.

"Actually, I did get some new ice trays at Sears." Gabe said, on his way to the kitchen. "The ones that came with the apartment were old and cracked."

Tex followed him. "I heard you work at Sears; what do you do over there, man?"

"I sell tools."

"That's cool. I work for the city," Tex said, taking the first glass Gabe filled and turning it up, emptying it fast. He had come to the lecture stoned-as-shit, and the cotton-mouth was getting the better of him. "That's some far-out lemonade, man. Mind if I have another glass."

Listening to her boyfriend, Arti Rose felt embarrassed. She got up from the table and went in the kitchen to help Gabe serve the rest of the lemonade, after he watered it down again to make sure there was enough.

They all went out on the balcony for a bit, then down to the park. They threw the Frisbee around until the heat got to them, then agreed to get back together the next weekend, if not before.

Arti Rose felt bad that most of them would end up back at the apartment complex, swimming in the pool, and Gabe would be left out.

"You should come over," she said. "My mom wants to meet you anyway."

"Maybe sometime soon, but not today. Thanks anyway," Gabe said

Tex grabs Arti Rose's hand as they walk to his dad's car, an old classic, glitzy painted Chevy he likes to drive when he takes Arti Rose out, especially because it has bench seats. She feels that his gesture is more a display of territoriality than affection, and pulls her hand away, using it to put her hair in a ponytail with a rubber band that had been around her wrist.

"What's wrong?" Tex asks

"Nothin'; I'm hot."

"You want to get with Gabe, don't you?" Tex says in the car.

"What are you talking about?"

"Well, you haven't been trying to get with me lately, kid. Look at you; you're way over there. You used to sit so close I could barely drive."

There are no seat-belts, so Arti Rose easily slides over next to Tex. "I guess I've got a lot on my mind."

Tex is thinking- Yeah, like Gabe. But he doesn't say anything, just puts his right arm around Arti Rose and drives with his left hand. "I love ya, kid," he says, squeezing her close.

Arti doesn't say anything but pats his right knee with her left hand, holding it there all along the Avenues, until Tex gets close to the mall and his neighborhood. Then she says, "Tex I just can't keep doing what we have been doing; I'm afraid of getting pregnant. And I don't know if it is right anyway, with us not being spiritually mature or blessed in marriage."

Tex lets out a sigh, pulls his arm from around her, and turns the wheel hard to the left, heading for the newest edge of suburban wasteland. They are quiet all the way there, quiet as he walks her up the stairs to the second-floor apartment. When they face each other at the door, his blue eyes penetrate her grey-green eyes for a moment, searching for something. He makes that clicking sound with his tongue, as he touches the freckle on the end of her nose with his pointer finger. Then he turns and walks away, even though it is still a sunny Saturday.

Arti goes in to put her bathing suit on. Dave and Sis are in the pool. When Arti comes out the summer afternoon thunderheads are covering the sun, threatening rain. "Get out of there before lightning strikes!" she yells down from the balcony, toward her younger brother and sister in the pool.

Arti goes back in the apartment, opens the front curtains, and spends a little time putting blue and yellow and green on the new "landscape" she started for the painting class. It is not much of a landscape, but the only view she has to work with. There is a tree just outside the ornate black wrought-iron railing (which is striking against the sky) along the second-floor balcony outside. It is a young tree, without much shape, just a blob of green. Arti Rose enjoys looking at any little pit of nature. The blue of the sky is enough to stir her, even with the thunderheads that won't be still long enough to become a part of the painting, a painting that Arti Rose will never finish because her life is about to change more than she can begin to imagine.

Selling Candles in the Rain

Gabe calls on Sunday to ask a favor of Arti Rose. His church is selling scented candles, nationwide, and he needs help with the fundraising project. He just got a shipment in on Saturday. His favorite is bayberry, but he thinks Arti Rose will like the strawberry. They are in brandy-snifter glasses. He is going to sell them door-to-door around Southside later this afternoon and evening, if she and any of her friends want to help.

Arti calls Sunshine. Sunshine loves bouncing around Southside for any reason. The three of them go to a huge old brick apartment building south of UAB in an area that is rough around the edges, a bit run-down. A surprising number of students and young couples and lonely-looking old people sniff the snifters until they find something that makes them dig into their pockets for three bucks, or two for five bucks.

Sunshine and Arti's arms are just barely long enough to hold the heavy boxes, which are like cardboard crates. Sunshine finally refuses to hold one on her own and just bounces alongside Gabe and/or Arti, giggling while accompanying them to various doors, up and down the seemingly endless stairs, knocking and facing face after strange, new face.

Arti is especially grateful for Sunshine's presence when it starts to rain, and she is afraid the box will fall apart. They take either end and scurry to the VW, putting the candles in the trunk and waiting there for Gabe, listening to the radio and singing while he gets soaked. They sing especially loud when Melanie comes on, with her song from the peace movement, "Candles in the Rain".

"Lay down, lay down; lay it all down. Let the white dove…"

It was an adventure. Sunshine is up for it when Arti asks if she will help with the candles again a few days later. Gabe fills up her gas tank. Tex says maybe on the weekend, but he won't do anything like that after work, and neither will Dave or Will.

Arti hasn't been getting that many hours at Woolco, and she does not care. She hates the job, and their clothes suck. She has been thinking of applying at Sears. Gabe has been dropping hints, and it is close to where her mom works downtown. She asks Sue if she can drive her to work one day and apply at Sears. Sue says O.K., but she will probably have to hang out in the newsroom with her and/or go to a café until Sears opens.

Arti Rose takes a copy of *Jonathan Livingston Seagull* and reads the metaphor about spiritual flight and evolution of the soul, to the clank-clank of typewriters in the newsroom. She loves the smell of ink, a familiar smell since her mother owned a small-town weekly and let the five-to-ten year old Arti Rose "catch papers" as they came flying "hot off the press". In fact, she has fallen asleep on many a stack of warm newspapers and now finds her head resting on one end of her mother's desk at The News.

"Arti Rose, I think it's about time for Sears to open."

"Oh, yeah. See ya soon, Mom."

"Wait. I want you to meet…"

Arti Rose has to meet several middle-aged men with thinning grey hair and glasses down on their noses. She also meets one young reporter who blushes through his acne because he is young enough to go out with Arti but has been secretly seeing sexy-Mama Sue.

Arti drives the blue Duster to Sears. On her way out of the office where she has filled out an application and been interviewed, Arti sees Gabe. He is animated and smiling as usual, talking with a fellow worker in appliances, which is next to the department where Gabe sells tools.

"Hey Gabe," Arti Rose says, approaching him, blushing a bit.

"Well, there's my favorite girl. What are you doing here?"

"I just applied for a job. I used you for a reference."

"That's great! But I thought you had a job already."

"I hate Woolco. You are always saying Sears is a good company to work for," Arti explains. "Plus my mom works near here."

"Oh, so you rode with her."

"Yeah."

"Are you going to be downtown for a while? I would love to go to lunch with you ladies."

"Sure. I want you to meet my mom anyway."

"Yes! I may remember her, from witnessing downtown. How about I meet you two at the sidewalk café on The Green about 12:15."

"Cool."

Gabe and Sue recognize each other immediately; after all it was he who handed her the infamous yellow pamphlet, not far from this very spot. The three of them eat sandwiches and chat, Gabe smiling that charming pixie smile of his the whole time, leaning his lumbering body over his little salad plate, moving his long legs around, trying to get comfortable while staying out of the way of the four female legs sharing the same small, round table. He seems a bit shy around Sue, something Arti has not seen before. Gabe is usually the most self-assured member of her group of friends. His bashfulness doesn't last long though. Sue has a way of melting the shyness off anybody quicker than the noonday heat can melt the ice in their sweet tea.

"Sue, you'll have to come to the center with Arti Rose sometime," Gabe says when she looks at her watch and stands up, newspaper deadlines pulling at her feet like gravity.

"I would love to," Sue says. "I hear it's on Southside. That's where I want to live when I save enough money to pay down on an old house."

"Mama loves old houses," Arti Rose explains.

"Me too," Gabe says. "As soon as I arrived here, I started looking for a neighborhood that would remind me of San Francisco. I didn't want to be too homesick, and I'm not. I love it here."

"Well, that's great. We're glad to have you here. It's nice to meet you," Sue says, walking off.

"I'm going to the library, Mom. I'll pick you up at five," Arti yells.

"O.K.," Sue yells back, nearly a block away already.

Gabe, it turns out, has taken the afternoon off. Things were slow in tools anyway. He has an idea. Since Arti has the car, they could go to the Center and pick up some candles to sell in the shops downtown, until her mom gets off work.

Arti Rose cannot say *No* to Gabe; that fact is becoming increasingly obvious. She does not really want to lug big boxes of candles around on the hot pavement in downtown Birmingham in the middle of summer. But Arti Rose cannot say *No* to Gabe. In fact, when he smiles at her, she has to smile back. (*Yes* again, *Yes* again, *Yes*).

Come five o'clock Arti is back at Sue's desk in the newsroom, sweaty and tired but glowing, smiling almost as much as Gabe, who is standing beside her with a big, half-empty box of candles under his left arm, holding a bayberry-scented one out with his right hand, for Sue to sniff. Sue pulls three bucks out of her purse. She tries to get the crusty old fellow in the desk next to her to take a sniff of her new candle.

"Try over there," the old curmudgeon says, cocking his head in the direction of a glass enclosed area of several desks occupied exclusively by women. "Maybe they'll do a feature story about your candles for the women's page," he says, trying to remind Sue and company that this is, after all, a newsroom.

A few minutes later, when Sue has put some cleaned-up copy on the editor's desk and grabbed her purse, she and Arti Rose meet Gabe in the elevator. His candle box is empty, and his pixie smile has widened into an open-mouthed grin.

Sue drives the blue Duster, dropping Gabe off on Highland Avenue, taking the back-roads to suburbia for a change.

"Arti Rose, now *he* is nice," Sue says, as if her daughter doesn't know the difference between nice and not nice, and she is using Gabe to illustrate.

Arti Rose gets the job at Sears, in the Junior Bazaar department. She starts juggling the blue Duster with Sue. Sue just gives up sometimes and drives one of the *Birmingham News* cars that are available for reporters working on assignment. Nobody at the News minds; after all, she is Sue Cronkite.

Gabe and Arti sell candles all over town whenever they are not scheduled to work at Sears. Gabe ends up at the apartment complex sometimes, hanging out with Dave and Sis and Scotty-dog, just like one of the gang. Sue starts buying the bigger jars of spaghetti sauce. It never bothers her to serve up an extra plate for Gabe. When Gabe's not there, Will usually is anyway. Sometimes they are both at the apartment, because Will comes in with Dave after work and Gabe comes in with Arti.

It bothers Tex that Arti Rose is spending so much time with Gabe. He knows better than to act jealous and controlling. Instead, when he calls Arti Rose on the phone, Tex starts pretending interest in Gabe's religion. "Isn't there supposed to be another lecture, about what happens when Jesus comes back and all that?"

"It's really important to sell as many candles as possible right now, because the church is buying an estate in foreclosure, for a new headquarters and a place for Mr. Moon and his family to stay when they come to America," Arti Rose explains, telling Tex what Gabe has been telling her. "That's why Gabe is putting off finishing the lecture series. It's just a priority to sell the candles every chance he gets."

Gabe finally gets around to it after a few weeks. By then Will has had a chance to cool down from the argument about the mission of Jesus. Gabe invites the whole group, through Arti Rose, reminding her of all the best Saturday afternoon and evening rituals: the lecture, a light meal, lemonade on the balcony, Frisbee in the park, the folk sing-in and snacks at the Catholic church, open mike at the Cadillac Café. He says they will try to do as many of the fun things as they can manage.

Later Gabe tells Arti Rose that there will be extra people at the lecture, some young people from the church who are traveling and happen to be in the area. They are staying at the center for a few days.

They all go; everybody in Arti's group who has been to Gabe's place before goes. Dave even goes and takes Wendy. Wendy's parents have decided she can go with him to church functions only (if another family member accompanies them). They don't know anything about the Unification Church, but if Arti Rose is going with them Wendy's parents don't mind. They have not seen Arti since she was in high school, but they know she is a nice girl. And they do love Dave. They do not want to hurt Dave or Wendy by keeping them apart all of the time. So Dave has been going to church with Wendy's family, and taking Wendy with he and Will to Pastor Paul's youth rallies. Dave is not interested in Gabe's church, but he likes Gabe. And he is not lying when he tells Wendy's parents they are going to a church function on Saturday. In fact, if they go to the folk sing-in at the Catholic church afterwards, they will be going to two church functions.

Sue is surprised when her son tells her he is going to "The Center", because he already said one of Gabe's lectures was "enough" for him. But Sue can tell, since Gabe has been coming over to the apartment, that Dave looks up to him. Dave looks up to Will too, but Will is more immature acting than Gabe. Anyway, Sue thinks her teenagers need good young-adult role models, and Gabe seems to be one. She doesn't worry about them too much when they are with Gabe, which gives her more of an opportunity to kick up her own heels on a Saturday night.

A white van is parked at the curb in front of Gabe's apartment building when Arti's group gets there on Saturday. There is a red wheel-like symbol on it, with the words "One World Crusade".

Will says, *"One World?"*, in a tone like there is something bad about those words. He mumbles something about the book of Revelations.

A few straight-looking guys in ties are coming down the steps, smiling. One of them sticks out his hand, saying "You must be friends of Gabe's, here for a lecture?"

Will shakes the young man's hand but does not return his smile. Arti thinks this is unlike Will. She notices that, in fact, most of the guys seem edgy. Maybe Dave is just picking up on Will's vibe. But Dave has been in a funk anyway. He is not looking forward to the lecture. Maybe if they were playing Frisbee he might feel better. But whatever all is going on with he and Wendy has him in a funk. He would really prefer to be alone with Wendy right now, but her parents have decided to forbid it.

Wendy is cheerful in spite of her wan appearance; she is darker under the eyes than usual, but smiling a determined smile, glad to be out with friends. Arti and Felicia are in good moods too and smile at the two young men who are about to get in the white van. Leash offers her hand to one of them and introduces herself.

Arti Rose is a little shy about meeting new people, but Sunshine is downright paranoid (unless they are hippies). Kirby is acting weird too, hesitant, suddenly serious, a bit on the defensive. Maybe the short-haired guys bother him. The hippies might be outnumbered in this situation.

Tex is the only guy who does not hold back. He shakes hands with the strange young men, says "Cool van, man" to one of them. Tex is happy to be with his girl for a change; if this is where Arti Rose wants to be on a Saturday, that's cool with him.

Gabe seems ecstatic to have his half-dozen "brothers and sisters" of the One World Crusade staying at the center with him for a few days. Several of the clean-cut but rather rumpled and tired looking young people, all wearing a wearier-looking version of Gabe's perpetual smile, hang around the apartment, "the Center", while Gabe presents the final lecture of the series. Gabe explains that he did know they were coming until the last minute; they are traveling around on a candle-selling mission and just came into Birmingham to do a "blitz". He seems to think it is good timing.

Arti Rose does not understand why Gabe thinks his company came at a good time, until the lecture is over and each one of the One World Crusaders zooms in on somebody who is struggling with the ideas Gabe has presented. They also know the song that Gabe wants everybody to stand in a circle in the living room and sing, after the lecture. The song is about "Unity", and the words are repetitious enough for everybody to learn the chorus and sing along. "Unity saving the people; unity saving all nations." Everybody joins Gabe and the others in the circle, but Will and Dave and Kirby and Sunshine don't sing. Arti and Felicia and Wendy give it a stab here and there, a series of awkward efforts. Gabe just grins the whole time though, like something really, really great is happening. Gabe and the One World Crusaders conclude this circular sing-along with a song called "He Has Come." It mentions Korea and says "His face is like the sun and like the moon".

While they are singing, Arti Rose keeps staring at the poster on the wall of Mr. Moon in a suit, and his beautiful wife and their young son and daughter in kimonos. She figures Gabe meant to say that Mr. Moon is the second-coming of Christ, but he did not exactly say that. He talked about "the messiah" and wrote "Lord of the Second Advent" on the board. "The New Age has now dawned," Gabe said at the end of his last lecture, after explaining that the third blessing is finally being fulfilled, the family of God is uniting to "take dominion over the earth", establishing a foundation for the heavenly kingdom. "The *Lord of the Second Advent* will reign over heaven and earth with divine truth and fatherly love, and his kingdom will live forever," Gabe had said. Arti Rose does not know what to think of all that, but she likes the songs and thinks Mr. Moon looks very nice, with his family in the poster.

Arti likes the smiling faces of the One World Crusaders in the circle, too. Even though they have shorter hair and more conservative clothes than her friends, they seem like real hippies to Arti Rose, real love and peaceniks. She looks at Gabe's beaming face and feels shy when he looks her way, a bit overwhelmed, but happy to be in his circle.

Arti Rose wishes that all of her friends could be happy together at this moment, but some of them look like they want to leave. In fact, when they are done with the song, some of them excuse themselves politely. Dave is careful to shake Gabe's hand, reassuring him of the basic sense of friendship that they have come to share, but insisting that he has to get Wendy home before dark. Kirby acts like he can't wait to get out of there and offers Dave and Wendy a ride.

Will, who looks like he is about to burst, is obviously uncomfortable with the situation but cannot leave; he has important arguing to do with Gabe. Will genuinely likes Gabe but believes that Gabe has been seriously misled.

Tex is not about to leave his girl this early on a Saturday night, no matter how strange these church people are. Actually, they are kind of cool in a weird way. So he doesn't mind hanging out for a while.

Sunshine and Leash are enjoying the attention they are getting from a couple of guys with the One World Crusade, who zoom in on them after the lecture and song. They go out on the balcony to talk.

Sitting down in the living room and arguing with Gabe about the Korean man whose picture is on the wall, Will is even more emotional than he was after the previous lecture. Stuttering and stammering as he accuses Mr. Moon of being "the antichrist", Will rattles off biblical quotes, mostly from the book of Revelations. A pleasant looking woman in her mid-to-late twenties, with a long, flowered skirt and a former-hippy look about her, settles in a living room chair near Will, supporting Gabe's side of the argument with a sort of spaced-out, calm sincerity.

Tex is thirsty for some of Gabe's weak lemonade and has already made a beeline toward the kitchen. A chubby, sweet-faced woman, probably in her thirties, gets a glass for him and lingers in the kitchen, talking to Tex.

Another woman, around Gabe's age or maybe a little older, starts up a conversation with Arti Rose in the dining room. Arti sits down at the table with her. The young woman, named Faith, says she grew up in an Amish community. She is very plain-looking, downright homely in fact. The fact that she is petite, which could be an asset, just makes her look more plain because her loose-fitting skirt and blouse seem to swallow her up. But the more Arti Rose listens to her, the more she likes Faith. There is something genuine and unpretentious about her. Her face is rough as stone, but her eyes are gentle. And Faith has that now-familiar perpetual smile, a more subtle version of the pixie smile Gabe uses to disarm everyone he meets. Faith is much quieter than Gabe, more like a little housecat than a big, friendly dog. Arti Rose is not sure if Faith really wants to talk to her or if she is just doing her job as a "missionary", which Faith does pleasantly enough but without Gabe's brand of enthusiasm. Faith summarizes her life story, how she made her transition from an Amish community to the new religious commune, after she had left the family farm to go to college. Then she says something strange but intentionally reassuring.

"Don't feel bad if you join the Family and your friends don't," Faith says.

"The Family?"

"That's what we call ourselves," Faith explains. "Our church members serve as Heavenly Father's extended family, working with His son to fulfill the third blessing. God does not expect everyone to recognize His son at this early date. But if Heavenly Father is calling you to join us, to help build the kingdom, you will know that in your heart. Just ask. Pray," Faith says. "Look for a sign."

Not long after that, Will walked out. He looked upset to a point near anger, making a beeline to the door. He didn't even have Leash with him; she was still on the balcony, talking to one of the guys from the One World Crusade. Tex was just coming out of the kitchen when he saw Will heading past the opening to the dining room, toward the door.

"Excuse me," Tex said to the lady he had been chatting with, quickly following Will out the door of the apartment, as if to find out what was wrong. In truth, Tex was craving reefer; he needed to smoke.

Arti thought Gabe would follow them, but he did not. Gabe went out on the balcony, to talk to Felicia.

The sweet-faced chubby lady, who had been talking to Tex in the kitchen, sat down at the table with Arti Rose and the Amish girl, Faith. "My name is Millie," she said, introducing herself to Arti and sitting down.

"I wonder what's wrong with Will?" Arti Rose said. She wanted to go find out, but she felt surrounded and did not want to be rude to her new acquaintances.

"Your friend is probably under Satanic attack," the chubby brunette with the Nurse-Nancy manner said.

"What do you mean by that?" Arti Rose asked.

"This teaching that you have just heard is a very important revelation from God. In time it will change the world, for the better. Unfortunately, just as there are often political forces that resist change on the earthly level, there are spiritual forces that resist change. We don't see them, but spiritual beings influence all of us. If Satan is ruler of this world, as the Bible says he is, then you can bet he does not give up any of his subjects easily."

"But Will is a born-again Christian," Arti defended her friend.

"All the more reason for Satan to attack him," the somewhat annoying but oddly sweet-faced lady said, matter-of-factly, like spiritual warfare was a subject of everyday conversation.

"Maybe I should go talk with him," Arti said, suddenly wanting to remove herself from the situation.

"Actually, I think it would be better for you if you did not have too much give and take with him right now," round-faced Millie said, with a strange, motherly concern. "Would you like some lemonade? I bought some fresh lemons today. Gabe was drinking barely sweetened water with a bit of lemon and calling it lemonade."

"Yeah, I know," Arti Rose said, laughing a little.

"Uh, I think it's time to get out o' here, Art," Sunshine said, when Arti handed her a glass of lemonade on the balcony.

"Hi, I'm Nathan," a smiling young black man said to Arti Rose. He and Sunshine had been talking.

"This guy's pretty cool," Sunshine said, giving her new acquaintance a little smile. "He's from Berkeley."

"Really? Another Californian?"

"Yes. I was one of those infamous radicals involved with the not-so-peaceful peace movement on the Berkley campus, before the Unification Church family found me," the young man said in an accent unlike any Arti Rose had ever heard out of a Black person's mouth (not Southern at all, and obviously way better educated than most Southern Negroes).

"He is really interesting, Art; but I need to go. I'm actually sort of grounded; that's why my dad took the keys to the VW and I had to ride with you and Tex, remember? Will just drove off," Sunshine said, pointing toward the parking area near the apartments. "If Tex leaves, we are stranded."

"Where is Tex?" Arti asked.

"I think he's sitting on the steps in front of the building. Hey Tex," Sunshine yelled.

"Yeah, c'mon down," Tex said in his friendly drawl.

"Tex, why don't you stay a while," Gabe yelled down from his porch rocker next to Leash and a good-looking One World Crusade fellow, at the other end of the balcony.

"Appreciate the hospitality, man. I'm sure we'll be back soon, if Arti Rose has her way," Tex drawled, sounding like he took a toke since he went outside.

Sunshine and Arti made their way to Tex's old Chevy, leaving Leash behind. The One World Crusade guy had promised her a ride home later.

In the car, Sunshine gets on Tex's nerves. She is too hyper and aggressive for his taste in chicks anyway. Sunshine is all in his eight-track case, picking out a tape, putting it in the tape player without even asking him if it's cool. And suddenly she does not need to go home so urgently. Tex cannot think of anything he wants to do with her along; so he ditches them both at Arti Rose's mom's place (with a promise that Arti will see him again soon).

Sunshine calls her parents and tells them she wants to stay the night with Arti Rose. Sue is home, on a Saturday night, because the car salesman dumped her and went back to the mother of his children. Sunshine tells Arti that her parents want to speak with Sue. Arti Rose goes to her mother's bedroom, where Sue is sitting up in bed with her hair in that row of bobby pins she has been putting around the edge of her head nearly every night of her life since high school. The light is on because Sue is reading a book. There is a box of tissues on the bed, and when Sue looks up Arti Rose sees that her mother's eyes are red. Arti doesn't ask, because she really does not want to hear about the car salesman.

"Sunshine's parents want to ask you if it's okay for her to spend the night here," Arti says.

Sue gets up and walks out to the living room, where the phone lives on the nearest end table. She sounds more pleasantly agreeable than she looks.

When she goes back to bed, Sunshine whispers, "Your mom doesn't look like herself."

"Man problems," Arti explains.

"That car salesman is an asshole!" Sunshine hisses.

"Maybe we should go outside for a while," Arti says, then raises her voice and projects it in the direction of Sue's bedroom. "Hey mom; we're going out to the swings."

Sun and the Cross

Arti Rose and Sunshine stayed up all night that night, mostly outside. Once they went in for a bit, when Arti noticed the light go off in her mother's bedroom window. She got a quilt and a pillow from Dave's room and tried to bed down on the floor near Sunshine, who was on the couch. But Sunshine kept talking. Arti Rose was not sleepy either, and she was afraid they would wake Mama Sue. So they went back outside and walked around, finally settling on a bench in the garden area of a nearby church. They sat there and talked all night.

Sunshine rehashed all her sexual relationships, dating back to her first, three years prior, at the age of fifteen. There had been three in high school, a pattern of oddballs. She had worked as a helper in the guidance counselor's office, where she met her first lover and began to romanticize, even to idolize, the chemically imbalanced misfits of the world, from the damaged to the "gifted". If she talked all night, every night for a week, she might cover the adventures she'd had before Arti Rose even really got started dating boys. Arti had heard some of it before, but she got the boys mixed up in her head. There was the band geek who played trumpet but also wrote music and charmed her with his talent on the baby-grand in the chorale room. There was the long-haired guy from the Drama Club; he had been in "Twelfth Night". Arti had not seen that play, but she went to all the musicals, like *Oklahoma* and *Brigadoon.* Arti Rose went to the same high school and never knew any of Sunshine's boyfriends. Sometimes she thought Sunshine made them up, because they were hard to find in the yearbooks, not always in the same grade as Sunshine, sometimes not in the alphabetically arranged class photos at all. It was difficult for Arti Rose to picture the far-out characters Sunshine described, eccentric young shadow-dwellers who had never stepped into the high-school limelight.

Sunshine's contradictions and hypocrisies increasingly wore on Arti Rose. She didn't like to judge her friend but rarely agreed with Sunshine's often harsh judgments of others. According to Sunshine, all of the high school kids who had been "popular" (including Arti Rose's sorority-sisters, like Davie's girlfriend Wendy and her older sister) were shallow snobs. Only "freaks" (current slang for hippy or bohemian types) were cool enough for Sunshine. So she found very few of the One World Crusaders acceptable, which put Arti Rose on the defensive about Gabe's less-attractive friends (like Faith and Millie).

Arti often found herself tuning out when Sunshine talked about Kirby lately too. Sunshine's Kirby was not Arti Rose's Kirby, the Kirby of Methodist Youth Fellowship, the innocent young Kirby who once walked miles to put a poem on Arti Rose's door. The Kirby who used to be Arti's friend and had become, to Sunshine, "just an asshole". And Arti Rose had to admit, she really did not know who Kirby was anymore. She didn't want to think about Kirby (or Will, or Rob, or Tex). Arti Rose did not want to think about guys she felt disillusioned with, and she surely did not want to feel the disappointment in her own self, where relationships were concerned. So she was not a very good listener that night. Arti Rose was happy though, to have her best friend for company that long night when she would never have been able to sleep anyway.

When the sun was rising, Arti was talking about Gabe and the Unification Church and the One World Crusade and that Amish girl named Faith who said not everyone would recognize God's son when he comes again. Sunshine was not really listening to Arti Rose, but she was glad to be with her.

"They think that Sun-Moon guy is the messiah," Sunshine said, in a tone that said she had already dismissed the idea. "That black guy from Berkeley was calling him Master. I asked him if that made him a slave. He said it made him a disciple. Maybe him, but not me," Sunshine said.

While Arti was talking about the implications of the last lecture ("but what if he really is the *Lord of the Second Advent*"), and Sunshine was tuning her out (but enjoying the sunrise and just being with her friend outside on a beautiful morning that the sleeping world was missing), a visual miracle happened. The big, red ball of light centered itself perfectly, for a moment in time, behind the cross on the steeple of the church.

To Arti Rose, it was more than a thing she saw; it was a thing she felt, the sun rising inside her, shedding new light on everything she had ever believed and experienced in light of her beliefs. Just seeing and feeling what she was seeing and feeling, was like being born again. "It's a sign," Arti Rose said. "the symbol of Jesus is one with the sun. It's a sign about Jesus and Sun Myung Moon."

"Oh my God!" was all Sunshine said, just looking at the sunrise and thinking how great it was to be cool enough to stay out all night and watch the glorious dawn of a new day, while most of the stupid world was still sleeping.

When Sunshine went home, Arti Rose wrote in her journal about "the sign" of the sun and the cross.

Dear Diary,

I had been praying that Heavenly Father would give me a sign. I got one when Sunshine and I stayed up all night and watched the sun rise. We had been talking but got quiet for a while to listen when the birds started singing. It was a beautiful morning. The air was fresh and cool. There were wispy clouds on the eastern horizon and billowy ones on the west. Directly over our heads, the sky was clear and blue.

When the sun first started to come up, we were looking all around and smiling and bubbling with energy. Sunshine had been talking about guys, and I was thinking about Gabe. I started talking about it being a new day (Gabe is always saying that this is a "New Day...a day of hope").

We became still and quiet. We were entranced by the beauty of the rising red sun scattering pink and purple streaks of light among the wispy clouds. We began looking at shapes in the colorful clouds and letting our imaginations soar. Then we started talking again, naming things that we saw, which we interpreted differently. I saw a triangle of clouds and thought about the Holy Trinity.

152

Sunshine was not into thinking about religion, and she said the triangle was like the two of us forming a connection with the sky. Then she noticed something else while my mind was still playing in the clouds.

Sunshine suddenly grabbed my arm and yelled, "Look Arti!" She was pointing at the fully risen sun, which had come up directly behind the steeple of a nearby church. We had not really seen the cross before, but the new sun now made it bright and beautiful. It was a magnificent sight.

"It's a sign!" I said, feeling a new hope rising inside me. I began to say 'Thank you Jesus' over and over in my heart. I figured that would sound too churchy to say out loud in front of Sunshine, so I kept it between me and Jesus for a minute. Then when the sun was up fully behind the cross, I said, "The new day and the cross are one!"

Sunshine only said, "Gaaah," as the sun continued to come up, then, "That was far-out!" as it ascended beyond the cross. Then she said, "I'm not sure it was a 'sign' though."

I felt sad, but I understood. I tried to explain it to Sunshine as I felt it. "Jesus was the living Truth…God's Truth is infinite and eternal, but it can only live on this earth when it lives inside of a man. Jesus promised us that with His death, the truth would not die. In promising his return, He was promising the return of living Truth to our world. The Truth that Jesus was able to give during his life was equal to the bright star that led men through the darkness to the place of his birth. Today the world is full of people living in darkness. For this to be the New Day…the day upon which man and God will be united, the Truth must shine brightly enough to lead billions of people out of darkness. A star is no longer bright enough. The new manifestation of Truth must be as bright as the sun…rising from the East to bring birth to a New Day."

"I don't know about all that, but it was a cool sunrise" Sunshine said, walking back to the parking lot by the apartment, where she got in her VW and went home.

I thought about what I had seen and felt all day and into the evening…

> When darkness falls
> around the new sun
> and threatens to smother it…
> the light will take refuge
> on the mother moon,
> and she will rule the night..,
> and He will rule the day..,
> and there will be no more darkness.

Sun Myung Moon is truly the new messiah! And the new sun, or son, sheds a new light on the life and death of Jesus. Just as the new sun brightened the cross and made it visible. The new sun, symbol of Sun Myung Moon, and the cross, the symbol of Jesus, are one in my eyes (because of the sign) and in my heart (because of what I feel).

Armageddon in the Kitchen

Arti Rose is sitting on the floor by the front window of her mother's apartment one afternoon, trying to add some texture to the painting of the shapeless tree in her view. She is layering yellow ochre on top of the previously applied green, using a little flat metal tool instead of a brush, thinking about Vincent Van Gogh but not doing a very good job of emulating his style.

Dave comes in from work, dragging his sidekick, who is quite agitated at the sight of Arti Rose.

"D-did you know they've got Felicia?" Will verbally ejaculates, his gangly, sweaty body towering over Arti Rose.

"What? Who?"

"The O-one World Crusade and your friend, Gabe."

"I know Leash was still there when we left the other night."

"F-Felicia is still there."

"Well, if she feels that Heavenly Father is calling her…" Arti

154

Rose says, trying to give Felicia the benefit of the doubt. Maybe her motives could be changing.

"Heavenly F-Father? Are you crazy?" Will raises his voice, holds his arms out, then up so that he looks like a mad Jesus. "Th-this Moon guy is the Antichrist! The B-book of Revelations warns about a 'One World' organization."

"I thought that was communism," Arti argues. "Mr. Moon is anti-communist."

"You'd better start listening to somebody besides Gabe, sister," Dave says, shaking his head from side-to-side as he heads for the kitchen. "Gabe's a nice guy, but I think he's been led astray. You should ask Pastor Paul what he thinks about Gabe's lectures."

"Fine. I'll talk to Pastor Paul if you want me to. Obviously, if the Divine Principle is true, at least some people with biblical knowledge are going to recognize that. You didn't even go to half of the lectures, Dave," Arti raises her voice so that Dave can hear her in the kitchen. "So I don't know how you can say..."

"*I-I* went to all of them, every single lecture," Will carries on, still towering over Arti. "A-and I read *my* Bible every day. Th-this is straight out of the Book of Revelations. A-and the One World Crusade has got Felicia. Th-the Antichrist, the *d-devil* has got your friend Felicia."

"I am not sure the devil didn't have Felicia before. And I think she is more your friend than mine, Will."

"Sh-she *was* my s-sister in Christ," Will says. "N-now she is under the influence of the Antichrist. S-somebody has got to do something." Will opens the door and leaves, slamming the door behind him.

Arti Rose puts her painting tools in a jar of water on the window sill and joins her brother in the kitchen.

"Leash just likes some guy in the One World Crusade," Arti Rose says to her brother. "I didn't want to tell Will that, but it was obvious the other night. Will shouldn't have left without her."

"He said he told her to 'come on' when he got ready to leave Gabe's, but she wanted to stay."

"See," Arti says, opening the refrigerator.

"Next you'll probably be staying over there," Dave says, pouring tea from a pitcher into a glass.

"SO! I'm not sayin' I will, but so what if I do. It's none of *your* business!" Arti says, putting ice in a glass.

Sue comes in from work while her two oldest children are arguing in the kitchen. Sis trails in behind her mother like a little duckling, dripping water from that sagging crocheted bikini she practically lives in. Sue puts her purse on the end table by the phone, and enters the kitchen, Sis following.

"Mom, Arti's gonna join the One World Crusade with Felicia and some *black* guy and a bunch of other people who travel around in a white van with an antichrist symbol on it."

"Antichrist? Black guy? What on earth are you talking about, David?"

"Dave's just been listenin' to Will, who is upset because his girlfriend likes some guy over at Gabe's," Arti Rose says.

"A black guy?" Sis asks.

"Just a guy," Arti says.

"I didn't know there were any other guys over at Gabe's," Sue says.

"There's a whole army of them, Mom. They may not *all* be at Gabe's, but, trust me, there is an *army*. This so-called church is way more than a church, and it is *not good*. Gabe might be a good guy, but he has been misled. You can ask Pastor Paul; Will told him about it, and he explained it to us yesterday after youth fellowship. It's all in the Book of Revelations. Arti Rose can*not* see it, because she likes Gabe. You should see the way she *looks* at him, Mom"

"I don't know what you two are talking about, but both of you need to calm down and help me get supper ready. Whatever it is; it's not the end of the world. I've been hearing people talk about the Book of Revelations and the Antichrist and the Battle of Armageddon since I was a little kid, and the world has not ended yet. My father survived World War I, the Great Depression, and World War II. He also taught me not to listen to any of that crap about the Book of Revelations. They make up all kinds of garbage to scare people into going to church and putting money in the offering plate. And *I* have survived *two* husbands and *two* divorces and three sometimes-*crazy* children without the world ending. So quit your fightin' and set the table!"

Saturday, August 12-13, 1972

Dear Diary,

As I have heard the Divine Principle, even from the first moment that I read the pamphlet given to my mother by Gabriel Dane, I have accepted every word as God-given truth. It all makes sense in my head, and I can feel some sort of strange warmth in my heart every time I hear or read the Principle. It's beautiful. My thirsty mind has been soaking up Sun Myung Moon's revelations like a dry sponge that was floating on oceans of un-quenching ideas. Because this great truth has rescued me from my confusion and filled me with hope, can it not do the same for the entire world? I am sure that it can. Being idealistic and open-minded to new ideas, I have found it easy to see the truth of the Principle. I wasn't afraid of the sacrifices I would have to make either. So doubt and fear were not able to enter me as long as I stood alone...or with people who were only positive influences. Now I am dealing with negativity, even from people that I love. But I am not going to let Satan use them to blind me from the Truth.

Sunshine has always been a mixture of positive and negative, and (after rooming with her at State U) I have learned to ignore her negativity. We are friends whether we agree or not. She has never been religious, so I don't expect her to be too interested in the Divine Principle. Her negativity doesn't hurt me like what I am getting from my old boyfriend William and my brother Dave and his girlfriend Wendy (who was my "little sister" in our high school sorority). The three of them have been involved in the Jesus movement together while I was away at college, and now they are being negative about the Divine Principle.

Earlier this summer, I went on a camping trip to Jacksonville, Florida with Dave and Wendy. While my brother was surfing, Wendy and I got into a heavy rap about God. We climbed a sand hill with palm trees and flowers to watch the sunset. It was magnificent. We were on a spiritual high that was so overwhelming that we couldn't speak without bubbling and singing and laughing. JOY! God made the sunset and the palm-trees and the ocean and the sea-gulls and the shell-lined sandy shores to bring joy to man (just like it says in the Divine Principle). Wendy and I could really feel Heavenly Father holding us next to his heart that night. We really felt alive, and the whole creation seemed to be smiling. There was no darkness. The night filled us with spiritual light that opened our senses and broadened our awareness.

With the warm summer breeze blowing through my soul and the rhythmic roar of the ocean allowing me to feel the steady heartbeat of the cosmos, Wendy and I stared spellbound at a sky full of the brightest stars we had ever seen. They were brighter because they were reaching out to us, and we were reaching out to them…and God was there. God was shining in all of those stars…all of those millions of stars…and God was shining in the hearts of Arti Rose and Wendy. A Rosy Wind blew, and we felt a tremendous sense of oneness with the entire universe.

Wendy said, "How could anyone look at all those stars and not believe in God?"

We were in complete agreement. And when my brother came in from the surf, it was like the three of us were one. We all fell asleep looking up at the stars.

So I thought Dave and Wendy would really be able to relate to the "Principle of Creation", and I was eager to invite them to the Unification Church Center to hear Gabe Dane's first lecture of the series. That one was easy enough for them to swallow (along with Gabe's sweet lemonade). Other friends have been to the lectures too. William and Kirby have been the most argumentative, but everybody likes Gabe. (Felicia and Sunshine flirt with him, which may have something to do with William and Kirby's heightened tendencies to argue, however religious and intellectual their arguments seem to be). Tex is trying not to like Gabe (because he thinks I like him too much). My mom likes Gabe, but she hasn't been to the lectures. Nobody seems to be as interested in the Divine

Principle as I am (except to argue with the biblical part and the conclusion, which they have mostly been negative about).

During this past week the One World Crusade "bus-team" for the spreading of the Divine Principle has been staying at Gabe's. They are beautiful people, full of warmth and love and understanding. I thought this would be a perfect time to share the Principle with my friends.

William and Felicia heard all of the lectures this week. William was interested in the biblical interpretation, but he did not agree with where it led. Sunshine and Kirby came to a few lectures together but started fighting again (about personal stuff). Sunshine quit coming, but Kirby came back a few times to argue his agnostic point-of-view with Gabe. Even when Kirby and I were in Methodist Youth Fellowship together, in high school, he took an agnostic position.

"Either Jesus really is what they say, or it's the greatest hoax in human history," has been Kirby's conclusion for years. He's a good guy, but he's just not religious. Still, I wish he could respect me for my beliefs instead of calling me "gullible".

Felicia went from one extreme to the other, agreeing with William at first (when she came in like a yellow butterfly on his arm). Then she started taking Gabe's side. Finally Felicia crossed over when she got smitten with a One World Crusader.

William is disappointed about losing Felicia's attention, but they had not been dating for long anyway. William is a "solid-rock" Jesus freak and naturally would have to change some of his ideas in order to accept the Principle. Most Christians are expecting Jesus of Nazareth to return. So the idea of a new Messiah with the same mission, but a different name, is often difficult to grasp. (Impossible for William).

William looks like a Renaissance painting of Jesus (which means more like a fair and curly-haired European troubadour minstrel than the desert nomad the Jewish messiah really was). William carries a Bible translated from the Greek and so heavy that his skinny frame leans when he walks around with it, which he always does when he is at Gabe's, arguing with the One World Crusaders out on Gabe's balcony and on the front steps of the Southside building and in the park across the Avenue. He is a sight. William seemed to be enjoying having knowledgeable people to argue with about biblical interpretations until after he heard the last lecture of the series. Then he started getting negative. Sometimes I worried William might hit Gabe or one of the One World Crusaders with that big, heavy Bible of his.

The hardest part about all of this is that when William started getting negative feelings about the Principle he began radiating negative vibrations in my direction. William has such a huge influence over my brother Dave. Soon Dave and Wendy and my whole family began to reflect William. It's like they have all been surrounding me from every side and pushing me up against a hard cold wall and throwing darts at me. Darts made of cold and distant words and glances coming from hearts that once gave me love and warmth and harmonious give-and-take. It wasn't their fault. They are beautiful people and I love them.

It was Satan, and he was so obvious. He wanted to hurt me, and he did. Gabe and some of the One World Crusaders told me to watch out for Satanic attacks after hearing and accepting the Divine Principle. Sure enough, I was bombarded. The weird thing is, my close friends and family are still friends with Gabe even though they don't agree with everything he teaches and don't want to join his church.

Last night William even went to Gabe's with Felicia and Tex. Tex really wanted me to go, because we have not gone out together lately. But I wanted to stay home alone. The three of them went to a fellowship night at Gabe's. I said I wanted to be alone with Heavenly Father. Before Tex came to my mom's apartment, I had been arguing with William and Felicia. Felicia talks out of both sides of her mouth at this point, and William is just glad to have her around to argue with. But they were too much for me. I started crying and told them how much I love them and to please not let Satan come between us. They left with Tex when he came in his van.

I was alone...but not alone...I had been fasting all day, and I felt very light. I was very depressed. I could feel great spiritual activity in the room and I was seeing "everythings" (patterns of little conjoined and similar, atomic-like living things that I had perceived the world to be made of, when I had experimented with psychedelics a few times). The everythings were dark and drab this time (though I had seen them bright and glowing with light before). The room was filled with a depressing spirit...I cried for a long time, and I could feel Heavenly Father crying all around me and pouring out his tears for His suffering children on my soul. I wanted to comfort Him. I promised Him that I will never desert Him...even if I lose every friend and every relative that I have. He has been crying for thousands of years...We of this New Age must dry His tears...permanently.

Tex brought William and Felicia back to the apartment after fellowship at Gabe's, because William had left his car. They were all in good spirits. Felicia wanted to tell me all about it. I could tell "Leash" (her nickname) was wearing on the guys' nerves. Tex was ready to go crash in his own room, and William's parents were expecting him at home. They left her with me.

Felicia didn't even call home, but that's nothing new. Her parents never seem to care where she is, maybe because she is 18 and supposedly an adult. I'm still 17. My mom says to ask permission about things that go on at the apartment, but she was asleep. "Mama Sue" never has the heart to say No to kids who hang-out anyway. She listens to all their problems. I've heard her say she doesn't know what to do about all of that, but she "can at least listen". And maybe there is "safety in numbers" if they want to hang-out. I am like my mother in some ways, because I listen too...

Felicia said the fellowship was wonderful. They had a spaghetti dinner and singing and fellowship afterwards. She told me about the way they prayed with so much depth and sincerity in their voices...and the way they said "Father" with so much love, as if the word "Father" was a feeling that came from the center of their souls. She said that one of the older members from the bus-team had given his testimony.

Felicia said "Jonah" had been married and was a doctor when he felt a deep inner need to search for something. He divorced his wife and traveled around the country for a while, being led to certain places by spiritual experiences & dreams. He was finally led to a spiritual medium, and while he was with her, they saw a vision of Master Moon. It was a perfect vision, and this made it fairly easy for Jonah to find the Unification Church.

I was very moved by the story, and I asked Felicia what she felt as Jonah was talking. She said that she could hardly hold back the tears, but anyone would have been moved by his story. She said she wasn't going to take that as a sign from God that Sun Myung Moon is the messiah. I agreed with her. I told her that she should let God reveal it to her, because Satan can easily work in horizontal relationships (as Gabe had told me).

We talked until around 2:30. I told her something else I had learned from the last lecture, which she had not heard yet. I told her I had spent the evening alone, talking with Heavenly Father, and I had learned that it is true that God is crying.

"He wants His children back," I said.

"My God is not crying!" Felicia said.

It made me really sad. People just don't understand.

I didn't want to argue with Felicia, but I told her I thought we should go to the sunrise service at Gabe's. He had called to invite me when I didn't show up for the fellowship. I had already borrowed my mom's car-keys before she went out with the car-salesman. I wasn't sure she would come home before sunrise but she did, and now she was asleep. Felicia was still high on God and thought it would be a good idea to go to the sunrise service. We set the alarm for 4:30 and rested at either end of the couch.

I couldn't really sleep but pretended to so Felicia would stop talking. I didn't really want the alarm to wake up Mama Sue on her day off either, so I barely dozed off and kept checking the clock. I was really exhausted and had weird dreams even though I was awake. I had almost fallen asleep when Scotty started making strange noises. I jumped up and looked at him, and he was moaning and barking and jumping all over the floor. It looked as though the dog was possessed. At least I had never seen him act that way when he was just dreaming. Anyway, I let him out.

I could feel the power of spiritual forces in the room, and I realized that was why the weird dream flashes. The alarm clock rang. I shook Felicia and she said, "Wow; I feel kind o' strange."

We got up and washed our faces. Leash looked like a raccoon, with all the black stuff around her eyes. I gave her a washcloth and a bar of soap. Afterwards was the first time I had seen her without all that make-up. She looked so sweet and innocent, almost like an older version of Dave's girlfriend, Wendy. I told her she looked better without the make-up, and maybe she should stop bleaching her hair. Her darker roots were showing. She said something about the One World Crusade sisters not wearing make-up. Personally, I've been into the natural-look since I got out of high school.

We went out in the cool air and received a tremendous surge of energy. It was still dark, but there was plenty of light in the parking lot. Before getting in the car, we held hands under a tree in a landscaped area and prayed. I prayed that Heavenly Father would give us a sign that would tell us if Sun Myung Moon was really the Messiah, if he was really His true son, and if he had really come to fulfill Jesus' promise of return. We prayed that Jesus would know how much we love him and desire to work with him. I vowed that if this movement is against the will of Jesus I will not join it. Felicia did the same, and she pleaded for a sign.

Felicia was unusually quiet while I drove us to the little park across from Gabe's,. The One World Crusade was just gathering for their sunrise service. The light was dim, and the air was light. We stood in a circle and prayed with them. I felt strong, spiritual rushes, like I have felt at Mema's Pentecostal church. Felicia must have felt the Holy Spirit too, because she was trembling and crying. They weren't speaking in tongues or anything, like at Mema's church. But I still think the Holy Spirit was there. The Divine Principle says the Holy Spirit is the female aspect of God, and that makes sense to me. Maybe that's why me and Felicia were the ones who got filled with the Holy Spirit. She is trying to give birth to new spiritual children. That would put Gabe in the position of spiritual father in that Trinity, with God at the top. Then we would be at the bottom, making it a geometrical diamond shape like the Four Position Foundation in the Principle..

Anyway, there was some excitement around me and Felicia and Gabe at the sunrise service, but most of the bus-team just looked sleepy. I figured they wanted to go back to bed (or, in their case, sleeping bags). Leash followed them all back inside afterwards., but I didn't. Felicia came out on Gabe's balcony and waved bye to me.

It was Sunday. I figured I could be back in time for my mom to use the car if she wanted to take my little sister to the Methodist Church. Felicia was caught up in the spirit and didn't want to leave. I had to get the car back home, so I left Gabe's without her. Gabe didn't seem to mind (and I figured, with the bus-team visiting, there was "safety in numbers"). I don't know how safe any of the "brothers" were though, with Leash around...But there may be hope for her...New Hope for us all...

Tempted

Arti is stretched out on the couch, nearly asleep, with the rest of her family in their beds for the night. The phone rings. She know it's Tex; he is the only person that calls this late. And he knows she is probably stretched out on the couch, right by the end table where the phone lives.

Arti doesn't feel like talking, but she picks up anyway.

"Hi kid," the familiar voice drawls.

"Hey."

"You sound tired."

"Yeah, I had kind of rough evening, arguing with my brother and Will, about the whole Unification Church thing."

"Will *was* pretty freaked out the other night."

"Yeah. Now he's upset about Felicia?"

"What about her?"

"She's still over there."

"You're kidding."

"That's what Will said. I haven't talked to Gabe in a few days. Maybe he's got enough help selling candles right now, with Felicia and the One World Crusade. Anyway, Sears doesn't have me scheduled much this week; so I'm trying to catch up on some school work. I got an A on my sociology exam."

"Far out."

"Yeah. I'm not doing that well with these painting assignments though. I think I would do better if could just paint from inspiration."

"Well, that's what you should do then. You said the sunsets you turned in were cool."

"Yeah."

"You could paint sunsets on my van if you want."

"Really?"

"Sure. There's plenty of space. You could do a sunset on one side and a sunrise on the other."

"Wow. That's a cool idea. It would be fun. But what if I messed up?"

"You couldn't mess up that old rust bucket. Anything would be an improvement. I was thinking about painting a big peace symbol or some shit on it anyway."

"Really? We should work on it together then."

"Far-out. Let's do it this weekend. My dad's got a bunch of old paint in the garage.

"Say, Kid; I've been thinking. The city just hired an extra guy, and we don't really need him on the park clean-up truck. I think he'll probably end up cutting grass or something. The old guy who drives

165

the truck is a friend of my mom's; so I figure he'll keep me with him anyway. But it would be a good time for me to take a vacation right now. If you could get some time off, I would love to take you to Texas, to meet my grandparents and see their spread. Talk about sunsets; they have some great ones out there Kid. It's all sky."

"Really? That sounds cool. I've never been west of New Orleans."

"Well, ask your mom. We could leave after we get the van painted this weekend."

"O.K.. I'll call Sears too."

"I'll talk to you soon then. G'night Kid. Love ya."

"Love you too."

Next day Gabe calls. "Where have *you* been?"

"Mostly around here. At school some. I got an A on my sociology exam."

"Great. When are you coming over to the center?"

"I don't know. I heard Felicia was staying there now."

"Yes, she is. For now. I don't know how long it will last. She wants to leave with the One World Crusade, in a few days. Millie is working with her, trying to be a spiritual mother to her. But they don't take new members on the road. And I don't think Felicia is strong enough in her understanding of the Principle to stay here with me alone."

"So, she likes that guy she was talking to on the balcony after the last lecture?" Arti asks.

"Hmm. Let's just say there are some things she does not quite understand yet."

"You mean about the fall," Arti Rose says.

"Yes. The fall. So what's Tex up to?"

"He wants me to go on a trip with him, to see his grandparents and their ranch and all.

"Ranch?"

"Out in Texas."

"Don't you have to work at Sears? I was talking to the lady that manages the Junior Bazaar over there, and she said she really likes you. Says you're great with the customers."

"I am. I help them put outfits together. I love some of the clothes that are coming in for fall. But if she likes me so much, she should give me more hours."

"It is slow right now," Gabe says. "But it will pick up when the back-to-school shopping starts. So, are you going?"

"Back to school?"

"Well, that *is* something we should discuss. But I was asking about Texas."

"Oh. Yeah I think so."

"Hmm."

"What's wrong?"

"It may sound strange to you at this time. But if you believe in the Divine Principle, it is not so strange."

"What?"

"Do you remember how, in the Bible, before Jesus started his mission, he went into the desert to fast and pray?"

"Yeah. For forty days and forty nights."

"Right. Satan tempted him in various ways."

"Yeah."

"Well, all I am saying is be careful right now. If you are being called by God to fulfill a special mission, which I believe you are, you will most likely be tempted.

"Tempted?"

"Just be careful. Don't forget to pray. And I will be praying for you."

"O.K. Thanks."

"God bless you on your journey."

To Texas with Tex

Tex's mom and sister, both of whom live in West End, near a sleazy Avenue where Tex's mom works as a cocktail waitress, decide to go. Arti Rose has never met them and probably would have made an excuse not to go if she had. Tex's mom looks like she is trying to be Marilyn Monroe, several years past a little too late. The sister is an obese baby, a recent high school dropout who (unlike her mother) does not groom herself, and she whines constantly. Arti Rose ends up in the back of the old work-van (with Tex's sister's body-odor). Tex has at least tried to make it comfortable back there, with a new shag carpet remnant, a bean-bag, and big cushions from an old couch.

Tex and Arti Rose have been working on the van all weekend when they pick up his mom and sister. They are especially proud of the murals, which are large versions of the sunsets Arti Rose painted for her class, with one in warm colors on the driver's side and another in cooler colors on the passenger's side. Tex put a peace symbol on one of the back doors and Arti Rose painted a big flower on the other one. Arti Rose wrote "Love" and "Flower-Power" in fat, rounded bubble lettering. Tex wrote "Peace" and "Make Love Not War" in angular lettering with jagged lightening bolts extending from selected letters. When Tex's sister sees the van she says it looks "cool". His mom's eyes get big for a second, like she is slightly taken aback; but she makes no comment. Her dream ride would be a rich man's Cadillac; however she does not seem to mind getting into the front seat of her son's hippy van, with the window down. Tex's sister plops down on the bean-bag in back, with her bag of candy. The grossly overweight girl says she likes the comfortable beanbag; but she soon starts complaining about the heat, as there is no air-conditioning and there are no windows in back. Tex opens the vent on the roof and says they will get more air back there once he gets moving.

Tex and his mom seem to talk constantly, but they don't say much of anything. It is mostly small talk and kidding around, like they are best friends (a fact Arti Rose was previously unaware of, since Tex has never talked about his mother much). Arti had envisioned herself in the front seat next to Tex, proudly riding in their personalized hippy van with the windows down and their long hair blowing (his blonde hair complementing the warm tones of the mural on the driver's side, her dark hair blending with the cooler tones of the mural on the passenger's side). Instead she is stuck in back with his whiney sister who keeps begging for her "mommy" to trade places with her. Tex's mom claims that he needs her help with directions, since she has been back and forth to her old childhood home many times and knows all the best short-cuts and back-roads. Arti Rose does not complain, but she is miserable with the whole situation. She tries to sleep as much as possible, which is easy to do in the heat of summer, especially when they get to Texas. The ride through Houston (a seemingly endless concrete-jungle) is almost unbearable, but they manage somehow and bypass a few other crowded areas. Eventually they get to the middle of nowhere (where the east ends and the west begins).

When they get out at a gas station, Arti Rose hangs close with Tex while he pumps gas. Still waking up from a long nap, she says, "Hey Tex; where are we?"

"East of the sun, and west of the moon," Tex says, then laughs his maniacal laugh.

"Wasn't that the name of a fairy-tale?" Arti muses, gazing dreamily into the horizon.

"Yes it was, kid," Tex says, putting his arm around her waist as they go into the little country store for snacks.

"Wan' a soda?" Tex asks, fishing around in the big red ice chest that says 'Coca-Cola' in fancy white cursive on top.

"Tex, you know I hate Coke; it burns my throat," Arti Rose says. "Do they have chocolate drinks?"

"Sure, kid," Tex says, pulling a glass bottle full of creamy brown liquid from the cooler and handing it to Arti Rose with a grin (like he's giving her a Christmas present). He gets himself an orange Nehi. They stand in line behind his mother and sister, who are buying a mountain of snacks.

"Can I get an extra bag?" Tex asks the clerk. "And some napkins?"

When they get back to the van Tex hands the paper bag and napkins to his sister on the beanbag in back. She has already started eating a candy bar and has a bag of chips open in her lap.

"I don't want any of that junk in my new shag-rug!" Tex says.

"That's why I'm tryin' to eat this candy-bar before it melts," she retorts.

They finally arrive at their destination, which is a simple white wood frame house with a few large, old trees shading the yard. Neglected land stretches out in every direction, dotted with scrub oaks (the shortest trees Arti Rose has ever seen, barely bigger than bushes) and strewn with tumble-weeds. In the widest of blue skies, fluffy white clouds wander lazily toward the horizon like an endless herd of sheep. But there are no stock animals.

Tex's grandparents are reminiscent of the cleaned-up old farming couple in *American Gothic,* the famous painting of American homesteaders with a pitchfork. They are grim and work-worn, proud and puritanical, self-contained under their leathery faces. His grandfather is tall like Tex, in a pair of clean, dark-denim overalls with a short-sleeved faded plaid cotton shirt underneath, all starched and pressed with creases along the sleeves as well as the length of the legs of his overalls. Tex's grandmother wears a faded calico print apron over her neatly pressed shirtwaist dress, which is of a once-dark color faded to neutral. Her steel-grey hair is pulled back in a tight bun. They both wear brown leather lace-up's, with chunky heels on the grandmother's shoes, giving the short, sturdy woman an extra inch of height but no added sex-appeal. Her sagging breasts provide the only sign of femininity, barely supported and hanging nearly to her waist.

Arti Rose is hard-pressed to imagine Tex's mom (with her pushup bra and ample breasts showing wrinkled cleavage above a hot-pink tube-top, her too-short shorts squeezing doughy white thighs, her garish pawn shop glitter), having once been a little girl with these parents, on this hard land. Maybe it was the hardness of her early life that changed her, made her want to run away. It is easy enough to imagine her in a Western brothel. However, there are pictures of her in pigtails (brown, not blonde), on horses and helping with cows and a variety of other animals, a lot more than the few chickens that peck around the yard now.

There is a photo with a boyish Tex too, smiling by a pigpen with a sow and her sucklings, looking for all the world like a farm boy, like someone who might actually get up with the rooster's crow and work hard, someday. Arti Rose spends so much time staring at the photo of little Tex that the old woman gives the cherished photograph to the girl (maybe hoping in her heart of hearts that Arti Rose will be the one to save him, to give him back what the war took from him).

Arti Rose liked the old people, felt sorry for them and admired them at the same time. They held themselves with a self-respect that made it impossible not to admire them. They were like living statues of unsung heroes from a different time. They seemed almost set-in-stone, so quiet and self-contained that it was impossible to read them. One could only imagine. Maybe they had survived the apocalyptic dust-storms which devastated that part of the country during the Great Depression. Arti Rose was too shy to ask them what all they had been through, but she could see that they were cut from different cloth than anybody she knew. This was hard land, harder than the land of the fertile American southeast that had sustained Arti Rose's parents and grandparents through times when others stood in line for government food. These were old-fashioned Democrats who had counted on FDR to help pull them through. And they had lost children to the dust pneumonia that killed so many, during the worst ecological disaster in American history. Maybe they'd had enough land and grown enough wheat, at one time, to think their children and grandchildren would all be rich. But the land did not want that wheat, and it made them all pay, turned them and their neighbors into "the dust bowl". Their sons and older daughter had died eating and breathing that dust. And their over-protected and pampered youngest (this cheap looking, middle-aged seductress) was their only child. This obese whiner was their only granddaughter. This twenty-something Vietnam War veteran with the dishonorable discharge for drugs was their only grandson. The only pride they had left was in themselves, and they held it in the laced-up leather shoes that they continued to keep themselves firmly grounded in.

Arti Rose could see all of that with her heart. However, she only had a blurry, impressionistic school-book knowledge of the history and would not have been able to articulate it at the time. Arti Rose knew that Tex's grandparents reminded her of her own Mema and Pepa, only they seemed older and harder, sadder and more serious-looking than anybody she had ever seen up close. Sensing their deep loneliness, she sat with the old people a few times while they watched the news and read the paper. As conservative as they appeared, the pioneer stock Texans had taken up sympathy with the anti-war movement while their only grandson was in Viet Nam. Nowadays, permanently discontent with the powers-that-be, they shook their heads at about everything they saw on the news.

Tex's grandpa was particularly concerned about the so-called attempted burglary ("a bugging", he suspected) of the Democratic party's national headquarters. Few Americans were yet concerned about the incident, earlier that summer, at the Watergate building in Washington, D.C. But the old man was not satisfied with the investigation the government was doing, a government that he said was mostly concerned with putting itself back in power, during a presidential election year.

"I smell a rat in that hen house," Tex's grandpa said. "Probably a whole stinkin' rat's nest."

A few days into the visit, Arti is napping in a hammock, strung between two shade trees in the side yard of Tex's grandparents' house. She has been trying to read a copy of the Divine Principle that Gabe gave her for helping him sell candles, but it is too hot to read for long without falling asleep. Tex's mom and sister are asleep inside, in the only room of the old house that is air-conditioned.

Tex startles her with a gift of sweet tea, the ice clinking against a mason jar. "Wake up, kid. I wanta take ya for a ride."

"Where?"

"Just somewhere to watch the sunset, alone."

"That sounds nice, but it will be a while before sunset."

"So, we'll take our time," he drawls sensuously.

"Yeah."

They end up sitting on a river dam, smoking a joint and looking out into forever while the sunset colors the big sky.

"I wanta marry ya, Kid," Tex says, sitting cross legged with her hands in his, looking into her eyes with those baby blues, as blue as the Texas sky. "I'll inherit my grandparents' place someday, you know. We could retire here, or maybe even come here sooner. They're gonna need some help in a few years. In fact, they could use some help now."

"Help?"

"Well, the place is getting pretty run down, compared to what it used to be."

"So, you're saying you want us to get married and come out here and help them get back to farming this place or having a ranch or whatever it was?"

"Maybe. What d'ya think?"

"I think it sounds sweet, Tex. But I wouldn't say anything about it to your grandparents yet, if I was you. They look to me like they have decidedly retired, and retired the place as well. Maybe you should wait for them to say they want company out here. It's a nice dream though; ya gotta have dreams."

"Yep."

"Wow; what a sunset," she says, looking away from Tex's baby blues and off into forever.

Arti Rose is thinking about how hard it is to get Tex to do the dishes, back at his dad's place. She cannot imagine, in her wildest dreams, Tex working hard enough to keep up a ranch, much less make a living off it. No doubt the old folks are collecting Social Security; they obviously are not living off the land anymore.

When they get back in the van it is almost dark. Tex doesn't start up the engine. He gets out of the drivers seat and goes to the back of the van, opens the hatch on the roof, then takes Arti Rose by the hand.

"C'mon Kid," he drawls, tugging at her gently.

She gets out of the passenger seat and goes down on the new shag carpet with him. They start kissing, but when things get hot and heavy Arti Rose sits up.

"I don't want to get pregnant. We've got to stop."

Tex sighs, sits up, gets up and eases himself back into the driver's seat, starting the van up without saying a word.

"Plus I have been reading the Divine Principle today," Arti Rose chatters on once she has composed herself in the passenger seat up front, "about the fall being sexual."

Tex struggles to concentrate on his driving and lets out another sigh, trying to release some of the frustration he is feeling. "You really believe that Adam and Eve stuff, Kid?"

"You didn't hear that lecture, Tex. It makes more sense than the straight Bible story."

"You mean that Moon guy makes more sense than God?"

"I don't want to talk about it if you are going to be like that. You need to hear the rest of it; give it a chance."

"I don't know if it's really the so-called *Divine Principle* that's got you, or *Gabe*," Tex drawls, "but somethin's gotch-ya, Kid. You're not the same. It's not the same with us."

"I still love ya," she says, but it sounds like Arti Rose is saying those words to a close friend, not a lover.

Tex pushes his Traffic tape into the eight-track player. "This is what I think about all of that God stuff," he says when the band starts to sing "Heaven is in Your Mind". Tex sings the words out loud: "Take extra care not to lose what you feel. The apple you're eating is simple and real. Water the flowers that grow at your heel, guiding your vision to heaven; and heaven is in your mind".

Arti Rose understands what the band is saying about heaven

being in your mind, because when she was on that one LSD trip she saw things change as her thoughts changed. The world had looked like heaven one minute and hell the next, according to whether her thoughts were "positive or negative" (as Gabe would say). But she doesn't agree with the part of the song that says "the apple…is simple and real". It might be real, but it's not simple. If the apple is sex; that's a scary thought. Sex has become scary since she thought she was pregnant with Tex's baby. Tex as a friend does not scare her, but Tex as the father of her children is a scary thought. She does not share these thoughts with Tex, however, as they listen to the music. He plays it too loud anyway, like he is trying to make some point that she does not quite grasp. Somehow she has begun to see everything through the window-frame of the Divine Principle, and she feels safer that way.

When they get out of the van at Tex's grandparents' house, he tries to kiss Arti Rose again. She lets him hug her but turns her head upward to look at the big, Texas night sky. "Let's just enjoy all these stars," she says. "We never see this many in the city."

"I wish we could stay here," Tex says dreamily, holding Arti Rose as tightly as she will allow, until she breaks away and goes inside.

Arti Rose bypasses the den where Tex's family is gathered sleepily, watching an old black-and-white movie on TV. She settles in on a day-bed on the screened-in back porch. Maybe Tex will think she went to the twin in the guest room, where his mom and sister share the larger bed. She hears Tex arguing playfully with his sister, as she moves over reluctantly on the couch. Maybe he will fall asleep there without looking for her. She doesn't want to be bothered.

Before drifting into dreamland, she tries to imagine what it would be like if she and Tex lived on this ranch with his grandparents. They could probably use the help. But they didn't seem to be doing much with the place anymore. It was hard to imagine Tex doing the hard work to plant and tend and harvest whatever crop might grow on this arid land. Or would he take on animals, like the pigs in the picture when he was a boy? It was hard to imagine Tex doing anything but smoking dope and lounging around, listening to music. She knew he had a job involving some physical labor, doing whatever he was told to do, what he had been trained to do by the men he worked with in the city parks department. But she had never seen Tex at work. He bragged about how easy it was, riding around in a truck, picking up tree debris, stoned (even at work). Maybe in a different time Tex could have been a strong pioneer type. She had called him Johnny Appleseed when she'd first met him. He had the look of a weathered wild-man. But now she could not imagine entrusting Tex with her own survival and that of whatever children might come from them if they made a life together, here or elsewhere.

Moving In, Moving Out, Moving On

Back at home and work, Arti Rose sees Gabe at Sears first. They are scheduled for the same shift.

"So, Texas didn't swallow my favorite girl up, after all."

"Na," Arti Rose blushes, near speechless, having half forgotten how Gabe affects her.

"Say, do you have your mom's car? I mean, could you possibly help me sell candles after work? National Headquarters says we have almost reached our goal, but I've still got a few shipments at the Center."

"I take it the One World Crusade left. What about Felicia?"

"She left too."

"With them?"

"No. I thought I told you; they don't take new members on the road."

"Oh, yeah. So why didn't she just stay at the Center with you?"

"We tried that for a few nights, uh, days," Gabe says, blushing, looking around to make sure the sales people in the next department are not listening in. "*Felicia didn't understand the Fall,*" Gabe whispered, implying some sexually-related event or awkwardness.

"That's Felicia," Arti says, a bit embarrassed herself.

"I told her sleeping together is only for blessed couples; so she suggested we get blessed," he says, breaking through the embarrassment with that little kewpie-doll smile.

"She asked you to marry her?"

"In a way. But, even if I had wanted to, uh, marry her… that's just not how we do things in the Church. I'll tell you more about it later," he says, looking embarrassed again, glancing around. "So, do you want to help me sell candles after work? I'll buy you dinner."

"I don't know. Tex is supposed to pick me up."

"That's O.K...." Gabe pauses, looking down behind his wire-rimmed spectacles, freeing Arti Rose of his warm gaze, maybe praying for a second. "He could come with us."

"I'll ask him."

Later, Arti Rose stops by Gabe's department on her way out to the parking lot, where Tex had said he would meet her. She has not warned him about Gabe, but brings Gabe out with her. Tex looks stoned but says "Okay" when Gabe offers to buy a bucket of Kentucky Fried Chicken first. Gabe seems to think the van is a classic hippy-mobile; he walks around it, checking out the artwork, reading the lettering, grinning. The only time he stops smiling is when he reads the phrase "Make Love Not War", probably because of the sexual implication and maybe because Tex's lettering looks like something off a Black Sabbath album. Arti Rose lets Gabe sit up front with Tex. She pulls the bean-bag up, nearly between their seats.

At "the Center", Gabe puts the fried chicken on a platter in the middle of the dining room table. Arti Rose helps Gabe set the table. Tex puts ice in the glasses. Gabe dilutes his pitcher of lemonade and pours it in the three glasses.

They all sit down. Gabe and Arti Rose pause meditatively when they are seated, their hands still in their laps. Tex, his eyes focusing on the plate as soon as he sits (if not before), grabs the largest breast on the platter and immediately takes a bite (without even putting the meat on his plate first).

Gabe corrects Tex, as soon as he takes a bite. "We always bless the food before we eat here," he says. "And we serve each other before serving ourselves."

"Sorry, man," Tex says, swallowing and putting his hands in his lap, sitting up straight.

Gabe says a simple prayer, asking the "Heavenly Father" to bless the food, thanking God for the many blessings in life, including the "fine company". Afterwards Tex takes on ultra-mannerly airs, even cutting his fried chicken off its bones (ironic in the days of ads about KFC being 'finger-lickin' good"). Arti Rose is hungry and tries to relax and enjoy her meal, in spite of the strange tension she senses between the two young men.

Afterwards they hit a few of the newer apartment complexes in Tex's neighborhood. Tex carries Arti Rose's heavy box of candles at first. Then, getting competitive, Tex takes the third box out of the car. Arti is a little worried about Tex going to doors alone. He hasn't had a haircut or a shave for months, since that first date of the summer when he trimmed his hair and shaved his beard (maybe because of his new job and/or maybe to impress Arti Rose's mother). Now Tex is back to being a ragged looking, long-haired, bearded hippy who cannot get the smell of pot out of his clothes or his skin or his hair, much less out from under his fingernails (which are his favorite "roach clips"). Tex tells people he is selling the candles for a church that helps young people get off drugs. He hands out church literature and empties his box before Gabe, then starts helping Arti Rose sell hers.

"WO-o-oW," Tex says when they meet back at the car with their empty boxes. He is excited, high on the whole adventure, kicking his long legs around in those faded, thread-bare flared jeans.

When they drop Gabe off, he invites Tex back for the lectures he missed. Tex says "Okay". Tex is still on vacation from work; so Gabe teaches him the Principle of Creation the next day. The next night he teaches him The Fall, which completes the series (since Tex had heard the final lectures with Arti and friends). Arti Rose has sociology class. Tex shocks her by calling later that night and telling her that he is going to move into "the Center" with Gabe, the next day.

"Gabe needs help getting his new church started, and I like helping him," Tex says.

"So you're really into the candle selling thing, huh?"

"Yeah; you should o' been there, Kid. I sold way more than Gabe last night. The guy talks too much, ya know? It slows him down. I just told them I'm a vet, and this church is helping me out and helping a lot of kids get off drugs."

"What about the Divine Principle? Did you get the lecture about The Fall?"

"I get that they don't believe in sex before marriage, but I can live with that for now. Maybe if you and I both join, we can be blessed in marriage. You've pretty much been thinking that way anyhow; haven't you? It's not like we've done it in a while anyway."

"Yeah."

Arti Rose cannot believe how much energy Tex has. He seems like a different person, bombarding her with his enthusiasm. She is tired from working and going to class; so she gets off the phone with

177

him as soon as possible. When everyone in her family is asleep, and she is thinking about everything, she remembers that Tex has not been smoking as much pot as usual. He didn't smoke that much on the trip, because of his family. And this week he has been spending a lot of time with Gabe, which means he can't be smoking that much. That's probably why he has so much energy. Or maybe God has just gotten a-hold of him. Or both.

Arti Rose sees Gabe at work, and he invites her over to the Center on Saturday. He says he and Tex are going to sell candles Saturday afternoon, then go to that folk sing-in at the Catholic Church. Arti Rose has a hard time picturing Tex doing something like that on a Saturday night, especially without her. She says "Okay".

Sure enough, in the light of day, on Saturday afternoon, there is Tex at the Center, his duffle bag and sleeping bag rolled up in a corner of the living room. Apparently, Tex has been staying there since Thursday.

"I wanted the extra bedroom, but he says that's for the sisters," Tex explains, when Arti notices his stuff in the corner of the living room.

"But there aren't any sisters."

"We figure you'll be moving in soon," Tex says.

"Hmm," Arti Rose muses.

"That would be the next step, if you accept the Divine Principle," Gabe says. "Have you had any sort of revelation or sign from God about what you are supposed to do?" Gabe asks Arti Rose, matter-of-fact, but with a more weighted expression than she is used to seeing on his face.

"I did see something, the morning after I heard the last lecture. The sun came up and centered itself perfectly behind a cross on a church steeple. It seemed like a miracle, for the cross and the sun to be one. But it wasn't what I saw so much as what I felt when I saw it. I felt a warm rush of energy, like the sun was rising inside of me. And I felt that what I was seeing symbolized something about the relationship between Jesus and Sun Myung Moon, that God was trying to tell me to trust the message that I had just heard about Sun Myung Moon being here to fulfill the mission of Christ."

"Well, what do you think it means if you believe that? Have

you thought about what kind of responsibility you have if you truly believe, in your heart, that Sun Myung Moon is the Lord of the Second Advent?" There is force behind Gabe's words, demanding an answer.

In truth, Arti Rose has not thought about it exactly that way, in terms of her responsibility. In fact, she usually does not think about the Divine Principle or Sun Myung Moon for long before her thoughts turn to Gabe personally. When she thinks about it, she just figures she will go on helping Gabe in whatever way he asks, selling candles and stuff whenever he needs her help. "I think it means I am supposed to do whatever I can to help with this mission," Arti Rose says firmly, decidedly.

Gabe beams at Arti Rose, his face lifting but still projecting a weighted message. "Well, I would be honored to have you here, if you feel that you are being called to serve as a missionary for the Messiah."

"Here? O.K.. I see what you're saying. So, how should I go about this?"

"Do what I did," Tex says. "Bring your clothes and your toothbrush over here."

They look at Tex's duffle bag in the corner and laugh.

"Actually, that's usually how it's done," Gabe says.

"My mom thinks college is the most important thing in the world," Arti Rose says.

"I will be glad to talk with Sue about this," Gabe says.

There is silence for a moment, Arti and Tex looking at Gabe, thinking about that word "glad", then glancing at each other with pained but comical expressions. They figure Gabe does not know about Mama Sue's Irish temper.

"Actually, I will probably be at least as nervous as you are, because I am somewhat in awe of your mother," Gabe says, pausing for the sudden outburst of laughter from Arti and Tex to die down. "But I will be there for you when you break the news to her, if you would like for me to."

"I'm gonna need all the support I can get," Arti Rose says.

"How about tomorrow?" Gabe asks.

The three of them go selling, in the heat of the day, all Saturday afternoon. Most people are home; so they don't blitz through the complexes as quickly as usual. Before the heat gives way, Tex loses it and splits. Someone has just slammed a door in his face.

"Fuck this," Tex says, and just takes off walking. They have been working near his dad's neighborhood; so he won't have far to walk.

Arti Rose is driving her mom's car anyway, and the extra candles are in it. Arti thinks Tex probably wants some dope pretty bad at this point, but she doesn't say anything about that to Gabe. She hopes Tex doesn't spend the candle money in his pocket on dope, but she doesn't say anything about that either. She has never known Tex to be dishonest.

As the evening progresses, Arti Rose has to admit to herself that it is nice to be sort-of alone with Gabe again for the first time in a while. She does not care how hot it is or how rude the people behind the doors can be sometimes. She feels happy during those in-between times, when it's just her and Gabe. She never lets him see anything but a smile on her face. And when they go to the Catholic Church afterwards, to sing folk songs, it feels sort of like a date. They do, after all, hold hands in the circle. Gabe takes her hand later too, when they are walking back to the Center. He does this as a protective gesture at one point, when they are crossing a street; but he does not let go immediately when they get to the other side. Her heart beats so fast it feels like it is going to fly out of her chest. And she goes shy, beyond shy; she can barely stand to look at him when he speaks to her. She meets his eyes with hers, then glances down in deference. Words won't come out of her mouth unless she has to answer him, and then she can barely manage a whisper.

When they get to where the Duster is parked by the sidewalk near the Center, before Arti Rose gets in her mom's car to go home, Gabe lets go of her hand and looks her straight in the eyes.

"We need to speak with your mother about you moving into the Center as soon as possible," Gabe says.

Arti Rose is already flushed and feels a choking sensation at her throat. If she opens her mouth, she is afraid that no sound will come out and her face will turn blood red under the street lamp. So she just shakes her head in the affirmative, gets in the car and drives home, caught up in the soaring euphoria of having been swept off her feet.

Later, settling toward slumber, Arti Rose finds herself wishing she could be falling asleep in Gabe's big embrace. She checks herself, however, wondering for a moment whether she is really that much

180

different from Felicia (the bleached blonde boy-addict that just moved in and out of the Center). Not wanting to rest on that thought for long, Arti Rose prays, asking God to guide her, offering up her will.

The next day Gabe calls early. It is Sunday, after all, and Arti Rose, at this point, is the only local member of Gabe's new church.

"Tex picked up his things from the Center last night after you left," Gabe says. "He was reeking of marijuana and alcohol. He said he just couldn't hack it, too many rules and restrictions for him. Said he felt "like a bird in a cage". So he flew. Your boyfriend doesn't want to give up his lifestyle. He said half the people who opened their doors when we were selling candles Saturday were partying. It was too much temptation for him."

"Did he give you the candle money from yesterday?"

"I told him he could keep that, to cover gas for helping me out several days last week."

"That was nice of you."

"So, when are we going to talk to your mom?"

"Maybe today, if you want. It's easier to catch her here on Sunday than any other time."

"If she's not using the car, maybe you could pick me up. We could sell candles around the complex up there. That way, if we are in and out of the apartment, we should be able to find a good time to talk to her."

"Good plan, man."

"I've been praying about it."

"Me too."

Sue is up, putting a roast in the oven, like she has done before church every Sunday for as long as Arti Rose can remember. The sound of her cutting up onions and carrots and potatoes had Arti stirring before Gabe called. Now Sue will get in the shower. When she gets out, Arti Rose will get in, not to go to church with her mom but to get ready to go pick up Gabe.

"Mom, I need to borrow the car," she will say. "I'll drop you off at church and pick you up after."

It's so easy with Sue. Sue is so easy going, doesn't ask a lot of questions (maybe because the church is in walking distance anyway).

Sue doesn't argue, just yells in at Dave, then Sis, telling them it's time to get up if they want to go to church.

Dave says he'll go with Will a little later. Sis gets up just soon enough to get in Arti's way in the bathroom. Nothing new. They all manage to get ready for their day.

Arti drops her mom and little sister off at the United Methodist Church, drives the blue Duster to Southside where she picks up Gabe, then picks up Sue and Sis after church, with Gabe still in the car, a load of candle boxes in the trunk. When Sue opens the door to the apartment, the smell of the roast, which has been slow-cooking in a warm oven, makes all four of them salivate. Sue goes straight to the kitchen, still in her church dress, and takes the roast out of the oven. Everyone else joins her, to help any way that they can.

Sis is wearing jeans and a t-shirt, which she insists on wearing to church these days or else she won't go. Arti Rose is wearing her long, flowered cotton dress with the empire waistline and puffed sleeves. Gabe has on his usual preacher garb but has loosened the tie in the heat. When the table is set and the sweet tea poured, the four of them sit down. (Dave is still with Will at the evangelical church). They make light conversation. Gabe rolls up his sleeves and insists on doing the dishes afterwards. Arti Rose clears the table. Sue dries and puts the dishes away, making more light conversation with Gabe while Arti Rose wipes off the table. Then Arti sits down on the couch next to Sis, who is calling a friend on the phone, talking about meeting at the pool. Sis gets up and Gabe, done with the dishes, comes into the living room and sits down on the couch (next to Arti Rose, but not too close). Sue starts to walk past, to go to her room (where she usually reads and takes a nap on Sunday afternoons. Arti stops her, standing up and motioning for her mother to take her spot at the other end of the long couch (leaving Gabe between them).

"Mom, sit down; Gabe needs to talk to you," Arti Rose says, sitting back down as her mother sits.

"What? This sounds serious, all of a sudden," Sue says, lowering herself to the couch but not sitting back, not relaxing, just smoothing the hem of her dress at the top of her knees and angling herself to face Gabe, who scoots away from her just a bit, sits forward and folds his hands in his lap.

"It is kind of serious, Mom. I'm moving out," Arti Rose says from the other end of the couch.

"You're what?" Sue says sharply, disapprovingly.

Arti Rose's response is shakier, less confident than the announcement, but laced with emotion that threatens to explode into something more powerful. "I'm moving into the Center, with Gabe," she blurts out, sitting forward and angling her head toward her mother. Their eyes do not meet. Arti Rose sinks back into her corner of the couch when Sue speaks.

"You are doing NO such thing," Mama Sue says calmly but firmly, forcefully, not looking at Arti Rose but shaking her head back-and-forth. "You have not finished college. Now Gabe," Sue says, facing the young man. "That so-called Center is just a Southside apartment, not a church. What purpose would it serve for my daughter to live there with you. You are not asking to marry her, are you?"

"No, nothing like that. That's why I am here; to make it perfectly clear that we will be living strictly as brother and sister in God, for the purpose of serving as missionaries, doing the work of establishing a new church here."

"So you would not be sleeping together?"

"No. It is a two bedroom apartment, and we will be moving to a house soon, when there are others."

"Other missionaries?"

"Yes. The One World Crusade, a traveling branch of our church that visited recently, will be stopping by again soon for a few days. A lady who travels with them and has been in our church for a long time, will stay for a while to help Arti Rose get adjusted to her role in the Center."

"Her role as a missionary."

"Yes."

Sue turns to her daughter. "I have never thought about you being a missionary," she says in a calmer voice.

"Then why did you take me to Moonbeams when I was a little girl?" Arti Rose asks, still being defensive but realizing she is going to have to sell her mother on the idea. So she calms down a bit, and they talk around Gabe.

"Moonbeams?"

"In the Baptist Church we went to throughout my elementary school years. There was a missionary named Lottie Moon who was starting a church in Africa or somewhere. And they had a class for girls, called Moonbeams, with literature that featured pictures and stories about Lottie Moon's adventures. I didn't exactly decide that's what I would be when I grew up, but I did get the idea that it would be an exciting and meaningful life, being a missionary."

"I just thought it would be fun for you to be in a class with other girls. I remember going to one of their mother-daughter tea parties. It was just a social gathering with some of the nicer females in the community. I guess some mothers want their children to be ministers or missionaries. But I don't want you to be a missionary. I want you to stay home until fall, then go to college, get a degree, work a while, then marry and have some babies for me to play with. Normal stuff. I thought that's what you wanted."

"I'm sorry to disappoint you, Mom. I wish you could just accept this and be proud of me. I am going to be a missionary for the Unification Church. I am going to live at the Center, because it will be easier for me to help Gabe with the ministry. We won't have to use your car as much. It's not a big thing. I have lived away from home before. So, smile; okay?"

"I thought you had a boyfriend. What does your boyfriend think about you moving in with Gabe?"

"I am not 'moving in with Gabe', Mom. I am moving into a Church Center- no sex, no drugs, no alcohol."

"So Tex doesn't mind?"

"Tex believes in what Gabe is doing. He would live in the Center too if he could live without pot. You should be glad I am going to live in a place where nobody smokes pot, Mom."

"Well, nobody smokes pot here either; I don't allow it," Sue says, looking around Gabe, meeting eyes with her daughter.

"Mom, stop looking like somebody died."

"What will I tell my friends? People will wonder where you are, where you live? I don't want to tell them you are following a Korean who says he is Christ; that's what your brother says this is about. Is that what you are up to, Gabe? I don't fully understand your purpose here. I mean, you seem like a nice young man. I took the piece of literature you handed me. I welcome you in my home as a friend of my daughter's."

"Yes, and I appreciate that. I thank you for your kindness. And

I don't want you to think that I am taking advantage of you or your daughter in any way other than what God requires of me. I am doing what I am doing because I feel that God has called me to serve Him in this way. Your daughter obviously feels the same way, and I don't think you would want to be responsible for stopping her from doing God's will, if this is God's will for her life."

At this point Gabe picks up a small book of poetry and drawings from the coffee table. It is *The Prophet,* by Khalil Gibran. Gabe seems to know the book well. He opens it to a drawing of an archer, with a bow and arrow. The passage next to it compares God to the archer, parents to the bow, and children to the arrow. Gabe reads the poem out loud:

"Your children are not your children;
they are the sons and daughters of Life's longing for itself.
They come through you but not from you.
You may give them your love but not your thoughts,
for they have their own thoughts.
You may house their bodies but not their souls,
for their souls dwell in the house of tomorrow,
which you cannot visit, not even in your dreams.
You may strive to be like them,
but seek not to make them like you.
For life goes not backward
nor tarries with yesterday.
You are the bows from which your children
as living arrows are sent forth.
The archer sees the mark upon
the path of the infinite,
and He bends you with His might
that His arrows may go swift and far.
Let your bending in the archer's hand
be for gladness;
for even as he loves the arrow that flies,
so He loves also the bow that is stable."

Sue lets out a sigh, shakes her head back and forth, and stands up. "You'll have to excuse me," she says, obviously near tears. Sue exits the room and enters the hallway. They hear her bedroom door close behind her.

"She reads and naps on Sunday afternoons," Arti says before driving Gabe home.

Next day, while her mother is at work, Arti Rose gathers all her things and has Sunshine drive her over to Southside in the VW. They ride with the top down and make an adventure of it. At the Center, Sunshine helps Arti put her clothes in the closet of the apartment's unused second bedroom. Arti Rose gives Sunshine a few stylish mini-skirts, "hot-pants" (fashionable hip-hugger short-shorts), and mini dresses she could not resist buying lately at the Sears Junior Bazaar where she works. She keeps the long skirts and "granny dresses", which are also in style and will serve her better as a missionary. There are two twin beds in the room, and Sunshine says she wishes they could be roommates there, like at the dorm, but without it being a "missionary thing". Sunshine seems to hate the word "missionary", like it is about the most uncool thing a person could do. But she still loves Arti Rose, of course.

Gabe is at work. Sunshine takes Arti Rose to her sociology class at the junior college, to take the final exam. Sunshine hangs out in the student union, playing pool with some long-haired guys. Afterwards, they go to the apartment, to pick up a few things Arti forgot and touch base with the family.

"Mom, your other daughter's here: the *crazy* one," Sis yells from the couch, in the direction of the kitchen, where Sue is cooking dinner.

Arti goes into the bathroom and brings her bottle of Herbal Essence out. Sunshine flirts around with Dave, who just came out of his room and is putting a Neil Young album on the stereo, like it's about to be a party just because Sunshine is over. Sunshine doesn't sit down, because Arti already told her they won't stay long.

Arti doesn't want to get into an argument with her mother; so she heads straight to the door with her bottle of thick, green shampoo. "Bye Mama Sue; I love you. I'll see you soon," Arti Rose yells.

"Mom, you're crazy if you let her move into that apartment with Gabe," Dave yells toward the kitchen.

Arti Rose is out the door before Sue can get her tuna casserole in the oven.

Part II

Moonbeams

Center Life

Sunshine drives Arti Rose back to the Center and goes inside with her. Sister Millie from the One World Crusade is visiting again, having decided that Gabe needs support while taking on a new member (especially since his failure with Felicia). Gabe and Millie are back from selling candles and are setting the table for dinner. They invite Sunshine to join them. Millie has been improving Gabe's kitchen, and there is a stew in the new crock pot she picked out at Sears. Gabe seems a bit subdued, like he is reluctantly letting Millie be in charge. Arti Rose goes in the kitchen to see if she can help Gabe while Millie is setting the table. Everything is sparkling like in a commercial for "Mr. Clean".

"Wow. You must have bought some new-fangled cleaning products," Arti Rose says.

Gabe opens a cabinet door under the sink and shakes his head back-and-forth at the abundance.

"Guess they must have been expensive?" Arti Rose says quizzically, not sure why Gabe would disapprove.

"I guess Millie feels *cleaner* now," Gabe grumbles.

Arti Rose thinks, for a split second, that Gabe is referring to Millie's role as sex-police (making sure no dirty, fallen relationships are forming in Gabe's budding Center).

They go in the dining room, where Millie says the blessing. Instead of watered-down lemonade, they drink plain water with the meal. Millie offers everyone tea afterwards, bringing out a plain ceramic pot where jasmine tea has been steeping while they ate. She pours it into little matching cups with no handles, oriental-style.

"It clears the palate and sweetens the conversation," Millie explains.

"No tea for me; you ladies enjoy. I'll take care of the dishes," Gabe says, gathering things up from the table while Millie serves tea to Sunshine and Arti Rose.

Sunshine is curious about the little gold band on Millie's left ring-finger, with the church symbol, which looks something like a wheel with spokes.

"Are you married?" Sunshine asks.

Millie goes and gets a picture of her husband, a homely looking red-haired man, probably in his mid-thirties.

"When Master came to America for the first time," Millie says with stars in her eyes, her tone of voice as sweet as a mother telling her daughters a fairy tale, "he was anxious to perform a blessed marriage ceremony."

"Is Master what you call Mr. Moon?" Sunshine asks.

"Yes. He is called by different names, but Miss Kim's followers in San Francisco are from a more oriental tradition. Zen Buddhist monks who are teachers are called "Master", and Miss Kim's grandparents, like most Koreans back then, were Buddhist. But her parents were converted to Christianity by Protestant missionaries. So she grew up with a mixture of beliefs, which helped to prepare her for Master's teachings. The Divine Principle also incorporates ideas from Taoism; so Miss Kim was inspired to call our Father "Master", as a spiritual teacher of high status would have been called in ancient China, for example."

"Wow; that's a lot of information!" Sunshine says.

"Yes. Eastern religions are still fairly new to most Americans, especially in the Bible Belt," Millie says. "But Biblical dispensation is central to what we believe in the Unification Church. In the Western traditions, Sun Myung Moon would be more comparable to a Catholic "Father", or a Protestant "Reverend". In fact, he aspires to the Protestant Evangelical status of the Reverend Billy Graham; so "Reverend Moon" is the name they are putting on posters for speaking tours now. But Miss Kim was his first missionary to the United States, and she is my spiritual mother. So I call him Master, as she always has."

"Okay. I get it," Sunshine says. "And what y'all really believe is that he is the Messiah! But what about your husband? What does he call Mr. Moon?"

"We're both from the San Francisco Center, so he usually calls him Master too. Sometimes we call him Father now, like some of the other blessed couples. Anyway, as I was saying, Master wanted to bless twelve members of his U.S. church in marriage the last time he visited our country. The Blessing is for members who have been in the Family for at least three years, which few of us had been. So some of the blessings were conditional, more like engagements. In fact, my husband and I have not consummated our marriage."

"You mean y'all haven't done it yet?" Sunshine asks with a quizzical look.

Gabe drops something in the kitchen, making a lot of noise.

"That would be one way of putting it!" Millie laughs a little, to take the edge off (while shaking her head a bit, to show her disapproval of Sunshine's crudeness). "We were separated immediately after participating in the wedding ceremony with the other couples. All of us were sent on missions. I was sent with the One World Crusade, and he was assigned to start his own Center in another state, like Gabe."

"But you look so happy; I don't think I would be very happy about that," Sunshine says, shaking her head so much that her curls look even wilder than usual.

"I am happy to do whatever the Heavenly Father wants me to do," Millie responds, smiling, getting up to put away the tea service.

Sunshine follows the plump little woman with her eyes, still wearing that quizzical expression and shaking her head, wondering how Millie can stand to look so plain and frumpish, with her closely cropped hair and loose, shapeless clothing, and no jewelry or make-up (like somebody's stay-at-home mom on a sick-day, only she has no children or home). The whole arrangement makes no sense to Sunshine. Oddly though, Millie has the light, carefree air of a woman well-married, secure, almost matriarchal though she may not be thirty and certainly is not yet forty.

"Gabe, isn't it time for Divine Principle study?" Millie says, taking the tea set into the kitchen.

No answer is necessary. Millie is there to establish rituals, to create a routine for Gabe and Arti Rose to continue when they are left alone. Gabe gets several Divine Principle books and songbooks from the bookcase in the living room and brings them to the table.

"Uhh, maybe I'd better get going now," Sunshine says.

"At least stay for one song," Millie says, wishing she could somehow convey to Sunshine that there is fun, and (more importantly) heartfelt joy, in Center life, even with such a serious mission.

"Millie is quite the songbird," Gabe says, grinning, handing out the little songbooks.

Inside are some songs that Arti and Sunshine have never seen before and some that are familiar but altered somewhat.

"The answer, my friend, is in the hearts of men; the answer is in the hearts of men."

After the four of them croon the familiar Bob Dylan tune (replacing the words "blowin' in the wind" with "in the hearts of men"), Gabe suggests that Millie sing a special song of her choosing, alone. He brags on her musical abilities, saying that Millie wrote some of the songs in the Unification Church hymnal herself. She sings a hauntingly oriental-sounding song.

"Ko-o re-e a, hea-art o-of the earth;
you were cho-o-sen to-o give Him birth...
La-and o-of the-e morning sun;
from your hidden springs
comes a healing balm
for a-all men.

"He-e has come;
Hi-is face is like the sun
and like the moon.
A-and soon the world wi-ill kno-ow His light;
there will be-e no-o
night."

"Wow. You sing like an angel," Sunshine says. "But hey; I really gotta go." She gets up from the table, where she has been seated for the past hour or two. She needs to use the restroom but doesn't ask. Sunshine is getting that panicky feeling she sometimes gets, and her manners seem strained, forced. "Y'all can do your studying better without me here anyway. But thanks for the food and the tea."

"Thanks for helping Arti Rose move in today," Millie says.

Gabe walks Sunshine to the door. When he gets back to the table, Millie is discussing Chapter II with Arti Rose. Millie just wants to be sure the young lady understands the significance of "The Fall" before leaving her at the Center alone with this young man, who Millie obviously considers to be less mature in his understanding of the Divine Principle than herself.

Gabe is never very comfortable discussing The Fall and asks if he may be excused to retire to his room, as he is scheduled to work an early shift at Sears the next day.

Millie says that will be fine as soon as they have had an evening prayer. After Gabe prays and exits, Millie talks with Arti Rose a little longer, finally letting the girl go to take a shower and get ready for bed. Arti Rose is tired and turns her bedside lamp off as soon as she climbs into the twin bed opposite Millie. Millie appears to be reading the Divine Principle, but Arti Rose notices that the page she is staring at is covered by a photo. Millie isn't studying the Principle; she's daydreaming about her "blessed husband".

Millie turns over on her side, with her back to Arti Rose.

Arti reaches down for the canvas book-bag she had put under her bed earlier, and takes out her journal and a pen. She thinks she is going to write about moving into the Center, but what she is thinking about is Tex (which might be a sin, but ultimately she tries to keep it "centered on God").

Ocean-eyed lover

...memories of this silver summer will shine in my soul like those seven shooting stars...they are always there...millions of them lighting up the night...and one is always streaking across the sky...you just have to dream your dreams with the soft white sand as a bed for your back...and the sound of the sea...your lullaby.

Dream with your eyes open...stare at the stars until you are one with them and you feel yourself suddenly shooting across the sky...your spirit is free...and you spring to your feet and run laughing and singing in the face of the wind...your naked body being kissed by the cool summer night and the sea, as your racing feet send her wet droplets dancing all around you.

Remember lover...have you ever felt so beautiful and so free...so completely alive...you didn't feel alive because you were with *me*...I am not the source of life...I am merely an open channel through which life can flow.

Think about it lover...think about the Divine Principle and what we learned from the lectures...God made the creation so that man can feel joy...when man feels joy, God feels joy...when God feels joy He pours it our all over our souls, and we feel free and alive...we are alive when we are one with God's heart.

All fallen men receive joy from the creation...many are returning to nature...looking for the garden of beauty, joy, and peace...and yet few realize that they receive this joy from the creation because of the give-and-take that it allows them to establish with Heavenly Father and Mother.

Lover don't you see how much we have learned from the Divine Principle...don't you see how much truth has been revealed to us...isn't it wonderful to be able to understand?

Lover...we must be brother and sister in God...we must take all of the love that we feel for each other and give that love to our Heavenly Father...He is so lonely...We are His children and we have run away from home...and now we must return to Him.

We must step back into reality...Can't you see it, lover? We have been tripping our lives away...it's all been nothing but a game...a trip.

When we talked about getting married, we were like two kids playing house...but if we go home to Father...if we become one with Him...maturity...reality...perfection ...Life.

Playing House

When "Sister Millie" leaves, Gabe and Arti Rose finally get to play house. Not that they stray from the routine, the rituals Millie set up for them, the structured lifestyle that makes their abode a house of God, a "Center". But they are, in fact, a young couple (of sorts) sharing an apartment. Arti Rose has never shared a living space with anyone other than her family, except for the year she spent at State with Sunshine as a roommate. Living with Gabe, Arti Rose is as shy as a virgin bride. The fact that they do not sleep together only makes it worse, because she has to hold everything inside that she feels for him. When they are suddenly close, whatever the activity, she is all nerves and emotion, held in, under the surface and ready to explode.

When the two of them have a study session and Gabe suggests they take turns praying, or sing a song together, Arti Rose is so self-conscious that she can barely make an audible sound come out of her mouth. Her face feels flushed with heat (so that Arti Rose knows she has "turned red", which deepens her painful sense of embarrassment), and she has to fight back tears every time she tries to pray or sing alone in front of Gabe. And when they sing together, Gabe can barely hear her. Gabe is awed by this and calls her names like "little mouse" or "little bird". Sometimes he suggests they hold hands when they pray, ostensibly to comfort Arti Rose and make her feel more secure (but maybe secretly, possibly even sub-consciously, because he wants to feel her moist palms, to sense her racing pulse).

Regarding daily religious rituals, Arti Rose feels more comfortable reading and discussing the Divine Principle, because the activity is more intellectual and allows her to keep her emotions in check to some extent. Gabe, seizing an opportunity to boost her confidence, tells her one night, when they have been discussing "the Principle", that he had a dream a while back that may have been about her. In the dream, a new student of his was explaining the teaching to him in a way that deepened his understanding. Now he thinks the dream was a premonition about Arti Rose. When he first tells her this, Gabe feels magnanimous. But during a later study session, when Arti Rose opens up and sheds light on a passage that Gabe has never given much thought, he finds himself feeling a bit defensive. Arti Rose senses this and is less vocally expressive during their next study session, holding back in the one activity of her new life that she had started to flower.

In the kitchen, she has little confidence. Arti Rose always helped her mother (setting the table and making salads and tea), but she has done little cooking other than adding toppings to frozen pizzas on Saturday nights. Now Gabe, who always seems to be teaching her, senses her awkwardness in the kitchen and instructs her in that situation as well. One evening, when she is making a salad, Gabe teaches her a new way to cut up carrots.

"Don't chop. Slice," he says, taking the knife from her gently. "Easy does it. The carrot is not your enemy. See," Gabe says, sliding the knife through the carrot as easily as if he is slicing butter. "The secret is *love*," he says. "It's the Divine Principle, like everything else. They taught me this at the San Francisco Center. The oriental way." Gabe keeps the knife on the cutting board as it goes through the carrot, barely bringing it up off the wooden board to make the next paper-thin slice. "It's about oneness," he says. "The carrot is yin and you are yang. You stay close, focus, concentrate on sending your love-energy to the carrot as you breathe out. And there is no resistance; see. That way the ultimate value of the carrot is realized. It makes the highest sacrifice and fulfills it's very purpose for being here."

Gabe stands so close that Arti Rose can feel his breath on her as he speaks. She feels like the carrot, something brightly colored and self-conscious, stiff with nervous tension, melting like butter, falling apart. He is rearranging her, making her into whatever it is he wants her to be. And she is falling in love with him. She wants to be his wife. She hopes they can be blessed in marriage. Soon. But she cannot bring herself to express these thoughts, even to God.

One night Arti Rose is reading a pamphlet written by Young Oon Kim, about prayer. In the pamphlet Miss Kim says that "prayer is the sincere desire of the heart, whether uttered or unexpressed."

Arti Rose starts to worry that she thinks about Gabe too much, especially when she is trying to fall asleep. She even sleeps with a big teddy bear she brought from home. The big, fluffy brown bear is the last gift her real daddy gave her, the year after the divorce, before he married again and had three more children in a row and stopped bothering to give her anything at all. Arti Rose used to think of her daddy when she hugged the bear; now she thinks of Gabe. There is something so huggable about Gabe, but hugging is not one of their rituals. Even though he is in the next room sleeping, Gabe seems out-of-reach. Maybe he does not even want her like she wants him.

As days turn into weeks, Arti Rose tries not to think about Gabe so much when she is falling asleep. She prays harder, tries to control her thoughts, knowing God hears whatever her heart has to say. And one day, when Gabe is at work, Arti Rose walks to the Salvation Army and gives her big, brown teddy bear away.

That evening, when Gabe comes in the front door, parking his ten-speed bicycle in the entrance way, Arti Rose is just taking the chicken breasts with cream-of-mushroom soup out of the oven. It is a dish her mother made often when she was growing up. The recipe was on the soup can; so she did not need to wait for Gabe to come home and help her with dinner. She heats up a can of sweet English peas while Gabe is washing his hands in the restroom. Then he helps her set the table, carefully placing the hot dish on a folded hand towel at the center of the table-top, with a large serving spoon. They sit down across from each other, but there is none of the usual lively chatter from Gabe. He is obviously tired; his eyes lack their usual luster. After saying a quick prayer, Gabe wolfs down two pieces of chicken, along with most of the generous pile of rice, gooey from absorbing the juices at the bottom of the heavy glass dish.

"I'm full," Gabe says when he finally stops to breathe, looking up from his plate.

"You didn't touch your peas," Arti Rose says, looking at the little bowl of neat, round, light green peas next to his plate.

"I don't have room for another bite," Gabe says, pushing the bowl away, dismissing the peas.

"You are missing something sweet," Arti Rose says, suddenly tearing up, her eyes brimming with glistening moisture.

Gabe finally looks her in the eyes, for the first time since he arrived home from a busy day in the tool department at Sears (with a well-advertised sale going on).

"And how are those sweet little peas ever going to fulfill their purpose of creation if you don't want them?" Arti Rose asks, a tear falling against her will.

Gabe is quiet for a minute, studying her with his big, brown eyes as he chews. "Are you talking about the peas, or are you talking about yourself?" Gabe asks gently, his eyes widening and his voice suddenly soft, tender.

"I don't know what I am talking about," Arti Rose says, picking up her napkin and wiping her eyes. She gets up from the table abruptly and starts picking up the dirty dishes.

"I'll do the dishes," Gabe says. "You take some time for yourself. Do whatever you want. We can skip Divine Principle study for one night."

Arti Rose feels the hurt going deeper, despite Gabe's good intentions, because the evening one-on-one study sessions are when she feels closest to him. But she does not argue with him or say anything at all. If she speaks, the volcano of emotion that is rising in her will have to erupt. She puts her dishes in the sink and is careful not to touch him as he brings his own dishes into the kitchen. Gabe's big body is an imposing presence in any room but seems especially out-of-proportion in the little kitchen. And Arti Rose is all arms and legs, although lately she is blooming out a bit more, putting on curves that get between she and Gabe when they bump into each other. Lately, they seem to be brushing up against each other so much that Arti Rose has to wonder whether it is really an accident anymore. In the kitchen, she is suddenly aware that one of the little rushes of feeling that she often gets from Gabe's slightest touch would take her over the edge right now, as she is already near tears.

He senses her avoidance as she retreats from her usual place beside him at the kitchen sink. "I'm tired anyway," he says. "I think I will go to bed as soon as I am done with the dishes, maybe study and pray in my room for a while."

Arti Rose does not respond to his words. She doesn't even say good-night as she exits the kitchen and goes to her room, where she stays for the rest of the evening. The next day she is scheduled to work at Sears and Gabe has a day off. She catches the bus to town early.

When Arti Rose come back to the apartment, Gabe says they have to talk.

"I'm tired," she says, wanting to retreat to what feels like a room of her own.

"Take a few minutes to freshen up, then meet me on the balcony. I'll get us some lemonade," Gabe says.

Arti Rose goes into the restroom and splashes cold water on her face, brushes her hair out. She knows Millie would want her to put it up. Looking in the mirror, she knows she is beautiful. She wants Gabe to think so too, so maybe he will love her.

On the balcony, Gabe looks out over the park while he talks, barely turning to glance at Arti Rose occasionally. He is all about the church business.

"We have to start bringing in people," he says. "I know you are disappointed that none of your friends have joined. I am too. I have an idea for giving it one more shot. Then you've got to move on. I know witnessing at work is probably not the best idea, because if it got controversial we could lose our jobs. I'm going to start working the college campuses. You have a good background in Christianity, and I think you could witness to evangelicals. I want you to make an appointment with that youth Pastor some of your friends follow.

"Pastor Paul? I've been meaning to talk with him anyway. Told my brother I would."

"If you can get him, he will bring all of your friends into the Family. Otherwise you have to move on. I don't want you spending too much time on him, but it's worth a shot. I hear Felicia went that way…"

"Really?"

"She called me," he said.

Arti Rose suddenly has an uneasy feeling, like she's been punched in the gut. She realizes it may be jealousy, which is not right. She is not competing with anyone for Gabe. Anyway, Arti Rose has been making a conscious effort not to let negative thoughts plant themselves in her brain these days. Maybe Gabe misses her family and friends since they quit coming to the Center. Arti Rose certainly misses them.

"I'll go and see Pastor Paul. He is influencing a lot of young people, and God probably wants him to learn the Divine Principle," Arti Rose said, thinking especially about how her younger brother and his girlfriend might have suffered less lately, if they had understood "The Fall"…If the pastor they had been following had warned them strongly about the spiritual consequences of premature sex…

"Good. You start working on Pastor Paul. I am going to try and get us a spot on a local TV talk show."

"Wow. I've never been on TV."

"It's easy. Just smile for the camera and answer their questions," Gabe says, getting up, like there is nothing else to discuss. "Now let's go out selling door-to-door for a bit; I didn't make any money today…We'll get Italian food afterwards. I wanna stop in and see my old friends at the deli anyway."

Arti Rose still feels shy when they are out selling and going in the Southside shops where Gabe is familiar with the local folks. Arti Rose misses her old friends, and her family. And she misses Tex.

At night in her own little twin bed, in "the sisters' room" at the Center, Arti Rose finds herself thinking about Tex when she is trying to fall asleep. Memories of their sex-life (the only adult sex-life Arti Rose has known) pop into her brain like scenes from a pornographic movie (which she has never seen on screen but has lived this past summer in Tex's bed). Arti Rose tries to fight these thoughts with prayer, but she is too tired to concentrate while praying silently. And the apartment is too small to pray out loud without disturbing Gabe. Arti Rose sits up in bed and turns on the bedside lamp. She reaches under the side of the bed for her book-bag and takes out her journal and a pen.

Dear Lover

...you said that living in the Center made you feel like a bird-in-a-cage.

Oh dear lover why are you so blind...can you not see that the whole world is one great big bird cage?

It does not matter where you fly my luv-bird...even if you go to the top of the highest mountain where the air is fresh and the woods are beautiful and free of man's abuse...your soul is more polluted than the filth that foams from the mouths of our city's steel-making monster-machines...and you will flap your wings until you hit that cage on every side and fall tired and bruised into your own waste...

Lover please come back into our True Parents' nest...they are teaching us how to fly...and we will teach others...until every single living soul is free to fly...and at that moment our Father will open the door to this cage...and it will be destroyed

199

completely...forever...

Lover I miss you...please come Home.

Public Relations

Next day Arti Rose does not have any scheduled hours at Sears but Gabe does. She calls Mama Sue's apartment until she gets her brother on the phone, and they arrange to meet with Pastor Paul together soon. Otherwise Arti Rose just does some cleaning at the Center and tries studying the Principle but keeps falling asleep. At least Gabe is satisfied that she did something with her day. He doesn't seem to notice that the apartment is cleaner, but he is glad she made plans to witness to Pastor Paul.

Before going to Sears the next day, they go by the TV station to be interviewed. The interviewer mostly talks with Gabe, who keeps things light and informative. There is a new Church in town. The minister is Gabriel Dane, from San Francisco. Arti Rose Riddle, a local girl, is Gabe's first member. Her mother, Assistant State Editor for The News, took a pamphlet from Gabe when he was downtown inviting folks to his introductory lectures. When the interviewer asks Arti Rose why she joined, the shy girl goes into the new "witnessing" mode she is experimenting with (not the one that is going to work). She sits forward in her seat and begins a preachy spiel. Something about the terrible shape the world is in, and how young people need to do something to save it. Her face is flushed and she comes across as way too intense. It's embarrassing. They cut that part out. News-wise, it's just a "who, what, when, where, how" piece...forget the "why".

She doesn't do better with Pastor Paul (worse, in fact).

Dear Diary,

My brother David asked me to go and talk with Pastor Paul, his youth minister. Paul is a Southern Methodist, which is the conservative branch of Methodism. I don't think my younger brother understands that they are not as open-minded as the United Methodist Church our family has been going to since we were in

200

elementary school. They just happen to have a big youth group that long-haired kids like.

It did not help that my new friend Felicia, who went to see Pastor Paul with our old friend William (after she'd moved in and out of Gabe's Unification Center) told Paul that we believe Sun Myung Moon to be the second Jesus. (O should I say the-third-Adam? Most people who accept the idea of a new messiah have heard the whole lecture series first, which includes an interpretation of Biblical history leading up to it.)

I knew that Pastor Paul would be totally against this idea before I talked to him, but I was determined to be strong. And I thought Heavenly Father could use me to reach Paul.

From the second that Davie and I walked into Pastor Paul's office, I could sense that something was wrong. I had been around Paul before, at gatherings I'd been with Dave and Wendy before they broke up. Pastor Paul had radiated a lot of warmth and love. But this time the spiritual atmosphere around him was full of negative vibrations. Paul could not hide his pre-judgment of me. The Principle is so true when it says that our bodies are an outer reflection of our inner nature. Pastor Paul had the same look on his face that I remember seeing on my Daddy's face when I was a little girl, and he was about to scold me. Daddy was never a Bible-thumper though. This guy picked up his Bible right away. He started talking about his educational background too, trying to come across as an intellectual.

I wanted the air to be warm and full of love…I wanted Heavenly Father to be alive in the room…I could feel Him inside of me, warm and burning in my heart…I wanted to see Him in Paul and Dave's faces so that we could have harmonious give and take on a spiritual level…I wanted to pray before talking.

"May we pray?" I asked (when I could finally get a word in edgewise).

"Sure," Paul said from his comfortable office chair. He

seemed to warm up for a second. "Scoot closer so we can join hands," he said.

Dave and I moved the aluminum folding-chairs we were seated in closer to Paul. The three of us joined hands. Pastor Paul prayed for God to guide us, my brother and I (these two young people who had come to him). He did not seem to be seeking any further guidance for himself, but that did not deter me from my mission.

As soon as Pastor Paul had finished his prayer, I held their hands tighter instead of letting go, and I began to pray. I was praying that we could ease the suffering heart of God and bring His children back to Him. I could feel Heavenly Father struggling to reach out of me and into them…I squeezed their hands and tears rolled down my cheeks…"In Jesus' name we pray…and in the name of the Lord of the Second Advent," I said.

I had to say that. Maybe I shouldn't have, but I felt it and I didn't take time to think about that strong feeling before it was out of my mouth. I am often guilty of that. Or else I'm guilty of having a strong feeling and saying nothing at all. "Perfect relationship between heart and body…feeling and reason…" I've got to get it together.

Later I thought I should have said, "In your son's name." Pastor Paul said I had messed up my whole prayer when I said the part about "the Lord of the Second Advent". I knew he was wrong, because I could feel Heavenly Father very close to me. But I suppose I did "mess it up" for Paul, if it caused him to have negative feelings. I guess he would have gotten those feelings in the conversation anyway, because it didn't get any better. And my brother just sat there looking embarrassed for me. His face literally got red, and Dave is not shy; he never blushes. I certainly didn't change his mind. But he still loves me; he's my Bro. I don't think Pastor Paul likes me at all though. If Gabe wants to go and talk with him, he can. But I'm not going back.

I don't know. I will learn… I will grow. I did my best. I told Pastor Paul about the Principle and about Master Moon as best I could. I told him that I felt this to be Truth because I had opened myself and allowed Heavenly Father to reveal it to me without self-centeredly attempting to look into my own mind, which is filled with ideas learned from old teachings, to see the reality of a new Truth. Rather I felt the reality in my heart. I felt god's warm and shining light glowing inside of me each time I heard a lecture…each time I prayed…each time I talked to the people in the One World Crusade bus team…and each time I told someone about the Principle. I felt this glowing within as strongly as I had when I accepted Jesus Christ. I know the feeling of a heavenly spirit…I know the feeling of Heavenly Father's heart. Jesus gave me that feeling many times…the Holy Spirit…and the Father. I have felt God's presence, and I can recognize it quickly and easily. I have felt Satan's presence also. There is a tremendous difference. I know that God wants me in the Unification Church…I know that He wants be to be a follower of Sun Myung Moon…I know that Sun Myung Moon is Truth incarnate…the same Truth that Jesus was and is.

Just because I have not been expecting Christ to be a man born in Korea, doesn't mean that I should let the shock of an unexpected idea close my mind. That's exactly what the Jews did to Jesus. They had been looking for the Messiah, but when He came as a man with earth-shaking ideas that threatened their church, they closed their minds and killed Him to make Him silent. They wanted to see Him on the clouds surrounded by angels and Heavenly music. Reality??? They couldn't look reality in the face. It wasn't easy enough.

Christians today are the same. They "accept Jesus Christ as their Lord and savior," and they blindly believe that He constantly forgives them of their sins and has a reservation for them in heaven. Reality??? It's just not easy enough. They forget Jesus said that to enter the kingdom, one must be perfect. "You, therefore, must be perfect, as your heavenly Father is perfect." (Matthew 5, verse 48).

Christians just don't have it all together. Pastor Paul kept interrupting me and quoting scriptures. It was unreal. If I had been a preacher for years and knew the Bible backwards and forwards, I could have had a backup quote for everything I said. But it really wasn't fair. Paul quoted some scripture to me about all Christians knowing the very second that Christ returns. He said, "I am just not going to worry about it, because my Jesus has promised me that I will know when He returns."

I am sure that any *true* "Christian"...Christ-like being...perfected man would be in the realm of direct-dominion and would certainly know that Christ is here. But there are very few Christians who are really Christians...who are really as close to Heavenly Father as Jesus himself is. It is too easy to go to church every Sunday and sing in the choir and call oneself a Christian today.

I told Pastor Paul that he was right. If his heart is close enough to Jesus, Jesus will certainly reveal it to him. I told him that Jesus had sent me to tell him that the Son of Man has come.

For Paul to accept that...he would have had to humble himself a great deal...he would need a great desire to ultimately do God's will. But he didn't even want to listen to me...he wanted rather to save me from this "satanic plot". I think in many ways Paul was afraid. Pastor Paul is satisfied in that comfortable office chair he sits in, and he feels that he is doing God's will by teaching people about Jesus. These new ideas are threatening to him. He certainly didn't want to see any truth in what I was saying. If he did he would have to tell his congregation that Christ is here and we must listen to His complete Truth and live it...and begin burning the old world and building a new one with the ashes. The Heavenly Kingdom is supposed to be instant utopia...why who ever dreamed that we would have to work for it...

"To restore the world...
let us go forth with the Father's heart
in the shoes of a servant,
shedding tears for man,

sweat for earth,
and blood for heaven."
Sun M. Moon

...That is much more difficult than...
To restore the world
let us accept Jesus Christ
into our hearts,
and He will build Heaven
for us...
alone.

Poor misunderstood Jesus. My heart cries out to Him. He tried so desperately...and yet I feel that today Jesus still feels the same loneliness and frustration that His Father has felt since the fall of Adam and Eve. So many people speak in the names of God and Jesus and the Holy Spirit. So few people share their heart. We must comfort their tearstained souls. We must join hands with Jesus and become an army of true sons and true daughters of our Father.

Oh Pastor Paul can't you feel Him in this room (I prayed in the pastor's office, holding Paul's hand and my own brother's hand)...*can't you open your heart? Heavenly Father and the Holy Spirit- our Divine Mother- love you, brother Paul. My brother Dave loves you. I love you, too, as your sister in God. You are a good man...Please don't hurt Father like this...*

I feel negative energy coming from Pastor Paul as I pray, and he relaxes his hold on my hand. It was his idea to hold hands in the first place. Gabe says they don't hold hands very often in the Family because the energy is too vertical. So I release Pastor Paul's hand gradually, as I feel that he wants to let go of mine. But my feelings are hurt that this person cannot accept my heartfelt prayer to the same God that he prays to, just because my beliefs, my interpretations, are not exactly the same as his. My brother and I keep holding hands. But I cannot speak anymore after ending my prayer. I am crying so hard that I choke every time I open my mouth. My heart is burning…filled with spiritual fire…my face is flushed. I feel lonely…cold…frustrated. I have poured out my soul completely, but there was no harmonious give and take with Pastor Paul. I have not reached him at all. He shakes his head back and forth, getting up from his chair in a way that means he wants me to leave. He seems angry, and I do not understand. My brother does not say one word to take up for me or agree with me. I don't feel hatred from Davie, but he lets go of my hand and looks embarrassed, standing up and thanking Pastor Paul for his time and heading for the door. I just sit there feeling completely alone, wiping tears away with my hand, wishing I had a tissue for my nose.

Then Dave, standing in the doorway, turns and says gently, "Come on Big Sister."

Something in me feels bolstered, respected by my brother whether he agrees with me or not. This feeling is bigger than his embarrassment.

I get up and follow Dave out to his van, thinking I am thankful that he hasn't stopped calling me Big Sister. I am going to quit calling him Davie and start calling him "Big Dave". Will already calls him that. But we don't say anything to each other in the van. He turns the radio up loud, drops me off at the apartment. Dave is a high-school senior now. He had taken me to see Pastor Paul after his last class, which made him late for his after-school job. Dave is still helping Will put up antennas for Will's dad's TV company. No doubt Will is going to hear about this, as well as Felicia. But how much of what I said will any of them get?

I have to wonder if my brother even heard what I said to Pastor Paul, if he even followed my reasoning. (Maybe for Davie it was just an emotional experience, a passionate battle, a sort-of stand-off between me and Pastor Paul. And each of us had held our own. But nobody really won.)

Dave is not always a good listener when it comes to the finer points of things. But he has a big heart. He is a friendly guy who always manages to fit in with the local-yokels, talking lightly about the weather, sports, joking when the opportunity arises. Gabe is basically the same kind of guy, and he likes Dave a lot. Davie likes Gabe too, even though Gabe is a stranger-in-a-strange-land. At least San Francisco is somewhere Dave would like to go to. Davie does not want to go to Korea, and he is afraid Mr. Moon will take his sister there. He also agrees with Pastor Paul about not wanting to replace Jesus with the man they call "Master". Arti Rose says that's not what they are trying to do, but it seems like it to Davie.

Davie has been to church all of his life, but he has only recently been "saved" (which means he went to the altar and got down on his knees and prayed and cried and accepted Jesus into his heart). Dave is not about to give up Jesus (especially with all the heartache he has been going through since Wendy got scared that she might be pregnant and told her mom. So, of course, her parents would not let her go out with him anymore, even though they were kind to him which made it worse somehow. He got the feeling they wanted to talk to him in a counseling way, but he was managing to avoid that. Maybe she'd had a miscarriage or gotten an abortion, or maybe she was never pregnant at all (just scared she might get pregnant). Davie isn't sure, but the whole subject is too mysterious and sad to suit him. Last time they talked Davie felt so many things but didn't know what to say to Wendy, and he was afraid to ask too many questions. Lately, when Wendy has managed to sneak a phone call to Davie, he can't understand half of what she says. She has had to whisper since her parents took the princess phone out of her room so that she could get more sleep. A few times Wendy tried calling from their family-room when her mom was busy in the kitchen, but her speech was slurred- maybe because of the "medication for depression" she had mentioned. Then, the last time she got Davie on the phone, Wendy had said she was in therapy and getting "shock treatments" so she would "forget". Davie thought she meant him, and the hurt went so deep he had to make an excuse to get off the phone, fast. He stopped trying to call. He had been hanging up when her parents answered anyway. She probably stopped trying to call too. Lately Dave is usually at work and manages to avoid the home phone. Sis is usually in the pool, and Mama Sue is at work. So nobody answers their phone in the apartment these days, and Davie doesn't know if Wendy calls or not (since answering machines and voice-mail do not exist yet). It makes his stomach hurt to think about Wendy, so he tries not to. But Arti Rose doesn't even know all of that. He hasn't talked to anybody about it, except Jesus. All he has told his mom is that Wendy is having "health problems" (that was the term her parents had used when they intercepted his call and told him that she was not available to go out on dates). Maybe that's all there is to it anyway- when Arti got wind of it, she reminded him how much Wendy had been absent from school with some mysterious illness, before she ever went out with Davie. Mononucleosis maybe- which they used to call "the kissing disease". Or maybe it was just trouble with her menstrual cycle; Wendy was barely full-grown. Anyway, other people may be able to brush it off, like their break-up is no big deal because they're too young anyway. But Davie can't kick the feeling that whatever is wrong with Wendy is his fault).

Dave has grown up enough lately to know that he needs forgiveness, and Jesus forgives. Dave knows he needs Jesus and friends and family. And maybe he still needs his big sister to look after him the way she did when they were little and he thought nothing bad could happen to him as long as she was around. He won't say anything else about it, but he wishes Pastor Paul had gotten through to her. Mostly he wishes Arti Rose would come back home.

Dear Dairy,

...I had an extra Divine Principle book that Tex had left at the Center when he moved out, so I gave it to Pastor Paul while I was in his office. He had been talking about the Bible, and I told him it is like a new book, a new revelation that God is adding to the Bible through a new prophet. He promised to read the introduction..."with an open mind but a closed heart". That was when I asked if we could pray. I hoped his heart might open some before I witnessed to him. Earlier he had told me that he used to be agnostic, because he could never accept the Bible intellectually...he finally accepted it in his heart. But he was determined not to listen to me with an open heart.

The heart is the home of God. Imagine being tired and cold and lonely and wanting to go home...only to find that every door is closed and locked tightly.

Why is Satan doing this to God...to me...to them. He has cast a cold shadow on their hearts and built a wall between us...with all that I have inside of me I cannot break that wall. I know how God must feel. He must know this feeling with every moment...and yet He never ceases to pour His loving spirit out to His children. We must cast our umbrellas and walk naked in the showers of a new season. I can feel cosmic springtime blooming in my soul. I will never leave you Father...I will share your every tear...no matter how painful...and someday you won't have to cry anymore. Someday you will look at your children and smile...and the world will be a garden...filled with the sunshine of your smile.

A New Friend?

Arti Rose is lonely. Not that Gabe isn't good company, but she needs a friend. A confidant. Frankly someone that she can talk to about Gabe. At work, when things are slow, she starts wandering over to the edge of the Junior Bazaar, talking to the girl in accessories. The girl is African American, a year younger than Arti Rose, and cute as a button. Arti has never had a black friend before. She's only been acquainted with a few early integrators, at her schools and college, from a distance. As a young child, however, she did have a Negro maid that she loved as dearly as if she had been a relative. So Arti Rose has no feelings of fear or repulsion toward black or brown people.

Arti starts the conversation. "Hey; I love the new line of scarves!"

The other girl says, "Yeah; me too," and fingers a silky, multicolored one, with a swirling paisley design.

"That would go perfect with your dress," Arti Rose says, thinking her neutral colored A-line dress is awfully plain for an accessory department, though her curves certainly make-the-best-of-it.

"I know, but I can't buy anything right now," she says. "I'm starting at the University here in the city this fall. Whatever my grant doesn't cover, I'll have to pay for. So I'm savin' up."

"Good idea! I went to State U last school year, and the books were outrageous." (Arti Rose doesn't mention that the only check she wrote for expenses was the blank one her mother had signed for her to take to the bookstore. And Arti Rose, who had been careful to pick used books, had figured she deserved to throw a few record albums on the pile.) "I'm Arti Rose, by the way."

"I'm Posey May."

"Nice to meet you, Posey May. Wow; we both have flowery double-names. I guess that's a Southern thing."

"Sure to be." Posey May uses a phrase, and a drawl, reminiscent of Arti Rose's rural, South Alabama grandmother.

"Hey, you wanna go to lunch sometime?" Arti asks.

"I usually eat lunch at home. I don't live that far," Posey May says, then feels bad about seeming unfriendly. "You can come with me if you want to," Posey May says. "My Mama always cooks enough for a big bunch, just in case my cousins show up."

"Actually, I brought a sandwich…But I'd love to…If, you're sure it's okay."

"I was gonna wait till my shift ends," Posey May says.

"I'm done at 2:30," Arti Rose says.

"Me too. I'll check with you before I leave," Posey May says, smiling warmly." There was something about her that had made Posey May forget Arti Rose was white, while they were talking. Arti Rose was just…sweet. She had a humble way about her, like she didn't think she was better than anybody else. In fact, Arti Rose reminds Posey May of one of her favorite cousins.

Arti Rose perks up, feeling better now that she may have a new female friend. She gets hungry and wolfs her sandwich down in the break room first chance she gets, but doesn't mention that to Posey May after work.

"I'm starved; let's go to my house," Posey May says. She's glad to have a ride, since Arti Rose has her mother's car. The bus ride would have taken longer.

Posey May directs her to an area of the city Arti Rose has never seen before. Some of it looks old and run-down, and some buildings have bars over the windows. However, there are lots of mature trees, and some of the old buildings are beautiful to Arti Rose. Posey May points to a side street, and Arti Rose turns into a neighborhood. The houses are small, and not all of them are painted. Then Posey May points to a dirt lane, muddy from summer rain. Arti Rose turns and turns again when Posey May points to an unpainted shack, the neutral color of Posey May's dress.

"Oh, I love cedar houses," Arti Rose says quick, so Posey May doesn't have time to be embarrassed. "My aunt lives in one that her father built, in the country." (Arti Rose doesn't say that it's her great aunt and it was the family's pioneer home, built twice as big as this with a wrap-around porch and an extra "dog-run" breezeway built through the middle). "My aunt says cedar's not meant to be painted, because it stands up to moisture better if it can breathe," Arti Rose says.

"Really? I hate it," Posey May says, as they get out of the car. "My old daddy says he'll never leave this place his folks left him, and he won't change one thing about it. Says it was give to them by the rich white folks they worked for, and we're lucky to have it. I keep tellin' him I wish he'd have one of them new Jim Walter Homes built, like my cousins' family did."

Arti Rose notices a smell she does not like, as soon as she opens her car door. She wonders if they have an outhouse like her great-aunt too. But she isn't about to ask. "Wow; this is great porch. They don't make porches like this anymore," Arti Rose says, climbing the steps, admiring the unpainted rocking-chairs. "My cousins had a Jim Walter Home built too. It didn't even have a porch," Arti Rose says, remembering the first cheap, boxy pre-fabricated houses that started springing up on rural lots near her grandmother's home when she was a child (before double-wide trailers, and the more expensively elaborate pre-fabs that came later; neither of which held up like the old cedar "shot-gun" shacks that continued to dot the country roadsides for ages after they were built).

They work their shoes on the rug before the front door, to get the mud off. Arti Rose pays attention to her breath, hoping for a whiff of cedar. But what she smells when Posey May opens her front door is the overwhelming (and embarrassingly bathroom-y) smell of chitt'lins cooking. So that's where the outhouse smell came from. Hog intestines. The stuff country folk used to throw to the dogs, and the slaves. Arti Rose has heard enough about them to know what they are. But she's never smelled them cooking, up close like this. She has to resist the urge to gag, while Posey May is acting like everything is normal, introducing Arti Rose briefly as she passes through the sitting area to the opening to the kitchen at the back of the house, where her mother is cooking with the heavy backdoor opened (and the screen-door closed to keep flies out). Arti Rose follows her far enough in to see the people in both areas.

"Mama that's Arti Rose, from work," Posey May says from the cooking area.

A woman who looks old enough to be Posey May's grandmother shyly lifts a hand above her kettle, waving slightly as she says, "Pleased to meet you, Honey," as sweetly as she can manage, considering.

"Nice meeting you, too, Mam," Arti Rose says, embarrassed to be embarrassing the lady of the house, who adjusts the rag on her head, then drops her hands back down to her work.

"Just sit down out there, Arti Rose. Daddy and Little LeRoy won't bite. I don't spect you want no chitt'lins," Posey May says.

"Thanks," Arti Rose says shyly, sitting, "But, um, no thanks; I already ate."

Posey May sits at a little table back in the kitchen.

The front area is lined with with unpainted ladder-back chairs against the wall. The room is narrow (probably originally an open breezeway or "dog-run", like the one in Arti Rose's great aunt's old pioneer home, with rooms on both sides). Arti Rose is seated across from an older man who looks like he could be Posey May's grandfather, and a "brother" who is young enough to be Posey May's child. The boy is sitting stiffly and obediently next to the silver-haired man, both in unpainted ladder-back chairs. The old man's face is lit up with a look of alarm, like fear and anger and injured pride are rising in him at the very sight of Arti Rose. On looking at his face directly, she immediately senses that his discomfort has to do with her being white. Since she can't help that fact, Arti Rose tries to make small talk, blushing as she says something about the weather.

"Shor been rainin' a lot," she says, instinctively choosing the vernacular of her country relatives (since some of them are from share-cropper families who, before Jim Cro w laws and segregation, once had much in common with their black neighbors).

The very black man barely shakes his head in the affirmative. He looks as if his white eyeballs are about to pop out of his head, and he will likely explode if he speaks. There is no escape from the hot, animal aroma in the room, and the heat of apparent emotion rising in the large man, as the room has no windows (and the side doors, apparently leading to bedrooms, are closed- probably to keep the cooking smell out of clothing and bedding). It is stifling. Arti Rose contracts her body in the hard, stiff little chair as best she can. She takes the heat of her gaze off the steaming man with the flared nostrils and addresses the child, asking how old he is and if he has started school, and what he likes...

The boy enjoys her attention and gets up, moving about the little room gathering his favorite playthings to show Arti Rose. Some of them are made of wood.

"Wow; this is really cool!" Arti Rose says, spinning a wheel on a wooden car.

"My daddy made it; he's teachin' me how to whittle too," the boy brags.

"Well, you're a lucky boy," she says, sincerely, without motive but grateful for an opportunity to give the man some of his pride back.

Posey May, apparently starved, takes no time wolfing down the bowlful and brings a few extra pieces of corn-bread with her as she breezes through to the front door. "Come on, Arti Rose; I want you to meet my cousins. One of them reminds me of you."

"Probably Annie, cuz she's skinny like her," the little boy says.

"Don't say that! Daddy, when you gonna teach this boy the same manners you taught me!" Posey May says.

Arti Rose glances at the man real quick before exiting. He looks like he has eased down some, but he is shaking his head side-to-side, as if in general disapproval.

"Nice meetin' y'all," Arti Rose says as they walk out the door.

"I usually go over to my cousins' after work anyway," Posey May says, getting in the passenger side.

"Sure; I'd love to meet them. But I can't stay long. I have to pick my mom up from work soon."

Posey May points the way to a freshly built Jim Walter Home down at the end of the same dirt road. It is painted bright white and has no porch at all, just a concrete block to step up on at the door. Posey May walks right in, without knocking, and Arti Rose follows. The sisters are busy putting dishes and laundry into new appliances, and barely bat an eye when they come in. Posey May goes to the newly furnished den and turns on the TV, and her two cousins soon join her on a big, plush, upholstered couch. Arti Rose had sat on a matching, wing-back rocker when she'd followed Posey May in. The sisters don't seem to care what color she is, or even if she is there. Arti Rose watches and listens to their familiar, puppy-like play for a few minutes, glancing at the romance on their "soap". Then she looks at her watch and says she has to go. The girls just say, "Bye."

After that, Arti Rose tries to invite her new friend over, but Posey May cannot understand why the apartment where Arti Rose lives is also a church. "If I tried to go to any church other than our'n, my daddy would have a fit," she says, "and we have enough to argue about, with him being such an old fuddy-duddy."

Arti Rose doesn't ask why Posey May's parents are so old, or why they were both home in the middle of the day like retired grandparents (while Posey May works more hours than she should need to work if she has a government grant for college). Arti Rose can see that Posey May has big personal responsibilities (maybe even a child).

So Arti Rose and Posie May are just work friends, but that is something. Posie May is lightly acquainted with Gabe at work too, but she doesn't take him seriously.

"That big, white preacher man is a nut," Posie May says. "He make me laugh."

And that's how Gabe is at work, kidding around with his fellow employees when the customer traffic is slow. He tells people he's a minister on the side, but Gabe never goes into witnessing mode at work. He does tell Posie May she should come over for dinner some time.

"Na. I done heard 'bout yo' cookin', Gabe," Posie May says, giggling. "Think I'll pass."

So Posie May is acquainted with someone in Arti Rose's life, and Arti Rose has met Posie May's family. They can vent to each other about their situations, which makes work and life more tolerable. And when Posie May learns that Arti Rose likes to write, she even brings an important English paper in, now and then, for Arti Rose to look over and make suggestions in the break-room.

Christmas holidays are too busy to talk much at work, but Arti Rose buys one of those paisley scarves from Posie May's accessory stand. She doesn't say what she is going to do with it, but Arti Rose takes it to gift-wrapping. One of her high school sorority sisters is working at Sears as a holiday extra, wrapping gifts while she's home from University.

"This would look great on *you*, Arti Rose," her old friend and confidant, Betsy, says. "It would bring out your green eyes."

"I know, but it's a gift for a new friend," Arti Rose says, suddenly feeling guilty. She and Betsy had been close enough to exchange gifts a few Christmases ago when they were high school seniors. They had written a few times after going to separate colleges. Betsy had tried to discourage Arti Rose from smoking pot. But now that a few break-room visits have filled Betsy in on Arti Rose's new direction in life (including the fact that she has quit smoking pot), her old pal seems to think Arti Rose is "still going off the deep end…just from a different direction". And Betsy has no interest in visiting any church other than the one where she knows her old boyfriend (the one she has dreamed of marrying since puberty, *and will marry when she finishes college*) still sings in the choir.

Seems like Arti Rose is always leaving friends behind now, with her life moving forward so fast she can hardly keep up. Gabe says church leaders will be focusing more on witnessing and bringing in new members. He's thinking they will need flexible hours for fundraising, and they won't have time for their work schedules at Sears. So Gabe and Arti Rose give their notice, that they will be leaving their jobs after the holidays. But before she leaves Sears, Arti Rose gives Posie May that paisley scarf, boxed and wrapped in pretty paper and tied up with a red bow. They say maybe they'll get together sometime. The phone number at the Center is on the Christmas card Arti Rose gives Posie May. Posie May doesn't say anything about her phone number (if she has one).

"I'll probably keep workin' here till I get my degree," Posie May says, stepping over to a display of bags. "Want me to hold this one for you," she says.

"Oh, I like that one!" Arti Rose says. She's been trying to figure out what kind of purse to carry while she lugs those candle boxes around, fundraising. Maybe she's better off hiding an envelope or something. Lately she's been using an old make-up bag (since she doesn't wear make-up anymore anyway). "No, don't hold it. But I really appreciate the thought, Posie May," Arti Rose says.

"Sure!" Posie May replies, smiling warmly as her new friend walks away. "You stop by sometime."

The Family

When Arti Rose comes home one evening the apartment is full of people she has never seen before. Strangers. Oddly, Gabe seems more comfortable with them, more physically relaxed than she has ever seen him. And they are not the One World Crusade, not Unification Church members at all. This is obvious by their ultra-casual, hippy dress and manner. The apartment has a different vibe with this group of people in it, closer to how it sometimes felt when Arti Rose and her friends hung out. Gabe appears to be so blended in with them that at first glance Arti Rose thinks they must be old friends of his, visiting from somewhere else, and from a different time in his life, before he joined the Unification Church. But they are not old friends at all; they are new friends. And everything is about to change drastically for Arti Rose and Gabe.

It was like some hippy party without the dope. Several people, including Gabe, were lounged on the worn oriental rug in the living room. Leo Kottke, a young avant-garde twelve-string guitarist and singer-songwriter, was on the stereo. Come to think of it, Gabe had never even played an album on the old-fashioned console that came with the furnished apartment. He had listened to weather reports on the radio a few times, because there was no TV in the Center. Arti Rose didn't know he had any albums. But maybe these new people brought the album over. Anyway, she had thought there was some rule against electronic entertainment in Unification Church centers. As Arti Rose took a loaf of bread and a carton of eggs to the kitchen, she found herself wondering if Millie would approve of Gabe's new friends and their music. But he certainly seemed happy when he came in the kitchen to greet her.

"I met them at Southern College when I was witnessing there today," Gabe spoke conspiratorially to Arti Rose in the kitchen, as their guests listened to music and chatted, two rooms away. "They were so prepared I barely had to put out any energy to get them here."

Gabe was obviously high on the whole experience, boiling over from his day, brushing up against her in his big friendly dog manner. But he sensed that Arti Rose's blue mood had not changed much from the previous evening. He simmered down, softened his voice, made eye contact with her as he leaned on the kitchen counter and she put her packages down.

"I knew Heavenly Father would not want you and I to be alone here much longer," he said, giving Arti Rose a knowing look.

Arti Rose, still a bit emotionally drained from the good cry she'd had in her room the previous evening, acknowledged his look with her own eyes, but said nothing. Knowing looks had increased in volume between them lately. Their eyes had taken on the burden of expressing that silent but very intimate level where they had grown to be partners of a different sort, lovers who deny themselves the physical act of love but cannot deny the closeness that they feel. They were supposed to be "brother and sister" in God. However, they had become more like a husband and wife who, for whatever reason, do not sleep together. A tension had grown between them from holding their bodies apart, like the stiff wooden furniture in the old furnished apartment they shared. However, in a way, on some level, they had fallen, like Adam and Eve. There was something forbidden between them, and it was beginning to be painful.

"I got on my knees and prayed really hard last night," Gabe continued, his long body lounged against the counter, leaner than she remembered it being when they first met, like he had hungered somehow, in spite of the food that they shared daily.

Arti Rose lit up a little, gave him a less pained expression, a small but sincere smile that came from her heart and shone through her eyes, a look of love. She never loved Gabe more than when she felt that he truly loved God. And she could not imagine anything more wonderful on this earth than a handsome young man who added to his own strength by accessing God in prayer.

"Today I felt like Heavenly Father had just gathered them up in

His hands and placed them in my path," Gabe continued. "There they were, in the middle of the campus," he said, "sitting on the grass, talking about God. They had never heard of the Unification Church. They asked me so many questions that I essentially taught them the whole Divine Principle."

"Right there on the grass?" Arti Rose put the eggs in the refrigerator.

Gabe shook his head in the affirmative, suddenly feeling a bit defensive.

"You didn't tell them the part about the Lord of the Second Advent did you?"

"They figured that out for themselves. These people are very well-versed..."

"Are they going to stay for dinner?"

"I'll order a pizza," he said.

That was a first. It was also the first time strange new people came for dinner and crashed on the floor, stayed the night, stayed the week, the month, just stayed. But it would not be the last time that happened. It was the beginning of a new way of life, the next level. It was the birth of a "Family".

"Sisters"

I liked the new people, but once he brought them in I was soon basically over Gabe without him yet realizing it. Gabe and I had been living alone for a few months; so I could not help feeling betrayed. We could no longer share a private closeness, a feeling which, for me, had fulfilled a deeper need than the physical. Giving this up was more painful than sacrificing the sometimes-satisfying sex that I had shared with my former lover "Tex". The initial presence of new members in the Center was a source of deeply felt emotional pain, however unexpressed, barely even acknowledged by my own self. The pain resided on that same invisible plane of existence where my deeply felt intimacy with Gabe had lived and was now being buried alive. With little understanding of my emotional landscape at that point, and conditioned to "accentuate the positive and eliminate the negative" (as Millie had put it in her sing-song manner), I interpreted my own sadness as selfish, even evil. I felt guilty and quickly stifled the jealousy that rose out of my pain, like some ugly weed in the garden, some fallen feeling of Satanic origin. I argued silently with my own emotions, reminding myself that no matter how strong my attraction to Gabe, how deep and unrequited my feelings for him, I had joined the Unification Church because I felt the calling of God in my heart. And beyond my emotions, the Divine Principle made sense to me. It was, after all, Sun Myung Moon who gave my faith and my life a sense of direction; it was the Master that I followed, not Gabe. So I swallowed the gall and welcomed each new face with that soon-to-be trademark "Moonie" smile (though the media had not yet nicknamed us "Moonies"). I had gotten the idea that "the purpose of the whole is greater than the purpose of the self".

If Gabe did not acknowledge my struggle or show much consideration for me personally, maybe it was because I hid my feelings. But maybe on some level he harbored a secret desire to see me cry again, like I had cried the night before, when he and I were alone at the dinner table for the last time. For whatever reason, Gabe nearly pushed me to the limit that first night, hurting my feelings in every situation that we shared with Beth, her "boyfriend" Eddie, and their friend Jonathan.

First, lingering around the dinner table casually with pizza and a pitcher of lemonade, Gabe started up a game, a sort of contest, to see who was "the most well-read". He was spouting out the titles of literary classics, the new girl answering back the names of the authors at bullet speed, with the young men occasionally tieing with her but rarely beating her. I just sat there quietly, feeling left out and too embarrassed to participate even when I did remember that Ernest Hemingway had written *The Old Man in the Sea* and John Steinbeck had written *The Pearl*. I had not yet read Fitzgerald or Salinger and didn't know why I should have. Although, if I had gone back to State U in the fall instead of moving in with Gabe, I probably would have had *The Great Gatsby* on my nightstand instead of *The Divine Principle*. Beth, I would soon learn, preferred falling asleep to *The Chronicles of Narnia* (and other fictional fantasy based in religious myth).

For the first time, that evening, I felt like a hostage, not of Master Moon's but of Gabe's. It was like being forced to play with a couple of trivia geeks on the game show "Jeopardy", against my will, with only one category, not of my choosing. When the flush of embarrassment started to cool down, I felt mad at Gabe. Was he purposely trying to make me (and Beth's "boyfriend" Eddie for that matter) look undereducated? If not, why were we playing this game? Did Gabe feel the need to impress his new friends informally before standing up at the chalk board and presenting the Divine Principle lecture series? Were Gabe and his new friend Beth just showing off to each other, sharing a common interest? That would have been okay, to a point. However Gabe went on with the game past that point, setting himself and Beth apart from the rest of us.

As the evening progressed, I could not help feeling that there was a hidden message in Gabe's behavior, and it was directed toward me. We had gotten close, but I was not Gabe's choice. I was someone who had come to him. He had accepted me as a gift. And we had grown together. However, it was time to nip it in the proverbial bud, that thing that we had become. Something had opened up in me; I had fed him my sweet tears for dinner, flowing like nectar, like honey poured over peas that he would not eat, like a dessert that he did not want, had not chosen or asked for, however tempting. He could not allow it to happen again. With the help of God, he would bring others to the table. So he visited the local college of his choice and, scanning the grounds, picked someone else with a wide, smiling mouth and high cheekbones, with almond-shaped eyes and dark, well-shaped eyebrows, with rich brown hair framing her face and falling down her back. But Beth was different, still wearing her jeans. She had a tougher, tomboy appeal that must have seemed safer to Gabe.

The feeling of being rejected, set aside, festered in Arti Rose as the evening progressed. The whole group went back to the living room after finishing off the pizza. They went right back to lounging in a room where Arti Rose had never lounged. Her blue jeans long gone, Arti Rose sat in her long skirt, with her hands folded in her lap, in one of the stiff little chairs that Gabe had seated her in the first time she came to the Center. Now Gabe (in tan polyester pants) and his new blue-jean wearing friends played on the worn oriental rug, lounging with the records and books they had brought. They wrestled around a bit. Eddie, Beth's "boyfriend", especially seemed intent on challenging Gabe physically, in a decidedly playful manner. Beth joined in like one of the boys. At one point, Gabe shocked Arti Rose by straddling Beth's backside, rubbing her shoulders and making a comment about her "strong peasant back", (a physical attribute that the small-boned, narrow-shouldered Arti Rose was sure she did not have). Jonathan, the quieter of the three newcomers, rescued Arti Rose to a certain extent, by taking a chair opposite her and retreating from the wrestling match (where Gabe had the advantage of being larger than any of them and in his own territory).

No matter how much it hurt to watch Gabe make a fool of himself with the new girl, Arti Rose would not allow jealousy to influence her manner in dealing with Beth. Maybe it helped that Beth actually looked like she could have been kin to Arti Rose, with the long, dark hair framing bright, clear eyes. They could easily have been mistaken for sisters, and later would be. Maybe God was trying to give her a kid sister of a different sort, Arti told herself. When Beth's behavior, wrestling around on the floor with the young men, seemed inappropriate to Arti Rose, she realized how much she herself had changed. She was not unlike Millie, the lady who had spent a week training her in Unification Church rituals and manners.

In the days to come, Arti Rose would carry herself differently than she ever had before, taking on the role of house mother; so that even Gabe himself began to defer to her at times. Sometimes all it took was a look.

That first night it was the way she exited the scene, taking the newest female member with her, presumably to show Beth the "sisters' room" where she would be sleeping, in the twin bed opposite Arti Rose. If Beth was going to be her new roommate, her "sister", Arti Rose, in her own gentle way, intended to take the girl into her own hands. She was sure Millie, and Millie's spiritual mother "Miss Kim", and Mother Moon herself (along with Heavenly Mother), would want it that way.

About Gabe, however, Arti Rose was just not so sure anymore. Sometimes there were intimate moments, glances between them that carried the weight of a deeper connection. But most of those moments were shared, that feeling quickly dispersed.

Once the group went to see Dr. Zhivago, a movie based on a book about the Russian Revolution. Gabe sat between Arti Rose and Beth, with others on either side. Arti Rose burned inside, being so close to Gabe in the dark theater. Afterwards Gabe jokingly remarked that the two main female characters, the wife and the comrade/lover of the doctor, reminded him of Arti Rose and Beth. When he said which was which, Beth argued teasingly that she was not a blonde. Arti Rose did not tease, as she felt the sacrificial nature of her role manifested more clearly and falling like a weight from her heart to her belly.

At least Arti Rose did not have to fear pregnancy, as when she had realized her mistake in mating with Tex. But the new members Gabe had brought in started calling Arti Rose "Mama-san".

Changes

Gabe shipped Eddie out as soon as he had been through a week's worth of Divine Principle study sessions and accepted Sun Myung Moon as the Lord of the Second Advent. It was customary to separate couples who had been in a "fallen" sexual relationship prior to joining the Unification Church, which Beth and Eddie apparently had been, to some extent. And with Master Moon and his family having recently moved from Korea to live at the newly purchased Belvedere Estate in Tarrytown, New York (which the nationwide candle-selling mission had paid for), Center directors with good connections in the church were being allowed to send select new members up to live and work at Belvedere. Usually, only trusted longtime members were sent to be that close to the True Family. However, Gabe was able to convince his friends in the church hierarchy that Eddie's excellent educational background at private religious schools and a Methodist college had prepared the newcomer for this special mission. (Not to mention the fact that, besides having read at least some of the Bible and various philosophers and theologians, Eddie had read *The Lord of the Rings*.)

The whole process got Eddie more pumped than the time his dad took him to New York to see a ballgame at Yankee Stadium. The young man was blown-away with excitement. He seemed to be way over Beth, apparently not too sad to be leaving her behind. The stars in his eyes were actually planets, satellites that were set on a new course, ready to revolve around the bright One from the east, whose golden smiling face shone like the sun. We all envied Eddie and showered him with blessings as he flew away from us.

There were more new members coming. We were hot news on the campus where Gabe had recruited our new members. Two popular sophomores and a respected upper-classman had left the Southern College campus to live at the Unification Church center. One had gone to live with some man named Sun-Moon that they were calling The Second Coming of Christ. Word got around. People were curious. Posters and pamphlets were placed around campus with information. Southern College students (especially old friends of Eddie's) showed up for lectures, which were given at regular times now, sometimes being taught by Jonathan or Beth or even the blushingly shy Arti Rose.

Things were changing, but Gabe kept some of the fun parts of the old Southside routine going for a while. Gabe and Jonathan and Beth and Arti Rose walked to the Saturday night folk sing-in at the old Catholic Church, and "open-mic" at the Cadillac Café afterwards. The young priest (who was also a counselor at UAB) went to the café, and a few of his friends went along too. People would get up and sing or recite rambling, free-style poetry. There was even a near-convert from that Southside group who tried staying at the Unification Church center for a while (for as long as Gabe could stand him). Sometimes Gabe was so casual with folks in the outside world that they thought Unificationists were like Unitarians (free-thinking church types) but with a commune.

The Ones that Got Away

Harold was the first computer geek I ever met. He was an unusually short-haired, conservative dresser, a skinny, brainy guy who talked constantly, dominating every conversation with technical information nobody understood. He was probably one of the first computer geeks to live in the South. In fact, I had never seen (or maybe even heard of) a computer before I met Harold. Harold's computer (or the computer he worked on) took up an entire room at the nearby university. He loved taking people on tours, talking on and on in geek-speak while showing off the oversized jumble of metal and wires (visually not entirely unlike a laundry room full of washers and dryers, in the musty basement of some old building). The computer was a fulltime job for Harold, because something was always going wrong with it. But Harold believed in it; he knew the computer was the way of the future. The machine itself was Harold's messiah. With all of its flaws, it was still a gift from God, a new beginning full of hope and promise. Harold was a prophet of sorts, heralding the more technological aspect of the New Age. Gabe could barely tolerate the competition. I remember his pained expression, when Harold would get started talking about how computers were going to take over the world. I don't think Gabe doubted the validity of what Harold had to say. But the kid was too much. He talked like someone from Star-Trek, saying "affirmative" or "negative" all the time, instead of yes or no.

Harold would have slept on the couch of the Unification Church center for as long as Gabe would have let him. He was like an alien who finally felt that he could fit in somewhere, among people his age who dared to believe in something that had not yet found its place. If he was not with other computer geeks (because there were too few then), at least he was with other hard-working futurists, people who were willing to make sacrifices to bring a vision of a better world into reality.

One evening when we were supposed to be studying the Divine Principle and Harold would not stop talking about his computer (thinking out loud, just talking to himself really, trying to solve some puzzle, work out the latest glitch), Gabe asked him to please leave, told him he could not live in the Center.

"We can still be friends," Gabe said. I remember how embarrassed and sad Gabe looked, to be in that position where he had to turn a brother out. Later I heard somebody say that Harold took his few things to the computer room at UAB and just camped out there, sleeping on the floor, working on the machine night and day.

We didn't see Harold much after that, but there were other people who came and went. Eddie, Beth's former boyfriend who had excitedly shipped out to meet the new messiah a few months earlier, left the Belvedere Estate in Tarrytown, New York, where Sun Myung Moon and his family now resided (thanks to the hundreds of candles that thousands of us had sold across the U.S.). When Eddie came to the Center one day, some of us thought he might be moving back in. Eddie, however, was just visiting. When I asked him what it had been like, meeting "Master" and living in his presence, there was none of the old excitement in Eddie's face or voice.

"He's just this middle-aged Korean man, with a mission," Eddie said. "No disrespect intended. But I left because I felt like I had spent enough time being basically a gardener, which was my job at Belvedere. At this point, I need to finish my education."

There were some out-buildings at Belvedere estate where Master began to train his leadership. Gabe was sent up for a few weeks, and he put one of the new brothers in charge. Samuel had followed the original group from the Methodist college in, so humbly he was hardly noticed. It seemed odd that Gabe would choose Sam, but Sam was probably the person he felt least threatened by. Gabe was big and loud, and Sam was small and quiet. Sam was not likely to take over. And as soon as Gabe got back, he sent Sam up to New York for training anyway (so there was no confusion about who was in charge). I'd had to help Sam quite a bit when he was left in leadership position, so we'd bonded. He wrote to me after he was sent away:

Dear Arti Rose,

I love you sister. I wish you knew how much you've helped me grow and how much strength you give me. I doubt that I would have been able to direct the Center without you there to give me your understanding of the Principle.

I've really been up and down since I've been here but today things really started to come together. Friday I started very positively but by 3:30 I was very negative and remained that way until late Sunday. Friday the weather was beautiful. We went to N.Y.C. for our weekly rally with N.Y. Center. This rally was near the place we had the last one. I could only witness to one person in 4 hours. He was really nice. He was my age and thinks a lot like me, but he didn't feel God really existed and felt the world would self-destruct before it could unify. I talked to him for about 45 minutes. He shared his lunch with me and we really had a good rap, but I wasn't able to convince him to come to a lecture. I couldn't even approach anybody when I got there. He thinks a lot of things I used to think, and Satan was able to use it as a base to attack me and he did a good job too. I was ready to start thumbing for home. I felt like I wasn't growing much here or learning

225

much of the Principle and so many questions were coming up that there weren't immediate answers for. I wanted to leave and get away from everyone I knew so I could study the Principle for a couple of months by myself. Saturday night it turned too cold to thumb in the clothes I brought (strange) so I decided to wait until it warmed up some. I had already set a 10 day condition but doubted I would stay. I couldn't pray and I felt terrible both times Master was here. (He spoke on "faith & reality" Saturday and Sun. He told us big things would happen by 1980.) Sunday night before I went to bed I realized I wasn't being patient in trying to understand. Much discipline and patience are necessary to understand the Principle. This morning understanding started to come. I'm glad it did because I was really getting torn inside. I was looking for too much too fast. I got a very good letter from Beth today. She has been a good spiritual mother to me so far, but I can tell she is struggling too. We met in a philosophy class before, and we were both very skeptical, questioning everything. She really wants to learn and to share what she learns, but only as it becomes clear to her. I want you to make sure she is patient. I want you to realize this is too vast to expect overnight answers and make sure the rest of the family can realize it otherwise they'll become troubled as I was. I was ready to head for California or Oregon and find a job and read and study for a few months but I know I couldn't do something that would hurt any of you. I love my family too much. I'm telling you these things because I think we've been to enough of the same places in life that you can understand me. I hope you can learn from my experience. I'm glad the curtains are up now. Master wants all the Centers to be really nice. I hope I get to see how the new Center is coming along, but I may get sent somewhere else. Master has a lot of new missions planned.

 I hope you're not falling back on being dependent on Gabe for all your directions. You must continue being a motherly subject when necessary. I know you can do it. Take care of my family when I am gone. I wish I could express how much I love you and my other sisters and brothers.

 This letter is for you, the other for everyone.

 Love in Their Names,

 Samuel

 P.S. If I went on & on it may be the coffee. I hate to admit it but I'm drinking at least 2 cups a day. Got to have that little hit of speed *to stay awake in lecture.*

 Jeepers, Arti, I forgot to mention how it is really drag city only getting an occasional letter from Beth and nobody else.

Sami

New True

 Soon another new brother and a couple of new sisters (mostly quiet, studious, types from the local Methodist and Baptist colleges, where most of the "witnessing" was done) stayed, content to sleep on the floor in sleeping bags. Everybody who did not have a job (and some who did) started selling buckets-full of cut-flowers on the streets, under Gabe's direction.. He picked the flowers up fresh from a wholesaler most mornings, in buckets. Then they had stacks of smaller, bathroom type plastic trash-cans, at the Center. Individuals put a little water in those when they divided the flowers, then hit the streets. Some new members had cars and soon got the job of dropping others off in neighborhoods or at office buildings, then picking them up at some park or other designated meeting place later.

 Gabe had rented a big old brick two-story in Mountain Heights. It was a whole new scene, a real commune, a pretend extended family, a group of friends with a common agenda, working and living together in a big, old brick house with character, perched among overgrown oaks and magnolias, dogwoods and azaleas, on the side of the mountain. It was cool, hip, fashionable (as odd as those terms may seem when used to describe what amounted to a sort of ashram or mixed-gender monastery). It was the early '70s. People with no intention of joining the new church, moving into the commune (or following Rev. Moon in any capacity) came for dinner, sat on the floor around the low oval table that Gabe built for traditional oriental-style gatherings, told stories and laughed.

 "The family" sang and prayed freely, openly, joyously, inviting God and others into their circle. They had celebrations, the first being "True Parents Day", one of the family-oriented holidays invented by "Father" Moon for the "children of the new age". The Birmingham family worked together to prepare for the holy day, cleaning the center, practicing songs, writing poetry, creating skits to inspire and entertain their guests. Everyone invited friends and family members. Few parents attended however, because most were not pleased that their children had left home and/or school and/or jobs and/or relationships to join the group.

Mama Sue did come to the True Parents Day celebration, along with Arti Rose's younger siblings, Dave and Sis. True Parents Day is one of several special holidays in the Unification Church, rituals for honoring various aspects of family life and life on earth, based on the values set forth in the Divine Principle teaching. The most holy day is called "God's Day". Another holy day is called "True Children's Day", and another is "Day of All Things" (a sort-of heavenly Earth Day). They are all meant to be celebrated in both joyful and worshipful ways, returning love and joy to God, and honoring those who set the highest standards of exemplifying God's love on this earth.

"True Parents Day" was especially tricky and hard to explain. In the hoped-for ideal world of the future, it would simply be about honoring parents, who would naturally be "true" to one another, to their children, and above all, to God. But in a not yet restored world, the celebration centers around honoring the "True Parents" of that church, who symbolize the God-centered parents that its members strive to become.

Regular parents who were not members of the church were generally regarded as potential converts, brothers and sisters in God but fellow sinners, fallen parents still living in the mass culture of the fallen world. Rev. Moon and his family were set up to be role models for a future when all parents and families would center their lives around loving God and each other and serving the earth and all living things (both physically and spiritually).

Friends and family of church members were invited to the celebration. Gabe told us to tell our parents that it was "a feast honoring parents". Once the guests had arrived and the festivities were under way, little was explained about the role of Rev. and Mrs. Moon, who were always subjects of controversy for parents of members. But some poems, songs, and prayers naturally included expressions of reverence toward the "Father and Mother" of the Unification Church.

However awkward at times, the attending parents all seemed to enjoy socializing with the group while refreshments were served, with everyone sitting in a big semi-circle of folding chairs around the open living room. They smiled warmly, clapped, chuckled, sometimes laughed out loud, and sometimes were moved to tears as the group entertained their guests, sometimes individually, sometimes in pairs or teams. But the aura around Arti Rose's family changed as she read a poem she had written especially for the occasion. At first they were glowing with pride as she stood before them in her long, flowered dress, their beautiful daughter and sister. Then, still smiling, they blushed warmly for her, with her, as she spoke softly with her gentle, shy voice. As the celebration continued, however, with others reading poems more obviously written for Mr. and Mrs. Moon (whose portrait decorated a table serving as a sort-of altar, with fruit and flowers, in front of the otherwise austere room) emotions changed. The open hearts of some guests soon realized who the words were meant for, and Arti Rose's family was hurt by words that were not intended to hurt them but did nonetheless.

Arti Rose noticed the change on her brother's face first, as his smile always seemed to outshine anyone else's in most situations. At one point Arti Rose's brother drew her attention with a strange gesture, suddenly lowering his head and lifting the neck of his t-shirt to cover the lower half of his face. He kept his t-shirt there until people were clapping, but Davie did not clap. His usually glowing countenance appeared darkened, his face fallen into a frown. Arti Rose interpreted the vibe she was getting as more of what Dave had dished out at the introductory lectures, when Gabe had met with opposition from her brother and William. Now Arti Rose thought her family was suddenly, once again, uncomfortable about her having a new savior, besides their beloved Jesus. Caught up in her new religious fervor, she never even realized that her siblings were embarrassed for their own mother, who did not feel personally honored by her daughter on this day that she had been told would "celebrate parents". When her family's goodbyes were polite but heavy-hearted after the affair, Arti Rose thought they were still feeling that they had lost her. And she had so wanted them to feel included in her new life. She felt some sadness as they were leaving, but also felt glad that they had at least come.

Arti Rose had no time to herself to reflect on the mixture of feelings, to sort out what might have gone wrong, to reassure her mother, her family. The group had to clean the center and get to sleep.

Arti Rose had to get to work at her new fulltime job (in the office at the medical lab where Beth had gotten a job testing bodily fluids), first thing the next morning. It would be a long time before Arti Rose would understand how much her poem, along with various things said at the celebration, had somehow hurt her mother.

For the Father

When you are young
each new season takes you on a trip
into a world not yet discovered
or even expected in your dreams.
Then one day
you hold all of those worlds.
They declare war
inside the universe that is you,
for they are all so different,
so incompatible
that your spirit can only scream out
in confusion,
fighting desperately for its own survival,
its own peace
in the midst of a senseless hell
that it seems to be dwelling in.
You stand back,
looking at all of those worlds.
One of them shines
like the brightest star you have ever seen,
and you know that
this one is your reality.
So you take all of those
senseless, empty worlds
and tear them to shreds,
with love and truth and beauty,
with all of the spiritual and physical energy
that your life can radiate.
You run to the Father
with open arms

and the tears of a loving child.
You step into that new world,
your life becoming an eternal sunrise;
you have heaven.

A.R.T. 1972

A Mother's Tears
by Sue Cronkite

I visited the Center, sometimes just dropping by unannounced. It was a warm and friendly place that attracted many young people with bright, fresh, inquisitive minds. A clean-living situation, there were no drugs or alcohol, even tobacco was not allowed. I never heard any dirty language, which was refreshing. There were separate sleeping quarters, with no sex allowed. The boys painted the walls, the girls made curtains, and they had a nice stereo system with good music, (some youthful, dreamer-type albums, a nice selection of classical, and jazz). In the living room was a picture of Moon and his wife, smiling, placid Koreans. Other than that there were few decorations, sparse furnishings, no TV to distract from studying Moon's teachings.

I kept trying to tell myself that the youngsters would "go back" to college at the end of a year's devotion to the Unification principles. One young lady was a music major who had dropped out toward the end of her junior year at a local Baptist college.

I listened to what they said and read some of the literature. But I did not fully realize to what extent my daughter was being pulled away from me until I was invited to a "feast" being held "in honor of parents". The center was decorated with fresh flowers and colorful fruit. The living room had lots of folding chairs, and the young people entertained us with skits, songs, poetry. We were served oriental type dishes, with mostly rice and vegetables, not much meat. I was not the only parent there. Two couples came, parents of girls who shared the crowded bedroom with my daughter. Other friends and family members came too, including my son and younger daughter.

They called themselves a "family". That didn't bother me too much. But at the "feast day in honor of parents", it began to dawn on

231

me that the youths weren't honoring us (the other couple and me), they were honoring the Moons, their "true parents".

When they prayed they breathed "Father" fervently, and I had assumed they were praying to God. At the parents' day feast it seemed to me that they were also praying to Moon, that the picture of the Moon couple represented their "true parents" and that I and the other parents had only been invited because we were a part of the past, which they were slowly and symbolically breaking with. We were being excommunicated from the family circle. It did not include us anymore. I was not my oldest daughter's "true parent"; that honor belonged to a Korean whom she had never seen. It hurt, very badly. I smiled politely and was as friendly as I could be and went home last. My car was down the street about two blocks when the tears started. It had been a long time, and there were plenty of tears to shed. I stopped the car on the rim of the mountain and looked down at the city. It felt as if someone had died, and I couldn't quite figure out who.

Misunderstanding

Gabe should have done a better job of explaining the meaning of True Parents Day to Mama Sue and the other parents who attended the celebration. He realized this later, when he started getting flack from Nanette's parents (who would, several years later, pay a large sum of money to have their daughter "kidnapped" and "deprogrammed" by a renowned psychologist who specialized in getting American youths out of cults). Maybe he should not have invited parents at all, but it was their first big celebration in the Heights house, and he had thought it would be a good time for parents to see them at their best. In fact, the church's president had sent a letter to all Center Directors, advising them to do just that. The house was at its cleanest, the food at its tastiest. What better time to invite parents? And telling them it was a celebration to honor parents was a good way of getting them there, and not much of a stretch. (Of course, it was imagined, that's what it would be sometime in the future, once the heavenly traditions were established and all the young members were blessed in marriage, with children of their own.) Maybe Gabe should have told the brothers and sisters to write special poems for their own

232

parents, as well as the "True Parents". He had just told them to prepare something to present for their guests, like a poem, song, or skit. He had trusted that they would consider their guests, especially those whose parents were coming. There had been no rehearsal. And, actually, Gabe himself was surprised, (as he seemed to be often these days, since moving to the Bible belt) at the religious fervor of some of the newer members. Things had been much more low-key at the San Francisco center, more light-hearted. The whole thing seemed to be getting away from him here. There were just so many decisions to make these days; it was impossible to get everything right, all the time, for an increasingly large group. Sometimes he found himself wondering if he really wanted the local Family to get any bigger, but of course he did. That's why he had told the brothers and sisters to invite their own families to True Parents' Day. Master had said many times that members who brought their own families into the fold were especially blessed by God.

Truth-be-known, Gabe had been eager to invite Sue Cronkite to the Family's first celebration in the big house. She had been so kind to him, letting him borrow her car when he and Arti Rose had so many candles to sell (for the church's nationwide campaign to buy the foreclosed Belvedere estate for the Moon family). Gabe only had a bicycle at the time. Sue had welcomed Gabe into her home many times, since Arti Rose had joined. Gabe admired Arti Rose's independent, intelligent mother, and secretly harbored a sort-of crush on the single woman. He had even fantasized about being blessed-in-marriage to her, if she would join the Family. The president of the national church was around Gabe's age, and he had been blessed in marriage to a forty-year-old woman. Sue wasn't even forty yet. If Sue would just get used to visiting the Center, maybe Gabe could get her through the lecture series. Surely if she understood the Divine Principle, Arti Rose's mother would join. So, of course Gabe invited Sue to their first celebration in the new Center, which just happened to be True Parents' Day. Later Gabe realized it would have been wiser to wait until one of the other church holidays (True Children's Day, or Day of All Things). Gabe never knew that Sue had cried after the celebration, but he certainly heard from Nanette's parents (who seemed more mad than sad).

Arti Rose did not know how her mother had felt until years

later, when she read Sue's unpublished manuscript.

After the move from the Southside apartment to the Heights house, Gabe quit his job at Sears to run the Center full time. The new level of financial responsibility was a shock to the young man. He tried various ways of dealing with it. Gabe had been getting brown rice and lemons in bulk from a Southside food co-op since shortly after he moved to Birmingham. Now he tried soybeans. His first experiment was a nearly inedible onion soup with soybeans. With no meat or stock, the soup had very little substance or flavor, and the beans were endlessly hard, no matter how long he boiled them. "The family" ate the soup all week anyway, barely complaining, getting more lightheaded every day, the discussions about the spirit world getting increasingly far out. Later Gabe got a grinder and put the soy in meatloaf, which was better. Some of the girls were trying to be vegetarians, but Gabe said it was not good to be obsessed with food, better to appreciate whatever was available. Gabe did most of the cooking in the new center at first, while the rest of us worked and/or went to school (which some had not yet given up on). Sometimes it bothered me, coming home exhausted to find Gabe lounged out, reading "Be Here Now" or some such. And it really bugged me when he pawned my clarinet to pay a bill (not that I ever played the squeaky thing, which I certainly had not mastered though I had owned it since fifth grade). But it was *my* clarinet. Gabe looked embarrassed when I noticed it was missing from the closet in the sisters' bedroom. When he explained, I did not bother protesting, and neither of us ever retrieved the instrument.

Beth quietly got a job at a lab on Southside, testing blood, etc. She told me about an opening they had for a typist, which paid better than Sears. I'd had a typing class in high school. The man who owned the lab had a grossly overweight wife and an obvious weakness for pretty young ladies. Looking back, it is one of my earliest memories of a sort of seduction that I was learning to practice in the world of men. Selling the candles, I had learned to use my rather intense eyes, my smile, the warmth of my heart and spirit, in a way that made me irresistible, hard to say no to, it seemed. And, (although I would have denied it at the time), as outwardly innocent as my projected self appeared, on some level, I was aware of and exercising a new kind of sexual power. All it took was an interview, a closed door, and my green eyes glowing at his brown ones. The guy hired me, in spite of the fact that I had no previous work experience as a typist and barely passed the timed test.

I sat for hours every weekday, typing address after address on bills, at a snail's pace. Meanwhile the bills got paid at a snail's pace. Once, when the man's wife stopped by with their two young children, I heard her whining to him about how slowly the bills were getting paid. Evidently she did the books. Instead of firing me, a less spaced-out (understatement), more mature lady who was a kind of office manager there operated my billing machine at high speed for the last hour of every day, while I did some of her filing.

I was a slow-moving day-dreamer (a fairy girl, floating just above the earth, barely touching the ground), but I was not the worst in the Center. Nanette, a demure, doe-eyed student from Southern, was so dreamy that I could get little done when we were teamed up for a task. Gabe first realized this when we went to a fabric store to buy material for curtains and did not return for several hours. The "ecology" movement was trending, and the store had a selection of fabric prints featuring large animals peering from jungle foliage. As I looked for the right fabric to make curtains for the Heights house, Nanette stared at one animal print after another, until I joined her. I had been ready to check out but got drawn into her fixation on the animal prints. Sucked into her dreamy aura, I moved from one print to the other with her, until we were both captured by the face of a great lion. I don't know how long we stood looking at the great golden face, talking softly about the spiritual quality its intense gaze seemed to exude. I remember my own soft-enough voice taking on the even softer, airier quality that Nanette spoke with. Finally I added one of the prints to the stack of fabric I was holding, and went to the cashier. Back at the Center, Gabe did not seem to appreciate the lion print, asking only how much we paid for it. When we tried to hang it in the living room, saying it reminded us of Christ, Gabe told us to put it upstairs in the sisters' room if we wanted to. As we were walking up the stairs, I heard Gabe half-jokingly make a comment to one of the brothers about Nanette and I being "a couple of space-cadets". At that point, Nanette and I were close enough to the '60s to feel almost complimented by the label; it was still hip to be a space-cadet. Most of us had smoked pot before,

235

and many had experienced another dimension via experimentation with psychedelics. I had only done half-a-hit of "yellow sunshine" LSD one time, a year earlier, but I had hung onto the high. (And maybe, with so many spiritual sub-cultures emerging in our generation, multitudes of us were trying to hang onto the high). A little further into the '70s, however, with the wider culture headed for the reactionary materialism of the 1980s, the media would nickname our church "the Moonies". This was not only because our leader was named Moon. People on the streets came to characterize us as "Moonies" because of the dreamy, wide-eyed, open facial expression most of us wore, perpetually smiling, often with a full-moon glow.

Nanette, as well as most of the group that joined when we moved into the Heights house, did not work in the outside world, except to sell the fresh carnations that Gabe started buying in bulk. Letting the new members stay in school, at least initially, was the most effective way for Gabe to appease their parents. Putting flower vendors on the street was the easiest way for Gabe to get a little cash out of the students with odd schedules. He took them out selling, tried to train them. But some did not have the personality for it. Jonathan did OK, except that he would stop to get into theological discussions and intellectual arguments as often as he could find anyone capable of such. (In fact, Jonathan soon found an "order" of priests that interested him more than the Unification Church. In the most friendly and respectful manner possible, and without drama, he suddenly moved into a local monastery of "St. John of the Cross"). The newer convert from Southern, Jonah, was just too quiet, too small and meek and mild and homely to sell much of anything, although he made a wonderful brother around the Center, helping out wherever a hand was needed. Then came plain Jane, a chubby, pimple-faced brunette who was such a well-organized, tidy house-frau type that Gabe started letting her do the cooking. She was a more practical, down-to-earth character than most of us. She kept her best friend Amy with her for company; they did the shopping and cleaning. Gabe started getting potentially profitable PR projects in the outside world, like a booth at the International Fair downtown. The One World Crusade was coming, and Gabe wanted to impress Art Shoman, the charismatic leader of the traveling group

The One World Crusade

The One World Crusade arrived the week before the International Fair, in a caravan of several white vans with red wheel-like symbols painted on the sides, a score of kids in their late teens and early twenties pouring out the doors, sounding like the tower-of-Babel. There were several who spoke English, but half of that group had British accents. Then there were the Germans, the French, the Spanish, the Japanese. They were mostly moon-faced and smiling, except for one big German girl who was as sour as sour-kraut. Their leader, Art Shoman, even though he was a Yankee, was as fired up as a Southern evangelical tent-revival preacher. But he was not like the revival preachers at Arti Rose's Mema's backwoods Pentecostal church. Art Shoman was almost as good-looking as Billy Graham or some TV evangelist. He had the face of an eagle, set on a compact body that moved with a dancer's grace.

Rallies were the specialty of the One World Crusade. They came fully equipped with loudspeakers and microphones. There were a few guitar pickers in the group too, a big loud British bloke and a sexy Spaniard. First thing Art Shoman did, (after he met Sue Cronkite for lunch, charmed her sufficiently, and hooked up with the press), was to set up a rally at Southern Methodist College. Being "the creative type", Art Shoman went to work designing fliers with the liberal-arts college in mind. After the evening meal, he kept the large dining room packed full of young people sitting on the floor, got everyone pumped up about the impending rally, and taught them some new songs he had written himself. His style was different from the traditional Korean that Millie had borrowed for her gentle, intricately slurred, heart-stirring melodies. Art Shoman's songs were upbeat, American-flavored, hand-clapping energizers.

> "The Day of Hope is Dawning
> In the middle of the night;
> The sons of earth are calling
> To the one and only light.
> Out of the East He is coming,
> Burning, beaming, bright.
> Into our hearts, hope's returning;

Oh what a wonderful sight!
The day-ay of hope,
The day of true family,
Day of joy, day of delight!"
(clap-clap!)

Everyone in the group had red palms by the time they were done accompanying themselves with the rhythmic clapping that was as important to Art Shoman as the singing. "Ta-tum, at-tum, at-tum" went the beat, like a drum. And after practicing songs, the dishes still had to be done. Then it was not easy getting to sleep when Art Shuman had gotten them so wound up. Most stayed up late, studying the Divine Principle, talking quietly downstairs. Art Shoman and Gabe seemed to be night owls, but Arti Rose and Beth had to rise early for work. They called in sick on alternating days, so that each of them could attend at least one of the rallies that were held daily that first of the two weeks that the One World Crusade stayed..

Most of the rallies were at Southern, since some of the members still attended school there. The local Baptist college did not want the group on campus anyway, nor did the Bible college; (so we had to sneak around at those places). Something about the words "One World" reminded biblical literalists of warnings in the book of Revelations. (And if they'd known the whole story, Rev. Moon would quickly have been labeled an "anti-Christ"). So Art Shoman figured the best strategy was to concentrate on the more liberal, Methodist college. Obviously, from Gabe's success, the harvest was good there; so why not take advantage?

With the One World Crusade in town, Arti Rose got tired, from working, selling flowers, entertaining guests, rallying and witnessing and teaching, helping with domestic chores. By the time she was able to attend one of the rallies at Southern, Arti Rose was beside herself with exhaustion and operating on an adrenalin high that made her feel like she was starting to come down from a drug high.. "Ding-y" was the word they had used around the dorm, after staying up all night on speed (to "cram" before exams). Warding off the feeling of tiredness, Arti Rose threw herself into the rally unselfconsciously and with all her heart. It was like an out-of-body experience for the normally shy girl, like being possessed by the holy spirit after a Pentecostal preacher had wound you up and wrung you out.

That was when Kirby, her old buddy and unrequited flame from Methodist Youth Fellowship (and her friend Sunshine's former lover), showed up. Evidently Kirby had witnessed a previous rally or rallies, since it was the third day the group had been on campus at Southern. They had sung a few songs, with Arti Rose up at the microphone by the British bloke, shaking a tambourine. She spotted Kirby's unmistakable lion's mane across the green, with a group of students around him. He was lifting a wooden structure, a man-sized cross, onto his back. Then he proceeded to walk across the green, stooped forward, carrying the cross with the other students supporting and following him. An extra shot of adrenaline increased the volume of Arti Rose's voice as the group sang an English version of the Korean folk-song,

"Tongil".
"Our cherished hopes are for unity;
Even our dreams are for unity.
We give our lives for unity;
Come along unity.
Unity saving the people;
Unity saving all nations.
Come here quickly unity; Come along Unity."

Arti Rose couldn't have felt less united with her old friend Kirby, who seemed to be mocking her. Her voice took on a pleading, heartfelt tone, like a country-western singer. Little did she know, Kirby and his irreverent pals had planned their drama after the first rally, which had happened while Arti Rose was busy typing medical bills at her day job. Although she kept singing, Arti Rose's heart was breaking. By the time Kirby had carried the cross all the way across the green and put it down, Arti Rose was visibly in tears and stepped away from the mike. Kirby, remembering that he was basically a nice guy, walked over to her and said "Hi". She wiped at her tears and talked through the ones that kept coming.

"These people came to America from all over the world, Kirby," she said, in a pleading, argumentative tone, ready to take him on like she had in the old days. The British bloke stepped into her aura, cool as a cucumber, offering his hand to Kirby, along with a heavily accented greeting. Kirby blushed, taking the guy's much bigger hand while the Englishman went on in an overbearingly friendly manner that left Kirby taken-a-back. Arti Rose, at this point, was choking on tears that would not stop. She politely stood her ground, wiping her face with her hand when she had to, until Kirby walked away. Then she went to the van, letting the French girl take her place at the microphone.

Later that week, when Gabe said they would need long skirts for the International Fair, Arti Rose went home to her mother's sewing machine (and her delightedly welcoming mother's help with the machine's persnickety bobbin) for the weekend. Figuring the other girls would wear ethnic garb, she chose a classic early-American pattern, but the fabric she chose for her long, full skirt was an easy-care cotton-knit in a bright, modern color. She took her time, having chosen challenging patterns to make a blouse with a lace-trimmed collar and cuffs, and a gored skirt with a fitted and fastened waist-band. No details were spared.

When Monday came, Arti Rose still needed to do the finishing touches on her outfit, by hand. There were buttons and snaps, and a hem that seemed a mile around the bottom of the flared skirt. With her siblings at school and her mother at work, Arti Rose was blissfully alone for the first time she could remember since she didn't know when. Arti Rose played some of her favorite albums, which were still there, and she played one her brother had bought recently. Since he'd never bought such a spacey album before, she wondered if Pink Floyd's new hit- "The Dark Side of the Moon"- had any special meaning for Davie... Arti got in a bit of a funk, facing feelings she'd been too busy for.

Arti Rose missed her brother and was glad to see that he seemed happy when he came home from school, like he'd had a good day. Davie had always been popular at whatever school he went to, and that had not changed. Sissy was popular as well, with too many kids following her home as usual. And Mama Sue, who went to work very early, came home around the same time as Arti Rose's siblings. All were hungry and congregated in the kitchen.

Sue had been teaching Sissy how to cook, so they hovered over the stove together.

Davie impatiently set the table. Arti Rose had made a pitcher of tea earlier. Davie poured tea over ice in four glasses, then turned the pitcher up and drank the rest while Arti Rose tossed a salad in the middle of the table.

"Hey Bro! That's rude!" Arti said as he drank from the pitcher.

"I'm thirsty, Art."

"Yeah, but that's for everybody! You wouldn't have done that if Daddy Dick was here; he'd tan your hide!"

"But you can always make some more, Sister! I've missed your sweet tea," Davie said.

They all sat down at the little wrought-iron set of table-and-chairs meant for a patio, where they ate and lingered, chatting lightly about their day, laughing at Davie and Sissy's antics, listening to Mama Sue's stories. Nobody tensed up like they had whenever Daddy Dick had gotten on his proverbial soap-box and preached at them condescendingly from the head of the big table in their former home. Arti Rose did a little preaching, but it was more like she was talking to herself out loud, trying to convince herself to go back to her work of helping God's cause of "building a heavenly kingdom on Earth". She told them about the "One World Crusade" and all of the different kinds of interesting young people, from other countries. Her enthusiasm for the cause was not new, but she was clearly not as wound-up as she had been when she moved out. There was a spacey-er, dreamy quality to her spiel. As happy as they were to have her with them, Davie and Sis felt like Arti Rose was already far away, and it broke their hearts. Their faces took on a weight beyond their years, but just for a moment, as they had already learned to hide their tears. When their sister talked about the church that was pulling her away from them, Davie and Sissy started picking at their food. Getting stomach-aches at the dinner table was not a new feeling for them. However, without Daddy Dick to turn his critical eye and tongue on them (and force them to stay at the table until they had eaten every bite) they picked up their plates and fled to the kitchen. Doing the dishes was a chore their stepfather had insisted they do. But it was a chore they had learned to love, for the time it gave them together, away from the tyrannical ruler who had not considered the kitchen his realm.

Mama Sue saw her daughter as tired. "I hope you know you can stay here and go to JC, if you want to," she said to Arti Rose as they finished eating their dinner. "You could make up credits you missed and go to the university downtown, near where I work. This is a big city. There are all kinds of different and interesting students from all around the world, right here."

They all worked in the kitchen cleaning up afterwards, playing and kidding around, like old times. It was the kind of family Sue had wanted (but couldn't have when Dick ruled her roost). It was a joy to have her eldest daughter be a part of it, if only for a short time. Maybe she would cherish the memory and move back home.

When the kitchen was clean, Davie and Sis settled down to do their homework by the lamps at either end of the long couch, with their books and notebooks, pencils and pens. Mama Sue went to the sewing machine's wooden extension table, by the front window, with Arti Rose following to show her mother the work she had been doing to finish her outfit.

"I don't think this kind of hem is going to work on cotton knit," she told her daughter. "It will shrink some when you wash it, and this will pucker. Then it won't hang right." Mama Sue handled the hem, showing Arti Rose how the fabric was already curling between the tiny, careful stitches she had made inches apart. As with the shorter, A-line dresses Arti Rose was accustomed to hemming, she'd placed some tucks where the wider expanse of fabric was brought up to a narrower part of the skirt. "The tucks are too bulky, with this fabric," Mama Sue said. "I think you need to trim a few inches off the bottom and do a little hem with the machine, like they're doing with t-shirts now. I'd take it out and start over, if I were you," she said.

So Arti Rose stayed most of the week, working on her outfit alone some, until the bobbin would get loose and tangled, and she would get frustrated and decide to wait for Mama Sue to come home. She did other things, like reading and writing in her journal and just resting. When the phone rang during the day she didn't feel like answering. The few times she had talked with Gabe he'd sounded impatient. She didn't understand why he thought he needed *her* with all of those other people there. He had plenty of help.

When Arti Rose was finished with her outfit, and it had passed Mama Sue's inspection the evening before, she called the Center. The One World Crusader who answered offered to come and pick her up. She said okay, gave him instructions, and left the apartment in a One World Crusade van while her siblings were at school and her mother was at work. When Arti Rose got to the Convention Center, she was well-rested, as well as well-dressed. There were only a few more days to sell flowers in her bright, flowing, light-green skirt and pale-yellow flowered-blouse, at the International Fair. The French and German and Japanese sisters of the One World Crusade had already been stealing the show for days, raking in the cash with their moon-faced smiles and interesting accents. Beth said she had been making excuses for her at the lab but wasn't sure Arti Rose still had a job there. And Gabe came right out and told her, when he got Arti Rose alone, that she had really let him down.

The first evening Arti Rose was back Gabe wasted no time getting in her face, in the sisters' room where he really did not belong and would not have allowed any of the other brothers to go. She was putting her sleeping bag and suitcase down on the only space that she could find on the floor, next to Beth's things on one side and the things of a strange girl from some faraway land on the other side. She felt so puzzled by this man, who was expressing his disappointment that she had not been by-his-side while the International Fair was getting started at the Convention Center, when he was setting up his booth, as minister of the first Unification Church in her home city and state.

From Gabe's under-articulated point of view, with Arti Rose by his side he had a more legitimate standing in the community. Most of the students from Southern who had joined the group were out-of-towners, Gabe himself was an out-of-towner, and all of the One World Crusaders were from way out-of-town. Besides being Gabe's first member, Arti Rose was a Southerner, a local girl, a home-town girl whose mother was on the editorial board of *The News* daily. Arti Rose, not being a worldly grown-up, was oblivious to the significance of all of that.

Little did Gabe know, Arti Rose was in the midst of a very private personal identity crisis. She was tired of the pressure of being part of his presentation. Before anyone else had joined Gabe's Unification Church Center, Arti Rose had walked the pavement with him, stood by his side as he shook hands with people all over town, even appeared with him on a local TV talk show. She was a quiet presence, but someone lovely and well-mannered that he could introduce proudly, someone who helped to give him legitimacy in a community where he was trying to gain respect and establish himself.

The One World Crusade was fine for the big show, but before the doors of the Convention Center were opened to the public, when civic leaders were milling about, setting things up, Gabe had wanted it to be just he and Arti Rose at the Unification Church booth. Unfortunately, he had failed to communicate his vision to her in a way that would have made her feel personally valued. Though Arti Rose had always been proud of her mother's position in the community, and more recently had sometimes felt proud of her place beside Gabe, she did not feel that she *herself* was important.

Arti Rose had been lost in the crowd lately. She had no deeply felt sense of mattering all that much to anybody but God. In fact, being confronted by Gabe, Arti Rose was shocked that he had more-than-noticed her absence. If Gabe could have just said that he had missed her, Arti Rose would have been his again. She had not been alone with him in so long. He had not looked her in the eyes this way, full-faced, with no one else around, since it was just the two of them, at the apartment on Southside that had been his first Center. And now he was looking at her with anger and frustration, just because she took several days off. Clearly he did not understand, had not understood that he had lost her long before he had to set up his booth at the Convention Center without her by his side. She had not been *his* since the night Beth moved into the Southside apartment (and Gabe gave Beth a back-rub on the living-room floor right in front of Arti Rose, who had been faithfully following church rules by restraining from touch with the man she loved).

Admittedly, Arti Rose had been head over heels in love with Gabe when she first moved into the Center; she had surrendered her heart and mind and will to him. However, all of these months since the others started moving in, her deepening sense of dedication had not been to Gabe, but to God. Increasingly, God was all that she could keep near. In the crowd, her relationship with God was the only sustainable intimacy. And as difficult as it was for her to face an ever-growing crowd, Arti Rose had come back to the Center out of love for God, out of dedication to a cause she believed in. If she had been inconsiderate of Gabe by leaving when she did, it was only because she was no longer doing this for Gabe. Whatever important thing she had been to him had gotten lost in the crowd. And she was out-of-touch with his needs. She was even out of touch with her own needs. She just went home to use her mother's sewing machine. But once she was there, the couch felt like a luxurious bed compared with the floor she had been sleeping on. And her family had given up the fight. They were just glad to have her back for however long she wanted to be there.

Arti Rose had enjoyed relaxing with her family over the weekend. Mama Sue had helped her with the sewing like she used to. And when Arti Rose's natural family went to school and work on Monday, she had enjoyed having the apartment to herself. She had taken the dog for a walk, written in her journal, rested and calmed herself.

"What were you doing all this time?" Gabe fumed.

"It wasn't even a whole week."

"But it was a very *important* week."

"I was sewing and writing. You said I needed a costume. And I haven't had a chance to do any writing lately."

"Well, it must be nice to just decide to take a break and do some writing. Wish I had time for that."

"Gabe, before the One World Crusade got here, you had your own little vacation, quitting your job at Sears, hanging around the Center reading "Be Here Now"; so I don't want to hear it.

"I have to be well-read in my position," he defended. "But you wouldn't know about that."

"What's that supposed to mean?"

"Well, I know you're not very well read," Gabe said thoughtlessly.

"Oh, this from a guy who advised me to drop out of college. When do I have time to read around here?" Arti Rose said, getting defensive, emotional, almost loud before she stopped to think about the crowd downstairs. "I don't *have* to read, but I *have* to write," Arti Rose asserted, taking a deep breath afterwards, wishing he would leave so she could write in her journal and release some of this excess emotion. She knew she needed her rest for whatever tomorrow would bring.

Gabe was quiet for a moment. "I needed your support; that's all," he said, backing out of the room.

Arti unpacked her nightgown, put it on, and crawled into her sleeping bag. Later the other girls came up and crawled into theirs. Still holding onto the pain in her heart, the only feeling Gabe had given to her alone for months, Arti Rose pretended to be sound asleep while the other girls whispered their prayers and made little comments to each other about their day. As the sisters unrolled their sleeping bags on the wood floor, Beth put hers next to Arti's. When the house was still and quiet and dark, Beth curled up to Arti Rose's back and slept close. Arti Rose sighed, feeling the pain of Gabe's hurtful words leave her as she exhaled and slept soundly.

The next night, after the group had spent the day selling flowers and handing out literature at the International Fair, a middle-aged Art Shoman scanned the living room full of glowing young people sitting on the floor, and picked Beth and Arti Rose, like flowers from the garden that was "The Family". They left town the next day, with the One World Crusade, and there wasn't anything Gabe could do about it.

Art also took a new girl who had just joined, a friend of Beth's from Southern. Barbie Winn was a striking fair-skinned blue-eyed blonde, a tow-head, with soft white curls falling around her face and all the way down her back to her waist. Barbie was more outgoing, more outspoken than the reserved Beth or the shy Arti Rose. Barbie was, in fact (though she seldom told it) a cheerleader turned hippy.

Looking back from this writing, it is so obvious that the older, more powerful Art Shoman took the most dazzling young women that Gabe had attracted into the organization. Gabe was left with the homlier, nerdier types, and a few space-cadets who were less likely to attract new members into the local church. But Gabe himself would soon be transferred to a large city in the upper Midwest. With "Father" (as Art Shoman called the man that Gabe had called "Master" Moon) residing in the U.S. now, "the movement" was on the move, and the only constant was change.

Gabe did not look happy the day Beth and Arti Rose left him. (But they would meet again.)

YOUR EYES

look at us
With a beam of radiance
That shows us your heart,
Thus reflecting God's Love.

We will miss you Sister,
As our heart wishes to
Unite us all as one.

But as you leave
We wish you joy
In your mission
Seeking the Father.

We know you will be one
With the heart of Heavenly Mother,
Loving all mankind
As brothers and sisters.

With unification as our goal,
And even though you leave
In your physical body,
We write in spirit because of this.

Our love goes with you,
And your love returns;
So all receive joy from God.

your spiritual family forever

(Penned by someone at the Center, & given, from the group, in farewell.)

Letting Go
by Sue Cronkite

As hard as it was for me to accept my daughter's decision to join a pseudo-Christian church led by a Korean, I tried to understand and respect her. She was, after all, a separate person from me, a nineteen-year-old now, old enough to vote and make various other adult choices.

Driving to and from work, listening to the radio, I often heard her favorite songs, (from albums she had played at home). In "Stairway to Heaven" by Led Zeppelin a verse says:

"Dear Lady, can you hear the wind blow, and did you know,

"Your stairway lies on the whispering wind.

"Your head is humming and it won't go, in case you don't know,

"The piper's calling you to join him."

Of course I thought about Jesus Christ as "the piper" when I heard the song.

In another of her favorite songs, by the Moody Blues, I could identify with the hopeful words:

"Someday the world will be, in perfect harmony, a planet with one mind..."

Everybody wanted harmony in the world. My daughter had the right ideals (even if Moon, the self-ordained messiah, was off-his-rocker). I tried to be proud of her for working hard for her ideals.

"She's a missionary, with the Unification Church," I would tell my family and friends who asked. "She lives at the church center."

I would have preferred to tell people she had gone back to college, but I tried not to let that disappointment show. It was a little embarrassing though, when she came into the newspaper to sell flowers. I knew we had a rule against it, and told her, but then one of the secretaries bought some mums. Even after she left with the One World Crusade, the local Moonies came by to visit with me, and sold a few carnations in the building as they came and went.

Every time they came I would imagine my boss stomping out into the newsroom and telling them not to sell flowers--or imagine hearing him ask my daughter why she didn't get a job. But he didn't.

He was pleasant. I still worried though. I would recite my resignation speech in my head every time she came in. If one person in that newsroom had been rude to her I would have flung myself at them and chewed them out. I fully expected to have to, but I never did.

When the One World Crusade came to town, the leader of that branch of the Unification Church came to the newspaper seeking publicity. Closer to my age than the other church members I had met, he seemed like an intelligent adult, which brought a sense of reassurance to me.

After he met with the religion editor, we went for a cup of coffee and talked. He explained that he had been in the church for a good while, but it was still a relatively new movement and likely to be misunderstood. He said he was an artist by trade but sincerely believed in the Principle and wanted fervently to help young people.

I discussed some of the things that bothered me about the movement, the insistence that Moon was the messiah and the recent upsurge in candle selling. The boxes were large and obviously heavy.

"Oh, that's a fund-raising method for a special project. It won't last long," he said.

I suggested the young people needed more sleep, that getting up at 5:30 a.m. to pray, then heading out on a full day that frequently lasted until midnight did not seem responsible. They should have more restrictions on their time, so they could have more time to sleep, I said.

"My daughter needs more time to herself," I told the One World Crusade leader. "She has always been very energetic, then withdrawn to rest. She's not resting and she seems to go at fever pitch. I'm afraid she won't hold up physically."

He convincingly pooh-poohed my worries. "Youth has almost boundless energy," he said. "Don't you remember how it was?"

We both laughed at that. Everybody can remember the time of their youth, when they slept little and tried to crowd all the living they could into every day. I had fun sharing a few memories from my own youth, with this man about my age, over coffee in the lounge at the The News. We liked some of the same music. And he was from a city where I had lived with my children's father when we first got married. I attended the University there, while my husband worked in a factory. Charlie and I liked going to the big band dances there; we even won prizes for our "jitterbug" (a gymnastic swing-dance).

He said he and his wife fell in love when they were in high school, eloped against their parents' wishes, had two children, separated, then got back together after he joined the church. Before joining the church he had traveled and lived in various places for a while, living a bohemian lifestyle, seeking inspiration as a sort-of beatnik artist. He credited Moon's teachings for motivating him to reunite with his family and said that ultimately the same teachings would inspire my daughter to value her family above all things. So I should not feel that I was losing her, he said, just allowing her to grow and have a youthful adventure.

He promised to watch out for my daughter.

Northwest Florida Bound

Mama Sue came to the Center to say goodbye to me the day the One World Crusade left town. Her little red-headed, short-skirted self looked to me like she was flirting with the OWC leader, Art Shoman, like he could have just about brought her with us. I guess if the man wasn't already married, he could have changed her name. He did change mine, or at least simplified what I was called.

"Let's just call you Rose, to avoid a mix-up," Art Shoman said, once I had left my hometown, my family and friends, and most of my identity behind. He said "Arti" had been his nickname when he was younger.

"When you blush, you look like a rose anyway," Art Shoman said.

Of course, I blushed when he said that. But he was always sweet-talking the sisters, mostly in a fatherly way it seemed to me. Some thought differently. Right away he made Barbie his personal secretary. That must have been what she wanted, because before we left town, she had gone to a beauty shop and had her gorgeously long and wild white-blonde mane cut and styled so she looked thirty or forty, like Art Shoman. She started dressing like my mother, in fashionable '70s office attire, including little heels and make-up (which very few of the other sisters wore). She rode in the front passenger seat of the van Art Shoman drove on the way down to Florida. And when we got there, she was too busy with her secretarial duties to go out

250

witnessing or selling with the rest of us. Then it wasn't a week before she came crying to Beth and I, packing her things, saying she was taking a Greyhound bus home because this "preacher-man" had "made a pass" at her. With all the time Barbie spent following Art Shoman around, I had not gotten to know her. There were rumors that she had tried to seduce Art, and he had sent her home. I did not know either of them well enough to comment, but I thought we should be careful not to judge. I showed Barbie some sisterly sympathy as we said our brief goodbyes. Since Barbie had followed Beth into the movement, I was a bit worried she might try to take Beth with her. But Beth hung tight with me, with the One World Crusade, and with Art Shoman.

In North Florida I feel closer to my roots. My accent takes on its original drawl and twang, matching the locals. My manner changes too; I am somewhat less shy, a bit more sure of myself. I feel more freedom to express myself, be myself in this group where I am not overly attached to (or in love with) the leader (who is older, free spirited, and a bit detached himself). Even my approach to religion changes. There is something happening on a personal level, a different kind of closeness to God than I have known before. And the witnessing I do, teaching the One World Crusade, does takes on a higher level of emotional excitement, a sense of urgency. Believing we have the "Second Advent" of the Christ on earth with us is what sets us in motion and keeps our wheels turning, like the wheels on the white vans we ride in. Being the most authentically Southern American girl in the group, I add a note of the Bible Belt revival spirit. It is harvest time, and we are hunters and gatherers for God. "Praise the Lord" (of the Second Advent)!

Tallahassee

The Tallahassee, Florida center was a long, low concrete and stucco house in the suburbs. The center director was a quiet, compact, understated fellow who had only collected a few followers of a similar style. They sort of blended with their wallpaper while the One World Crusade took over the place, spreading our sleeping bags out in the various bedrooms, setting up a big chalkboard for teaching in the

Florida room. The German girls even took over the kitchen, rolling out homemade dumplings. But the main one who took over was Art Shoman. He had us selling flowers all over town and witnessing on the campus of Florida State University. And there he was with the loud speakers again, setting up rallies every day, making speeches, leading songs, giving lectures right on campus like some visiting professor or author. He had a way of intellectualizing and using words like "philosophy, ontology, system-of-thought, movement, subculture, phenomenon". A bit of a chameleon, Art Shoman could worm his way into any situation.

It was all fun to me. I loved Florida, the campus, the low, rolling hills of Tallahassee, the green suburbs, the water-colored sunsets, the flowers. My mother grew up in NW Florida, and I had spent my early school years in a small town north of the Gulf-coast and near the Alabama line. After we moved closer to the East-coast, my siblings and I spent our summers at our maternal grandmother's rural Florida-panhandle home. And we spent most summer Sunday mornings at the tiny, backwoods Pentecostal church where Mema was what our moderate, Methodist mother called "a holy-roller".

So I was in my element in Tallahassee in spring of 1973, humidity and all, a rose in the right soil, blooming in the sunshine. And I felt freed up by the move, unbound, loving everyone but not too close to anyone. As soon as we had left Gabe, Beth had attached herself to Richard, the second in command of the One World Crusade, a tall, handsome young Englishman with the bearing and the confident, reserved manner of royalty. Most of the brothers and sisters were jealous of their close friendship, the privileges of working partnership and casual togetherness that came so easily to them with Richard being "team captain" and Beth being his chosen assistant. But I was glad to be free, just to be in love with God, unburdened by the emotions that had plagued my relationship with Gabe.

Most of the brothers and sisters secretly dreaded selling door-to-door. Not so for me and Kimeo, the lone Japanese sister who spoke little English but made more money than anyone else on the team. I liked selling with her best, because she charged forward on her side of the street, leaving me alone until our appointed time to meet. She spoke little English, so we did not get bogged down in conversation.

I can still remember being dropped off, with Richard driving the van and Beth sitting up front, studying the map, making notes for him, acting as "copilot". There may have been a few butterflies as I grabbed my product, opened the big sliding door of the van, and jumped out. The international team, imagining ourselves to be fighting the battle of Armageddon (the biblical final conflict between good and evil) used old military words like "blitz" and "kamikaze", thrusting fists to encourage charging into a situation with an attitude of selfless service to the cause. Though I did not fear death in the suburbs of Florida's capital city, a certain amount of rejection was always in store. The mission could be nerve-wracking. But some of my favorite times were working alone, selling flowers or candles or ginseng tea door-to-door, in well-landscaped neighborhoods, singing as I walked fast or ran or skipped, light as a butterfly, spotting four-leafed clovers in the grass along the way.

Kimeo first showed me how to do this. I had never heard of "Zen" back then, and it was not a word that Kimeo ever uttered to me. I had heard "go with the flow", and Kimeo embodied that concept for me. Though she could not explain the special talent to me, I watched her work, studied how her energy stayed concentrated in-the-moment. She was positive dynamic motion, something barely touching the ground and yet somehow one with it, speaking few words of explanation yet collecting so much green that she could have been harvesting lettuce instead of money. And she had such a connection with nature, picking wildflowers and clovers along the way without stopping to daydream, just reaching out for them here and there. At the end of the day she almost always had at least one four-leafed clover. She sometimes pressed them in books, sometimes gave them away. As a child I had spent lazy, day-dreamy days searching for four-leafed clovers. Under the influence of Kimeo, I developed an uncanny ability to find them at a glance, barely stopping to reach down and pick the magical symbols of good luck. Kimeo had taught me, through her example, a different kind of awareness. The Divine Principle taught us about "spiritual senses, corresponding to physical senses". Something about the way Kimeo moved, the way she worked, taught me to watch and listen to everything along my path. The four-leafed clovers called out to me, from the thick mats of St. Augustine grass, over-watered by suburban sprinkler systems and summer rain. For some reason, they seemed to want my attention, my recognition. I took them as gifts from

God, who was my new playmate. Pressing the delicate green leaves carefully between select pieces of literature I carried, I saved them to glue to cards and letters later.

I was convinced it was God who gave me the four-leafed clovers. I had never heard of the Tao or Zen Buddhism, and Kimeo never explained whatever religion or philosophy she had grown up with to me. But I learned about the flow of positive energy that came with a heart-centered focus, with unhesitant movement, with fearless faith, with joy. There was love in that flow, and I found it. I gave it while I was taking it. There was power too. I could have taken anything; I just chose to focus on the clovers. I took money also, for whatever I was selling. People opened their hearts and their wallets to my smiling face. I gave the money to Art Shoman. And sometimes I took people. I gave them to Art Shoman also, to Rev. Moon, to the Unification Church. I intended to give them to God. Now I'm not so sure about some of what I did with people back then, but then I felt sure. Everything I did with the One World Crusade felt as right as picking those four-leafed clovers.

I learned how to get in the flow and stay in it for a while, like riding a wave but longer. I did it by staying positive whether someone bought my product or slammed their door in my face. I had God with me; my mood was not dependent on anyone else's reaction to me. My energy was flowing in a predominantly "vertical" current (between God and I), which made the "horizontal" connections I made with others flow more easily. I was learning to put Divine Principle concepts into practical use. And I was happy. There was always a song in my heart; some I had learned from the group, some popular songs, some I made up myself.

"Don't you want God to be a part of you, to live at the heart of you?" was a song I made up and sang to myself, to imagined others, and to God, as I skipped along.

Pop Art

Art Shoman designed a psychedelic poster, announcing his lectures on "the spirit world and psychic phenomenon", and had us put them up all over campus. He used one of the classrooms to present the first chapter of the Divine Principle, emphasizing the part about the spirit world. The heavenly world beyond was described as being connected with Earth (with corresponding "spiritual senses") but more like the original Garden of Eden, vibrating at a "higher frequency". Students were told that they could access that finer realm while on Earth, in their physical bodies, through relationships with the creator (described as "Source Energy" with the heart and love of "True Parents"). Yin-yangs were drawn on the board, while God was described as positive and negative energy, male and female. The yin-yang symbol was emerging in popularity in the West, especially in the silver jewelry found in "head-shops" (boutiques featuring hippy fashions, drug paraphernalia, psychedelic art, and avant-garde musical recordings) frequented by the young. Few, however, had actually studied oriental philosophy (especially in the South, the "Bible Belt").

We brought students who wanted to hear the rest of the lecture series back to the Center for dinner. Some of the students were high (or hung-over from highs they were trying not to come down from, trying to extend with their own mind-states). The pop-art poster that had attracted them to the campus lecture had reminded them of something they had seen on "acid" (LSD) or "'shrooms" (psilocybin mushrooms commonly found in cow manure, prevalent in pastures in rural NW Florida, just outside Tallahassee). Maybe Art Shoman had tripped, or maybe he had been inspired by popular pop-artists like Peter Max (who depicted a dreamy version of Earth, glowing with brightly-colored beings living in harmony with nature). During dinner we talked one-on-one with new students, often taking conversations to cosmic levels. Having a relationship with God was sometimes depicted as being as far-out as an endless drug trip, a "high" conveyed by the One World Crusade's youthful energy, warm-hearted acceptance of others, and open-faced smiles.

After dinner Art gave a condensed version (more like a high-energy sermon that started out appealing to the intellect and ended up with an emotionally-charged bang). Art Shoman was animated, moving his hands constantly as his voice rose and fell and rose again, like the pied piper's flute, guiding the students through the Principle of Creation, the Fall, the Mission of Jesus, History as Restoration, and today as the dawning of a New Age being ushered in by a new Messiah. It was a real mind-blower, with a lot of singing at the end, like some

Pentecostal revival meeting that opened up people's hearts and got them crying (most were mentally and emotionally exhausted by the end anyway).

Rose could relate to this style, having been subjected to many Baptist and Pentecostal revival meetings. After Art Shoman's presentations, she personally singled people out, helping some of the potential converts "pray through", advising them to accept the Lord of the Second Advent into their hearts, as their personal savior. When someone expressed conflict, because of a loyalty to Jesus, Rose told them about her vision of the sun and the cross, rising in oneness. It was a lot to take in, but the Spirit was there. Rose knew how to access the Holy Spirit and convey it, from the heart.

Rose could feel the fire, and she helped others to feel it, especially a young man named Danny Hart. He had driven all the way from California in three days, high on speed and caffeine and the restless energy of his youth. Trying to come down and relax, once he had reached his destination, Danny had stopped at Florida State to look for some pot. He saw our psychedelic poster plastered here and there. The art reminded him of an acid trip. Thinking the lecture might be a good place to connect with people who were getting high, Danny went. Then he followed Art Shoman back to the Center for a free meal, dragging his girlfriend Sabrina (who wore all black and claimed she was a witch). The only thing they offered him besides food was ginseng tea. Some of the sisters looked good to Danny, and he was getting sick of his girlfriend. Rose was especially hot, he thought, in more ways than one. She was on fire for the Lord. Danny had been raised Lutheran, up near Germantown in Maryland. He didn't know much about Southern religious ways, but he liked the spiritual high so far. Plus he liked the ginseng tea. He had been crashing, and he seemed to be getting his energy back. He still wanted some pot, but he was sufficiently distracted from that mission at the moment (especially since Rose had focused her holy-rolling, glowing attention on him).

"I drove day and night for three days, just to get to Florida," Danny told Rose, his blue eyes drooping at the lids.

"I think there was another reason," Rose said, with her heart in her throat. "I think you are one of the *chosen ones*."

Danny not only heard but also felt what she said. He had been numb for a while, and it was refreshing to feel something. Maybe it was God that was choosing him, or maybe it was this beautiful girl. Either way, it felt like irresistibly powerful love.

"Well, then I don't have any choice do I," he said, intending to be serious but feeling foolish as something about Rose's eyes filled him with a warm glow. Looking at her, he could not hold back a smile that came naturally to his wide mouth and full, pink lips.

There was a persistently sneaky gleam in Danny's lazy, blue, bedroom eyes, dazed and glazed over, not clear-eyed like the usual converts. Rose figured he would need a spiritual house-cleaning, but she was up for the job (if he should decide to stay with the group, which he did). Danny had been sleeping in his Toyota Supra. So a floor to stretch out on, under a ceiling fan that whirred all night, seemed a luxury.

The sisters tried to make Danny's girlfriend Sabrina comfortable, giving up bedding to make a pallet for her. Rose stayed up late listening to the newcomer's occult ramblings, trying to steer Sabrina's thoughts from darkness into light. Eventually their conversation took on a more personal tone, with Sabrina ranting nervously about her boyfriend's recent loss of interest in her sexually. Rose tried talking with her about "the Fall", explaining that, according to the Divine Principle, God had not meant for spiritually immature people to be in sexual relationships. Rose found it difficult, however, to hold Sabrina's attention long enough to make a point. She had noticed earlier, when the lights were on, that Sabrina could not tolerate eye contact for any length of time. Rose usually did not bother witnessing to anyone for long when that was the case, but Art Shoman had asked her to take Sabrina under her wing. Finally Rose felt drained by the effort and went to sleep. Sabrina tip-toed through the house until she found Danny and tried to sleep with him. When he rejected her, she tried snuggling up next to one of the other brothers. Next day, when Art Shoman got word of this, he put Sabrina on a Greyhound bus with a one-way ticket home, cordially inviting her to visit the Washington, D.C. center when she got there. Sabrina was flattered when Art Shoman explained that he felt the church's national headquarters would be a more suitable situation for a classy young lady like herself.

Danny could not have cared less; in fact he was relieved about Sabrina's departure. He had met her at Johns Hopkins University in

Baltimore, where neither of them were doing anything but partying away their freshman year. Since he had a car, they had impulsively decided one day to see the U.S.A. Danny had gotten pretty good at turning reefer with the spending cash his businessman father sent him. So they got by, but the relationship had gotten old fast. Sabrina's looks were a turn-on, however her mouth was a turn-off. And it got worse when he showed an interest in other chicks, which had been inevitable in California (and no less inevitable in Florida).

The German girls went goofy over Danny from day one. He was, after all, a big blonde of German descent. With so many shaggy young men in the world at that time, the sisters were not shocked by the fact that Danny's nearly shoulder-length hair was matted in back, (like he had not put a comb through it in months).

" 'es goot," the German sisters said of him, shaking their heads in the affirmative when Rose asked what they thought of the new brother.

Rose would not have chosen the word "good" to describe Danny, but there was something about him that she liked. He had a natural, unselfconscious self-confidence. Danny did not hold back; he bubbled over with energy, injecting every activity with a contagious enthusiasm. He could be overbearing though. The brothers showed some signs of feeling threatened by Danny, although they were generally friendly with him. There were mixed reactions to Danny. He had an obnoxious but infectious laugh. His large bones did not fold comfortably to sit on the floor, oriental style. He dragged his big shoes noisily when he walked. He played popular, secular songs on his guitar, accompanying himself in a loud voice that, besides being out-of-place (with some of the sexier, profane, rebellious lyrics), was often off-key as well. But some popular songs of that time were inspirational (practically hymns). Danny got everybody singing, laughing, clowning around. With a serious mission on the shoulders of such young people, the relief was needed.

Art Shoman identified with Danny's exuberance, his fun side, and his stubborn, very American independence. However, Art disliked the young man's overbearing physicality and manner (or lack of manners). Perhaps Art Shoman, who was a man of smallish feet and barely medium build, felt somewhat threatened by Danny. But, no doubt, Danny could be of use to him, an asset to the team. Though he was clearly not Art Shoman's cup of tea, he entrusted his prized Rose with the assignment of being a "spiritual mother" to Danny.

"The new brother sticks out like a sore thumb," Art Shoman said quietly to Rose, conspiratorially, after prayer meeting one morning. Everyone else had left the prayer room. Art Shoman had kept her to discuss Danny. His expression was sour. "Did you see how his big feet were sticking out in the middle of the circle? I have tried talking to him; he does not listen to me. But you; you are such a flower," the man said, changing his expression, smiling as he looked into Rose's eyes. "You are a sweet, southern lady. Let's see if you can make a gentleman out of him for Heavenly Father. If anybody can do it, you can" he said, laughing a bit.

Art Shoman liked the newcomer better after the first evening Danny went selling. Flowers were wilting too fast in the Florida sun, and roasted peanuts in brown paper bags were the new commodity. Art had loaded Danny's trunk with the fragrant packages and sent he and Rose off with one of the British brothers (a well-mannered chap). Art had taken Rose aside first and spoken with her.

"Make sure you go to every door with Danny; don't let him go alone. And tell him not to spit in people's yards. Have you seen him doing that?" Art Shoman made the sour expression again. "Disgusting habit, spitting. I tried to speak with Danny about it, but he is as stubborn as a mule."

The English brother took the other side of the street. Danny shuffled his feet loudly along the sidewalks, spitting casually in nearly every yard. Rose could not bring herself to do anything more than ask if he had a cold.

"Huh? Na; I'm fine," he said, oblivious to why she might be asking that, spitting again soon after, barely conscious of a habit he had taken up in early adolescence when he noticed an older cousin spitting and thought it made him look tough.

Danny was not tough on the inside; he was a basically a big baby, a mama's boy. Little Dapper Dan had grown up in Frederick, Maryland where his father had a fine shop selling expensive suits, sometimes to politicians who came from nearby Washington, D.C. Danny's school-teacher mother had kept him squeaky clean, well-dressed, groomed, churched, given piano and guitar lessons. His country cousins back home had seen him in bow ties and polished shoes. So he'd had to work hard at trying to be tough like them. Growing up near the Potomac River, Danny had out-fished, out-hunted, out-gambled the best of his country cousins (and drank them under the table too).

More recently he had worked hard in the gym at Johns Hopkins University in Baltimore, building up his body. Standing behind him, as he charged from door-to-door walking so fast she could barely keep up with him, Rose could not help looking at his backside. He had not yet cut his hair, but someone must have at least given him a comb, as the slightly-wavy blonde locks fell nicely over the back of his neck. He must have also been told that he could not wear jeans out selling or witnessing, but his navy blue corduroys were skin-tight. And his shirt was a western cut "body-shirt", cornflower blue to match his eyes, with navy blue piping that accented his shape. (" 'es goot," the German sisters had said).

"Our church is helping kids get off drugs," Danny said, loudly and convincingly, at door after door. (That was certainly true of him.)

We went back to Danny's car to refill our box at the end of every block in the subdivision. When we ran out, we crossed the road and helped the English chap finish selling his. I say "we", but it was mostly Danny. I just stood beside him and smiled sweetly, shaking my head in agreement when he said the church got kids off drugs.

Art Shoman was so thrilled with the cash we brought back that he made a big deal about Danny being the top seller, giving him a robust pat on the back and leading the group in cheers and applause.

Needless to say, Art Shoman was convinced he had made a wise move, pairing his Rose up with the new brother. Not that he meant for us to be a couple, in the fallen sense. He trusted me to know better and to keep Danny on the straight and narrow path as well. Although, no doubt, Danny would be looking for every chance to stray; Art Shoman could see that in his eyes. He could also see the dollar signs. The kid was money, a keeper for sure. And Art Shoman did not keep every kid who tried to jump aboard the One World Crusade vans.

Rose, however, had mixed feelings about Danny, until the night she was assigned to cook dinner for everyone. She preferred Kimeo as a selling partner and Beth as a witnessing partner. Danny was too much responsibility; he required guidance. And he did not listen very well. On this occasion, however, the whole team went out selling and left her with a mountain of hamburger meat, fresh vegetables, seasonings, pasta, French bread, and Danny. Art Shoman had caught Danny alone earlier that day, sitting in his car and smoking a joint. He had confiscated Danny's pot and temporarily suspended him from contact with the public, having realized that Danny needed a deeper understanding of the Divine Principles before he represented the Unification Church and its founder. The German sisters who usually did the cooking were sent out selling that evening. And Rose was left behind to get dinner ready for everyone. Rose had never been in charge of cooking for this group before. The kitchen was unfamiliar, and she was a nervous wreck until Danny took over. He charged into the kitchen, with his big, noisy feet and muscular frame, and started throwing food around like it was a game, a sporting event. That perpetual grin on his face soon eclipsed her worried expression. He tossed a big onion at Rose and told her to cut it up, then threw some bell peppers her way. He started banging huge pots and pans around. Soon he had something cooking that was starting to smell like sauce, and she was washing and cutting up piles of fresh of vegetables for a huge summer salad. By the time they had cooked the pasta and were pulling the garlic bread out of the oven, Rose relaxed enough to realize that, in spite of the fact that she was dripping sweat, she was also having fun. And she might be falling in love. She even felt a little jealous when the group got back and the German sisters came in the kitchen to fuss over Danny and his sauce. Later she might have made Danny a little jealous, sitting next to the handsome Italian brother who critiqued the sauce while Rose listened indulgently (and ate hungrily).

There were, undoubtedly, undercurrents of energy and emotion that flowed between various members of the group, those currents between Rose and Danny being among the strongest. There was little alone-time, however, for individuals or couples. So the feelings were usually repressed, expressed only as appropriate, as allowed, within the various rituals of a well-structured and busy routine. Sometimes when they were singing in circle formation, Rose and Danny looked at each other, their eyes shining with love for the God they were singing to. Sometimes they gave, and took, a little of that love, for each other. Rose knew in her gut that it wasn't quite right, when Danny's blue eyes narrowed into a seductive stare. Then she would look away. Sometimes, however, when they were in a prayer circle, Danny opposite to her so that Rose's eyes naturally met his when their bowed heads rose, their eyes shining clear and bright from prayer, she glimpsed a future world, a different life, blue skies and oceans and maybe even the eyes of her children to come.

Heading North

The One World Crusade left Tallahassee after a few weeks, heading Northeast. First stop was Atlanta, where the center director was a hospitable southern gentleman, tiny of stature for a man but big-hearted, with a large, old rented house in a historical district and a church family of a half-dozen or so. His last name was Rose; so we had something in common from the beginning and enjoyed conversing, sitting on the big front porch together for a long time after dinner one evening. Oddly, we had another thing in common besides the name; we had both seen the light, the blue light. When we were talking in the dim light of evening, I saw the little flash of blue near his head and told him about it. He was one of the first people I ever told about the blue light, and I was surprised when Mr. Rose said he had often experienced the same phenomenon. I must have "seen" the tiny flash of flame-blue hundreds of times since, with no explanation and a repeated "hunch" that it has a spiritual source. (My daughter, now grown, also says she occasionally sees the blue light).

Art Shoman took over in the Atlanta center, as usual. The quiet, rather meek group who lived in the Center there seemed to enjoy being supercharged by the One World Crusade, with our rousing, somewhat militaristic style. When we got in a circle and sang "Tongil", the Korean song of Unity, we were as likely to thrust our fists as we were to lock arms and sway. I tried not to look at Danny while I sang, glancing instead at my new friends in the Atlanta center, as my grey-green eyes lit up with something as unexplainable as the blue light.

Back on the road, we stopped briefly to sell and witness in beautiful, old Southern coastal towns like Savannah and Charleston, with their charming architecture and humid Atlantic breezes. We stayed overnight in Myrtle Beach, at the vacation home of the parents of one of our One World Crusade brothers, who cooked "spoon bread" from his mother's recipe. Art Shoman gave us a day off, and we all got sunburned at the beach. I was red from embarrassment before my lily-white skin turned red, as Art Shoman seemed to be gawking at me in my two-piece suit with teardrop-shaped peek-a-boo holes on either hip. I had bought it for my high school club's senior trip to Panama City Beach. The elastic was worn sufficiently to make it droop below my navel. After a while on the beach, I realized that the only way to stop Art Shoman from staring at me was to close the distance between us, engaging him in conversation so that he had to look at my eyes instead of my brightly-flowered bathing suit, which both amused and attracted him. When I remember talking to him up close like that, nearly naked, all I can think of is how big his nose looked and how hard it was for him to keep a straight face no matter how serious I happened to be about whatever I was saying. He would burst out laughing over things I said, even when I was not trying to be funny, just making observations about people and nature and what I thought God might think. I was trying very hard not to be self-conscious that day, and while everyone else swam and played Frisbee, moving faster than I could afford to move with so little elastic holding up my bottoms, I talked to Art Shoman and the life guard. At the end of the day my skin was red and I was in terrible pain, but I knew I was adored by Art Shoman, a man I had previously kept my distance from, a man who would have a great deal of control over my life for at least another year.

During the One World Crusade's trek North, I brought a "spiritual child" into the church while we were witnessing in a military-base town in one of the Carolinas. Danny and I were talking to random people on the street, and a tall but rather boyish looking soldier with wide-open, clear eyes showed an interest. I locked eyes with him and spoke to him from my heart, sharing my love for God and belief in our church's teaching and mission. On leave at the time, he began choosing to hang out with our group instead of going to the bars with his buddies. I thought that was a good choice, having walked through a maze of those bars myself, with my bucket full of flowers wilting from smoke and alcohol fumes (my spirit wilting with despair at the decadence and degradation). The young soldier (having already served overseas during the Viet Nam war, which was about to end) would get involved with our church to such an extent that he left the military as soon as he could without repercussions. I would cross paths with him toward the end of my journey with the church, when he was no longer a soldier but a member of the Mobile Fundraising Team for our national church headquarters. Later he would go to seminary. Eventually he would leave the church and work in law-enforcement, marry for life (and become a proud father and grandfather). Since I had witnessed to him, he considered me his "spiritual mother" and never forgot my name. Reaching out to me on social media (around the time of his retirement from civil service) the veteran credited me for having helped him choose a better path than some of his buddies had taken (as they had struggled to transition from military to civilian life, during an era of social unrest).

Traveling up the East Coast, the One World Crusade stopped in Maryland. We visited Danny's family home, on our way to a gathering at the church headquarters in Washington, D.C. Danny's parents were so glad to see him that they didn't seem to mind his rather large, unusual group of "friends". They welcomed us into their home, where Danny quickly took the brothers downstairs to play pool. Art Shoman sat in the spacious living room with Danny's father, mostly agreeing with the man-of-the-house, a successful businessman who was an outspoken political conservative. With Rev. Moon being South Korean and anti-communist, cold war politics was not a difficult subject, even for a not-so conservative character like Art Shoman.

I hung out in the kitchen with Danny's mom, along with most of my church sisters. Danny had introduced me to his mother as his "special friend". I talked with her while she wiped her stove, a smooth-top model (decades before glass stoves were popularized). It was white, like her blue-flowered Corning-ware pots and pans. She wore a blue-flowered apron too. I had not seen anyone quite so "Ozzie and Harriet", so "Leave it to Beaver", since childhood. If her kitchen had not been so overwhelmingly decorated in blue, I would have thought I was seeing in black-and-white. Had she been in this kitchen since the 1950s? Danny's mom was not like my own liberated mother, who would have been in the living room talking politics with the men (though she might have served them coffee with cake she'd cooked the previous Sunday). At that moment, probably homesick and in love with her son in spite of myself, I felt like I had come face-to-face with the old-fashioned "American dream" machine, a woman apparently contented in her role as a housewife.

Oddly enough, with my mother being ahead of her time, I could not rebel by admiring the liberated, working woman. Whether or not I was aware of it, on some level, I was idealizing the domestic goddess.

Soon we were on our way, Danny and I and the rest of us, pit-stopping in Washington, D.C. We were only there long enough for Art Shoman to be trumped by the national church president, Mr. Nolan, who happily took his pick of our group (including both of the British brothers, the French sister, the brother from Italy, the African-American brother from UC Berkley, and the young Southern gentleman whose parents had a house in Myrtle Beach. We got to keep everyone else American, along with Kimeo, and the German sisters (the tall, big-boned sour-dour Olga and the short, fat and friendly Helga). Art Shoman took what remained of his branch of the One World Crusade to the Detroit, Michigan center, where his wife and kids lived in a big, old brick house with a colorful (in more ways than one, since Detroit was predominantly black) cast of characters who made up "the Detroit Family".

It would be a new adventure, one that Sun M. Moon would enter into (in the flesh).

Rev. Sun Myung Moon and his wife, Hak Ja Han Moon

Rev. Moon speaks at Belvedere Estate (his home in the U.S.) and at Madison Square Garden, N.Y. 1974.

BOOK II

Become the Moon

Part I

The Family

Heavenly Father...

i want to walk the road that travels to the fields
of your mind...
Long & dusty...the road may be
And I may find fields that have been parched
by the burning fire of Your Heart...
misused and alone...barren

But I will not come unto You
with a saddened heart & feet that are weary...
i will come dancing like a gentle brook
that is clear & cool...
gushing through the dusty furrows & stirring up soil...
uncovering new life...
seeds that have been buried deep in the fields of Your Mind
since the day when Your dream was young
The seeds can open up now...
breaking through the walls of fear that held them in...
They did not know
if their opening would find
Warm sunshine kisses of Life
or the frozen darkness of death...

Do not fear, my Father...
Your dreams can blossom forth now...
with vibrant color...
I will kiss them each morning
that they may unfold into the newborn day.
i will protect their
precious petals from all pain
by surrounding them with
the strength of your Love
& the rainbow radiance of
Your Joy...

A.R.T. '73

"Home Away from Home"

As spring of 1973 saw summer coming, in a great, far-northern American city, a white One World Crusade van, with me (Arti Rose Riddle) inside, drove up to an old two-story red brick house so familiar looking that if had been on a hill, and in a better neighborhood, one might have mistaken it for the Unification Church Center I had left, earlier that spring, in the South. Art Shoman, the charismatic thirty-something leader of the young crusaders (who were mostly in our late teens and early twenties) said the back door of the house would be open. As we started unloading our things, a woman came out of the screened-in back porch to greet us. She was a motherly-looking brunette, a homely housewife type, a bit overstuffed, frumpily dressed, but friendly and welcoming to most who filed through her door. As I approached however, I saw something change in her face, something suddenly contrasting with the open arms and smiling mouth. It was the expression out of the eyes that took me aback. In fact, it was the fact that she appeared taken-aback that took me aback. Wide-open for any motherly friendliness I might be about to receive, I had the distinct impression, instead, that her big, brown eyes were somehow shocked at the sight of me. All of her body language and energetic aura said that she was immediately and suddenly defensive toward me, maybe threatened, especially as her husband drew near. Since her reaction happened before she had time to think about it, she consciously corrected herself, softening soon enough to play her role and welcome me in a way that looked okay (but did not feel right to me).

Remembering this much later I realize that, especially when my face was flushed, I was a sometimes-stunning beauty in my youth. Any natural woman would have felt bewildered to have her husband bring home such a creature (though I was barely more than a child). I also realized in time (after later seeing pictures of Audra as a teen, when she and Art first fell in love) that she had been similarly striking, with her glowing fair skin framed by a thick mane of long, dark hair that had flowed in waves down her tall and slender body.

At the moment I met the middle-aged looking, motherly (but seemingly cold) Audra, I was un-groomed and felt grubby from the journey. I was unaware of my beauty but felt suddenly aware of my loneliness. The woman of the house I was moving into not only appeared to have mixed feelings about taking me in; she also looked like she had seen a ghost. Art Shoman both helped and hurt the situation, introducing me proudly as "our Rose" while he mixed the two gestures of offering his wife a friendly peck on the cheek while reaching his hand in my direction to unburden me of the suitcase I had been carrying. I lowered my head as I said a shy "Hi" to Audra and "thanks" to Art, careful to keep the corners of my mouth turned up as I removed my black coolie slippers, leaving them among dozens of other shoes on the back porch.

Once inside, I wanted to hide. Two large rooms, connected in the middle and taking up most of the second floor, belonged to the sisters. The room to the right of the stairs had been reserved for the One World Crusade girls. I made myself at home there, finding a corner for my things, and settled into my sleeping bag. Art Shoman had already told us we could have the next morning "off". Pretending sleep whenever anyone tried to beckon the sisters downstairs, I managed to avoid the broader situation until well into the next day. Then, out-of-sync, I embarrassed myself by making an entrance and having to be introduced into a situation where most had already made themselves familiar.

It was Sunday, and only "the Family" and the new One World Crusade residents were present at the brick house, no guests. Arti Rose felt like a guest, however. The group was having a "free day" to recuperate from the trip and get adjusted. Before coming downstairs late Sunday morning, the Rose of the One World Crusade probably spent too much time grooming herself, then felt more self-conscious for wearing a dress she had never worn before. She had bought it at a thrift store back home, on Southside, near the Center and the lab where she and Beth were working. They had been looking for some appropriate, ladylike clothes, and the vintage dress caught Arti Rose's eye. It was cut-to-fit, polished cotton, lavender and lace, high-necked, long-sleeved and hemmed just below the knee, like something from the 1950s or early '60s (reminiscent of Audrey Hepburn, in a black-and-white film). Arti Rose put her long, dark hair up in a bun. Then she went downstairs, carefully, moving more slowly than usual because the fitted cut of the dress left little room for freedom of movement and made her feel stiff. She walked into the large family room where a dozen or so young people were gathered casually (most wearing the t-shirts and jeans that they were only allowed to wear on their days off). They were lounging around an old baby grand piano that looked like it had seen better days and might have come with the house. The only other significant piece of furniture in the room was the large blackboard standing pedantically between the front windows. Otherwise, there were folding chairs, mostly folded, lining one wall. Arti Rose was thinking of getting one for herself, hoping no one would notice her before she got a chance to sit down. The black brother, who had just started to play something, stopped, the room silent as he looked up at her, his eyes widening at the sight of the slender but curvaceous figure before him.

"You must be Rose," he said.

She blushed, smiling and nodding in the affirmative at the young man who had spoken to her.

"You're shy?" he said quizzically, looking surprised that such a flower would hang its head. "Don't be shy. I'm Jermain."

"Nice meeting you. Y'all don't stop the music, please," Rose said, looking around at the group, still blushing, folding her hands in front of her as her narrow, rounded shoulders curled forward. "Sounds good!" she said sincerely, hoping to take the focus off herself, though all eyes were on her as she stood at the outer fringes of the gathering.

"Thanks. We're all into the music here. I used to be a stand-in for a group called *the Spinners,*" Jermain said proudly.

"Cool," Rose said, recognizing the name and easily imagining Jermain dancing in-sync while singing harmony with several other smartly dressed black guys.

"And Dawna here has quite a voice," Jermain said, turning his head toward a young African-American girl, around 16. Dawna's "Afro" (a very popular hairdo at the time) made a soft mane, like a richly hued halo around her warm brown face. Her beautiful white teeth glistened in a smile that emanated from her big brown eyes as well.

"Was that you I heard? You can really hit the high notes like that? I thought you were going to crack a window," Rose said, looking at the little girl with the big voice.

Dawna laughed. "That was probably me," she said. "But I'm not the only one who can sing around here. Audra is like an opera singer, but most of us are more Mo-town."

273

Audra was not in the room at the time, neither was Art Shoman. Arti Rose was relieved about that, as she would have felt even more like an embarrassed school kid, with a teacher (and the principal) in the room.

"We try to be true to the old Mo-town tradition," a thirty-something, brownish but Caucasian, hippy-looking woman said. "I'm Jade. And, by the way, don't think for a second that Jermain's nickname might be Jerry. It's 'Main'," she said, turning attention back to the singer.

"That's right; 'cause I'm the main-man in the band, Sister," Jermain joked, breaking out in a little peacock strut for a few steps (long enough to get a laugh, and some phrases of agreement chiming in like harmony with his brotherly bragging.

Arti Rose smiled at Jermain, but her attention was mostly still on Jade (who was almost an old-rose but seemed enviably more relaxed and comfortable with herself than our new-girl-in-town). She felt both better and worse, meeting Jade. Jade was dressed in loose, well-covering but sensually comfortable, colorful, stylish clothes, and her black hair fell around her face and hung down her back. She even wore some make-up and big, hoop earrings, which gave her the look of a gypsy. Though she was well into her thirties, and somewhat coarse compared to the more freshly blooming Rose, Jade's comfort in her own skin gave her an earthy, more subtle but grounded glow.

As the blushing Rose demurred at the edge of the group of a dozen or so, Jade urged her in, patting the seat of a fold-out chair next to her. Rose quickly excused her way through the parting sea of bodies, taking the seat with a sigh of relief. Jade, feeling a rush of motherly warmth toward the shy girl, put an arm around Rose. "You are so cute," Jade said, giving her a little squeeze, then letting go and refocusing on the "Main-man" in the room, watching as the piano player danced his dark fingers up and down the white keys, like jazz, like he was trying to decide what to play next but delighted to be improvising in the meantime.

Just then Danny came downstairs with his guitar and his songbook, "Hits of the '70s".

"If we could just get this guy to sing on-key," Jermain said as Danny approached.

274

They all laughed, including Danny (who laughed the loudest).

"If everybody sings along, hopefully you all will drown me out," Danny said with a grin and a chuckle, thumbing through his '70s songbook, starting to plunk at his guitar again. "Here's one of John Denver's tunes everybody will recognize. I changed the words, but hopefully I'll at least get some help with the chorus by the second or third time around."

"Almost Heaven
In the family;
Brothers, Sisters
Lovin' everybody.
Glad we're all here,
Where we all belong,
Getting close to Master;
He's going to take us home.

It's a long hard road,
To the place we belong,
Up in heaven
With the Father,
Master's going to lead us home.

Everyday we're
Getting closer;
Master's heart is aching,
Wants to drive us faster.
Not much time left,
Satan soon will yield;
Just one way to beat him,
Fighting in the field.

It's a long hard road
To the place we belong
Up in heaven, with the Father,
Master's going to lead us home.

God's voice is there
Every day as He calls us,
Principle reminds us
That there's one truth,
Just one way.
And when we hear it spoken
How we wish mankind had followed yesterday...
Yesterday.

It's a long hard road
To the place we belong,
Up in Heaven
With the Father,
Master's going to lead us home."

With Danny's energetic presence taking center stage, Rose relaxed and joined in. The group spent the afternoon singing around the piano and guitar, expressing their hearts in creative song, becoming more and more at ease with one another. By dinner time they were friends and family, brothers and sisters in God, praying together, then sharing a meal. When they went to the dining room, arranged like a cafeteria with lots of family-sized tables, Rose sat next to Jade. While eating, they told of where they came from, how they had discovered and joined the Family.

"Art is my spiritual father," Jade said. "He witnessed to me in a bar; I was a prostitute," she said easily and freely between bites, almost bragging, smiling a bit, laughing at the irony of her life.

"Really? Wow," Rose said, without judgment, without turning away even slightly. When she did turn her open, clear-eyed face away to look at her food and take a bite of rice with chicken and vegetables, taking time to mix in a little kimche from the side of her plate, Rose almost let herself wonder what Art Shoman had been doing in a bar, talking to an attractive prostitute who looked like a gypsy. Before the thought could form itself, Jade spoke casually between bites.

"He and Audra weren't together at the time. They were married but separated. She had joined the Family. He had joined but left for a while. He was struggling when I met him, but that just made it all easier to listen to. He wasn't preaching, you know. I couldn't have stomached a preacher, much less one on a bar stool. Ha!" she laughed a little, again at the irony. "Anyway, it was all he could talk about. The movement. The Divine Principle. Audra and their kids. The whole crazy, crucial question of whether Father was the messiah, the Second Coming. And Art wasn't religious in the first place. He was bohemian, an artist type," she said. "I found it all very interesting. Anyway we became friends. I could hardly wait to meet his family, which meant I also met The Family. And here I am," Jade said, putting her hands up, opening them out so she jangled her big, hoop earrings and nearly hit Dawna (who was on the other side of her but just giggled a bit, her big, white teeth glowing when she smiled).

Everyone worked together cleaning up after dinner, then settled into sleeping bags upstairs, mostly reading or writing letters (Rose wrote in her journal) until lights were out, then whispering a little. Rose had a hard time falling asleep after the excitement of her first full day at a new Center. But when she finally drifted off, the sleep was deep and satisfying. She was at home in this house, with her new Family.

Weekdays usually involved putting on street vendor's badges and selling inexpensive products (like candles or flowers, candy or peanuts) and/or "witnessing" (handing out literature and talking to people about the Unification "movement", which Art Shoman preferred to call the organization), often on college campuses, sometimes at cultural events, like festivals. The group grew naturally, with so many enthusiastic young people recruiting every day. It was as easy as making new friends, as natural as falling in love.

They were a big, extended family, living in a rambling, old, rented house. The boys slept in the attic. The Shoman family, which included an elementary school-aged boy and a middle-school aged girl, used two of the four bedrooms, on the back side of the second floor (while the "sisters" used the two adjoining bedrooms that faced the street). Remarkably, they all shared two bathrooms (with the Shoman family allowed to leave their personal things in the one nearest their rooms, while the "youth missionaries" carried personal grooming items in and out). They all ate meals together in a big dining-room with lots of various-sized fold-out tables arranged restaurant-style (and sometimes put together to create one long table, for special occasions when everyone would squeeze around it, elbow-to-elbow). It was quite cozy until "Rev. Moon" came to America and started "mobilizing" church members for his various "campaigns"; then everything changed.

But let us dwell awhile, at the big, old, brick house.

Food Rose Remembers

It was my second morning at the Center, a Monday. I had heard from some of the sisters that we had no specific plans for the day, as yet. Some of them were getting laundry together. I came downstairs and found Art Shoman and a few One World Crusaders gathered casually in the breakfast nook/office area off the back porch. The room smelled of coffee spiced with cinnamon (from Art Shoman's habit, I would later learn, of shaking cinnamon over used coffee grounds when he made a second pot). Art was sitting at one of several card tables with folding chairs, glancing through a newspaper and talking with British "team leader" Richard Williams about plans for the week. The younger Richard had pen and paper and a serious look on his face. Art looked up and smiled at me with a kind of goofy smile that made his nose look even bigger than usual.

"There's our Rose," Art said.

"Good morning," I said, a bit shyly, glancing at the handsome Richard, pausing like I expected instructions or orders.

"Relax. Have a bagel," Art said. "They're over by the coffee pot."

Being from biscuit country (before bagels had achieved a more widespread popularity), I had never eaten a bagel, much less a bagel with cream cheese and grape jelly. I found it challenging to keep the grape jelly from sliding off the cream cheese, but the struggle was worth it. One of Art's favorite foods, the bagels were a standard on mornings when Helga (the German sister that Audra Shoman chose, early on, to help in the kitchen) did not cook.

Most mornings the One World Crusade was out the door and on the streets so early that we barely noticed what we grabbed to eat on our way to the white vans out back where we gathered to pray before being dropped off for whatever mission we might be assigned to for the day. When we had the occasional, more leisurely day, around the Center, I sometimes visited the kitchen for the treat at odd times, chatting with Helga. She was sweet as grape jelly, plain and doughy and round as a bagel, fat as cream cheese. I envied her for having been picked as an assistant to Audra (as it was difficult to feel at home, to be a real member of the household that clearly, basically belonged to the "blessed couple" and their children). If Audra was in the kitchen, when I went looking for my favorite treat, I would act as though I had just come to visit, until Audra offered something.

"There's a bowl of fresh fruit on the dining room table," Audra would say, sending me on my way.

We were all assigned kitchen duty on occasion, in teams, with the assignments posted on a bulletin board, in the office area of a little side-room with a big window (probably originally built to be a breakfast-room). However, I sometimes helped Helga with the dishes and such, randomly. (Now I realize she was a bit envious of me for getting out, witnessing, bringing "spiritual children" as we called new students of the Divine Principles). She was especially interested in hearing about my adventures and problems with Danny (who was considered my "spiritual child").

Danny liked Helga too, and he would often show up in the kitchen (though he preferred strawberry jam). I couldn't help thinking Helga reminded me of a younger version of Danny's mother (a round-faced, ample-breasted lady of German descent who had been in her kitchen when the One World Crusade had stopped by their home in Maryland, on our way north).

Though Helga looked the part of a cook, I don't believe she had a chef's command of ingredients. Audra did the grocery shopping and created the menus and the recipes. The meals were the standard Asian-oriented fare of Unification Church Centers, based around rice (which was bought in quantity), with a mix of vegetables that varied (and did include fresh seasonals), and small amounts of meat, mildly seasoned. There were also the more American (pre-made sauce over refined wheat noodles) meat-stretching standards, such as tuna casserole or spaghetti. It was not unusual to have a standard, restaurant-style breakfast with scrambled eggs and toast, hash-browns or tater-tots, and maybe even watered-down orange juice, but bacon or sausage or ham were rare. Meat, in any substantial form or cut (such as a steak), was practically nonexistent, though the group was not vegetarian. The food was not the fare of a Chinese restaurant, either, as there was little grease or oil of any kind. The cooking was mostly water-based, but too much rice, or pasta, was added to result in soup. A mildly spicey version of a Korean dish called "kimche" helped, whenever the food turned out bland or boring (though I don't remember hearing anyone complain, even the almost nightly guests who came to hear Divine Principle lectures and were invited to eat with the church family afterwards). The jars of kimche (pickled cabbage, with varying peppers and/or carrots, etc. added for color and spice) were abundant and could be a side to any meal. Kimche was also a cultural novelty for most American guests, giving us something light to talk to guests about at the table (after a serious lecture). Helga taught me to make kimche, after I had wandered into the kitchen a few times, looking for a jar when there was none on the table. (Later, after Rev. Moon came to live in the United States, I would hear that his favorite lunch was a "Big Mac" hamburger from McDonald's fast-food restaurant, with a side of homemade kimche.)

When we went out for selling or witnessing, the team captain would usually grab a bread-bag full of sandwiches (peanut butter and jelly, or cold-cuts with mustard) from the kitchen (I often helped to make those too). We were allowed to spend money that we made on non-alcoholic beverages.

Some days were so cold, once the Michigan winter came, that I remember spending about as much time in White Castle burger joints as I spent standing on street corners selling the long, slender boxes of (sometimes frozen) chocolate-covered thin-mints that became our product that time of year. "Let's sell this box full, then we can go for hot chocolate," I'd say to a selling partner. That would pick up our pace, even on snowy days.

Celebratory food, from a few occasions, also stands out in my memories. Once when the national church president, Mr. Nolan, visited, he and Art Shoman showed off by taking the Family out for dinner at a nice restaurant. They put us in a special room with long tables. We were told that we could order anything on the menu, including one beer ("Father likes to have an occasional beer" was the word going around the tables, in whispers). There were no speeches that night, no formal prayers. I had not acquired a taste for beer and did not order it. Some were ordering steak, but I had Chicken Cacciatore (with a whole chicken breast, all to myself). Another memorable part of the evening was that beer option I declined, as it was the only time I remember seeing alcohol (and seeing people consume alcohol) at a Unification Church event. Had it been wine, I might have ordered a glass. (My only experience enjoying alcohol, at that point in life, had been taking sips from bottles of fruity Boone's farm wines that had been passed around at pot parties at college, to curb the cotton-mouth). I noticed Danny ordered a beer and seemed to be enjoying laughing out loud, even more robustly (and sometimes obnoxiously) than usual. Mr. Nolan, on the other hand, seemed a bit embarrassed (sitting next to an increasingly loud Art Shoman), like he felt guilty about having been talked into something that was not kosher. Jade was acting out a bit too. (I wondered if a few folks hadn't managed to get more than the one beer we had been offered).

On another occasion, they may have had rice wine at the True Parents Day celebration, on the great lawn at Belvedere (the estate in Tarrytown, NY where the Moon family resided). I seem to remember hearing the word sake there for the first time (*or was that when I watched the movie "The Last Samurai"?*). If wine was on the lawn at Belvedere, it would have been doled out in plastic cups the size of shot glasses, by some strict, older blessed sister (like the Millie who had been sent from National Headquarters to Gabe's center to train me in church manners, when I'd first joined). Anyway, though there were rumors, I never saw alcohol or behavioral evidence of it. There was a large, raw tuna at Belvedere that everyone was talking about. It was heavily marinated. I took a tiny bit, just to see what all the buzz was about. I was there with the national Mobile Fundraising Team, and pretty homesick at that point. So I would have preferred the fried bream of my Southern American childhood.

Interestingly, looking back, I was never in love with the food. However, my style of cooking, as head-of-household in later adulthood, was largely influenced by the Unificationists, if for no other reason than the necessity of thrifty nutrition. I now use brown rice, rather than white, and usually add a legume to my sparsely-meated vegetable medleys. Fresh out of the Moonies, I tended to add soy-sauce to dishes that turned out bland (from low-fat/ low-sodium), but now I am more likely to add some Cajun spices or put hot-sauce on the table. I'm thinking about making my own kimche again and have bought some pre-made since it is now being touted for its probiotic properties.

Life on the Streets

My pitifully white, "Scotch-Irish" (as my mother's family called us), skin got its healthiest tan ever on those city streets. Maybe God did me a favor, putting me so far north for my first summer as a fulltime Unification Church missionary. The tan came relatively painlessly, gradually. By "Indian summer" I could have almost passed for an Indian (except for the sprinkling of freckles across my nose). My long, slender legs got strong and muscular too. Fearless, we were, on those streets.

The team leaders, driving the white vans, used to drop us off in pairs, in various situations. The most extreme were the freeway exits. The lights could be long where an exit landed at a major through-street. Sometimes we would park our buckets of flowers (in water) several feet back, away from the curb (under a bush or tree, if available), and carry half-a-dozen or so. We would pray. Then we would approach cars, going right up to their windows with our eyes still shining from prayer, the corners of our mouths perpetually turned up. My attitude was to project love to each person (from my heart, through my eyes, my smile) individually, for just a moment, then move on down the line of cars until someone responded. When the timing was right, on a good day, someone would hand me a dollar, and I would hand them a flower (sometimes three, for two dollars) at almost every light.

If I had a lot of literature, I offered them a pamphlet or flyer. If I only had a little, I just showed it to them, told them we were a church, helping young people learn to live a God-centered, drug-free way of life.

It was a way of interacting with many people, quickly and lightly. At the end of the day, we were exhausted, but, on a good day, our spirits were high.

The mood back at the center was celebratory, with Art Shoman making a fuss over the highest sellers. I usually made over $100. Danny made closer to $200. He was more aggressive, forceful. He covered more ground and focused better than I did (as he was not naturally inclined to get into conversations that involved too much listening).

I was a daydreamer, and I got into (sometimes deep) conversations with my selling partners (and/or non-members on the streets, etc.). They called it being "too horizontal". The trick was to keep the prayer going ("stay vertical") and be a channel for God.

"Nobody can say 'No' to me when I'm high on God," Danny bragged, glowing from a good day selling.

It was a power trip for him. But he could go off-center easier than anyone I knew at times. If someone was smoking pot in a car he approached, he might take a hit or even buy a joint (or take one in exchange for flowers- though he never admitted it to me).

Once when I was selling with him, his eyes got a glazed look and he said, "They won't be back to pick us up for hours; we could go to that motel over there."

"We need to pray," was my response.

He laughed, to make me think it had been a joke. "No. I'm sorry; you're right," he said. "Let's pray." He moved closer to me then, trying to look serious with that impish look on his face, stretching his hands toward me, palms up like he wanted us to hold hands while we prayed.

It was an endless challenge, being his "spiritual mother". Sometimes I went along with the hand-holding thing, though it was usually considered "too horizontal".

Jermain was as challenging as Danny to work with, but for different reasons. Jermain was very black. His skin was even darker than it probably would have been if we had not been out selling flowers in the sun so much. I was not as self-conscious about working with him as I would have been in the South (where mixed-race couples were rarely seen back then). The thing that made me uncomfortable about working with Jermain was not that he was black. His apparent discomfort with himself was what made me uncomfortable. On the streets, he was clearly ashamed of being an African American man and would go so far as to pretend to be something else. His attempts at Caribbean or Ethiopian or whatever accents were the stuff of comedy routines, but more painful than funny to me at the time. He lied about where he was from, and people did not buy it. Consequently, they did not buy our product either. I don't know if he behaved so outlandishly with other selling partners.
Maybe it was just me.

Maybe I made Jermain uncomfortable and self-conscious because my skin was so white, and I had a Southern accent. I had grown up in the Jim-Crow South, meaning that if I looked particularly ladylike that day, it could have appeared to some that he was my servant, my "boy". As a post-Martin Luther King city suburbanite, however, that thought never occurred to me, as I had no conception of that way of life beyond having had black "maids" as babysitters, when I was between the ages of five and ten. We had lived in a small, NW Florida town then, where Mama Sue owned the town newspaper. That era of my life ended around the time Sue Cronkite became a correspondent for a big city newspaper and took us with her on assignment to Mobile. We got to see Antebellum homes along the "Azalea Trail". Mama also took my brother and I to see the movie "To Kill A Mockingbird", which was about the wasted life of an innocent and wrongly convicted black man, narrated by a girl around the age of my younger brother. I don't know if our maid could have gone into the theater with us in Mobile, Alabama in 1963. Jonni, a recently hired teenage black girl who was the last of our two consecutive maids (the older "Atlanta" having been our beloved maid for the several years prior) stayed in the motel room with my howling baby sister.

I never thought about any of that at the time. And, probably for purely practical reasons (not much money at the end of the day), Jermain and I were not often assigned as selling partners.

Jermain struggled with his sexuality too (moving in and out of the Center, because of "fallen" relationships outside, sometimes comically bragging that he "fell" when he came back and one of his confidants- myself included-would ask where he had been). Consequently, Audra didn't like him being paired up with the younger black sisters (who were her teenage foster kids).

Jermain would usually end up paired with One World Crusade guys with European accents (and he would revert back to, comically but sadly) faking that "Jamaican-maahn" accent. Jermain was a natural performer anyhow. Maybe it worked better that way; when Jermain was selling with foreigners, he could pass himself off, more believably, as a foreigner.

The tragedy of that sinks in more, at this writing, with the Black Lives Matter movement rising up nearly half-a-century later, against the murders, by police especially, of so many African American males (even pubescent boys) who have sometimes done little more than frighten someone with their appearance, triggering a violent response simply because they were black.

Grouping and pairing us for selling and witnessing was an everyday juggling job for Unificationist leaders. Since we often worked in the inner-city, sisters were considered safer with a brother, and Rose was often assigned to work with Danny. It was easier to get Danny to stay focused once Art Shoman decided they could keep ten percent of their earnings for personal expenditures. Life was more fun that way. The sisters and brothers went shopping on their days off, the whole lot of them converging on a K-mart (or wherever the van let them out). Rose bought a stylish coat that Danny helped her pick out. It was brown, fitted at the waist and hung to mid-calf, with a hood, and a ribbon trim with an embroidered floral pattern in fall colors. The fabric was a cheap synthetic, but Rose thought if she took good care of it, the look might hold up. Danny liked her in it.

Sharon, one of the Detroit sisters who had joined before The One World Crusade arrived, had tried on the same coat. Sharon was a statuesque, short-haired, conservative-looking blonde: proud and superior in her bearing and in her careful articulation of the Divine Principle. She was one of Audra's girls (local, and still going to college classes), but Art was grooming her to teach first chapter, the Principle of Creation (the introductory lesson which had been Arti Rose's favorite since the first time she visited Gabe's Center back home).

"It won't be winter for a while yet, though," Sharon said, at the register, when she noticed Rose buying the coat. Sharon was a local girl, and probably had coats in her parents' closet at home.

Arti Rose's mother had warned her about the upper-Midwestern winters, nearly every time they talked on the phone. Mama Sue told the same stories over and over. She had followed Arti Rose's handsome young father to the same city where Arti Rose now lived. He had followed one of his buddies up to work in a factory that paid better than the mills down home. Sue had been in her late teens (like Arti Rose was now) and had enrolled in a University in the same city. She and Charley had gotten married. When Sue found out she was pregnant with Arti Rose, she insisted on going back home to be near her mother. (*"I aint havin' no Yankee baby"* was what Arti Rose's *grandmother said her daughter had proclaimed).*

"It was so cold, I could spit and it would freeze before it hit the sidewalk," Mama Sue told her daughter now, long distance.

"Don't worry Mom; I bought a coat with a hood," Arti Rose reassured her.

"Well, you'd better get some fur-lined boots as well; so your toes don't freeze in the snow and the ice and the slush."

"O.K. I will."

"You know you could just come on back home in time for fall semester."

Indian Summer

It was cool enough to wear a sweater at night, or early in the morning. The sun felt good on my tan skin, and I could still wear my favorite natural cotton peasant-blouse tucked into a knee-length (not the popular mini-skirt, but short enough to show off my muscular, suntanned legs) paisley print polished-cotton skirt. The skirt had a black background, with the flowery print in my favorite fall colors (reds and greens and gold). It was softly gathered, with rows of tiny elastic at the waist (showing my shape without being showy), allowing room for freedom of movement as I walked up and down the median of a busy street (carrying a bucket of flowers), or strolled a campus lawn (blending in with students, my long, wavy, dark-auburn hair hanging down my back).

One day, in late summer, I saw a lovely African-American girl sitting on a park bench on the front lawn outside the International House of a private, local college campus. I thought she looked like someone I would like to be friends with, so I sat down on the vacant end of the bench, as nonchalantly as possible. She was slender, with sharp features, and a graceful, sensitive manner. She wore glasses and had an intellectual aura. When she looked up from some paperwork she had been leafing through, I spoke. "Beautiful day, isn't it?" I said. "I'm Rose."

Her name was Colleen. She had a quick, bright smile, and a sense of humor that loosened her up, brought out her African-American side. During our conversation I found out that she had lived in the International House for the previous school year, and they had allowed her to stay through the summer. However, American students were only allowed to stay in the International House for one semester. Colleen had neglected to reserve a dormitory room, mostly because she had lived in a dorm before and "did not fit in". I had caught her with the dilemma on her mind, and she shared.

"I think the International House is the only situation I have ever felt completely comfortable in," Colleen confided, after we had talked for a while. "I guess I have always felt like a 'stranger in a strange land' myself, for some reason," she said.

"I know what you mean," I said. "When I was ten my parents divorced. After that my mom moved us every three or four years. I got used to being a stranger in a strange land. Now I never meet a stranger."

"That's interesting, because when you first spoke to me, I thought I knew you from somewhere," Colleen said. "I was relieved when you told me your name, because I was thinking I was supposed to know it already."

We both laughed, though her comment had not surprised me. It was something I heard frequently as the result of a carefully practiced art. Having to approach so many strangers, I had learned that I got the most positive reception when I acted like I was approaching a friend. I had come to believe, anyway, that on some level we are all one and the same. It wasn't unusual for someone to start confiding in me (after we had conversed for a bit) as if they knew me. (I wore my heart on my sleeve, so why shouldn't they?)

"You should visit the Unification Church Center, where I live," I said. "You would love it. It's probably a lot like the International House. We have young people living together from all over the world, studying and teaching the Divine Principle."

Colleen was ready to move in after hearing the first lecture and having dinner with us. She never even had to be convinced that Sun Myung Moon was the new messiah (the usual hurdle at the end of the lecture series). Colleen loved the way we lived, blacks and whites together. She could be her whole self with us.

I went with her to get her things, which were in three places: some at the International House, some at her mother's place, and some at her boyfriend's house. The International House was amazing, with art and artifacts from all over the world, books in different languages. Colleen spoke to one student entirely in French, and another in Spanish. She seemed so sophisticated that I was a bit intimidated. Her mother's place was a different story though.

I was not surprised that she lived in a wealthy neighborhood, even though she was black. She was so intelligent that I figured she had well-educated parents who were doctors or lawyers or maybe even corporate executives (since promoting "token" blacks was starting to become a trend with progressive companies). Colleen said auto factory owners' families lived in this neighborhood.

I didn't ask if her family owned a factory. It seemed unlikely in that day and age. The house that she directed us to was a mansion. However, she did not direct the driver of the van to the big house, but to a separate building that turned out to be servant's quarters. Colleen's mother was a dark-skinned black lady who had been a house maid at the residence for as long as Colleen could remember. Her mother was in and out while we were there, wearing a black and white uniform with a fancy apron. She was superficially friendly but seemed too busy to ask Colleen any questions. Clearly, she seemed to consider her daughter to be an adult who made her own decisions about her own life. There was no mention of a father, but I figured he must be white because Colleen's skin was much lighter than her mother's. It did not take long to gather Colleen's few things from the tidy room that she had once shared with her mother. Remarkably, there was a small piano.

I sat on the piano bench as her mother, standing by the door (for we had caught her on her way out) bragged about how well Colleen could play. I told her Colleen had played for us the first time she visited the Church Center. I invited her to come over some time.

Back in the van, Colleen talked (mostly in response to Jermain, who was so wowed by the neighborhood he could hardly keep the steering wheel straight). Colleen talked about how hard it had been growing up in a white neighborhood, going to a white school. Jermain was too taken by the shine of the place to be very sympathetic. He pointed out glamorous, expensive touches, like fountains with Romanesque statues, glitzy gold monogrammed entry gates, and some of the most expensive cars in the world parked randomly here and there. Colleen shook her head and tried to shush his gushings. She must have needed to vent to a black friend, to let someone who had grown

288

up in poor circumstances know that the people living in rich neighborhoods were not necessarily more contented.

"Don't envy these folks. They're not all-that! They just have a different, less visible set of problems," she said.

Well-trained to "accentuate the positive", I kept pointing out the natural beauty, allowing for appreciation of the experience of the lovely outing we were being blessed with, out for a drive through one of the most beautiful neighborhoods in the world. There were winding lanes with canopies of well-established trees, and beautifully landscaped lawns with circular driveways leading up to mansions that were sometimes well displayed, sometimes hidden behind foliage somewhere at the top of a hill. Maybe it was not heaven, but it looked like it to me and Jermain.

Then we went to another place, more urban, closer to the Center. Colleen's boyfriend was unlike any black man I had ever met. He lived in a loft. Once inside the place, I was awed by the view from huge windows facing the street, which was lined with brick buildings and colorful awnings over delis and sidewalk cafés, bookstores and art galleries. At least a decade older than Colleen, his home was that of a sophisticated world traveler, with African tribal masks and other carved, wooden objects decorating bookshelves alongside leather-bound classics. There was a smell, like exotic incense or essential oil of some kind that I had never smelled before. The place was sparsely furnished, in a spacious, modern style, with high tech stereo equipment that played jazz at a low volume. The apartment was scrupulously clean, the man well-groomed and elegantly, though casually, dressed (in a black turtleneck, with fitted black jeans, and leather loafers with no socks). He was very black but may have been from another country. He did not speak or even stay in the room for long when we arrived. He was either completely indifferent, decidedly (maybe respectfully) detached, or not happy with her, or me. Anyway he was hard to read (the epitome of "cool").

If Colleen and I had been in a vehicle alone, on the way back to the Center, maybe she would have talked with me about the relationship. Jermain, however (maybe sensing male competition, though he had not gone into her friend's loft with us), chose the ride back as a time to brag about his experiences as a stand-in singer and dancer with the Spinners. Back at the Center, per Audra's instructions,

Colleen settled into the room adjacent to the one I stayed in upstairs.

I wondered why Audra had not put Colleen in the same room with me. It soon became clear, however. Colleen was not from the One World Crusade.

Audra Shoman kept the local girls under her wing, in a way. Helga, the cook, was the only one Audra had taken from Art's One World Crusade brood. Audra kept her girls at the Center more. Some were still attending local high schools or colleges, and some helped around the house. One World Crusade girls spent more hours on the street than we did at the Center. We kept different hours; so we slept in a different room.

Beth, my original Unification Church sister, from back home, was admittedly not happy at the new Center. She had always managed to stay off the streets by clinging to the side of whatever man was in charge (first Gabe, then Art or Richard when we left with the One World Crusade). Of course, that did not work at the Shoman house, under Audra's watchful eyes.

Not long after Gabe was transferred to a northern Center (in a nearby state) himself, he personally came to visit us and took Beth back with him. Beth had been the only sister in my room with English as a native language. I was still assigned to sleep in the room with Kimeo (a Japanese sister who spoke little English), Olga (a six-foot tall German sister who was loud and cross), and the French sister who did not believe in wearing deodorant. It wasn't really the lack of deodorant that bothered me about her, but rather the compressed, masculine, almost military bossiness that all of the other One World Crusade sisters, besides myself and Helga, carried in their tense muscles, their sweat, their auras. Probably they had been chosen for the mission, sent from abroad by their various Center directors in their various countries of origin, because of these very qualities. I was clearly a misfit amongst them, yet no unkindness passed between us.

I would not have admitted to not loving any of my roommates at the new Center in the same way that I had loved the "best friends" of my girlhood, or my high school sorority sisters, or my college roommate, or the Unification sisters back home, or- for that matter- my own biological sister. I was not able to acknowledge the fact that I was lonely for a certain kind of intimacy, that I longed for a best friend.

There was a kind of "negative thinking" that we were trained not to allow ourselves, so that it became difficult to recognize the specifics of one's own feelings. Despite my unacknowledged personal loneliness, I did experience a broader, more cultural sense of belonging, a certain satisfaction in recognizing that there were sisters in the Center that I could have been best friends with, given less regimented circumstances. Sue Anne, for example, (small, fair-skinned, brown-haired, blue-eyed, bespectacled, soft-spoken, with a clean, clear aura of femininity) would have made a good elementary school teacher and was chosen by Audra as a nanny and tutor for her children. I sometimes thought Sue Anne and I could have been close friends if our schedules had put us together more often, in more intimate circumstances. We looked enough alike to have been related.

Colleen and I did not look related, but there was a similar sensibility about us. I had thought Colleen and I might be close, but she seemed intent on fitting in with the black sisters, like it was her new mission in life. Dawna and Sissy (who were only sixteen and, in actual reality, were foster children of Audra's rather than converts) seemed a bit flabbergasted but enjoyed Colleen's attention. They had limited abilities to converse with the older, more educated black girl with the white mannerisms (though they were proud to know more about the Divine Principle than she did). Colleen did not mind the awkwardness; what she wanted to learn from them was how to be a black girl. She sang robustly with them, laughed loudly, played. Jermain, smitten and busy showing off at the piano (being himself), was the sweetheart of their clique. And Colleen made a good selling partner for Jermain. She had no problem approaching all kinds of people, and Jermain relaxed and acted more like himself with her. Colleen was the big sister Jermain had needed. And Colleen was not impressed enough to "fall" for him, but simply enjoyed teasing and playing and laughing with Jermain. And they sang together, like angels.

The visit from Gabe, which had ended with him taking Beth back to his new northern Center with him, was painful in a way that I had too much pride to show and could barely even acknowledge to myself. I had been in physical pain anyway, because of an abscessed molar. One of my cheeks was swollen. However, I bounced around the Center in

Gabe's presence as if I was on top of the world. I even showed off my friendship with Danny (probably hoping to make him feel some small amount of jealousy, since his attentions toward other sisters, especially Beth, had wounded me so back home). I acted as if I had found my best friend in Danny (maybe my soul mate). Danny certainly looked good enough to show off, as a "spiritual child". However, in reality, I had mixed feelings about Danny (from having to deal with his shenanigans).

To Gabe's credit, he insisted Art give me a day off to see a dentist while he was there. Gabe even took me himself, waited in the waiting room, held my hand when I came out groggy and babbling.

Neither Gabe nor Art had argued with me when I opted to have the tooth pulled, however. The dentist had recommended a root canal and crown. I had called Art.

"I know it is a time when we need to make sacrifices, because of the New Hope for America campaign," I'd said to Art on the phone, mimicking his exact words from the speech he had given us after dinner the evening before.

"You do whatever you think is best," Art had said with a kind of emotional force to his voice, just like when he had given that speech.

Sacrificing my tooth was the best I could do at that moment, for the "New Hope for America" campaign. I also talked about it in the dentist's office, to all of the office personnel and anyone who would listen, under the influence of some opioid. Even when it was physically impossible to talk about it, I dreamed about talking about it. Rev. Sun Myung Moon would be coming to the city soon, to speak about changes God was working to bring about in the United States, and in the world.

Gabe tried to be his fun, friendly self, light and upbeat. However, the way he held my hand was with a kind of gentle sadness, a deep tenderness, like he felt sorry for me, and more. If he could have cupped my swollen cheek in his hands, looked into my dazed eyes, and told me that I looked terrible, that he was worried about me and did not think I belonged in the One World Crusade under Art Shoman, I might have felt better. I might have been able to be authentic, to tell him that I was going through a rough time, but I would be O.K. Instead, I just kept smiling that plastered-on smile, even with the physical pain and the weird, drugged feeling that cut me off from my body and my emotions even more than the lifestyle and the way of thinking had begun to do.

I never asked why Gabe came to our Center. Maybe Beth had reached out to Gabe. Maybe Gabe had needed help starting his new Center, and Art had said he could take her. Anyway, when Gabe went back to his new Center, Beth went with him. She was all I'd had left from my original Unification family, and the only Church sister who had ever felt free to scoot her sleeping bag over on a cool night, close enough to snuggle like real sisters.

Of course, there were days when I was assigned a female partner for witnessing or selling. However, there was always the feeling that too much talk was "horizontal" and distracted from the mission. The only way to freely engage in a long, intimate conversation with another female (without witnessing) was to remain downstairs after everyone went to bed, under pretenses of studying the Divine Principle. Then there was a tiredness, a dream-time spacey-ness to the conversation that took it way off into the cosmos, far away from human relationships and feelings that might not always be "positive".

There was a kind of high that came from talking about God, not unlike the drug highs I had experienced with my college friends (not that the lot of them had wanted to talk about feelings either- most were trying to escape). Sunshine (my college roommate) and I had talked exhaustively about our feelings. It had been too much, at times. From that perspective it was refreshing to have many "spiritual" relationships, with assumed potential for depth. There was the pervasive dream that one would, after all, eventually be "blessed in marriage" to another Unification Church member, with a whole lifetime to develop intimacy. So there was always hope, to temper the loneliness-in-a-crowd feeling, especially since one was young, and it was Indian Summer.

Sirman

My favorite place to be dumped off (by a One World Crusade team leader, driving a white van with the red wheel-like symbol on the side) was my mother's alma mater (State University, in that great northern city). My favorite people there were the young, black students (generally of the socialist persuasion) who sat together in the student lounge or the cafeteria, philosophizing. They tended to be male, and too angry and abstracted to hold the attention of most females for long. They were not as flamboyant or attention-seeking as the militant Black Panthers of the sixties. In fact, most of them were not political activists; they were just students who happened to be intellectually radical. I found them stimulating, challenging, fun to argue with.

Sharon started me talking to them. The tall, conservative blonde was a student at the University and had held a student government position before she got involved with the Unification "movement". Sharon had attended one of the introductory lectures that Audra managed to present on campus, as "A New System of Thought". She was one of Audra's girls, but Audra did not mind letting the One World Crusade give Sharon rides (since Audra spent much of her time shuttling her own children, foster children, and spiritual children to and from various schools around Detroit).

Sharon had a way of intellectualizing, using her hands as she articulated her ideas, slowing her speech down to word things carefully. I admired her but did not really understand the politics. She argued from a political point-of-view. I argued from a heart-centered point-of-view based in my Christian turned hippie turned Moonie ideals. Most of the really hard-core communists were not open to religion in any form, but they could relate to the utopian ideals of unification, a movement toward creating a different culture, a more all-inclusive family of mankind.

One tired evening, waiting to be picked up by the One World Crusade van, I sat at a circular table having a cup of coffee with a few young black men, one of whom I had conversed with several times before. The one familiar to me was as black as ebony and at least as hard as the stone. Nothing in his face gave. Anything he agreed with me about, he only used to try and sway me in his direction, though I knew he did not really want me. I was the enemy, mostly because I was white. He was flattered by my attention, and he liked sounding off at me, as I helped him attract the attentions of those around us. We had played this game before, and I had sat with him this time mostly out of tiredness. He would surely take center stage, and I could bide my time until the van came.

The energy shifted, however, as the coffee took effect and a newcomer, a lighter-skinned, bright-eyed deer of a young man, named Sirman ("Yes Sirman; not Sherman") responded to my tired arguments.

"The Marx/ Engels proposed path to establishing a Communist system depends too much on conflict. It just creates a different division; it doesn't eliminate division. What we need is unification, and the only way to establish that is through heart-centered, universal love, the kind of love that Christ understood and taught. Unfortunately, however, the Christian churches are divided and divisive. What we need is the sort of unification movement that Sun Myung Moon has started," I said (again).

"Ebony" was not any more fazed than usual, but Sirman was on the edge of his seat. By the time the van got there, I had talked him into joining us for an introductory lecture and dinner. He and Colleen, who looked so much alike they could have been brother and sister, made eyes at each other all during dinner and sat talking for a while afterwards, before one of the brothers drove Sirman home. He moved in with us a few weeks later.

Sirman was supposed to be my spiritual child, since I had witnessed to him first. That meant I was supposed to nurture and raise him in Unification thought and the ways of our "God-centered" lifestyle. I saw and felt that mission landing naturally on Colleen, since she showed such an interest in him and had the energetic exuberance to let her fresh inspiration spill over on Sirman. In my mind that feeling had nothing to do with them being black and me being white. Looking back, I think the timing was bad between Sirman and I. I had been in the movement for over a year, and he was not my first spiritual child. I was tired, like a mother with post-partum depression.

At the time, I probably would not have been able to articulate that tiredness I felt (or even think it, since my mind had been persuaded against "negativity").

I also did not understand myself, or human nature, well enough to be conscious of the fact that (although I had been on a new convert's spiritual high) I was basically an introvert. Colleen, for example, was an extrovert. Having been the first to witness to her, I was also considered Colleen's spiritual mother. However, if Colleen had been my baby she had never needed to suckle. Her attention had not turned toward me, on entering our Family, but toward her new-found siblings of color. Also, favoring females who were students at local schools, Audra had immediately taken Colleen under her wing. I had been relieved, not because I did not want a black sister hanging on me but because I did not want anyone hanging on me every waking moment. I needed time alone to recharge, I was not getting it, and I was getting increasingly desperate for it. I could not have articulated that need, but I did tell others that I liked writing in my journal. Most days I would not have chosen to go out selling or witnessing if I had been asked what I wanted to do with my day. I would have said I wanted to study or write. If I had been asked whether I wanted to sell or witness, I would have chosen witnessing. And if I had been asked where I wanted to witness, it would have been in the student union at the University, or in a courtyard or green-space of any college on a lovely day. Those were the places where I had met Sirman and Colleen. I had met others in similar spaces, sometimes bringing them in only to watch them fall away.

One student, who was also black and brilliant, felt torn between our movement and her family's need for her (as a first-born child in a large, poor family with a single, working mother). She was burdened with an extraordinarily intense need to succeed in getting a higher education and a lucrative career. In spite of all that (and maybe from a temporary compulsion to escape it), she somehow managed to follow me from that bench in the University courtyard, where I had so excitedly shared with her my high ideals for unification. She never seemed comfortable living in the Center, however, sometimes giving me a look across a room, like she was lost and wanted me to tell her what to do next. With *her* life. I could draw her into my prayer or study group, teach her a song that inspired me, share a poem from my journal, but I could not bring myself to tell her what to do with her life. When she went home for a holiday and stayed, it was my mission (per our Center Directors) to go and bring her back. I was dropped off at her family's factory-village shack, the van waiting outside to take us both back.

The van took only me back to the Center, my heart still too broken to utter more than a few words all day. It was not losing her that had broken my heart. It was what I had seen inside. The poverty. The love. The need. So many little children looking innocently up to their big sister. Such a sweet, tired looking old mother (who probably was not as old as she looked). And I could see in my new friend's large, clear, light-brown eyes that she was to take care of them all. There was a warmth in those eyes, a sparkle, but rarely a smile. And in her short time living with us, she had not donned the perpetual Moonie smile we were famous for on the streets. She could not escape this world by projecting the dream of a better one. There was no freedom in her youth, only responsibility, a higher responsibility than I yet knew. I thought I had taken on the world, but I could not look in the face of one small child in the clean but under-decorated and over-crowded shack that was her home and say that I could save them. Maybe their truly black and truly brilliant sister, with eyes so big they looked like they were trying to out-weigh her heart, could. I let her go. I can't even remember her name. She called me once to tell me the University had let her back in (after dropping all of her classes mid-semester to join the Unification Church).

She had opened up to the counselor, told her story, her conflict. They had a simple solution. She could get a full semester's credit by spending the rest of the semester with the Peace Corps. There was an opening at one of their camps in South America. Now she was working on her Spanish, she told me, looking forward to helping different kinds of people, forming cross-cultural bonds. That way she could put some of the ideals the Unification Church had reinforced in her into action and continue with the higher education she needed to help her own family out of the cycle of poverty. I thanked her for letting me know what was going on.

"We will always be sisters in God," I said.

"Thank you," she said.

I wished her well and had no doubt she would do well. But I never heard from her again.

Colleen was a different story. So was Sirman.

The Shoman's were starting to give me more leadership responsibility, and Art put Sirman in my selling group. The van dropped us off at a mall/ shopping center complex, with cardboard boxes filled with small paper bags of salted peanuts (slots cut in sides of the boxes, for handles). I was the group leader, but I had little experience with that job and all of the considerations involved. I was accustomed to being expected to inspire people, but managing logistics was not my forte.

And there were so many new people coming in I hardly knew their personalities well enough to know who would work well with whom when it came time to pair people up.

We had each taken a box as we exited the van, and the driver had left a few extra boxes on the sidewalk. Fortunately, I had worked the shopping area before. We were all wearing licensed vendor badges. I just sent people off in different directions (barely taking note of which way each of them had gone), telling them we would meet up at the food court, by the courtyard, at noon. I kept Sirman with me, each of us picking up an extra box (so that we were carrying four, one on each side of both our hips). We walked to the food court together, talking lightly about the day, the weather. I was not feeling particularly energetic or inspired that day. When we got to the food court, I placed my boxes on a table by double doors leading to an outside courtyard with landscaping and benches and a fountain at the center.

"You can just leave your extra box here," I said. "I'll watch our product, hopefully sell some in here, and I have the sandwiches in my box too, for lunch. You can sell wherever you want to, around the area, and meet back here at noon, or sooner if you run out of product."

Sirman hesitated for a second, gave me a puzzled look, like he wanted to say something but couldn't quite get it out. I didn't even ask.

"Man-se!" I said. (We used the Korean exclamation as congratulations for victory both before and after the fact). This meant that I had full confidence in him, which I did. And off he went.

I organized my table as casually as possible (since it was an eating table, not a vendor table). I put a few bags of peanuts and some UC literature at center of the table, stacked the three boxes in a chair next to me, and sat down. Stuck with too many supplies to carry, I hoped someone would notice my wares and stop to buy some. As I casually started eating peanuts from a bag, a young man walked up.

"Those peanuts smell really good," he said.

"They're fresh roasted," I replied. "Wanna try one?" I asked, offering an unshelled nut.

He took it, shelled it, commented that it was good.

"They're a dollar a bag, or three bags for two dollars," I said.

He reached into a pocket of his worn, faded jeans, and pulled out a dollar.

"Mind if I sit down here and eat them?" he asked.

"I don't mind," I said, immediately starting my witnessing spiel once he was settled.

He was about my age, a sort-of redneck-hippy looking character like guys I had known back home (maybe too simple or down-to-earth to make sense of what I was saying).

I used the word "movement", trying to make it sound more like a hippy thing.

"I can dig it," he said, sitting down, pretending to listen while he shelled and ate his peanuts and stared at me.

I felt more comfortable with him sitting there, since I figured it was unlikely that the Church had permission to sell in the food court. He had bought a big soda-fountain drink and placed it on the table. Trying to appear more casual and less vendor-like, I didn't set any boundaries with him. He hung out.

So, it became increasingly apparent that I (however inadvertently) was taking advantage of my leadership position (as I had seen so many others do) to waste a good part of the morning. The young man had little to no interest in the Unification Church. Around noon I offered him a piece of literature I doubted he would read and told him the group would be coming back for lunch and someone would need his seat. He wandered off as casually as he had approached, and I started putting sandwiches (from a bread bag I'd filled in the kitchen before we'd left the Center) on napkins from a dispenser in the middle of the table.

When they picked up sandwiches, I told my team members to replenish their boxes from the extras. We had a few more hours to sell before the van would pick us up, at the same spot where we had been dropped off.

They came and went sporadically, using some of their earnings to buy drinks and chips. We didn't gather to pray, and most went outside, into the courtyard to eat. I stayed put, watching the sandwiches and the two extra boxes of peanuts until everything was gone except for my own box.

When I was alone, figuring I should be the first one to meet the van, I took my box out into the parking lot. Most of the people I approached were heading back to their cars and had already been approached by someone from our group selling peanuts. I did sell a few bags before the van came, but not many.

Back at the Center, later that evening, Audra pulled me aside and reprimanded me in a way that did not seem especially harsh at the time but puzzled me. All I had done with the young man in the food court was talk about everything and nothing, for an hour or two (with him barely listening but obviously enjoying staring at me). One of the sisters, Audra said, apparently resented it. The un-named sister had reported to Audra that I had not bothered to sell anything and had ignored Sirman, my newly converted spiritual child, who was awkward and shy and had needed training on his first day out selling.

"I heard you were really *mean* to Sirman" she said.

"Really? I had no intention of being mean to him," I said, truly puzzled and trying to remember what I possibly could have done.

"Apparently that's how some of the others saw it," she said.

"Hmmm," I said, trying to imagine who, in the group I had just worked with, might think me mean, for whatever reason (my mind settling on a new sister, a bossier type who I had recently heard sounding off in the adjoining sisters' room, making negative, jealous comments about longer-time members who had special privileges). I shook it off, not wanting to go into gossiping mode about a new sister whose struggle I sympathized with. I tried to see my day from a different point of view.

"I never thought about Sirman needing that much help," I said. "I'll try to make it up to him. But since we're talking about Sirman, I will say that I think you should put Colleen in the position of spiritual mother for him."

Colleen had not been in our group that day. I just thought Sirman might have been happier if she had been.

"Because they are both black?" Audra asked, raising her voice a bit and looking hard at me, with a quizzical, somewhat accusatory expression. I had inadvertently put her on the defensive by telling her what I thought she "should" do with two of her subordinates. So, her tone may have had more to do with that, but what I heard was someone assuming that because I was Southern; I was a racist. This was somewhat of a rude awakening for me.

"No," I said, taken aback, feeling my face flush. "Because they are so obviously interested in being friends."

"You have been in the Family longer than Colleen," the imposing woman said, throwing her chest out and lifting her chin a bit (reminding me who was the boss). "She is not ready to be spiritual mother to someone that she has a natural attraction for."

(I thought of how they were always pairing me with Danny but did not present the argument.)

"They could fall, and we would lose both of them," Audra said. "So I need you to pay more careful attention to Sirman; help him along," she concluded.

"Of course," I said, wondering how she was being less racist, obviously assuming Sirman would be safer with me (as if I would be less attracted to a handsome and intelligent black man than a young black woman would be- when it was I who had brought him in).

Audra gave me a motherly (but more firm than tender, I thought) pat on the back as she walked away. I was shocked, flabbergasted, but mostly wounded (too tired to think until I got around to journaling, then too self-correcting to allow myself to write anything "negative" or judgmental).

What crossed my mind later was that the odd mix of mostly Yankees and Europeans that I worked with thought that, because I was from the South, I had felt entitled to send the black boy off to slave for a buck while I enjoyed my day doing what I felt like doing. It bothered me that anyone might be capable of thinking that way about me, when I had been selling and witnessing nearly every day, without complaining, from the first day I had sold candles with Gabe, a year earlier. If I had been black would people have thought that Gabe (and then Art, and Audra for that matter) had made a slave of me?

Maybe. My own mother probably felt that way about what I was doing; though, I figured, she was a bit of a slave herself. She had been a reporter for the *Birmingham News* at one time, living most of her life out on the streets covering any event they sent her to cover. Now she was an assistant editor, which meant she cleaned up other people's copy. *Maybe someday Mama Sue would be an editor-in-chief, giving other people assignments rather than taking orders, (writing pretty much at her leisure). Maybe someone would resent it and make judgments about her that might not be true.*

But those were little more than feelings at the time, barely formed into thoughts and not given the time-of-day. There was no place for negativity in my life, toward anyone including me. I didn't blame myself. I knew that if someone else had been assigned to be team-leader for the day, I would have been happy to pair up with Sirman as a selling partner. In fact, I had intended to pair up with him before realizing there would be extra product, the driver would leave, and someone would have to mind the store. I had made my decisions in the moment, but Audra had not asked for my side of the story. The incident had upset me. However, I did not let myself dwell on it for long. I drew Sirman into my prayer group, expressing my heart in prayer to help clear up any ill feelings before they had time to fester.

I never felt anything but a sort of comfortable friendliness between Sirman and I (except for a sort of shyness, which was a personality characteristic we had in comment, exacerbated by that event). He never told me, and I never asked him, if I owed him an apology about that day for some reason. I felt too puzzled to know what to say, at the time.

It occurs to me at this writing (with white men on trial for murdering Ahmaud Arbery in 2020- a young, black jogger that those men claim they thought was a robber in a white neighborhood in the American South), but never occurred to my nineteen or twenty-year-old self, that Sirman might have had the same issue approaching people as Jermain had. Some people (especially whites, even in a Northern city) might have felt accosted. But Jermain was blue-black and carried himself with a casual slouch (even a jazzed up, funky strut at times). He had little education and faked a Caribbean accent. I could see how some folks he approached might have been taken aback, wondering if he was up to no-good (like some of the street-kids in that high-crime city). Sirman, on the other hand, did not appear to be a street-kid (a hustler type). His skin was too light (for an African American) to have spent much time on the streets. And there was no funky strut or anything about Sirman that I would have considered off-putting to the average person at a mall in a middle-class, Northern American neighborhood. Sirman carried himself like a proud (but somehow also humble) gentleman, and he was so mild-mannered and articulate that I could not imagine anyone being afraid of him. (Nor did I understand, at the time, that African-American men live in fear of the possible consequences of other people's fear of them).

Yet, even at this very writing (half-a-century later), descriptions of how I saw and felt (and did not see, or feel) differences, may seem inherently racist to some. I hope not but don't know how any of us can get around it on some level (if not consciously, then subconsciously). Even people of darker-skinned races tend to discriminate according to color, within their own groups. Until the palette is blended, color is tragically one obstacle to "Unification" that the human-race will likely continue to struggle with.

Looking back, I was certainly not aware of any lack of particular attention paid to Sirman by me having anything to do with him being "black". I know I had nothing against his looks, as he was quite handsome. Oddly, I think my apparent neglect had more to do with the fact that I felt basically comfortable with him, as a person. "I'm Ok; you're Ok" was the feeling I had about Sirman. And once he was comfortable in the group (which did not take long) he was not demanding of my attention.

I do remember some good casual, but deep, talks with Sirman, when we lingered at a table after dinner, dropping our Divine Principle books to talk into the night. We were friends. I was proud to have brought him into the movement, but he was not my follower.

Art Shoman once confessed to me, not long before I left his Center, that he was "bored with followers". His expression said that he was beyond bored; he was burdened, depressed and oppressed by all of us (me included I supposed).

Sirman was the quiet type, and he may have seemed like a passive follower to some (but not to me, because I also was quiet, saving my assertiveness for situations that I considered to be worth the effort of turning my introspective energy inside-out). I knew Sirman well enough (from having met him at State U.) to know that his mind was very animated, questioning, active. He made a good student of the Divine Principle and comparative religions and philosophies. *(In fact, he was later sent to the Church's first seminary school in America, where he eventually became a professor. He was "blessed" in marriage to a light brown (but apparently Caucasian) woman- from Miss Kim's distinguished San Francisco Center-, had beautiful (racially non-descript) children, and has remained in the Unification Church throughout his life so far. (I know all of this now, from recently having quietly, secretly explored his public posts- including lovely little sermons he writes and shares, on his Facebook page.)*

Me & My Dreams

The truth about me was that I had not been looking for someone to follow when I joined the Unification Church, and that was probably true of most of my spiritual brothers and sisters as well (no matter how sheep-like we may have seemed to some- the media, in particular- who tended to portray us that way).

What I had been looking for (somewhat desperately after disappointing experiences) was an intelligent young man to love. Of course, I wanted a man that I was sexually attracted to, but I knew that would not be enough. It would not be enough that he wanted me sexually either. We should have something more in common, some higher ideal. I wanted a mate with the righteous political convictions and social ideals of the 1960s, but with a less selfish personal morality than the decade had handed down to my generation. I wanted a clean man, a man of faith whose conscience would answer to a higher authority (but his beliefs, our beliefs would have to make more sense to me than those of the religious culture I had grown up in). I had been looking for a young man that I could admire, respect, and trust enough to imagine marrying him. I had found Gabe. I had taken the initiative, asserting myself into his situation.

I was the first person from my state to join the Unification Church. I had been a young woman following my ideals, and following the natural order of things, taking her place next to a young man of her choosing. Ironically, I had chosen someone in a situation that did not encourage personal choice in mating. Our marriages were to be arranged by someone higher up (not unlike the way we were paired for a day of witnessing or selling). So we were all gambling, betting on ending up with someone like that fine young person who drew us in.

Meanwhile we attracted one person after another, looking to fulfill the same dream, two dreams really. One dream was for an ideal mate, the other dream was for a path to a more ideal world, a world worth giving children to. Beyond the dreams was a willingness to work to make them come true.

Meanwhile, both follower and leader I had become. Besides leading selling and witnessing groups, I had also started teaching, at that point. Art had assigned me to teach the second chapter, "The Fall," which was not my favorite (I preferred "The Principle of Creation", which Sharon, who was considered to be intellectual, taught). *I wonder now if it was deliberate, having me lecture about Eve's fall (which Sun M. Moon interpreted as sexual) to instill the strength I needed to lead the young men I attracted. Or maybe it was the image I projected, as if I, myself, had not yet "fallen".*

Audra once surprised me by saying, out-of-the-blue, "You have an aura of cleanliness about you."

(Here, standing before you at the black-board, teaching you about the Fall of Mankind away from God, is the pure Eve, restored to her original condition, glowing with the light of heart-centered love, and blooming like a rose in God's garden.

Sold.)

Key

Looking back, it seems like Art Shoman should have sent Sirman (since he was both black and a native of the city) with me to represent the Unification Church in our meeting with the city's first black mayor. Art wanted the mayor to give Rev. Moon, who would soon visit on his speaking tour, a "key to the city." Though we were of different races, however, Sirman and I were both generally easy-going, never really pushy. Danny, on the other hand, would have been a good used car salesman. Art knew he could count on Danny to close the deal (if he sent me along to keep him in line). I was very centered on the mission and made sure that we prayed beforehand. When we felt our hearts open up to the unmistakable, uplifting presence, we went forth confidently.

The mayor was a charismatic African American man. We went to a "prayer breakfast" where city officials met informally with community leaders of faith. After breakfast, when the mayor was mingling, we introduced ourselves to him, shook his hand, made our request. Later we followed him to his office, where we closed the deal. My hair was up, and I was dressed in my Sunday best; Danny wore a high-end suit from his father's shop. The mayor had the glow of new, untarnished power. (We had the glow of newer than new, pure and untarnished love).

Rev. Sun Myung Moon of South Korea, who was on his "New Hope for America" campaign, visiting a major city in each of the fifty United States of America, would have his (symbolic) "key to the city".

The Hand of God

Art Shoman kept the Family up late one night, talking about the new mission. The One World Crusade had been out selling flowers all day, eaten a late meal heavy with starches, and I was exhausted. We sat on the floor in the large, open living room (which had no furnishings other than a big chalkboard on a wooden stand). Most of us were fighting sleep (we called it "being attacked by sleep spirits"), but Art was fired up. At one point I saw Art Shoman's aura flash out around his head, like the sun, with rays in every color of the rainbow. I had never seen anything like that before (*nor have I since, but I have recently heard it called "the rainbow light-body"*). It woke me up long enough to hear the point he was making at the moment.

"It is time for us to ascend to a higher level of service," our One World Crusade leader (blessed-husband of the center-director) said. "Father will be visiting us soon, with a message of New Hope for our nation. An auditorium full of people, from various walks of life, will be expecting us to have something to offer them personally, spiritually, as well as avenues for them to serve, to join us in building the Kingdom of Heaven on earth.

"Father says we will be like the hand of God, branching out with five fingers: religious, educational, political, economic, and cultural."

On one level, the pumped-up preaching was inspirational, motivational. *But later, when burnt-out Moonies went home and told their parents, and the counselors their parents sent them to, these late-night sermons spent on the sleep-deprived were labeled as brain-washing techniques for deep indoctrination.*

Thinking about Art Shoman, however, what I remember best is his excitement about setting out to channel "the Unification movement" (as he preferred to call our church) into practical, social applications.

Black Christian Mothers

For a while, I was assigned to the political team. We were designated, usually in pairs, to attend various civic and community meetings. I was very excited and imagined myself being like a 1960s civil rights activist. I remember sensing, however, that I was being regarded somewhat suspiciously by the more mature black women who typically lead the groups that were organized to improve the city.

Maybe I was being overly sensitive, my heart wide-open and noticing every look, even the most subtle glance or change in demeanor. I remember feeling great admiration for the black, Christian mothers who (like me) were trying to bring the faith they drew their strength from into the practical work of politics. There was, however, a difference between us other than color. I was coming on the basis of idealism, and they were bringing their broken mother's hearts, their tired feet. They had their feet on the ground. And though my feet had been pounding their city streets, my head was in the clouds. Maybe if I had actually grown up on those streets (or if I had been more of a grown-up) they would have greeted me more warmly at their meetings. Maybe I just had my heart on my sleeve and expected too much. I hope I at least conveyed the supportive vibe that was sincerely intended. It certainly was not about me, but what I am remembering is about the girl that I was.

(*Now I realize that I must have wanted those women leaders to love me. They reminded me of my own family's most beloved black maid, Atlanta, who had kept an eye on me as a young child, while she cleaned and cooked at our house when my mother was working. As kind as Atlanta was to me, I knew there was some part of her heart that I never got*).

At the community meetings our church's political team attended, we said our Unification movement was interested in promoting racial harmony, and helping kids steer clear of drugs, premature sex, and violence. Nobody could argue with our goals. At the time I could not understand why the black, Christian mothers (who I came to admire more than any people that I met in this great, but increasingly challenged, northern city) did not warm up to me more. Yes, I was white, but I had black brothers and sisters by my side. Now that I am a mother, I understand that the cold-shoulder I got was about more than color.

The black Christian mothers of the inner city were passionately political because they were losing their children in new and various ways. Though the media had not yet crucified Rev. Moon and his "Moonie" followers, we were already perceived, by some, to be a threat. We wanted their children.

Now I look back at Art Shoman's attempt to channel me into city politics as a sort of civics lesson. After I had attended a few meetings, he had other ideas about how I should be serving the movement anyway.

Workshop on Race Relations

Art was clearly on a mission to be *the* church in our city working hardest on race relations, giving our name, *Unification (maybe a name originally coined to promote re-unification of North and South Korea),* a special meaning in the U.S. I had no problem with the ideal of unification of the races, except for the push made (in the meantime) for a kind of inadvertent emphasis on the negative. Personally, I felt that just living in a communal situation with African American peers, as closely as brothers and sisters, had already put me past the negative experience of growing up in the segregated South. Then there was this workshop, putting pressure on us to talk about the differences, the separation, the challenges to Unification. And, being from the South, I felt like I stood out, like I was expected to have some special story. It was not one of my best days in the movement.

We'd been recruiting students especially for the workshop, so our mix was mostly young blacks and liberal whites. I guess there was that expectation for a certain type of story and message. Art Shoman had us gathered in the big room where he gave his speech about unification being God's will for humans. We sang a few songs, both from the church and popular culture (which had plenty with that message at the time). Then Art asked for volunteers. The first to get up had their own, rather obvious political agendas. I knew some of the characters from having argued with them in the student lounge at the University. Sirman, who I personally had recruited from that camp of black intellectual radicals, got up and gave his somewhat awkwardly new (and more emotionally charged than intellectually grounded) argument against the Communist solution.

"Communism is too rooted in conflict," was our church's much repeated phrase, like a chorus in one of our North Korean born leader's favorite songs (and none of us had the experience to understand that message as well as he did. Although some black neighborhoods in the U.S. admittedly did have a war-zone feeling about them).

"We have too much conflict as it is, without a violent revolution," was Sirman's message. "What we need is a unification movement, and that is what we are offering here," Sirman said, obviously intending to expound on that idea (his long, slender hands opening, palms up…).

Art Shoman suddenly stood up, cutting Sirman short and taking his position in front of the seated group. "Thank you, Sirman," he said, as Sirman returned to his seat. "I appreciate the philosophical positions presented here so far. Now does anyone have a more personal story about how racial segregation has affected their life?"

Art seemed to be seeking my face as he scanned his audience. I not only saw but also felt his burning eyes settle on mine. Maybe that was just because my eyes were the most attentive, responsive. But I thought it had something to do with me having been raised in the South, during the era of Jim Crow laws and extreme segregation. I was, in fact, the only Southerner in the crowd. I figured Art expected me to have something to say. So I timidly put my hand up (like a sinner at a revival meeting where the pastor is asking if anybody is ready to come-to-Jesus).

I felt my face flush as soon as I stood in front of the group and opened my mouth. "I grew up in the South, but I never knew anybody black except the maids we had when I was little, until recently. I really loved one of our maids, whose name was Atlanta. She seemed like an aunt to me, or a grandmother. I missed her when we got a new maid, who was a teenager and not as considerate or affectionate toward me. The two maids we had were as different from each other as they were different from me, it seemed.

"As a younger child, I had never really thought about Atlanta being black much, until one day when one of my cousins used the N-word right in front of her. My cousin and I were sitting on our front porch with Atlanta, when a young black man drove by in a red convertible. Atlanta whistled and said something about how handsome he was. My little country cousin said, "But he's a nigger." I was not only embarrassed but hurt, as if I was feeling what my beloved black nanny was feeling. Except Atlanta may have felt angry too. I wouldn't have blamed her if she had, but she didn't say a word. I didn't either.

"Anyway, after that I was more curious about the differences. I wondered why I never saw where our maids lived. So one day, when I was nine-years-old, I wandered off the path when I was walking home from school. I had a friend with me, and we were more curious than afraid. We walked to "the other side of the tracks" (where I'd heard they lived), along a dirt road, to a neighborhood where everything was as brown as the people. After that I wondered why they were called "colored folks", because what had struck me most in that poor little neighborhood was absence of color. A brown dirt road had led to brown wooden houses with brown wooden furniture on porches, and rusty automobiles parked in yards. And that was all I saw of black people before the age of ten. After that we moved to a Florida city and quit having maids. I started watching my younger siblings after school, and helping with household chores while my mother worked.

"Then there were a few black kids at my schools after integration started…but I- I didn't really get to know them," I said, feeling ashamed of that. "Maybe if I'd been involved in sports, or chorus…" *That didn't sound right, I thought. Am I stereotyping?* "Or if I'd been smarter…The one black guy I remember from my middle school was so smart he was voted Most Likely to Succeed."

I didn't mention high school, when we had moved back to Alabama where the only black boy I knew of played sports, and the few girls sang in the chorus. "Then, when I was on my college newspaper staff," I continued. A black guy was voted President of the Student Council. I got a front page byline for my story about it, but it was labeled as an "opinion" piece. I was only a freshman, did not know the person I was writing about, and mainly bragged on the mostly white student body for being progressive enough to vote for a black guy. Then the new student President wrote a letter-to-the-editor, protesting the fact that I had barely mentioned his previous accomplishments and credentials.

"And that's all I have to tell about my experiences with black people before I joined this church," I said. "I did try to make friends with a girl I met at work down there, after I joined last year. I had been living in the suburbs and hardly ever saw black people. Then my Unification Church center director had a job at Sears downtown, and I got one there too. I made friends with a black girl at work, and I even went to her house once when she invited me…I- I don't think her dad liked me though." *Should I say I had felt like he didn't want a white person in his house?* "I tried to invite her to the Center…" …I looked at all the black brothers and sisters who had joined the Unification Church in the great Northern city where I now resided. I got choked up.

"Maybe I should have tried harder…"

Art Shoman stood up, cutting me off. "You sound like you feel guilty," he said, shaking his head. "Sit down, please."

By the time I got back to my seat I was crying convulsively. The floodgates had been opened. Someone mercifully gave me a tissue. The tears kept coming, off and on, for the duration of the event and even when I was back at the Center. It was worse when I tried to stifle the emotional geyser. I tried to keep to myself as best I could, especially around the guests at the workshop. But my new black brothers and sisters, especially my most intimate friends, kept offering me hugs that would re-open the floodgates.

I thought Art was mad at me. I wasn't sure what I had done wrong. Maybe he thought I *should* feel guilty. Had I tainted his workshop? Had he resented me getting so much attention (though I personally knew that I would have preferred to be invisible). It would be a long time before the experience would be mentioned between us. (*And now that I can look back and see how much I was emotionally manipulated in those days, I wonder if I didn't play into his plot, voluntarily taking the part of the white scapegoat- choking on the sins of the many, getting carried away…*)

The Fall

I had been assigned to teach "The Fall". I stood at the blackboard and taught the second chapter of Rev. Moon's "Divine Principle" most evenings that the Detroit Center offered lectures (usually several times per week). The interpretation of the Bible's first book (Genesis) was controversial, and I argued for it with the best of them. If "the fall" had not been sexual, why would Adam and Eve have suddenly felt shame and covered their genitals?

Rev. Moon's theory (said to have been a revelation, received in a state of prayer) states that premature sex, between spiritually immature partners, is the root of human suffering and separation from God. My argument was that even if the creation story is understood more as myth than actual history, this interpretation makes sense from a modern psychological viewpoint; we get our issues from flawed parents. Rev. Moon's "Divine Principle and its Application" teaches that we can return to God by concentrating on our individual relationships with God before "falling in love". Physically based relationships have a "horizontal" energy flow. When we first secure "vertical" relationships with God, "love" will not throw us off balance; we will be able to maintain our original axis. Then two spiritually mature, "God-centered" individuals will be ready to establish true and lasting love, building a solid foundation for God's ideal and fulfillment of creation: True Family. (This, of course, was not assumed to have happened in history except, theoretically, in the case of Rev. and Mrs. Moon and, subsequently, couples who were blessed by them. That, however, was not revealed until the last chapter of the lecture series which, at the Center, was not presented by me- or any of the other members of my status- but by the "blessed couple" there).

I am remembering my young self standing in front of a group of several new students of the "Divine Principle". My long, dark auburn hair is pulled back, away from my face, secured with a rubber band at the nape of my neck, and falling down to my waist in a wavy but tamed ponytail. I am wearing tiny pierced earrings, one silver stud in each earlobe. I wear no makeup. My eyebrows are dark and naturally well-shaped, giving my clear, grey-green eyes definition. I am tallish (5'8") and slender, without exaggerated curves. My long legs (once "skinny") have become muscular and shapely from pounding pavement, but I make no attempt to show them off. My dress is comfortable and feminine, not unstylish but certainly not provocative. I am pretty, but I am not particularly sexy. My Scottish features are somewhat severe, my countenance serious. My presentation is logical, but I speak from the heart. I am genuine, sincere. My skin is fair and flushes pink when I am the center of attention. This quality, along with my sincerity, mesmerizes. People can't take their eyes off me, as I am a rosebud, blooming before their eyes. They want to hear what it is that I am so passionate about, this "truth".

So much seriousness is difficult for such a girlish young woman to sustain; even a serious Rose is a rose. Nature calls. An Indian-summer day is irresistibly seductive. A young man, blue-eyed and fair-haired as a fairy-tale prince beacons, and he has a car. He is the only one in the group with his own car: a sporty Toyota Celica. Art Shoman gives them the day off, and Danny invites Rose to a park, in the country an hours drive from Detroit.

No one seems to notice that they go off alone, as a pair, which is taboo in this group.

"This is what God looks like"

It was a Saturday like no other that I had experienced under Audra Shoman (as "Center Director"). There was the feeling of freedom that we'd sometimes had, traveling with Art Shoman's branch of the One World Crusade. Looking back, with more knowledge of such things, it is obvious to me that, around that time, Art wanted us out of his house so that he could have his way with his "Audi", in more ways than one (for they would have a third child in nine months or so, whose arrival would steer my own fate).

No "team leader" hustled me out of my sleeping bag for Helga's freshly cooked breakfast, as she too had been given the day off. As the sun started sneaking its way around the blinds, I could hear the other sisters in my room chattering excitedly about whatever they were hoping to do with their day. Some had already been downstairs to the coffee-pot to recruit van drivers. They were organizing themselves into groups according to which shopping center or laundry-mat they preferred. I kept my eyes shut tight, pretending to be sleeping, hoping they would all soon leave me in a quite space where I could think my own thoughts and maybe write in my journal.

When things quieted down, I got up and snuck out to the little bathroom in the hall. Cheerful little Bessie. the short, round, dark-skinned black girl who was one of Audra's foster children, had been left with the Shomans' two kids (while Sue Anne, the official nanny, was given the day off).

Bessie was helping Theodore with a toddler's bathroom duties, guarding the cracked door to give him a bit of privacy.

I chatted with Bessie a bit, commenting on the beauty of the day. Bessie did not complain about having been given a job, when everyone else had a day off. She went to high school during the week, while most of us were out witnessing or selling flowers. I had been to Bessie's mother's apartment once, and knew why the girl was so cheerful about her life at the Center. Caring for one toddler, one nerdy bigger boy, and one sassy teeny-bopper on a Saturday was nothing compared to what she would have been doing at home. In fact, Bessie had ended up in the foster-care system because her school had reported the number of absences she had from staying home to care for her pre-school aged siblings while her mother worked.

"Hi Theo," I said warmly, crouching down to be at face level with the darling boy when he came out into the hall.

He flashed his bright eyes at me for a second, then complained to Bessie.

"I can't but-ton."

"Yes you can; let me show you how," Bessie said, crouching down.

I went into the little bathroom. Since no one knocked on the door while I was on the toilet, I decided to seize the moment to wash my hair. The Shoman's daughter, Shawna, used the same shampoo and conditioner as I. We weren't supposed to use the Shoman's personal things, but I could replace Shawna's balsams when they got low, I reasoned. I had done just that last time I'd had a chance to shop, so who knew which one of us the creamy liquid belonged to? We had the same long, thick, wavy hair, but our personalities were as different as night and day (I thought, lathering up in the shower, then putting on the thick conditioner to work the tangles out). Shawna, barely a teen, already acted more like Jade, who had been a prostitute. Maybe being a prostitute wasn't what had made Jade tough and brazen; maybe she had been tough and brazen from childhood, which made her suited for prostitution, but not hard in her heart, which ultimately made her unsuited...Maybe Shawna would be Ok, I thought, rinsing her balsam out of my hair. She wasn't a "blessed-child" though, born as she had been before the Shoman's were blessed in marriage by Father Moon. Theodore was a blessed-child. It was easy to see the difference, I thought, as Theodore shined with the innocence that the pubescent Shawna seemed to lack.

Drying myself off with my terry-cloth robe, I had only my

flannel gown to don before exiting the bathroom. Hoping most everyone was gone, I was surprised to run into Danny in the hallway, descending the ladder from the attic where the young men slept.

"Hi!" we both said, suddenly inches from each other.

I backed up in the little hallway, as best I could, self-consciously hugging the front of myself with my wet terrycloth robe (which was quickly drenching the front of my flannel gown).

"Why didn't you leave with everybody else?" I asked.

"Why didn't you?" he asked, his eyes doing that funny thing they had a habit of doing, going from clear and wide-open to dreamy and droopy.

"I just wanted to wait for everyone to leave so I could write in my journal," I said.

"Oh", he said, looking a bit disappointed. "Well, I was wondering. I looked for you downstairs," he said. "I thought you might want to go to a park; I know how you love nature," he said.

"I- I don't know," I said, feeling a bit cornered.

He backed off some, cooled his expression.

"Well, I was thinking of going fishing anyway," Danny said from inside his own skin. "If you want to come, you could bring your journal."

"That might be nice," I said. "I'll have to get dressed."

"I'll be waiting by my car," he said. "I want to check the fluids anyway."

"Ok," I said, backing into the sisters' room, nearly slipping in the puddle I had made with my long, dripping hair.

Getting into Danny's sporty little Toyota Celica always made Rose feel young again, maybe younger than she had ever felt. Most of her high school boyfriends had driven their parents' cars (except Kirby, who was all about the hippy business in his VW, serious and intellectual and ideologically motivated, even when driving around listening to the radio. Only the seriously meaningful songs were turned up, rarely the just-for-fun ones).

The One World Crusade vans had seemed cool at first, with their "Dharma Wheel"-like symbols painted on the sides. But the vans had come to be associated with the work of selling endless buckets of flowers on the streets, and/or "witnessing". Rose had been in Danny's car before, but only when they had been assigned a mission and she, being his spiritual elder, was in-charge. This time Danny was in charge, and he clearly intended to have fun. The music from his eight-track tape player seemed shockingly loud at first (they did not listen to popular music in the Centers or the vans), but Rose settled into the bucket seat and listened while Danny navigated, changed gears and accelerated, taking a freeway that quickly transported them from cityscape to countryside.

Danny stopped to get gas and snacks at a cross-roads store that advertised live bait, which he also picked up a carton of. Rose grabbed some fresh fruit and nuts, putting them in her roomy tapestry bag as they got back in the car.

Danny was excited, grinning, teasing Rose. "Wanna put these in your bag, too?" he extended the carton of wigglers in her direction.

"Eeeeh!" she squealed, moving her body back toward the door suddenly and clutching her bag. "I don't mind fishin' with wiggle worms, but I don't want them in my bag," she said.

Danny laughed, starting up the car. And the music was on again. "The Who", a cool band but not an album Rose would have bought. She liked some rock-and-roll, but Rose preferred the acoustic sound of folk-rock. Still, she enjoyed the diversion for what it was, even singing along with the first part of "Behind Blue Eyes", which was clearly blue-eyed Danny's favorite. ("Nobody knows what it's like to be the bad man, to be the sad man behind blue eyes…telling only lies…But my dreams, they aren't as empty as my conscience seems to be…") Neither of them were shy about singing, as they sang every day at the Center and in the vans, and even stepped up to a mike sometimes at rallies in public places. But Arti Rose was surprised at how much emotion Danny put into this particular song, like it had some meaning to him personally. She didn't have long to think about it though, as another song came on and another, and they soon arrived at their destination.

At a park they had been to with the group before, Danny parked near the lake and got his telescopic fishing reel out of the trunk.

"That's cool. We always used cane poles when Daddy took us fishing," Rose said, picking up her pace to keep up with the exuberant young man who seemed, solid as he certainly was, about to take flight.

At the lake, Danny seemed almost to forget Rose was there.

She hung out beside him long enough to see him catch a fish, which did not take very long as he seemed to know exactly where to cast his pole. He gently took the glistening creature off the hook, tossed it back in the lake, and continued casting, obviously delighted with his success.

Rose praised him a bit, admiring his first catch, then wandered off. Something shiny had caught her eye, and she started following a trail of stones which, when they were broken, revealed quartz crystal in shades of purple and rose. She may not have wanted worms in her bag, but she had no qualms about filling it with the beautiful stones. When she had tired herself, Rose sat down and pulled her journal from her bag. But before she had written anything, Danny surprised her, sitting down beside her in the wooded area, near a trail, where she was leaning against a tree.

Danny was lit up from the excitement of fishing, his blue eyes shining like the sunlit sky that framed his blonde hair like a halo. Rose shyly put her journal back in her bag and pulled out a stone to show Danny.

"It looks like a plain, brownish stone, but see where it's broken," she said, turning it in her hand until the light hit the quartz crystals inside.

"Huh," Danny said, looking around.

"I didn't find them here. They were over there," Rose pointed. "But this tree looked like a good resting place."

"The shade feels good," Danny said, still looking off in the direction Rose had pointed. Something had caught his eye, but it wasn't a stone. He got up and walked several yards away, picking a bit of Queen Anne's Lace. Sitting back down next to Rose, he handed her a single flower.

"This is what God looks like," he said, looking into her eyes as she accepted it.

Rose was grateful to have something else to look at, as she blushed and dropped her gaze from his. "Source energy," she said, using a Divine Principle term to describe the perfect pattern that radiated out from the center like rays of the sun, like everything.

"Exactly," Danny said. Then he started talking about physics and how he thought it related to the Divine Principle.

Rose hung on his every word, listening and supporting,

responding with her own insights. In a while it seemed that they were high on something, except their energy did not start to drain like it would have if they had smoked pot. They didn't get hungry. They just kept talking about God until the sky started to change colors. Then they walked back down to the lake so they could see the sunset reflected on the water.

By the time they got back to the car it was nearly dark. When Rose settled into her bucket seat, she thought Danny would start the car, but he did not. She looked at him, sitting in the driver's seat, and he was looking her way.

"I just want to look at you for a little while," Danny said.

Rose smiled at him with her eyes, and they sat gazing at each other in the twilight as dusk turned to dark and other cars left the park.

Rose had a funny feeling, like butterflies in her stomach. "Danny, I think we should go now," she said.

"Ok, but can I just kiss you first," he asked sweetly.

"Well, I guess a little kiss wouldn't hurt," she said, not really thinking, just kind of wanting to move things along.

The kiss was not a little one, and if there had not been bucket seats Danny would have been on top of her. In fact, he practically was on her. Then suddenly he was really happy, like something had happened. He got out of the car, like he was going to take a leak. Then he was jumping up and down, whooping and hollering.

Rose was putting herself together, pulling her loose cotton peasant blouse down, checking to make sure her jeans were still buttoned, smoothing her hair when a car drove up and a park ranger got out with a flashlight.

"We were just leaving, sir," Danny said, getting back in the car and buckling his seatbelt.

"You okay, young lady?" he asked, shining his flashlight at Rose.

"Yes sir," Rose said, feeling embarrassed.

"Well, I just wanted to make sure," he said, moving his light away from Rose. "I just heard some commotion and thought I'd better check," he explained.

"Park's closed anyway, except to campers," he said to Danny, who already had the keys in the ignition and cranked the car as soon as the man backed away.

"Can we play something quieter?" Rose asked as soon as The Who came back on.

Danny stopped at the gate, reaching over Rose to get a tape out of the glove box. He could see that she was a bit upset.

"It's okay" he said, patting her on the leg before he pushed the Beatles tape into the tape player.

Rose wasn't sure it would be okay. An hour ago Danny would not have felt free to pat her on the leg, and they were on their way back to a place where that was strictly against the rules. What they had just done (though "parking" was not a new experience for either of them) was taboo for unblessed couples (who, according to the Divine Principle, had no right to be couples) in the Unification Church.

"Let it Be" came on.

Rose turned the volume down. "How are we going to explain ourselves when we get back to the Center?" I asked.

"Shoman said it was a free day. So, we went to the park; so what. We're both sunburned. I'll just say we stayed to watch the sunset...Then the battery was dead, and I had to find someone to give us a jump," Danny coolly planned out-loud as he accelerated on the highway.

Rose turned the volume back up on the car stereo.

Danny would have turned it up louder, but he "let it be"...

When Danny parked his car amongst the vans in back of the Center, Rose was busy taking a hair-tie off her wrist, pulling her hair back like she usually wore it, (though she had left it down to dry that morning and later left it to be kissed by first the breeze, then Danny). When her long locks were secured at the back of her neck, Rose gave Danny a glance. For all his bravado, he looked suddenly anxious, hesitant. What's worse was he had lost his luster. If Rose hadn't known him better she would have thought he looked guilty. She put a hand on his shoulder. It was her fault, she thought; she was his "spiritual mother", the person entrusted with the job of giving her spiritual brother (newer in the faith) guidance. She was clearly in the position of Eve, with him being something of an Adam in God's eyes. They had just spent a day in the Garden. But looking at Danny, he must have felt more like the lustrous Lucifer, with his light tragically put out.

Fortunately, on opening the doors of the car, they could hear a rather chaotic gathering on the large, screened-in back-porch. Some people were perched on the steps, and some stood in the yard close to the porch where Art Shoman was giving an informal, but apparently important, speech.

Danny and Rose separated and worked their way shyly, carefully into the crowd, where their spiritual brothers and sisters were too busy listening to Art Shoman to ask questions. He was talking about plans for the winter and said they would be moving before Father's arrival on his public speaking tour across America. He and Audra had been out looking, and they had found a school for teaching and another building that would be converted into a dormitory. Shoman said we were all going to have to work hard to pay for our step up in the world, but we would have more legitimacy and Father would be proud of us. He had thought we deserved a day off, before starting our new mission, and he hoped we had all enjoyed our free-day.

As Shoman finished his speech, and everyone started working their way inside, Rose glanced at Danny (once they were on the lit porch) and thought he looked like she felt: detached and awkward in the crowd, shy to the point of shame, as if he felt afraid that his naked face might reveal his aberrant actions.

Rose tried to avoid other people's eyes. Sharon (the tall, imposing blonde who, though she intimidated some, was, like everyone else, used to Rose's readily offered warmth and openness) said, "What's wrong, Rose? Don't you think it's cool that we're getting our own school?" Sharon, obviously inspired by the speech, was glowing.

"I'll miss this place, though," Rose forced a sad smile, as her heart felt strangely heavy (though it had nothing to do with the house).

Rose made her way to the sleeping bag in her corner of the One World Crusade sisters' room, as quickly as she could. She was hungry, but did not want to mingle in the kitchen, where people were raiding the fridge. Rose brought her journal and pen out of her bag before she settled down and shut her eyes. She drew a mandala of dots, swirls within swirls, then added a stem, to resemble Queen Anne's Lace.

All she wrote was, "This is what God looks like."

"the winter of our discontent"

I have a hard time remembering the sequence of significant events from that exceptionally eventful winter of my youth. We moved. "Rev. Moon" came to town during his "New Hope for America" campaign. Also, besides his speaking tour, there were rallies for his "Forgive, Love, Unite" campaign, which had to do with President Nixon and was in all the big newspapers across the U.S. (The national church actually bought full-page ad-space for a written version of Rev. Moon's "Forgive, Love, Unite" speech, which was intended to help the nation through the Nixon crisis).

Though I had grown up with a newspaper woman for a mother, I did not read the papers while I was in the "Moonies" (the name the media gave us, soon after our "Master" or "Father", who was given the title Rev. Moon, came to America). Art Shoman reading the paper every morning was a familiar sight at his table by the big coffee pot in the dining room of the brick house. Audra seemed too busy to join him in that ritual most mornings, as she ran the domestic scene. Sometimes Jade (a friend from Art's "former life") sat at his table and read sections of the papers as he cast them aside. Once I tried looking over Jade's shoulder, just to see the headlines and maybe enter their conversation. Jade, who sometimes treated me affectionately (as if I were just a sweet child in her worldly eyes) gave me a cold shoulder, and I never tried that again. Jade looked like a gypsy, with her long, black hair and big, hoop earrings. She often bragged that she used to be a prostitute, until Art witnessed to her and took her off the streets.

Jade was territorial around Art, which Audra clearly did not mind since Jade was part of their inner circle and had a particularly strong bond with Shawna, their pubescent elder child (who'd had Jade for a babysitter from a young age).

Art Shoman gave us little news-bites, when they related to our "movement" (as he liked to call it, because it sounded more political and philosophical than religious). He was delighted when the media catchword, "Moonies", began to spread like wild-fire. We were famous (or infamous).

"Some of us who are a little bit older used to be called 'Flower Children', and they weren't always nice about that either," he said, standing on the big desk at our school. "But we didn't care. We were proud to be recognized, and we wore our nickname like a badge. I want you to do the same," he said. "This brings us more into the mainstream. We're going to start singing more mainstream, popular songs too, as we develop our musical program here at the school."

Art was grinning, glowing, full of himself and his high ideals. "Our center is going to stand out, in Father's eyes, because we are going to express our unique talents here. The Divine Principle tells us to be one with God, but also to perfect ourselves as individual expressions of God. So, within our massive, international movement, this center is going to be a unique expression of our city's historical and natural musical talents, with the fresh faces and soulful voice we have right here, in our school, today.

I looked at my roommate, Celi, and she was glowing. She was finally hearing what she and her parents had understood to be the purpose of her presence here. Jermain (who had been a stand-in for the "Spinners", a popular rhythm-&-blues harmony and dance group) was glowing too. I surveyed the room, and most looked exactly as I felt: excited, but a bit apprehensive. We all loved to sing, but most of us had little or no experience as performers.

Sometimes it seemed to me that Art Shoman was from a different planet. I liked that about him, because he fed my dreams. However, his vibe did not transmute for long when I got dumped out of one of the white vans (which he no longer even stooped to drive, must less jump out of in the "kamikaze" style often alluded to). The nickname "Moonies" may not have looked so bad when we made the headlines, but it hurt when someone who might have bought a flower for "a church youth group, helping kids get off drugs", now recognized us and scoffed.

"Get a job, Moonie," was a particularly cutting remark I remember.

To me, it was a job. I was a missionary for a new church. I did not understand why people I had grown accustomed to approaching with warm smiles, and getting warm smiles back from, were suddenly turning as cold as the weather.

We had no TV in the Center either. So all I knew of the news was what people were saying on the streets. Our nation was in a state of discontent, even despair which translated into seething hatred of our president. People needed a father figure, but it was increasingly difficult to find anyone with enough innocence to open their heart and trust our Unification Church Father. I started to see that people figured Sun Myung Moon was like a politician, out for money and power. Moon was also clearly right-wing (with a militaristic anti-communist stance that stemmed from having lost his homeland, North Korea, to a dictatorial communist regime), and the bigger voices of American media tended to lean left (as Nixon and his right-wing cronies were investigated for their crimes).

With little understanding of what was going on, I started going to pay phones, calling my mother with the little bit of change people were willing to give up. The cynical newspapermen she worked with did not like Rev. Moon either. She told me that, for her generation, it did not help that Rev. Moon was from a nation we had been at war with in her youth. And here he was, taking their kids out of college and putting them on the streets to beg for him while he strutted around in fine suits, his chest thrust forward like some slant-eyed rooster.

"I don't like him either, but I like you and I like your friends," Mama Sue said. "I know y'all mean well. I wish you would come home, though. I miss you so much. I visit the Center here, because it makes me feel close to you. They don't eat enough meat, so I buy meat on sale and take it to them. They don't seem to know how to cook anything but rice either and it doesn't have any taste. I show them how to cook the meat so they end up with drippings to make gravy from. Then they can cut the meat up and stretch it out…"

"That sounds so good, Mama. You're making me hungry," I would say, remembering her Southern style of cooking.

Getting off the pay phone with Mama Sue sometimes triggered a visit to a fast-food joint for warm comfort-food. I would often go to a White Castle, using a bit more of my change to buy one of their little palm-sized burgers and a hot chocolate to warm up. At the end of the day, I didn't have much money to hand Art, back at the Center. The phone calls and the food were not expensive, but the time (not spent selling) was.

The "New Hope for America" campaign felt hopeless to me. Art Shoman went from giving inspirational talks to leading the kind of "motivational" pep rallies that time-share salesmen later became infamous for. He tried to appeal to our competitive side, but I did not have one. When we came in at night, counted our earnings and turned them over, Art would write our respective names with the amounts on a black board (which was usually used for Divine Principle lectures). Danny seemed to thrive on the competition, often showing a total over $100. My totals were sometimes as low as $40. And when I was assigned to work with Danny (though that had always upped my game before) neither of us did well. We would stop to gaze into each other's eyes, maybe steal a kiss. Once he even tried to get me into a motel that was on our assigned selling route. I said "no", even though I was cold. Then we sometimes ended up sitting in his car, but the feeling was not the same as it had been at the park. His eyes did not look clear or bright to me. One time he even had a marijuana joint. He said they had been smoking in a car he'd approached while selling at an intersection. He had asked them for a joint and given them a flower in exchange. I said I didn't want any, so he didn't smoke it around me. But I could tell he had already smoked some, maybe when he went to the restroom at a gas station.

Sometimes I felt like the devil was after us, like Father said in some of the speeches that were being published in little books now. I had one I'd been reading which was entitled "New Hope for America". We were supposed to sell them, but sometimes I just gave them away (that way I would at least get a smile). I was tired of selling.

Before the Shoman's bought the new buildings, we had balanced selling and witnessing days. Now we were selling nearly every day, in colder and colder weather. We went from selling flowers to peddling frozen thin-mints on icy, sometimes slushy street corners, even in near blizzard conditions. I got addicted to chocolate and sugar, trying to get a lift by snacking on our product (prying the frozen mints apart so I could let them melt on my tongue, one at a time).

I couldn't get warm that winter. It was like I could never quite thaw-out, even when we went inside. The school we occupied, during the daylight hours when we were not selling or witnessing, was cold. The Shomans said the heater needed repair, but when I look back now I think they could not afford to heat the place, with the new mortgages they had taken on. The dormitories we slept in were warmer, physically, but colder spiritually than the big residential home we had lived in before (which was not in the best of neighborhoods and had probably been a rental). There we had felt like a big, extended family (even fitting around one, long table when Art Shoman had first brought the One World Crusade to join Audra's Unification Church Center).

The dormitory building had a small apartment which the Shoman family occupied, between the male and female wings but closed off. I never went in the brothers' wing, but our wing only had one common area and that was the laundry room. It had a sink, and Colleen was often in there washing her pink down-vest out by hand, even using an old toothbrush on the dingier parts around the neck and pockets. All the black girls gathered around her, laughing and joking. Colleen had succeeded in getting some authentically black sisters out of the deal, especially with Audra's foster daughters Dawna and Bessie. I tried but never quite fit in with their group, although I got along well with them individually. The black girl who was my roommate was not in that clique either. She was as much a misfit as me, and I think we might have gotten close, whispering to each other as we did from our separate bunks, if it had not been so obvious to both of us that she did not belong there. Celia (who I affectionately called "Celi", trying my best to make her feel like a sister) had not been in the One World Crusade, and she had never lived with the Family in the big, old brick house. She had just suddenly appeared when we got the school and moved into the dorm.

From what I gathered, Celia had met Audra in some sort of singing group or class affiliated with her college. Audra was practically an opera singer; the windows shook when she sang. Audra had convinced this seemingly sophisticated black girl's parents, who were professional people, that Celia would be getting in on the ground level of a new performing arts school that was going to take off. Celia would get teaching experience, as well as opportunities to perform for large audiences. She would also get free room and board, and she could continue her classes at the local college. (The sad thing is, I think Audra really believed our organization could offer all that, so much did she believe in her husband's vision and in the spiritual power that was the source of her faith).

Art Shoman was in rare form when we first got the school. He wore black turtlenecks (like a beatnik artist type) and a denim leisure suit (like a dressed-up hippy). He mostly kept his brown hair short and neat, which was practically a rule for all the brothers as well (though the style of the day, for young people, was longer, which meant the boys usually had to cut their hair soon after they joined). At the school, Art liked standing on top of an old solid-oak teacher's desk, giving an animated speech or leading us in song.

Song became such a mission that I sometimes think of Art Shoman with a conductor's wand, though he never used one. He used his hands like one. His vision had to do with reviving the music heritage of our city which, a decade earlier, had been a creative center for popular music by African American artists. Somehow he hoped to revive that spirit by the time Rev. Moon came to town, and maybe have us perform before Father's speech. At the same time he said he was talking to "Gladys Knight & the Pips", a popular, black family singing group, just in case we did not get up to caliber in time.

Back at the dorm, Celi was on cloud nine, singing like an angel as we got ready for bed. Finally, she had stuff to talk about. Usually it was me talking about the Divine Principle, and her not having a clue. But music? She could talk about that all night long and put you to sleep singing a lullaby.

"I love Gladys Knight and the Pips," she said. "Maybe if we get them, and we have learned their songs- which I already know most of, by the way- we do background harmony- as if they don't do enough harmony,but we could back them up- and dance around them on stage…"

She went on like that until we both drifted off, dancing our way into dreamland.

The school did not have an auditorium. There was a large gathering room, which could be used as a cafeteria or an auditorium, according to how the folding chairs and/or tables were arranged. We used it as a cafeteria so our singing and dancing practice was done around these obstacles, after the evening meal, when we came in from selling. Then, on teaching nights, when we invited students of the Divine Principle to eat with us before classes (which took place on various levels, in various classrooms), we also practiced our songs on these students.

We were singing popular songs about brotherhood and love, which was not unusual. We had a Unification Church songbook full of popular songs that had been altered. Bob Dylan's "answer" was Blowing in the Wind but our answer, to his song full of questions, was

"In the Hearts of Men". The American church mostly borrowed from 1960s folk singers. But Art Shoman had us borrowing from Soul, R & B, and Rock. He wanted us to stand out in the eyes of Father, as a more "dynamic" branch of the Family (reflecting his own personality).

Art and Audra knew who had exceptional singing voices, as we sang every day. Audra had a powerful voice that she had been training in local classes, where she had met Celia and Jermain, and she had been taking one of her foster daughters, Dawna. Those were the only trained voices amongst us. The rest of us sang more from the heart than the belly. We knew nothing about professional singers' use of the diaphragm, and Audra was not the one conducting us (as she stayed at the apartment with her children when we practiced, evenings).

Art went fishing for trained instrumentalists. There was an old, untuned upright piano at the school that some of us played with. Danny was the only one in the group who'd had lessons, and he preferred to play his guitar. Danny was not especially talented on either instrument and only played when he had readable music to look at. We were all fondly familiar with the fun but often comical sound of Danny, hiding somewhat in a remote corner of the Center (where some of us would delightedly join him, if our time was unscheduled) singing at bit off key as he struggled to play from a music book entitled "Popular Songs of the Seventies". (As we did not have radios, record players, or tape players in our Centers, and so many of us had been following the proverbial pipers of our time when we joined the Movement, Danny's awkward sound plucked at our collective heartstrings. Art had always been tolerant of him on the One World Crusade, but Audra had sometimes chastised him for choosing songs that were "off-center" when they were less about universal love and more about romantic love or (that dirty word, in the fallen world) sex. Jermain was another one that got chastised when he cut loose on the piano sometimes, playing by ear and making up his own, sometimes "fallen" lyrics. But they were about all Art had to work with. Harvey had played drums in junior high, and he was inclined to start drumming on a table, or the top of the piano, when we sang. He had used a practice pad for school lessons, and never owned a whole drum set. Art bought one for him and, to keep the rest of us from feeling like he was showing favoritism (when we all knew Harvey was Art's favorite anyway), Art said it was also for his second child, Jonathan (who would be going into junior high the next school year).

Danny played guitar and piano, and Harvey played drums, on "Get Together". And Jermain played piano on "Lean on Me". Danny looked like Ringo Starr, who was the goofier looking Beatle but had great bangs and a nice body. (Danny didn't have Ringo Starr's big nose, but his lips were big and his eyes ridiculously bedroom-y at times (displaying his struggle with off-centered thoughts, to a comical extent). Harvey, a white guy with wire-rimmed glasses, looked like John Denver and had his perpetual smile and breath-of-fresh-air, cosmopolitan-country hippy style. Jermain was a lean, very black guy of medium height, and he was a natural dancer with a fantastic sense of rhythm and a charming smile. Jermain could carry a tune, too, but so much the power behind his voice did not match the energy of his physical movement. And when Jermain played the piano, it was part of a dance which could not be pinned down. There was no predictability.

"I don't know how you ever did stand-in for the Spinners," Art Shoman would say to Jermain when he went off into a James Brown type shuffle. (The Spinners were carefully choreographed, matching their every move to perfectly harmonized vocals).

Danny was the only one who knew anything about electronics. He always set up the sound systems at our rallies. He set up an area in the cafeteria/ auditorium of our school, so that featured musicians could be amplified.

Art had Danny playing the guitar part for "Get Together" by the Youngbloods. Harvey played the understated drum part. The rest of us were supposed to dance around while singing the song. We practiced on Divine Principle students when they sat at tables after meals. We wove in and out, singing directly to their faces at close range.

Needless to say, sometimes people looked as if this made them feel a bit uncomfortable. Some of the male students seemed, by their facial expressions, to be enjoying this part of the routine in (what would have usually been considered) an inappropriate way. Unification Church sisters did not usually dance around or display their bodies in obviously alluring ways.

Rose herself had grown accustomed to attracting people with her face, her eyes, while steering them toward her mind, her heart, her understanding of the Divine Principle and ultimately of God's heart reflected in the Family. In witnessing and teaching, she had pulled young men to her (to a certain extent) for what she felt was God's purpose, but she had not held onto any of the spiritually younger students, before Danny.

Now Rose struggled, trying to let go of her attachment to Danny, as she felt separated out, ironically lonelier because of it. Though she had not taken Danny into her body, certainly Rose had taken him into herself in a way that had changed her. Even Audra, who had never appeared to pay much attention to Rose, commented one day (when they were both in front of the big mirror in the girls' restroom at the school, washing their hands at neighboring sinks) that Rose was "beginning to look more womanly". Rose only knew that her clothes were getting tighter, probably from all the starchy foods that stretched their meals. If anything, Rose felt that she was losing her glow from the inside, which had been her real beauty.

Dancing around in the cafeteria/auditorium, to an audience of Divine Principle students, Rose found herself glancing at Jade, the young woman who had been a topless dancer when Art Shoman converted her. Jade obviously felt comfortable gyrating around tables, singing inches from people's faces with a smile that was both intimate and distant, warm but artful. "The Moonies" were becoming famous, in the media, for "plastered-on", "moon-faced smiles", but Rose had always felt her smile coming from within, from her heart, and she had seen her brother's and sister's that way.

Now Rose felt drained from a day of selling in the cold, and found herself singing soullessly, trying to imitate Jade's sinewy movements and seductive smile. It did not seem to matter whether they ate their white rice or pasta-stretched evening meal before or after their performance (meant as practice for when Rev. Moon would come to town on his speaking tour). The energy this dance required dimmed the power of her heart, which had been the very source and force behind her untrained singing voice.

All Rose really wanted to do at the end of the day was to curl up on her bunk (hug her pillow and think about Danny). She knew she should be praying, but all she could see when she closed her eyes was Danny, standing up in front of the group with his guitar. Of course other girls were fixated on the instrumental performers as well. Sisters sometimes talked about the brothers they liked, in the laundry room or when they were paired up for selling or witnessing.

"Who would you want to be 'blessed' to if you had to pick one of the brothers?"

A black girl would usually say "Jermain", or a white girl would usually say "Harvey". Most knew, on some level, that Rose liked Danny. So they wouldn't say Danny, though she knew a few liked him. Usually they would laugh if she said she liked Danny. He was comical and fun, everybody's go-to for lightening up. Which made it hard for Rose to understand why she felt so heavy, weighted as she was by this new love. She thought it was due to "The Fall" and wondered if she would ever recover.

One of the rare times that winter, when Rose was not-so-alone, in this feeling of being separated out by love, was when they traveled to another city for a rally, and she got to spend time with Beth (her first and best sister from back home).

In the big, windy city, Beth was at Gabe's side. Strangely, this fact felt more comforting than painful, now that Rose was in love with Danny. Gabe had taken his rightful place in Rose's heart, as her spiritual father, brother in God, and familiar old friend. Gabe had once said, when he took the Family to see the movie Doctor Zhivago. that the wife of the good doctor, in the story, reminded him of Rose, and the comrade (and lover) reminded him of Beth. Their roles in Gabe's life and mission had changed since then. Beth was the first-lady in his new kingdom. And Rose really had no idea how Gabe thought of her now.

Gabe did seem glad to see Rose, when the white One World Crusade vans with the red stylized karma-wheels arrived at his Center. Rose was glad to see Gabe too, but she did not feel the magnetic pull that had drawn her irresistibly to him before. He had put on weight, and so had Beth (who had also cut her previously long, dark hair). At this new Center together, Gabe and Beth seemed to be perpetually sharing a huge bag of cheese-puffs.

Rose did not eat cheese puffs, and she had only "filled-out". Her dark auburn locks were still long, though usually tied back. Rose was still beautiful, but instead of a Rose that had opened (which, in fact, she had, to some extent, with Danny) she had closed around her secret, diminishing her rose-y glow. Rose did not feel (and maybe, on some level, where shame had slithered in, did not want to be) very attractive. She had started wearing anything she could get her hands on to stay warm, except for the new coat Danny had helped her choose (watching patiently as she had tried on one after the other). It had been the first time that past Indian Summer when Art Shoman had given them ten-percent "incentive pay" for their week's work. Since then, the stylish coat, a long and fitted wrap coat with a tie-belt and hood, chocolate brown and accented with embroidery in bright, fall colors, had been discovered, hanging in a shared closet in the sisters' room. Sharon had asked, with pleading eyes and a humbled head and voice, if she could borrow it.

At the time, Rose seemed adequately coated, as she had been wearing a hand-me-down, short and shabby grey plaid coat trimmed with dingy, wooly-looking fake fur that could be pulled up around the neck. Audra had cast it into the sisters' room one night, and Rose had picked it up when no one else did, the next time they were all bundling up to go out selling. Rose was afraid if she wore her new coat it would just end up looking as shabby as Audra's cast-off.

Sharon, an elegant, golden lovely, borrowed Rose's new coat one day, and wore it proudly all winter. Rose had wanted to save it for special occasions, like the rally they were having with Gabe's group, but she could not bring herself to ask Sharon to give it back (and Sharon never offered). Sharon apparently did not have a coat, though this seemed odd since her parents lived nearby, she was still in college and always wore stylish new pants suits or long skirts or dresses (which Rose's coat complemented beautifully).

Rose just tried to keep herself warm. She bought a bright green knit toboggan, which was plain but brought out her stunning, dark-browed green eyes. She pulled the cap down over her ears and tied her shabby coat collar up around her neck with a grey knit scarf that Audra had thrown into the sisters' room, along with the coat. She bought herself leather gloves and boots lined with rabbit fur, and layered her knit tops under a green, button-up sweater. She had one nice garment: a pair of green tweed wool pants, with a wide waistband, pleated, baggy legs with cuffs, and big pockets. She had bought them back home when she and Gabe were both working at Sears (Gabe in appliance sales, and she in Junior Bazaar). Maybe he recognized them when she wore them to the rally, or maybe not (as the trousers had hung loosely on her body back home, but now fit tight).

Beth wore a puffy down jacket which, Rose thought, made her look even more like an Eskimo than she already did. Beth and Rose both had dark hair and black eyebrows, but Beth's eyes were almost slanted, especially when she smiled. At least Beth's jacket was a feminine color, deepest pink (which matched her wide mouth). Otherwise, with the jacket's shapelessness and the boyish cut of Beth's hair, she could have been mistaken for one of the brothers. Beth had never worn make-up, but she had beautiful skin.

"I need to use the restroom," Beth told Rose, when they stepped into a fast-food joint for a hot-chocolate.

Rose wondered why she'd had a drained feeling around Beth, ever since they had jumped into the same van and started clinging to each other. Beth seemed tired and distracted.

"Do you have a tampon?" Beth asked, as they went into adjoining stalls.

"Sure." Rose took one out of the zipper area of the open cross-body bag she carried her Church literature and money in. "Art lets us keep ten-percent of our earnings," Rose said. "He calls it incentive pay."

"That's cool," Beth said.

"So, what's it like with Gabe, these days?" Rose asked from her stall.

"It's Ok. We're close…maybe too close. I try to support Gabe, in ways that I think our Mother would support our Father. But Gabe is not our Father; he's not even who we thought he was, Rose."

"Hmm." Rose did not know what to say. She had seen Gabe's strong side, and his weak side. "Maybe he's struggling," she said.

"Oh, Gabe is struggling all right," Beth said, coming out of her stall and going to the sink.

"We all do," Rose confessed.

For the rest of their time together, selling on the streets and dodging snow flurries by darting into White Castles for mini-burgers and hot chocolate, they talked about Gabe and Danny. It wasn't happy talk. Beth had set the tone, venting about her old friend and Center director in a way wives complain about their husbands, with a negative shake of the head and a slight but ironic smile. "He's not perfect, but he's mine," was Beth's clear message.

Rose commiserated, venting what she had held inside. Her message was, "I thought he was mine, but now I'm not sure. And it is fallen of me to want him anyway."

Rose didn't know what Beth was thinking about or dreaming of, if anything other than what she talked about. Beth had never been as open as Rose, and she was clearly holding something tight in the space around her, even as they curled up together when they napped on the floor of the van.

Rose knew what she was holding tight in the space around her. Danny, however had other people in the space around him. Besides his stage cohorts, he had two new side-kicks. One was a young girl, a new foster daughter of Audra's. Darcy was sixteen, still wore her tight jeans and shape-showing sweaters, had blonde hair down to her waist, and followed Danny around with a quiet femininity that made him feel like the important one.

Danny's new male side-kick (if he was male, as some were calling "Cat" gay) was at least out of high-school, but also followed Danny around like a new puppy. Art and Audra insisted on calling the new guy "Thomas", but he called himself "Cat" and so did most people. Cat was obviously mixed ("high-yellow" was the older term) with a leonine Afro that circled his head like a dingy halo. Like Danny, he could never be completely tamed. Cat had moved in quickly after hearing the Divine Principle lecture series, but he had quietly refused the ritualistic haircut, which usually happened at the Center, after the first week. Art Shoman, secretly a lover of rebels (since he was one himself) picked his battles with some and didn't figure it was worth fighting with Cat about his mane.

So, we may not have looked like hippies, standing next to a crowd of protesters, but we had Cat. When we locked arms in front of the Convention Center, we could have been mistaken for a Sunday School class, but Cat stood out as our symbol of free-spirited universal brotherhood. A more pervasive symbol that day, however, was the American flag, more likely to be worn than waved by the general population of youth during the Viet Nam War era. Our leaders, Art and Gabe, held large flags high while the rest of us waved small flags. The protestors yelled "Fuck Nixon!" while we sang "God Bless America".

Nixon managed to get into the building alive. I really had no idea what was being said and done inside. I was just following my leaders, who were following our church Father. Rev. Sun Myung Moon had started a national campaign, called "Forgive, Love, Unite". Full page ads, displaying a speech written by Rev. Moon, were in every major newspaper in the United States. And the person he was praying for America to "forgive" was our President: Richard Nixon.

A Child is Born

I got singled out. Not sure why, because they had never included me in their inner circle. Thing is, Audra just gave her to me and disappeared, had things to do at the school.

Now I think it's because they thought I was pure; (Audra's one real compliment had been telling me, "You have an air of cleanliness about you."). Maybe they thought Marin would turn out like me instead of like their eldest (whose personality seemed to be turning out like her original babysitter, Jade).

So there I was suddenly, living in the laundry room of the Shoman's apartment, where they had placed a cot and a crib. There were diapers nearby, and bottles of formula in the fridge. Most of the time Marin just slept. I read. I couldn't open up enough to write about what was on my mind, which was Danny. Somehow nothing that I owned felt like mine (including my journal, and mySelf) in their apartment.

I took comfort in a newly published book they had given me: a collection of speeches by "Rev. Moon" (as the media was calling our church Father now). *New Hope for America* was the title, and Rev. Moon had given the speeches in cities he had been to recently, on his tour to the greatest cities in each of the fifty states. He would be coming to our city soon, and the Shomans had chosen me to be the usher who would first greet our Father when he entered the great hall. I had already found a suitable suit, when we went to a mall on one of our free-days. Other than that, I didn't get out with my brothers and sisters much that winter, except when we participated in the big, national campaigns.

We went other places besides the rally, in a neighboring state, at the Republican National Convention. We also traveled in our white vans to New York City (for Rev. Moon's speech, to a full house, at Madison Square Gardens). And we went to Washington, D.C. for a "Forgive, Love, Unite" rally in the park across from the White House (which President Nixon, himself, ended up attending).

In spite of all the excitement, I passed the winter in sort-of a fog. My life went back and forth between the sleepy boredom of attending a sleeping infant, and the over-stimulation of participating in group gatherings orchestrated (mostly by Art Shoman) to have the high-energy of pep-rallies and rock-concerts.

Art apparently had a similar feast or famine dilemma with his energy levels, because most of the time he seemed to be resting, trying to recharge at the apartment, watching TV. When his wife and children were home, Art was often irritable, snapping at them from his spot in front of the TV as they bustled busily about the apartment. Audra almost never sat down.

Sometimes, when the baby was asleep and Rose came out to make herself a sandwich, Art seemed to sense her loneliness. (Maybe, in his own way, he was lonely too.) He occasionally invited her to join him in the cozy den, which had a big, comfortable couch and a thick carpet. But they never really talked. Art was usually concentrating intently on whatever story he watched, which usually had a science fiction or political plot. Rose could never find a feminine character to identify with, and usually drifted back to her cot in the laundry room after eating her sandwich.

Once Rose came out when she had been crying. It had never been unusual for Rose to cry. For as long as she could remember, especially since her parents started breaking up (before they divorced when she was ten) Rose had released her emotional suffering by cleansing and comforting herself with tears. It wasn't unusual for her to be hungry afterwards either. At home she would have made herself a banana sandwich and poured a glass of milk. Mama Sue always kept a good supply of milk, bread, and mayo, usually some bananas, and often a bag of sour cream and onion potato chips (which Rose requested as a favorite snack, along with Little Debbie Swiss-cake rolls, apricots, dried beef curled up in a juice glass, and sliced pickles). Arti Rose never asked for anything particular at the Shoman apartment. In fact, Arti Rose did not exist at the Shoman apartment, except in

Rose's dream world. Whoever they thought Rose was, the Shomans were projecting onto her for their own purposes. Sometimes Rose felt at home with the children. Other than the baby, however, the kids were rarely at the apartment. They were in school. Ironically, with all the family circles being drawn on blackboards, at classes the Shomans taught, there was no nurturing "atmosphere" of "love" and "joy" felt by the one adult who spent the most time in their home (namely Rose). There was little sense of "family", and there were too few family rituals in the apartment. Rose's sense of isolation, in the corner of the laundry room where she dwelled with the mostly sleeping infant, made her feel as if she was being sucked into a black hole in some far corner of the universe.

Audra and her children must have been somewhere else, surely and securely gone, maybe to Audra's parents home at the lake when the unfortunate incident happened. For whatever reason, Art acted differently. Maybe he sensed that Rose had been crying, maybe he actually looked at her swollen eyes as she sat at the other end of the long couch, eating her bagel with cream cheese and grape jelly (the one Shoman snack she had learned to love). His deluded male ego must have thought he could be of service. Or maybe his actions were self-serving. Most likely, it was some of both.

Anyway, he leaned her way, stretched out his hand, scooted over (when she, shocked and confused, did not respond), took her hand and pulled gently as he lowered himself onto the still new-smelling rug.

"Come 'ere,' he said. "It's Ok. Relax." He patted the carpet beside him. She lowered herself.

"You look so tense," he said, barely looking at her, stretching his orchestrating hand out in front of her along the soft rug. "I just want to give you a massage…there, lie on your stomach. It's Ok."

Rose went along with it and was beginning to relax when Art did something that made her tense up more than ever. He raised her loose t-shirt, still reassuring her it was Ok, and undid her bra, saying he could do a better job without that in the way. Maybe she did need a massage, Rose thought, raising her arms up, putting her hands under her head, trying to get comfortable and relax. But before she could settle into what (giving Art the benefit of the doubt) he seemed to be offering for her own good, she felt his hands go astray. He started running them up and down her sides, with the tips of his fingers, from under her arms (which tickled, but she froze against that response) all the way down to the waistband on her pants. Then he brought his fingers back up, resting them to fondle where the sides of her breasts were smashed out under the weight of her body.

Rose tensed, saying, "I think I'd better get up now."

Art moved his body, which had been straddling her (though not seated on her). "Suit yourself," he said. "I was just trying to help."

"Thanks, but I'm going to check on the baby now," Rose said, going back to the laundry room, locking the door, getting in her cot, and praying Audra would get home before the baby woke up.

When Audra was home she often took Marin, gave her a bottle and played with her, even took her to bed with she and Art sometimes. Maybe Art felt neglected.

For whatever reason, what had happened had happened, and though they went along as usual for a while, things would never be the same.

"The Holy Spirit is a Woman"

I was so nervous the day Father came for his speech. I couldn't eat; my stomach was full of butterflies. I was told to stand at the top of a hand-rail where He would come up the steps of the great hall, and in through the big doors. It was dusky out. He was flanked on all sides when he got out of the limo. So I could barely see him until he was upon me. His entourage went into single file on the sort-of ramp area where he came up. So he did walk very near to me, though he was focused on staying close to the strong-looking man in front of him (and another of the same followed). Rev. Moon did not turn his head to the right, where I stood so near. Nor did he divert his eyes in my direction to give me even the slightest glance. His focus forward was that of a laser beam. He looked very hard to me, like stone.

As soon as he and his apparent body-guards had passed, a little old Korean lady, holding a purse on her arm, stopped at the top of the railing and looked right into my eyes (as I had hoped "Father" would do). With the warm familiarity of a grandmother, she gave me a sweet smile while reaching into her purse for a mint, which she pressed into my hand as she passed. I don't remember her saying a word. Someone soon told me, "That was Miss Kim" (the author of the first translation of the Divine Principle into English, the first Unification Church missionary to the United States, and the founder of the UC Center in San Francisco where Gabe, my spiritual father, had joined).

I had never, in my life, been more in need of a mint.

"His Face is like the Sun and like the Moon"

We did not perform before Rev. Moon's speech. Art had decided we were just not up-to-par. Or, at least, that's what he said, not very nicely, in a tirade he subjected us to one evening at what had been rehearsal time. *(Later I heard there were threats of lawsuits from popular songwriters, especially in the folk-rock genre, who did not want their lyrics altered and their tunes used to promote Rev. Moon).* Getting the famous black family Motown group "Gladys Knight & the Pips" was Art's unfulfilled dream. So he hired a black gospel choir from one of the local churches instead. They were quite primitive, and the contrast with the restrained, almost prim Col. Pak (who introduced Rev. Moon at length) was almost comical.

Father's speech was very close to what I had been reading in his closely held and cherished book of recent speeches from that "New Hope for America" tour. His appearance and manner, however, were different from what I had imagined. He spoke in Korean, and he was thick, like a wrestler (not a particularly elegant man). Though his interpreter Col. Pak was lean and intellectual-looking, calm and dignified, while trying to translate some of the emotion expressed (though it came out in a sort-of military, cut and dried style), Rev. Moon was obviously an evangelist. His style was nearly as emotionally and physically expressive as the holy-roller black choir. He yelled (in Korean), sweated, stomped around, gestured dramatically. And his face was practically that of a contortionist. Every emotion imaginable was expressed there. There was just no doubt in my mind that, whatever he was saying (which had the word "God" in it a lot), he meant it on a gut-level. Ironically, his style came close to those sweat-wiping, suit-wearing Southern Baptist and Pentecostal preachers I had turned my back on when I'd left Alabama. (Not that I had ever completely doubted them- just broadened my mind beyond their limited, dogmatic perspectives and emotionally manipulative, sometimes fear-mongering, methods. Unlike internationally popular Billy Graham, however, Rev. Moon did not do an "altar call" (herding the audience forward to be "saved") at the end of his speech.

After the speech, the local family met the "Father and Mother" at McDonalds, at Father's request. (We had heard that Father loved McDonalds and ate a Big-Mac for lunch most days, but with a side of kimchee instead of fries). I bravely sat at a table near them. They radiated such warmth, and I wanted to radiate that warmth back to them, to give them joy (as the Principle said we were meant to do for our Parents, and for God). True Mother seemed a bit shy, but so was I. I stayed in my seat but aimed my camera first at Mother, who smiled but diverted her eyes, and then at Father because he was already grinning at me, making it easy for me. This made up for his stone-faced entrance earlier. In a more relaxed mode, he really did look the part of a big Papa Bear, huggable and fun (down-to-earth).

Father was quick to laugh at Art Shoman's easy antics. Art and Audra had their children with them, which took the heat off the rest of us. The bubbly spontaneity of the children kept us all entertained, so Art and his family stayed at the center of Father's attention. Art was beaming with pride. He had clearly wanted to stand out as a great leader in Father's movement, as a true son. Somehow, they seemed to speak the same language without actually doing so. And in this situation, at a McDonalds eating fun food and just relaxing in our shared afterglow, little language was needed.

After the True Parents left, Art gave all of the brothers and sisters medallions Father had left as gifts for us. They were burnished, heavy brass, larger than silver-dollars, with the "horsemen of the apocalypse" etched on, hanging on a strip of leather. I treasured mine but never wore it around my neck, as Art Shoman did sometimes when he wore a turtleneck. I kept it in a bag Audra privately gave me.

The bag was from True Mother, Hak Ja Han Moon. It was a carry-on travel-bag with both a hand strap and a shoulder-strap. The brown vinyl looked like leather at first glance.

"This is from Mother," Audra said. For a moment she made eye contact with me, and I felt really special (for a second, before Audra's wandering eye wandered off). Maybe True Mother had noticed me as an usher at Father's speech, or when I sat near them at McDonalds. I had been chosen, deemed deserving of something that our True Mother, the restored Eve, had carried as she stood by the side of our Father, the restored Adam (the new Messiah!), on his mission to save mankind. But the moment of feeling special did not last. When Audra saw my eyes light up, she quickly looked down, pointing to a little torn place on the shoulder strap (which I might never have noticed, otherwise, and would not have found difficult to mend when or if I did notice it).

"Mother is photographed everywhere she goes; so everything she wears and carries has to be perfect. She went shopping for a new bag while she was here and told me to give this to one of the sisters," Audra explained, her lazy eye soon giving up its attempt to focus on me.

"Thanks," I said, as Audra turned to her next task.

Once again I felt lesser-than. Everything I wore or carried did not have to be perfect, because I was not perfect or sinless or true. But maybe someday I would be "blessed" in marriage by the True Parents, and my children would be born sinless and true. Maybe I would buy them real leather travel bags, and they would be ambassadors for world peace, protected wherever they might go (by the horsemen-of-the-apocalypse).

But wait, aren't the horsemen supposed to bring war and plagues, etc., even though one of them supposedly represents Jesus Christ? I never liked the Book of Revelation anyway. Revival preachers in the South used that to scare people into coming to the altar. When I was a kid I went to the altar for nicer preachers (when I was inspired, not scared), and when they sang heart-tugging songs like "Come Home".

"This I Pledge & Swear"

Another gift we all got from the Father was a laminated copy of the "Children's Oath". It was not much bigger than a driver's license or credit card, made to fit into a see-through sleeve of a wallet like a child's school photo, with a symbol like the sun (with twelve light or dark rays, according to where the eyes focused, and a circle of light at the center).

The print was on both sides of the card, and so tiny that only young eyes could read it without magnification. We said it often enough to learn it by heart, but I carried the copy Reverend Moon had given me for years, transferring it from one wallet to another (until those spaces got filled with more normal, sometimes required symbols of card-carrying adulthood in 20-21st century American society). Eventually it was tucked into a pocket of an old canvas back-pack full of memorabilia and pushed to the back of my closet. But it will never be discarded by these hands.

As small as my palm and as light as a feather, the "Children's Oath" is one of the heaviest things I ever carried.

CHILDREN'S OATH

1) As the center of the cosmos, I will fulfill our Father's will (Purpose of
    creation), and the responsibility given me (for self-perfection). I will
    become a dutiful son (daughter) and a child of goodness to attend our
    Father forever in the ideal world of creation by returning joy and glory
    to Him.   This I pledge.

2) I will take upon myself completely, the Will of God to give me the whole
    creation as my inheritance. He has given me His word, His personality,
    and His heart, and is reviving me who had died, making me one with Him
    and His true child. To do this, our Father has persevered for 6,000 years

the sacrificial way of the cross.   This I pledge.

3)   As a true son (daughter), I will follow our Father's pattern and charge
*   bravely forward into the enemy camp until I have judged them completely*
*   with the weapons with which He has been defeating the enemy Satan for*
*   me throughout the course of history by sowing sweat for earth, tears for*
*   man, and blood for heaven, as a servant but with a father's heart, in*
*   order to restore His children and the universe, lost to Satan.*
*   This I pledge.*

4) The individual, family, society, nation, world, and cosmos who are
*   willing to attend our Father, the source of peace, happiness, freedom,*
*   and all ideals, will fulfill the ideal world of one heart in one body by*
*   restoring their original nature. To do this, I will become a true son*
*   (daughter), returning joy and satisfaction to our Father, and as our*
*   Father's representative, I will transfer to the creation peace, happiness,*
*   freedom, and all ideals in the world of the heart.   This I pledge.*

5)   I am proud of the one Sovereignty, proud of the one people, proud of the one land, proud of the one language and culture centered upon God,

proud of becoming the child of the One True Parent, proud of the family

who is to inherit one tradition, proud of being a laborer who is working

to establish the one world of the heart.

I will fight with my life.

I will be responsible for accomplishing my duty and mission.

This I pledge and swear…

President Nixon and Mama Sue

I didn't talk with my mom much. We didn't have cell phones then. I don't remember there being more than one common phone per dwelling. There was, of course, a phone in the Shoman's apartment. It was not in the laundry room, or anywhere that I could have had much privacy. I don't really remember calling Mama Sue there, but she may have called me. She did tell me later that Art Shoman had promised her, when I left with the One World Crusade, that he would take care of her daughter. Maybe she had his phone number. Still, I don't remember being in contact with her very often during that time.

Not having been a mother myself, I could not have known how much Mama Sue missed me. I knew she visited the Unification Church Center near where she worked (the one I had left). The sisters there reminded her of me. She had made friends with them. They got used to her stopping by with donations of fresh food, and sometimes staying a while to show them how to cook what she had brought. Sometimes Sue stayed for one of their lectures. She came to respect their system of thought, but she never agreed with all of it.

Sue Cronkite had grown up Baptist, married a Methodist, and

was still a member of a local Methodist Church. Having grown up in a rural community where there were few other cultural outlets, church had always been Sue's favorite place to socialize. She also drew inspiration from the Bible and varied church literature (especially a publication of daily meditations). Her father, however, had taught her to "take all that with a grain of salt". So, she pretty much seasoned everything she heard or read (from any religious or philosophical persuasion) to her own taste. At the time, she was reading St. Thomas Aquinas. She shared some of his ideas, and some of her own, during the discussions she got into with the young people at the Center. They understood that Ms. Sue was not likely to join their church. However, she showed them respect, and they came to think of her as a friend that they could trust.

Someone may have told me that my mother was going to be in Washington, D.C. when we went there for the "Forgive, Love, Unite" campaign. I don't remember whether I had been told, or whether I was surprised when I first saw her in the big hotel we all stayed in. She was staying in a room with the sisters from the Center back home. I was thrilled to see them, warmed from the inside out. I stayed by my mother's side for the duration of that experience. Once we even had some time alone for a few hours, when the sisters went to a big meeting to prepare for the rally.

I remember talking to my mother as if I was witnessing to some stranger, babbling on and on about "New Hope for America", showing her things I had underlined in the book of Rev. Moon's speeches that I had been reading. She listened patiently, never really agreeing or disagreeing much, just giving me her attention. She kept repeating, "It's so good to see you, Arti Rose."

I don't remember talking to my mother about the infant I had been taking care of. I don't remember talking to her about Danny either, although I did introduce her to him when our whole movement went to see the Washington Monument. Danny was hanging out with a little group from our own Center, including Darcy and Cat, who always followed him around lately.

Danny tended to follow Rose around (whenever he caught sight of her, outside the Shomans' apartment). Maybe Mama Sue sensed a special relationship there; maybe not.

It was a massive crowd by the time they got to the park across from the White House. Then Rose was following Danny, who came in handy because he was aggressive and bigger than most people, and he plowed a path. Mama Sue followed Rose and Danny straight to the center of the crowd. When they got to an area where the big-wigs of the church had created an inner circle in the middle of the crowd, Danny approached Art Shoman, said something, then turned and pointed to the lady from the press. Art recognized her and excitedly waved she and Rose in. Sue Cronkite needed to be as close as she could get to Mr. Nolan (leader of the Washington, D.C. Center and the national church) because the newspaper she worked for expected a story. Mr. Nolan was only a few feet from Sue Cronkite with the giant candle that was supposed to burn for the duration of President Nixon's term.

Many Americans wanted Nixon impeached, and there was speculation that he would likely resign before that would happen. Rev. Moon did not want that to happen. Nixon had been the first American president to visit China, and he was a staunch anti-communist. The leader (who had survived the split of his homeland and started his church in a North Korean prison camp) appreciated Nixon in a way that Rose did not understand at the time. Sue Cronkite, who did not particularly like Nixon, nevertheless lived in a conservative state and worked for a newspaper that had endorsed Nixon. Though Rev. Moon was a foreigner, his position regarding President Nixon was not far from that of many southerners. So, Sue went with the flow. She wouldn't be expressing opinions anyway, just giving them the who-what-when-where-why-& how. And, hopefully, getting a picture.

"My feet are cold," was about all Sue said, hiking her shoulder bag into place and pulling her little spiral note-pad and pencil out of the outer flap. Her Canon SLR manual camera was hanging around her neck, loaded with a fresh roll of black and white 35mm film, flash secured on top.

Making a Memory

"You should have boots and gloves on Mama," I said, looking her over as if for the first time.

I was not accustomed to telling Mama Sue how to dress. Before leaving her for college and then the movement, I had been barely more than her little girl. And when we were getting ready, back at the hotel, I was incessantly babbling about the Divine Principle (stuck in "witnessing" mode, which was the only way I had related to anyone not in the Unification Church "Family" for the past year-and-a-half).

Mama Sue had at least brought a silk scarf, which was tied under her chin, Audrey Hepburn style. Her shoes were the little leather heels she wore to work, with sandal-strap backs. I tucked my right arm into her left, hoping to help her keep her balance in the grass, hoping to help keep her warm too. She did at least wear a coat.

"Mom, don't you have a pair of gloves in your purse?" I asked.

"Wouldn't be able to take notes, much less pictures," she said, glancing down at the camera hanging at her midriff. She had adjusted the aperture and shutter-speed as soon as they'd settled into their place in the inner circle of the crowd. Most people in the crowd had little candles and were passing around lighters or sharing their flames. Sue, however, had enough newspaper reporter paraphernalia to juggle, without adding a candle to all that. (Besides the fact that she was not, really, one of us Nixon supporters and had some doubt about my understanding of who and what I was indirectly giving my allegiance to, politically).

I lowered my right arm (which had been linked with her left arm, in comrade position), and took her bare left hand in my gloved right hand.

"Wish I'd brought my tape recorder," Sue Cronkite said. "Maybe I'll take a picture when Mr. Nolan lights the candle. How does he spell his first name?"

"I'm not sure, Mama."

"I'll call him," she said.

Mr. Nolan was going on and on, a flashlight on him with the big (still unlit) candle, reiterating the points made in Reverend Sun M. Moon's address to the nation, "Forgive, Love, Unite." The church had bought full-page ad spaces for the address, which had been printed in every major newspaper in America (including the one Sue Cronkite worked for).

"Did you read Rev. Moon's speech, Mama," I asked, whispering in her ear. "It's the same message."

"Hadn't yet," she said. "I've got that paper in my suit-case but haven't had much time to read."

(With her daughter talking so much, I heard in my mind).

"I'll give you a copy in a brochure," I said. "You can put it in your purse. It'll be easier to read on the plane that way."

She seemed to relax after that, somewhat, though still tensed from the cold. Then, just when we thought we would freeze to death, wondering why they didn't just go ahead and light that candle, Mr. Nolan started us singing the Unity song, first in Korean then in English.

"Our cherished hopes are for Unity;

Even our dreams are for Unity.

Come here quickly Unity; come along Unity.

Unity saving the people;

Unity saving all nations.

Come here quickly Unity;

Come along Unity."

The singing warmed us up a bit, and was repeated continually, getting more and more spirited, louder and louder. Then something I had heard rumors of, but never really expected, happened.

There was a bustle of activity from the edge of the crowd, moving us out in a wave as someone pushed his way toward the center. There was cheering that we did not understand. I thought Rev. Moon must have come, but I had heard he was in a different state, on his speaking tour. Then I saw something that seemed like a dream. Either we were delirious from cold and exhaustion, or President Richard Milhous Nixon was standing next to Mr. Nolan, in his pajamas and robe, right in front of us. Here was the man most of America had come to hate, his name the dirtiest word in everyday conversations over coffee and beer. He looked like anybody's grandpa, up getting a glass of warm milk when he couldn't sleep (which he probably had not been able to do, in the White House across the street, with all of us singing). Mr. Nolan was lighting the huge candle, which had four wicks.

"Four more years," the crowd started to chant, getting louder and louder.

Nixon, for once, was speechless. Tears broke out of his eyes and streamed down his face. We were close enough to see them glinting in the candle-light. I let go of Mama's hand as she lifted her camera to her face and took a shot.

The President of the United States was almost sobbing, but saved face by lifting his arms into the air, Nixon-style, and shouting, "Thank you...Thank you."

Then he shook Mr. Nolan's hand.

Sue Cronkite was taking pictures. Someone had gotten between her and Nixon. She took her camera from around her neck and lifted it high, taking a shot she could not see, but hoped would be right-on.

Various church leaders with megaphones had begun parting the waters so that Nixon could move safely out of the crowd. Suddenly someone's body shoved against Sue Cronkite, causing her to rock on the loosely sandaled heels of her work pumps. She nearly lost her balance and, though the crowd held her up, she did drop her camera. Before she could pick it up, President Nixon stepped on it. She managed to get it back, intact, but the flash was cracked.

When the President of the United States was safely back across the street, and in the White House, the rest of us exited the park in a relatively orderly fashion (excited, but ready to get out of the cold).

Back at the hotel we perched on beds and chairs for a while, talking about the experiences with our faces aglow.

Sue Cronkite read Rev. Moon's "Forgive, Love, Unite" address and worked on her story. She didn't want to wait until she was back home to write it. She wrote it by hand in her stenographer's notebook, then called it in, dictated it. The Associated Press picked it up. It was in her paper, and others, the very next day.

Maybe it should have moved people's hearts. But most people thought Nixon was a war-mongering crook, and Rev. Moon was just another gook-kook some of the hippy kids were following. At least I got to spend some time with my Mama.

Cast out of the Garden

Things went downhill rapidly from there, once we were back at the Center. I was stuck in the Shoman's apartment most of the time. When I got out, it was only to go to the school, which was always cold, or out selling in the snow or slush. When I wasn't in the Shoman's apartment I was always cold, no matter how much coffee or hot tea I drank at the school, and no matter how often I got off the street to guiltily dodge into White Castle burger joints for hot chocolate. In contrast, the Shoman's apartment was always too warm, and I wanted to sleep as much as the baby. Plus I figured it was better to just stay in the laundry room, where the baby was anyway, and I could avoid Art Shoman.

One day, when Audra was home, she asked me to come out and have a cup of ginseng tea with her, at the kitchen table. My stomach fluttered, as this was not a common ritual. Something was up. If she had intended it as a pleasantry, this was not going to happen. I was clearly near tears, a few sips in.

"So why are you depressed, Rose. Do you need to get out for a bit, maybe go witnessing for a change, or just do some personal shopping?"

I could not speak. The tears were starting to come. I picked up a napkin.

"It's not uncommon to get the winter blues here," she said. "Is that it, do you think? Or has something happened? You can tell me," she said.

"A few things have happened," I said, composing myself but feeling flushed. It was like I had opened the flood gate, then closed it; but there was still a crack in the dam.

Maybe I had too recently seen my mother, and that's who my subconscious hoped I was talking to. On a conscious level, I was so not used to Audra acknowledging my presence for any reason other than to instruct me regarding my duties, that I had not bothered to think the possibility of this moment through. And I was so bottled up. I had only hinted to Beth about what had happened with Danny. And I had told no one about the incident with Audra's husband.

"A few things have happened," I said. Then, with my hands shaking I spilled the tea and told all.

Audra just listened, offering nothing more than her napkin, to help wipe up my tea, until I was done.

Her face was blank, with that lazy eye (which had maintained its focus while I talked) wandering off to the side when I quieted down.

"Well," she said, getting up from her chair. "We'll have to make some changes." She patted me on my tense shoulder before gathering the teacups. "Don't you worry," she said in a voice so even-keeled that I could tell nothing.

I went back in the laundry room and read until I slept on my little cot, with the sleeping baby in her bassinet beside me. In a little while Audra came back, having picked up her older children from their schools. She had Sue Anne with her, which was not unusual. Sue Anne was Audra's usual after-school babysitter, but she lived in the dormitory. I heard the usual commotion in the apartment, and it was not long before Audra peeked into the laundry room.

"Rose, you can gather your things," Audra said quietly, not wanting to wake the baby. "You will be moving back into your room in the dorm," she said in the same tone she used for instructions she doled out almost constantly, as the Center Director. "Sue Anne can watch the baby, with Shawna's help. I'm trying to get Shawna to take more responsibility for her younger siblings anyway, and it's time she bonded with the baby."

(Time you bonded with the baby, too, I was thinking).

I had my old dorm room to myself now, as my old roommate had left when she and her parents had realized the Shomans were not going to make her a star. She had not even sang at the big auditorium before Rev. Moon gave his speech.

I had only been back in my dorm room for a few days when the Shomans invited all of the sisters into their apartment for tea. When we had perched here and there in seats around the den and dining area-room, with some of us settled on the rug with as much ladylike finesse as possible, Audra stood and spoke. Her husband, seated at the dining table, was the only male present.

"The reason we have gathered all of the sisters together here today is that we have learned of some incidents related to The Fall. Of course we are all fallen, as were our original parents, Adam and Eve, but we all know that our True Parents are here to remedy that. Meanwhile we all struggle with our fallen nature at one time or another along our path. So we are not here to single anyone out. Please relax."

Some of the sisters giggled. I did not.

"What we are here to do is to learn which ones of you may need more help than others, in this regard. It is our responsibility, as the Blessed Couple in charge of this Center, to help each of you prepare for your own blessing in marriage by our Father. So, in order to get to know you better, we are asking, and you may answer with a simple raise of your hand, 'How many of you have not yet lost your virginity?'"

Helga, the chubby, sweet-faced German cook (who'd had an obvious crush on Danny since the day he'd joined) raised her hand, and blushed.

"Only one virgin?" Audra sounded genuinely surprised. Even her teen-aged foster daughters had not raised their hands. "Well, that's a sign of the times."

"Ok." Art Shoman said, getting up from his chair. "You can put your cups in the kitchen and go out to the vans. Some brothers are waiting to drive you to your selling spots. It's a nice day, so let's push our product. We need to sell the mints before spring, since they are not a warm weather product…"

"I need Sue Anne and Rose to stay behind to help with the children, please," Audra shouted as we headed for the kitchen (and most, for the door).

I knew I was not the babysitter anymore; so, of course, I was being singled out.

As soon as Sue Anne had left to pick up the older children from their schools, I was asked to sit down at the kitchen table with Art and Audra.

"You're not a virgin?" Art asked, bold-faced and in obvious disbelief.

"Well," Audra said. "Don't worry about that, Dear. You are no exception, and we don't want you to feel singled-out. But we think you would be happier with a different mission at this time. And we have been asked to contribute one of our members to the Mobile Fundraising Team, which serves our national headquarters under the direction of our church president, Mr. Nolan. We considered sending Danny, but he is our highest seller and Art needs him for that mission here. Also, Danny is the newer member, and not as strong in faith as you are. This new mission is an honor, and we would not send you if you were not one of our stronger members. All of the brothers and sisters here respect you, and this change will be presented to them as a noble sacrifice on our part and a sort-of promotion into the national church for you. Your new church Center will be in Washington, D.C. but you won't be spending much time there. Mostly you will be living in camper-trailers, in various campgrounds. So you will get to 'see-the-USA'. Ha-Ha," Audra said, lightening up by referencing a TV ad for an automobile company.

With that Audra got up, picking up her cup and mine. I followed. No discussion.

"You can go back to the dorm. Take the day off. Start organizing your things for your new mission," Audra said as she showed me to the door of her apartment, with an air so light and matter-of-fact practical that one would think her husband had never sneakily touched my breasts.

Part II

M.F.T.

&

D.C.

Mobile Fundraising Team

I don't remember how I got to the campsite, or even exactly where I was. It was somewhere much warmer, somewhere I had not been before, flat and dry with lots of sky. Maybe Kansas; I remember going there (and lots of other corn and wheat-fieldy midwestern places). It must have been Spring by then because there is a photo of me in an ankle-length tropical-flowered cotton dress with an empire waistline, fitted at the bodice, with short bell-sleeves that ruffled. My hair is short, freshly cut, and I am smiling, still new to the MFT, and not yet miserable. The "Team Mother" who'd just cut my hair must have been miserable when the "Team Father" said, "Did you have to cut it ALL off?" It had been quite long, and quite beautiful (even tied-back, as I usually wore it, in a pony-tail down my back). That amount of thick, wavy, deeply and richly-hued reddish-brown hair could probably have been sold to a wig-maker for more money than I would make selling flowers for some time.

All the sisters on MFT had short hair. There wasn't even a shower at that particular campground, just a faucet on the outside of a building with toilets inside. There was no hot water. I don't remember restrooms inside the little camper trailers we slept in, either. Maybe there were small johns. I do remember kitchens, because I sometimes had to cook for the team.

It was not an easy life, but the scenery was priceless. I remember sleeping outside sometimes, in my sleeping bag, under a canopy of stars so bright and infinite in number that I would fall asleep with my soul singing, "My God how great thou art". Usually we slept inside though, sometimes as many as eight sisters in a little camper. We took turns with the various pull-out shelf-like bunks, and there were usually sisters on the floor as well. None of the spots were very comfortable, but we were always so tired from selling that we would crash hard and sleep all night.

MFT life was often compared to the military, but our battle was said to be with "Satan". One Team Leader I worked under was obsessed with Satan and often ended the prayers that sent us off to sell each morning, by pounding his fist on the dashboard of the van and saying, "Crush Satan!" Then we would jump out of the vans, "kamikaze" style (a WWII Japanese military term he used), with our buckets of flowers to sell. Rex also used the European military term "blitz", when he wanted us to get in and out of a situation where we'd been selling (like an office building or topless bar or factory or apartment complex) very quickly.

When the Team Mother who had cut my hair was sent back to her original Center (having earned, through service, the blessing of marriage to her husband from before they had joined) I was promoted to Team Mother. This meant that I sat up front next to Rex, in the vans, and sometimes stayed behind with him to make plans, shop for the group, etc. We were the Team Parents, which made us mates, of a sort, though there was no sex and, as far as I was concerned, no attraction.

When I look back now, I can see that the young man was depressed. He was not a very attractive person to me, though he looked fine in the wheat-colored linen blazer he wore most of the time. Some of the other sisters were seemed taken with him (in their subtle ways), bragging about how "strong" he was. He was tall and slender (but dense of muscle, wiry), with dark hair and glasses. I would not have found him unattractive (in spite of the scar above his upper lip, which went well with his sort-of bull-dogish, pug features) if his personality had been different. Maybe he thought he was unattractive, because of the "hair-lip", and hated both himself and the women he expected hatred from. Or maybe it was just me; his style rubbed me the wrong way. Besides his Hitler-style speeches (not filled with hatred for anyone but Satan and Communists, but too negative to inspire my gentle soul) he did not seem to have much to give. He was always nodding out, even sometimes at the wheel at redlights and such. He would drop us off at a shopping-center parking-lot with our flowers, go somewhere and nod out, and leave us there all day. I had never been treated like that in the Unification Church before.

A few times I remember being at a shopping-center that closed, sitting up against a building in the dark, just waiting half the night for him to pick me up. This not only happened when I had a selling partner, but also when I was alone a few times. There were no cell phones then, and there was no one besides Rex to come and get us, no one (in the middle of nowhere) to call (except the police, if there was a pay phone, though I don't remember ever calling them. I do remember cops stopping to ask if I was okay sometimes. Or if I had a street-vendor's license, which I did- complete with tax identification number, since

Rev. Moon was already being threatened with tax-evasion charges, which he would eventually do time in federal prison for, despite the tax-exempt status of churches in the U.S.).

Our team leader was not the only depressed person in our group. A few of the sister's were obviously depressed, and it was my job to boost their spirits. I started getting depressed myself. People weren't buying our flowers, or our story, like they had when I'd first joined. They had heard about our Korean, messianic leader. and what they had heard was not good.

I had read some of the articles, standing in line at grocery stores where the sensationalized stories sold magazines displayed in check-out lanes. Some stories included out-and-out lies, even in respected publications. For example, the scenario I described, several paragraphs above this one, might be taken out-of-context, edited to make it appear that the MFT team leader had "pounded" on a person rather than the dashboard. (The terms "yelling and punching" were used by *Time* magazine, to describe indoctrination methods.)

Rev. Moon had an evangelical style, and he sometimes raised his voice and did karate-chops or fist-pump power movements in the air while speaking (especially when he was trying to inspire us to "fight" Satan or Communism). We considered ourselves crusaders, "Christian soldiers" fighting a spiritual Battle-of-Armageddon. However, I never experienced (or saw, or heard of from any other member) violence from the hand of anyone in the Unification Church. And the pictures of our leader were apparently hand-picked to give a distorted, one-sided image of Rev. Moon (being presented by our media to the American public). Imagine, for example, if Billy Graham (that era's internationally beloved Christian evangelist) had been presented to the public mostly with hand-picked pictures from the moments during his sermons when he furrowed his brow against the decadence and divisions degrading humanity. Imagine, also, if he had been foreign, wearing the face of enemies from the East that the United States fought during the twentieth century. And imagine how American parents, who had worked and saved and borrowed money for their children's college educations, felt when their kids raised money for some new church that was being called a "cult". And Moon's family appeared to be better off than their own, rich even, living like royalty (no matter that it was their church's choice to house

Rev. Moon's large family in an "estate", with grounds big enough for many missionaries to live there and for many to gather occasionally- that's not how the media presented it- Unification Church missionaries were characterized as "slaves" who had been "brainwashed").

The MFT was mostly selling in small towns and rural areas where everybody knew everybody, people did not think outside their traditional religious boxes, and they did not trust foreigners (especially someone who'd settled his family into a large estate in NY, while wayward American kids sold flowers, etc. to foot the bill). With so many negatively slanted stories in plain sight, on the front pages of newspapers we saw in stands at the very shopping centers where we tried to sell our flowers, it became impossible for most of us to keep our spirits up.

The irony of our wider culture's rejection of our leader was not lost on us. We knew the whole story. Sun Myung Moon had grown up in a North Korean village whose family and nature oriented and ethical beliefs and practices had been eclipsed by the wider spreading Christian missionary movement. Like indigenous people in our own country and the world over, he had only been raised with traces of his ancestral heritage. And the irony was that he had graciously taken what our culture took to his (in the little Presbyterian missionary Church that was the center of his community), and he had brought it back to us, mixed, in his "Divine Principle", with teachings from his Eastern traditions (so well grounded that they went with quantum physics, the new science of the twentieth century). And yet we were not so gracious as he, who extended himself (paying us back by coming here as a missionary in his maturity), trying to help complete the admittedly incomplete (yet somehow closed-minded) religious foundation of our culture. Judeo-Christianity has always been an open-ended religion, trying here and there to close the book anyway (like some unsatisfied married person who can't quite stop looking and waiting and hoping for "the one", but is too committed to the sacred ideal of what they already have to accept the next volunteer). We knew we were living in the land-of-the-free and the home of many cults (though they would not have called themselves that), long perpetuated in the name of religious freedom. And they were pointing their fingers at us?

Rex dropped me off alone more than I was used to, maybe

because the selling spots weren't busy enough to support two sellers. I developed a sort-of addiction. I guess it had started back at the Center, when we sold those chocolate-covered mints. I seemed to crave chocolate more than ever. I would go in a store to use the bathroom, grab a candy bar, take it in the bathroom and eat it in the stall. I had never been a thief before. When I tried not to do this, I would go in and go to the bathroom, then come out thinking I was doing better, but end up grabbing something chocolate on the way out (sometimes paying for it, sometimes not). When I stole something on the way out, I was so ashamed that I would look for a wooded area to hide and eat my chocolate. Then I might sit there for hours, thinking maybe I would just stay there and live in the woods, like a homeless person.

When I think about it now, I wonder if Rex had a hidden addiction too, maybe to some drug that made him nod out, or some form of alcohol that had no lingering scent but caused him to have angry outbursts. The thought never occurred to me until a decade later, when books about addiction and co-dependency started showing up in the "self-help" section of bookstores.

Toward the end of my stint in the M.F.T., I started calling Mama Sue often. There were pay phones at most shopping-centers. We would just chat sometimes. Or sometimes, when I was feeling particularly needy, I would go on and on about how I thought I needed glasses (which I had never worn). This was usually after I had been selling door-to-door in neighborhoods a lot. We had no cell-phones with GPS. The team captain might give us a map or draw a sort-of outline of where we were to go, and tell us when we were to meet him and where. Then we had to go by those little green signs with white letters, at intersections. It was hard to read them from a distance, and I thought that if I had glasses it would be easier. I had to give directions to subordinates who were dropped off with me. Often we had to walk all the way up a street before seeing that it was not where we were supposed to be at a given time. I remember being obsessed with talking to Mama Sue about how I thought I needed glasses, which the team captain must have said we could not afford. When she sent me money for glasses, it would only cover the cost of those on a cheap rack of ugly ones that were not in style. I just wanted simple wire-rims (like the Beatle, John Lennon, wore). The only metal-rimmed pair, on the discount rack (where most had plastic frames), was bright gold (not real gold, but meant to match a matron's jewelry, with eighth-of-an-inch wide frames). They had an odd, sideways oval piece over the nose that soon broke. If we had even been in the same town, I would have insisted on returning them, but we were long gone.

The optometrist had said I had 20/20 vision (which I do not doubt, because I never needed glasses before or after, until the typical reading glasses of middle-age). I still could not see the street signs from a neighborhood block away (which would have made my job easier, more efficient, and more lucrative for the church). The glasses had helped some. So I called my mother from pay phones more often, telling her I wanted contact lenses (thinking that would eliminate the problem of style, and maybe my selling would improve if I looked more like I used to). On some level, I must have resented working so hard and not having the money to buy something I thought I needed, in the fashion that I wanted. But I never complained about not having my own income.

I think I mostly wanted somebody to care how hard my life was, somebody to help take care of me. Maybe I had "leftover dependency needs" (something I would read about later in self-help books). I talked obsessively about needing contact lenses. But I don't remember telling my mother how miserable I really was. I could barely admit it to myself long enough for it to register in my brain. I did tell her that I didn't like my team captain. It felt good to call him an "asshole". My Southern-lady mother was not one to cuss casually. She was, however, a word person, a writer, and some words just fit. We had both started calling my step-father an asshole before she divorced him. I thought we had invented the word, because it was not yet widely used, especially not in the South. It just fit because what came out of my step-father's mouth sometimes would have been more suited to the other end. Not being able to say that word now, as the team-mother of a straight-laced religious group, it felt good to tell my mother what an asshole my team-captain was.

My misery was not all the team-captain's fault though. Not having a home life is a hard thing for females, I think. Also, I think females are happier with a balance of males and females in a group; it is probably a hormonal thing. At that time the MFT teams were all led by males, but the team itself was either male or female. Ours was female. Sometimes a male team would show up at a campground where we were staying, and we would have energetic songfests and picnics. The young men never seemed unhappy together; they even wrestled and played like pups. We were happier when we had a few days with brothers other than Rex, and so was he. Otherwise the sisters were hard to cheer up.

Being the Team Mother, I tried to boost morale. But my own morale was not high. None of the eight sisters in our team were cheerful, except Fanny. Fanny brightened things up, but Rex told me he thought she was "too loose". He told me to get her to tone it down and be more like True Mother (who appeared passive, at Rev. Moon's side).

"She is too much of a subject, when she is supposed to be an object," Rex said when he talked to me privately, about Fanny.

I wasn't sure if Rex was talking about Fanny or me. "The Divine Principle says the subject-object positions in relationships are interchangeable," I said. Then there was an argument, a power struggle. My mother was a liberated woman, and these were liberating times for women. I was not about to sit quietly and let someone tell me that women were supposed to be "objects". That was a misunderstood word in the English interpretation of the "Creation" chapter of the Divine Principle, which was based on quantum physics. "Source energy" was described as having a flow, from positive to negative (with "negative" being structurally and metaphorically feminine). I had drawn those symbols on blackboards many times before MFT, when I taught Divine Principle. The arrow (symbolizing Source energy) did not flow one way. It came back, from the feminine side of the yin-yang, as well, which meant the power generated by the feminine was equal (or even stronger, as it contained both what the male or positive side had given, *and* what the female or negative side of the charge was giving back).

Brothers in charge never wanted to hear that. They mostly wanted to keep us sisters in our place. I couldn't control Fanny, nor did I see any reason to. She had a rear end to match her name, and there was no hiding it. But her perpetual smile was natural and innocent and not forced. It did not matter that she had a chipped tooth right in front (just as it would not have mattered that he had a hair-lip, if he had smiled with his heart). Fanny was my one joy on the MFT. She loved food and actually seemed to enjoy helping me cook. Having been the oldest of a large brood, she knew how to stretch meals and make them flavorful too.

Still, instead of Fanny being a source of joy for the entire group, the other sisters seemed to resent her as much as Rex did. Maybe because her energetic nature gave her a dominant vibe. Maybe because she and I were close. But it seemed to me that they did not need much of a reason to resent me. As long as I was in charge of them to a certain degree, they resented me for that simple reason.

I became most keenly aware of their resentment the evening of the day Rex had dropped me off at a mall, telling me to buy coats for the sisters. We were going to North Carolina, and it would be cooler up in the mountains. Then we were going up to Pennsylvania and New York. Father would end his speaking tour at Madison Square Gardens, and the whole movement was going (for the inspiration of course, but also to help fill the house). I felt this coat-shopping mission to be a daunting task, without the sisters along to help. Rex said we needed them to keep selling, if we were to come anywhere near reaching the financial goals that the National Headquarters in Washington, D.C. was setting for the M.F.T.

I had no doubt that God put a particular rack of coats right in front of my eyes that day. I had been all over the mall. I was tired. I had, of course, tried on a coat that I liked. It was a light camel-colored wool wrap with a tie belt, dress length. But there was only one. I asked the clerk at the department store to hold it for the rest of the day. I went to lunch, wandered around some more, listlessly, wishing I could take a nap somewhere (which Rex was probably doing in the van). I went into a little boutique. The proprietor was very nice. I told her my dilemma.

"I think I have just the thing," she said. They just came in, so I still have the whole line, every size. She took me to a rack at the back of the shop. There was a row of navy-blue wrap-coats, similar in style to the light camel one I had seen earlier, but car-coat length. They were not wool, but the synthetic fabric had a nice look and feel. I tried one on, and it was warm. It looked good in the mirror too. When I counted them, there were seven, progressing in sizes just as the sisters did. I would need one more, but the coat I had found for myself earlier would make it a complete package. It was miraculous.

"I hate to take your whole line," I said.

"That's Ok," the lady said. "In fact, I will give you a discount since it is for a missionary group."

It was God's doing, I thought. I expected the sisters to be happy, but, as usual, the only one who lit up (when I pulled the coats out of their bags back at the trailer) was Fanny. Fanny, though she had an outstanding fanny, was not the biggest girl in the group. She found her size, put it on, smiled her genuine smile, then took it off again because it was too warm to wear a coat for long. A few of the other sisters were looking, less enthusiastically, for their sizes. A few were not looking at all. I fished through the pile. When I proudly presented my extra-large coat to the correspondingly-sized sister (who had been the most challenging to shop for) she retreated to a corner and cried. Another sister said, "I'm really not into the uniform look."

"What look are you into?" I asked, looking at her short hair, khaki skirt, plain white blouse, and Earth Shoes.

"Oh, whatever," she said.

I opened the little closet we shared (but none of us used much, as we lived out of suitcases kept in a bin built into the side of the trailer). The lady at the shop had let me keep the hangers. The coats fit in the closet. And when we reached a cooler climate, nobody complained about having one in her size. Meanwhile I had told them that if anybody needed a longer, somewhat dressier coat for a special occasion, they could borrow my camel one (which was size Medium and could be wrapped tightly or loosely or left open). Nobody took me up on that offer until Fanny had to go home for a funeral. Her father's.

Fanny did not come back. Her mother needed her to help with her younger siblings while she went through crisis. Fanny was not leaving the Church, she said. She would stay active with the local Center where she lived.

My sense of loneliness became too much to bear. I knew I had reached the end of my rope.

One morning I refused to get into the van with Rex. He had given one of his "Crush Satan" speeches at the picnic table where we ate breakfast before going off to sell. I cleared the table, put dishes in the trailer, and started cleaning up while everyone else was loading the van then getting in. I finished cleaning up but didn't go out to the van. Someone came to get me.

"I'm not going," I said. "I don't feel well."

Next day I did the same thing.

Rex came to the door. "You look like you are feeling fine," he said. "Come get in the van!" he said, in a commanding tone.

"No," I said. "I am never getting into a van with you again."

Next day Mr. Nolan, president of the Church, flew out from D.C. The rest of the group was out selling, except for Rex, who had picked Mr. Nolan up from an airport in a nearby city. Rex had brought the leader to our campsite, dropped him off, then drove back out to pick up the team.

I had never met Mr. Nolan before but had seen tapes of him giving speeches. I had not known that he was coming. He knocked on the door of the camper trailer where I had cooked a tuna casserole for the team and dozed off while reading. I wondered for a moment, when I first opened the door, if I might be dreaming.

"Mr. Nolan?" I asked.

"Yes. Nice meeting you, Sister," he said.

"Would you like something to eat or drink?" I asked, wondering if I should invite him into our cramped quarters.

"No, thank you," he said. "I was hoping we could talk." He stepped back and motioned toward a picnic table, then seated himself, motioning for me to sit across from him. Which I did. "What's going on?" the very large, kind-faced gentleman (who, in spite of his commanding appearance, was probably only around thirty years old) asked twenty-year-old me.

I felt a surge of terror, followed by every emotion I had been holding back. It all came out.

"I joined this movement because of love. Love is what motivated me. And I am not doing anything anybody says, until I feel Love," I said, quivering like quiet thunder, warning of a storm of unpredictable magnitude.

He was surprisingly calm. "Yes. I am familiar with your spiritual father, Gabriel," he said. "And, of course, Art and Audra Shoman. Their styles of leadership are very different from most M.F.T. leaders."

I don't remember him saying much else about my predicament, but somehow I understood that he understood. He started talking about having met my mother at the rally across from the White House, having read her story. He had talked with her on the phone later and asked her for an 8x10 darkroom print of her photo of himself presenting Nixon with the big candle. Whether it was his intention or not, the solid and serene Mr. Nolan distracted me from my rising emotional storm and led me gently toward the setting sun. When Rex brought the team back we gathered for a prayer, ate tuna casserole around the picnic tables, sang for a while, and slept.

When the team left to sell the next morning, I stayed back and went to the airport later with Mr. Nolan. We got on different planes, as he was on a mission, visiting various troubled teams to boost spirits and motivate the M.F.T. during a crucial time of fundraising.

I was in Washington, D.C. very soon after that. There, Mr. Nolan said something about my mother having called him every so often when I was traveling for the O.W.C. or M.F.T. That was why I was sometimes told by leaders to call home. My mother's communication with the national church president, and the fact that when I called her she could call me back from the "WATS Line" at work (which allowed us unlimited free phone time) made my story different from the stories of other increasingly unhappy young members (and their frustrated parents).

Worker Bees & Grain-ariums

I remember being in a great dining hall, where Mr. Nolan and his forty-year-old wife (mature for an American Unification Church member, even a leader at that time) held court in their quiet, confident, self-contained (while ready-to-serve), centered and relaxed way. I was invited to sit with them the first night there, at the Washington, D.C. Center's main building, which was the national headquarters for the church. I was introduced to Ms. Kim, the church's original missionary from Korea (who had given me a mint at our less formal meeting, when I'd ushered at one of Rev. Moon's speeches).

Ms. Kim sat at a table next to the Nolan's, with an American gentleman of mature years. Mr. Nolan introduced me to Ms. Kim, mentioning to her that my mother was a journalist. Ms. Kim then introduced me to her gentleman friend (a "professor"), saying, "We are writing a book together." Young Oon Kim's little red cloth-covered hardback book of around 200 pages, entitled "The Divine Principle and

364

its Application", was my most cherished book at that time of my life. I was aglow with the mild-mannered attentions of these super-stars of our movement. Being out-of-my-league with them, however, my own attention gradually turned away from their increasingly administrative conversation, to the younger brothers and sisters mingling around the dining hall.

The person who first caught my eye was an obviously new member, still dressed in the fashionable hippy garb of the day, with a new short haircut that had not yet grown out to the in-between, not long or short, shapeless and style-less look that most of us sported after sacrificing ourselves to the cause for a while. She too was aglow, the new life-blood for her own age group. Looking at the new member, I (who would soon have my twenty-first birthday go unmentioned and unmarked, except by a card from my mother which reached me after-the-fact) felt old.

There was one familiar face in the dining hall, from my earliest days in the movement. Millie, who had come that first week for an extended visit, to help me adapt to Center life as Gabe's first member, was now living at the D.C. Center.

"Hello, Arti Rose!" Millie's strong but feminine singing-voice rose from a nearby table. "You must come with me after dinner," she said. "I want to show you my new baby boy. His father is watching him for the moment." Millie looked even fatter and frumpier than I remembered. (But, now, I probably looked like she had then).

There was no waiting around to meet the new girl after dinner, and somehow I knew we would never be the sort of friends (or "sisters") that Beth and I had been anyway. I followed Millie to the suite she shared with her "blessed" husband and their new baby. The pale, red-haired infant was sleeping. Millie introduced her elfish-looking red-haired husband as he left to get dinner for himself before the dining hall would be closed.

Millie made tea and we sat. I told her the story of all that had happened since I had spent that week with her when I first joined, learning church etiquette, domestic tips, and the role of sisters in the church. She had been a role model, a motherly figure (though probably less than a decade older than me), and a counselor. Now, over a cup of tea, I unloaded on her (with no forethought or motive) like an old confidant or a psychiatric patient stretched out on a couch (neither of which I had ever been to her). What she had been to me was a visiting "spiritual mother", a substitute for someone who had not existed for me in the Center I first joined. Though we both remained seated, it is a wonder to me now that she herself was not flattened by my sad tale (which included the part about Art Shoman touching me inappropriately). Instead, she showed no empathy and little sympathy, and no real warmth. She ruffled her feathers a bit, defensively (as if she was the Church itself).

All that Millie said, in response to my tragic tale of disillusionment, was, "Well, you most likely would have been through worse if you had continued your relationship with the young man you brought to the Center. What was his name? I think you called him 'Tex'."

So we were talking about romance, I suddenly realized. I thought it best to shift the conversation away from myself.

"Yes; Tex. I knew I couldn't marry him," I said, shaking my head briefly, then trying to brighten the tone. "Congratulations on your blessed marriage. I think I remember you saying you knew your husband before?"

"He was at my Center in San Francisco for a while," she said.

"With Ms. Kim," I said, vaguely remembering the story and the picture she had been so proud of when I had met her (before the "blessed couple" was actually living together. Millie had said, back then, that their marriage was "conditional" and would not be "consummated" until they had fulfilled separate missions). I remembered Millie staring at her wedding picture late at night, as I was falling asleep thinking of Gabe when I'd first joined.

"Yes. Ms. Kim recommended us for the blessing."

"Were you in love?" I asked.

She looked taken aback.

"Well, no," she said. "But I used to get a feeling sometimes, seeing him across a room. I wasn't sure what it meant. I just knew he was special."

She did not seem to want to dwell on it, and started clearing up the tea cups, saying she needed to change the baby's diaper, opening the door and giving me directions to the guest room where I was staying temporarily (in a real bed, like some dignitary). It occurred to me, as I lay thinking, that Millie might not be happy, and I certainly had not lifted her spirits. I thought I might make it up to her somehow. Maybe I could have babysat for her, given her a break sometimes. But I never saw her at close range again.

I slept in "the big house" that night, but the next day I was moved to a row house in Georgetown where a "blessed family" lived on the main floor. The large group of brothers and sisters crowded the upstairs bedrooms, and there was a "grain-arium factory" in the basement. At the time, "terrariums" were newly popular plant environments, usually in glass cylinders. Our product had no living plants. Instead we started with grains, or sometimes layers of colored sand, and added various natural decorative things, like dried flowers, stones, shells (or any combination of the above). The top was corked and they were packed in the original boxes that the glass cylinders had come in. We then took these to the streets. They were the heaviest things I had sold since the boxes of scented candles (in "brandy snifters" that Gabe and I had carried all over town, when I had first joined). The grain-ariums were fun to make at first, and they sold well in the office buildings around D.C. But both the factory and the house I lived in were so crowded that I felt over-stimulated and withdrew deep into myself, feeling disconnected from what should have been an interesting town to live in.

Early on, during my stay there, Becky (the house mother at the grain-arium factory) told me that I would be taking a day off from selling. A sister from the-big-house would be coming to take me on an outing, show me around town. The main thing I remember about that day, besides the bustling streets of Washington, D.C. at lunch time, was that the sister took me to a busy little café, owned by the church. She was pretty and graceful, like a ballerina, and had a pretty face framed by a short, neat, pixie haircut. Her manner was gentle and sweet. I remembered the Shomans comparing me with her when she had visited our Center once, but I did not see myself in her fairy-light air. She had originally been a "spiritual child" of theirs. They had apparently called her and asked her to keep an eye on me when they heard I was in D.C. At the café she proudly escorted me to, I had a cucumber sandwich with cream cheese on whole wheat bread. It was the best experience of my time there, but I don't even remember the girl's name. It was just that I let myself imagine, for a little while, that we were normal girlfriends going downtown for lunch, with no agenda except to enjoy ourselves. Since that was never the case, she did fulfill her mission of showing off one of the church businesses, as if to say, "This is another cool thing our church is doing in this town". I did not think the sister running the tiny café looked happy, but the cucumber sandwich she made was something new and made me happy for a while.

Later we had a more serious mission. We visited various members of Congress in their offices. I remember us sitting primly across from one rather pudgy and casually slouched gentleman's desk, but I do not remember which state he was Representative of. He was apparently a Republican, as he did not mind signing Rev. Moon's petition to "Forgive, Love, and Unite" under President Nixon, who had not yet resigned (despite threats of impeachment). It took the important fellow a while to sign. I had the feeling he was keeping us in his office as captives, enjoying our attention.

Later I learned that this was a mission that Beth would seek out, transferring from Gabe's Center in the Midwest to work as a "lobbyist" for Rev. Moon's conservative (anti-communist) political interests. If I had shown any interest, I probably could have been assigned to that mission (and must have been being considered for it, probably by Mr. Nolan). I had no interest, however, in anything but going home for Christmas. I kept mentioning that dream to the few people who reached out and showed an interest in me, but I was not getting encouragement from anyone but my mother (who I had begun to call with increasing regularity now that I was somewhere with a house phone).

Madison Square Garden

It was the biggest event I went to during my time as a Unification Church missionary, and I felt nothing. I was awed-out, over-stimulated, under-whelmed. I could have been watching TV for how connected I felt to that crowd (which appeared to be a full house) and the little Korean man strutting and shouting in a foreign tongue on that far-away stage. I remember seeing some old friends in the crowd, but they were far away and my thinking was that they probably would not have recognized me anyway. My hair was an in-between length and had no style, and my body had plumped out and lost its shape. I was wearing an outfit I would never have worn before MFT. I had picked the dress out because there was a whole line of sizes I could buy for my troup, and it was a polyester fabric that would not wrinkle in our suitcases. The color was beige-y and bland, with tiny, horizontal orange stripes, mostly covered by a homely beige sweater that I felt comfortably invisible in.

The only old familiar I remember re-connecting with there momentarily was the now shockingly lovely lady who had been my homely-looking team mother when I had first been banished to the MFT. It was she who had sheared my locks. Now she stood before me, tall and slender and dressed in a classic little-black-dress, with a mane of shoulder-length blonde curls. Her animated face was made up with color highlighting her cheekbones and brightening her blue eyes. Artisan silver earrings dangled and flashed out from her locks as she flitted about in the crowd, bubbling like champagne. When I asked where she was staying now, she proudly said that she had returned to the home she and her husband had built together in the Oregon countryside before joining the church. They continued to be affiliated with the Unification Church in a nearby city, but her husband had returned to his job at an architectural firm there. They had earned "the blessing" by serving as missionaries for a time and would be allowed to renew their vows in the international mass wedding that Rev. Moon would be orchestrating in South Korea.

"Well, congratulations on your blessed engagement. You look great!" I said, as she flitted away. (Nice for her that she knows who she will end up with, I was thinking, scanning the crowd, spotting a group I had once lived with but not seeing Danny Hart).

Our "family" from the D.C. Center stayed in Manhattan long enough to sell some of our grain-ariums on the busy streets. However, so many local "Moonies" swarmed the streets there, selling flowers and trying to hand out literature, that nobody seemed to want anything to do with us. I only sold my product when I focused on showing off the grain-ariums themselves (which were a novelty) and not mentioning who or what I was selling them for. If anyone asked, I would say I was with "The One World Crusade" (the lesser-known, traveling branch of our church that I had served with under Art Shoman) and not mention the Unification Church (or Rev. Moon) if I could avoid it. When the subject did come up, some folks told me that various of our members had tried to sell them tickets to see Rev. Moon speak at Madison Square Gardens, then handed them free tickets the week before the event. Discarded tickets still littered the streets.

Merry Christmas

I wanted to go home for Christmas. I told Becky that every time I saw her. Becky was the house-mother whose "blessed family" (including her husband and their infant and toddler boys) squeezed itself into the master suite on the main floor of the Georgetown row-house (where I slept on the floor upstairs, and crafted grain-ariums in the basement). A whole herd of young people lived in that house. Needless to say, Becky always looked tired and overwhelmed. She was not an overbearing or intimidating person. Nor did she possess a natural aura of authority, as Audra Shoman had. Becky was petite and pudgy, with the same nondescript brown hair most of us had, and plain, serviceable shoes. She did not wear the plastered-on smile that us "Moonies" on the streets became famous for. Her face had a sweet but concerned expression. I even thought I detected guilt, like she thought she was supposed to be taking care of all of us though her family obviously drained her. I don't know what her husband's position was, outside the Center, but he was not a powerful presence in our Center. I think Becky was supposed to be in charge, but she was not a powerful presence either. In fact, she seemed to be hiding from our stampeding herd when we rushed in and out. When I did see her, I did not mind approaching Becky, asking to use the phone in their suite when I wanted to call my mom. She knew the call would not be expensive because we could hang up right away, and my mother could call me back from the WATS-line at the newspaper.

When I told Becky I wanted to go home for Christmas, she squeezed her eyebrows together. "You'll have to talk with Mr. Nolan about that," she said.

I thought that had to do with money. Becky's family seemed poor to me, because their living quarters were tiny and cluttered with baby equipment. I figured the money we made, selling grain-ariums, must have gone into the National Headquarters pot just like the Mobile Fundraising Team money had. So, I was essentially still on the MFT.

(And I still was "not feeling any love", except what little sympathy Becky's eyes offered, which felt more like guilt over having nothing, at the end of the day, left to give).

In Mr. Nolan's office, I felt like I had been sent to both the Principal and the Guidance Counselor.

"If it's the money, I'm sure my mom can pay for the ticket," I said.

"The problem I have with this is not financial," he said. "It's spiritual."

"I'm Ok, spiritually," I defended.

"That's good to hear," he said. "However, in my experience with family members who have been…depressed, they can become vulnerable to Satanic attack when they venture outside the protection of the Church family. I just don't want that to happen to you."

"But my mom is friends with the Church," I said.

"That's true. Maybe you could stay at the Center there, and just visit with your family. I could arrange that by giving you a temporary mission there."

Clearly he was trying to stick to "Principle", and he (being in the position of my "higher center", and representative of the Father) was supposed to keep me in his realm.

"I want to stay in my mom's house for the holidays," I said. "She bought a house that I haven't even seen yet. It's on Southside, not too far from the Center."

Mr.Nolan reluctantly agreed, advising me to be careful. "Satanic attack can come in many subtle forms," he said in his mild-mannered but rock-solid way. "I will be praying for you."

Part III

Home is where the

Heart is

Twin Strangers at the Airport

It was always strange being a Moonie alone, like being an alien. Suddenly one was aware of how different everyone else appeared. I had kept to myself at the airport and on the plane, reading, not talking much to anyone, like someone from a foreign country in an odd costume, reading a different language than that spoken by those around me. I was tired of extending myself to "witness" about Rev. Moon's "New Hope for America" campaign. I was drained. So I just sat back and observed. At the airport I wondered, for a moment, whether Mama Sue had forgotten what time to pick me up, as I looked for her but did not see her. Truth was, we did not recognize each other immediately. In fact, we had already walked past each other, and I was looking for my suitcase (actually *her* big, beige, seemingly indestructible Samsonite, which I had borrowed two-and-a-half years earlier) when she and my sister approached me. Mama Sue had already spotted it (in the pile of checked baggage that came off the plane and moved along the belt inside the airport), before she had sorted me out from the crowd.

For a second, I thought some strange woman was stealing my luggage, as my changed sister stood between us while my mother reached for the oversized, hard plastic, horizontally rectangular suitcase and heaved it toward her petite body.

"Ouch," she said, as the bottom landed on her thinly loafered toes.

Our faces suddenly found each other then, and there were immediate smiles and hugs. I took the suitcase I'd grown the muscles to carry, put it in the trunk of the same blue Duster my mom had bought the year I'd left home (now sporting a few dents, and looking less sporty). We chatted comfortably in the car, bubbling over lightly.

But I was still a bit shocked at how different they had looked (as they surely had been at the first sight of me without my long locks and slender figure, wearing ugly glasses, without stylish clothes or any sign of caring about my looks).

My sister was nearly full grown. She and Mama Sue looked like sisters to me, although my mother was 41 and my sister was 14. I wondered who was wearing whose clothes, because their outfits looked interchangeable. Both were in jeans that fit tightly everywhere above the knees, then flared out somewhat (but not into the huge bells we had worn earlier in the '70s). Their little knit sweaters were also tight and decorated with embroidery in the neck and chest areas. My sister, whose long hair was straight and naturally blondish, was obviously wearing no bra under the baby blue sweater that showed her small, perky breasts. My mother had been covering the gray in her naturally reddish-brown hair for years, and now the red highlights were brighter than ever and spilled like waves of molten copper, contrasting with her green sweater and landing in curls at the top of her breasts. She, at least, was wearing a bra. I was a bit shocked, however, at how sexy my mother looked. She wore her trademark Hollywood-matte rose lipstick but less eye make-up than my sister, which somehow served to make her appear much younger than her years. And, with my sister looking older than her years, I couldn't help saying, "You two look like sisters."

They had looked at each other and laughed. "People say that all the time," my little sister said. Seven years my junior, she was still smaller than me but had about caught up with Mama.

I had turned out taller, like my grandmother on Daddy's side. Usually I was slender, "like a model", but I had put on weight. Even my face was fuller, making my high cheekbones less prominent. And I had made a thing about "needing" glasses (which Mama Sue had sent me money for, but not enough for the newer styles) when I'd struggled to read neighborhood signs, a block ahead, while selling door-to-door (and giving directions to others) as a team mother for the MFT.

My hair was short-ish and tucked behind my ears, to hide. It had not been cut or styled since that first MFT team-mother had chopped it off. My clothes had been chosen simply to cover my body modestly and travel well. I had no style. I was wearing the navy car-coat Fanny had left behind when she had borrowed my dress-length camel coat to go to a funeral she'd never returned from. I looked like a nun on vacation, or an AWOL soldier. These strangely sexy-looking female relatives had been happy to see me anyway, with four arms open to hug me in what was, at first, a group hug. Somehow their bubbly effervescence seem to come from the same cup. They were together, and I was still alone (maybe more alone than ever, I secretly feared).

I had stepped out of one world into a high-speed aircraft that took me to another world. I was an alien, not from another planet but from another culture (a sub-culture, a "cult"). And the first and most obvious difference was that the females where I came from were discouraged from flaunting our sexuality, and the culture I was visiting encouraged its females to appear youthful (while aging) and sexually attractive (from a tender age). From my Moonie perspective, I had entered the Satanic realm.

I did, however, feel the Love. So, there was hope for a new beginning. Also, as a big bonus (for the first time in my entire life) I had my own room. It was the smallest room in the house, other than the bathrooms. I had no complaints. Perched on the Northeast corner of the top floor, I could see rooftops and treetops from the one window on the East side, to the left of the foot of my bare-bones twin bed. There was a small closet with a shelf over the clothes-rack, and a bedside table with a drawer (and that was it- no bedroom set, no pictures or decorations, and only flat, yellowed blinds on the window). I slid my suitcase under the bed, continuing to live out of it for a while (since I might be leaving any time- going back). At first the only things that came out of the suitcase (besides basic personals) were my reading material and journal, which went on the bedside table and in the drawer. Free to read and write all I wanted, I stayed in that room so much that my 19-year-old brother David, who lived in the basement, joked with the English-professor neighbor about having Emily Dickenson reincarnated and tucked away upstairs.

My maternal, country grandmother, getting wind of the news, made the only trip I remember her making up the state to our big city. She brought an antique mahogany bedroom set in the covered pick-up truck she'd borrowed from my uncle. It was the set my mother had grown up with. Mema'd had it refinished and glazed with a rosy varnish (like my hair it was dark brown, but reddish in the light). The set, a double-bed with high headboard and posts (carved in swirls that trimmed out each piece), had a matching chest-of-drawers and a sit-down dresser with an adjustable oval mirror. The icing on the cake was a handmade quilt of many colors. The quilt was lined with a warm blanket, covered with cotton on both sides. An Americana patchwork printed sheet covered the underside. The decorative top was made from squares of cotton prints of the gingham and calico sort that farm animal's feed sacks used to be made of, saved from scraps of clothing my mother had worn as a child. The scraps were arranged semitrically around a larger, rectangular and regal looking filigree print in cool green (like wall-paper in the Queen's palace), and that showpiece was surrounded by a neat rectangle of uniformly sized, deep red squares. Nobility and peasantry seemed suddenly represented there, on more levels than met the eye.

So, the humble, little room became a source of pride, a space worth showing off to friends and worth settling into, owning. It was a gift that made me feel my worth to both my grandmother and my mother (as it had been Mama Sue's before, and she seemed glad, though maybe a bit envious, for me to have it). It healed a wound I had carried for a decade, since my mother left my father with intentions to give us a better life. I was ten then, and all the priviledged and pampered girls had "princess" bedroom sets in creamy, off-white French provincial, with ruffled spreads and matching, pastel-covered canopies. Mama Sue had said that she was going to buy me a canopy bed (though I don't remember asking for one). But when she remarried, my little sister and I got second-hand twins from the Salvation Army which we had until I left for college. It had been one of many unspoken disappointments (probably shared by my mother, who has always struggled financially, whether married or single, despite working hopefully and tirelessly toward her dreams and even excelling as a woman in her field at that time).

Needless to say, I didn't go back to the Unification Church in Washington, D.C. after Christmas (as I had told Mr. Nolan, the American Church's president, that I would). I had not consciously planned it that way and would not admit that I was not going back to the Unification Church for some time. There was, of course, a Center in my mom's neck-of-the-woods. The Family was not the same, with exception of one or two who had joined just as I was leaving. I had been the house mother, at the time, the spiritual elder of that group, which meant that they had deferred to me. Though I remained loosely affiliated with them and visited them from time to time (as my mother had grown accustomed to doing), they held little sway over me and seemed to assume that I had my own mission (which, in my mind, I also gradually came to feel that I did).

My younger siblings were in trouble, a fact that my mother must have been aware of on some level but had little energy left over (after her job) to be attentive to.

Still stuck in missionary mode, during my first week home I tried to teach the Divine Principle to my little sister and her strange, semi-runaway friend who was staying with her for the entire two-week Christmas and New Year's vacation from school. The fifteen-year-old friend of Sissy's looked like a full-grown woman (busting out of her clothes) and smelled of a sickeningly musky perfume. She also shaved her eyebrows, then drew black arches over her eyes. She would sit in front of my sister's dresser mirror, plastering layer upon layer of make-up over her fair, freckled skin, and trying to do something with her baby-fine reddish hair, for hours on end.

I found a child's blackboard, among my toddler cousin's playthings (Mama Sue was Aunt Sue to her younger brother's daughter). I took the A-B-C blackboard (and some chalk I found in a catch-all drawer in the alcove, on the main floor) up to my sister's room. She and her friend never seemed to mind letting me in, somehow enjoying my attention while managing to stay in their own teenage dream-world (and thinking I was a bit of a weirdo, however sweet).

My sister had the large, airy and sunny room that was built out over the front porch, with windows on three sides. Her full-size, white, antique wrought-iron bed always had at least one cat (sometimes Smokey, but usually Snow Kitty) purring on one of my grandmother's homemade quilts. The antique, manual pedal-style sewing-machine was also in a corner of my sister's room (and was well-used by both she and Mama Sue). Since sewing had been my main hobby as a teen, I could not help being interested in the fabrics and patterns in an old trunk next to the machine. I often perched lightly on the chair there. The "mission and purpose" I continued to have in mind, however, was to teach these wayward girls the Divine Principle. So I would prop the little blackboard on the trunk, moving fabric scraps around to hold it up while I explained what I wrote there (using the most ragged scrap I could find to erase, when I needed to outline the next topic). I explained the Principle and Purpose of Creation, the Fall (especially the Fall, which was the young Eve's doing and, according to Rev. Moon, due to pre-mature sexual indiscretion), and Restoration. All with my sister's radio blaring and the girls going about their business (mostly primping and playing with the cats) and giving each other glances while stifling the snickers and giggles that gurgled forth when I finally left the room.

Crazy as I may have seemed, in the context of a seemingly typical teen-aged girl's room, it was not what went on there that filled my heart with a burning sense of mission (and more than a Moonie mission) regarding my sister. It was what went on very late at night, and very early some mornings. Somehow these young girls had hooked up with a young woman, my age, who included them in her night-life. According to my very worldly brother, this young woman (who lived in the part of town where there were nightclubs with topless dancers) was a junky and a prostitute. When our mother was home, she often wore herself out talking to Sissy about why she should stay away from Bobby Jean. What I could not understand was why Mama Sue did not talk to Bobby Jean herself. Maybe Sissy had learned not to talk to Bobby Jean when our mother was home, but I was home all the time. We had a phone downstairs in the alcove by the kitchen, and a phone on a little stand in the hall between our three bedrooms. I answered it sometimes and started my own relationship with Bobby Jean. First, I was friendly with her, making small talk while she waited for Sissy to wind up whatever she was doing and come to the phone.

Then one day, when I felt an opening there, I spoke to Bobby Jean from my heart, appealing to her better nature. I asked her to please leave my little sister alone. Apparently…she did.

My other mission was with my brother, David. He had been my best friend, my playmate, since I was two years old. He was nineteen now. Davie's territory was the basement of this great, old house that Mama Sue had bought as a fixer-upper (for a mere twenty-four thousand, during an economic downturn that resulted from a petroleum shortage) while I was gone. On my arrival, after awing me through the historic neighborhood in the hills, the big front porch with rocking chairs, the living room with a fireplace, and the dining room with a great table, Mama had yelled down the stairs from the dining room to Davie's basement "apartment".

"We're coming down, son."

A light came on. A cool breeze wafted up, carrying familiar smells.

"David likes sandalwood incense," Mama said, not mentioning the musky, almost skunky smell it attempted to cover.

"Does he run the air-conditioner in the winter?" I asked.

"No. It just feels like it," she answered. "Something about the design of the house, with this part being on the back of the hill. It feels good down here in the summer," she said, like a tour guide, pointing out the highlights.

There literally was a cold wind blowing up the stairs as we went down, apparently from no source other than Mother Nature herself (though no window or door was open). The bottom of the stairwell opened to a small den, with an L-shaped couch where my brother was sprawled on the side of the L that we faced. His strangely sallow-looking face was surrounded by a halo of long, sun-bleached, light-brown hair. (Maybe it's the lighting, I thought, noting the yellowed lampshade on the end-table, and the lava lamp, with its ever-changing red blob, in the center of the cypress-stump coffee-table.)

Davie scooted up, smiling at me, but he did not get out from under his stack of old homemade quilts, polyester blankets, and Native American wool wraps.

"What's up, Art? Great to see you, big sister," he beamed with a strange glow that seemed to come straight from his heart, bypassing his weakened looking body.

"I would get up to hug you, but I'm not feeling good and it might be contagious."

"Well, it's great to see you anyway, Brother. I like your pad."

"Thanks," he said proudly, glowing in a strangely similar way as the black light poster of a big ocean wave, that he had displayed in a corner under an elongated, bare, dimly lit dark bulb.

"He's going to the doctor tomorrow, if I have to take him on my lunch hour," Mama Sue said.

"I could take him," I said, sensing a need. "But my driver's license needs renewing."

"Maybe I should take a day off," Mama Sue said. "But it's nearly impossible, working for a daily."

"I can drive myself to the doctor," Davie said.

"But *will* you?" Mama Sue asked, pleadingly.

I had sensed, in my first five minutes inside my mother's new, old house, that I had a mission here. I would be the one to cook breakfast for my brother, wake him with coffee, prod him into seeing a doctor. He had hepatitis.

I had been in the hippy scene long enough, before joining the

Moonies, to know that hepatitis was spread by sharing needles to shoot up junk (heroin and the like). I also knew that, like Neil Young said in his song, "Every junkie's like the setting sun." I did not know, for sure, how Davie had gotten the hepatitis. But I knew that I could not let my brother go down that way. I became his nurse, cook, and counselor, besides just enjoying hanging out with my oldest best-friend. Since it was not likely that I would catch his disease, my portions of the meals I cooked followed his down the stairs, where we sat and ate at the cypress-stump coffee table, playing gin rummy for hours afterwards (like we had as kids).

There was a woman called Bootsie (more suitable for a cat, I thought) who phoned my brother often. I thought he was getting drugs from her, and suspected they were lovers too (though he never said she was his girlfriend). She came to his back-door entrance one day, and I met her. She had a manly build, but her breasts were large, and she had a big mane of processed hair encircling her hard-looking, made-up mask of a face. I was shocked at how much older she looked than my brother. I was friendly to her, trying to focus on the heart that I had experienced (by looking innocently into the eyes of thousands, while on my Moonie mission) as universal. At some point I knew that I would do for my little brother what I would also do for my little sister. The laundry room was on the bottom floor, near my brother's apartment. So I would answer the phone there, or the back door, when my brother was not around. Eventually I would appeal to Bootsie's better half, asking, "Please leave my little brother alone."

When that happened, Davie didn't even seem to notice. Maybe Bootsie disappeared from his life, or maybe she just became less visible. Anyway, there was always another female at his door, though I don't remember any who followed looking quite so tough. And he later claimed the hepatitis couldn't have come from a needle. He said it was more likely he had picked it up when he and Gabe traveled to Mexico (shortly after Gabe left the Moonies, and only a season before I did), and then to California (where Gabe had settled). Gabe had not gotten hepititis, but Gabe had stayed out of the water (while Davie surfed) and never ate raw oysters (which Davie said he had eaten just before he started feeling sick). I hoped what he was saying was true, but I suspected that my brother had acquainted himself with harder drugs than marijuana since I had been away.

Later I would learn that he had often stopped at cow pastures, picked psilocybin mushrooms out of cow manure (sometimes boiling them and adding the liquid to fruit-flavored kool-aid that he even shared with our drug-savvy, teeny-bopper sister when they traveled down to the Florida panhandle). Some of the artwork and poetry Davie left on scraps of paper around his room (which I sometimes rescued from the trash when he got around to cleaning) was pretty far-out (playful, yet profoundly symbolic). But my fear that he had been a needle junkie (of the heroin addict variety) was probably part of the whole exaggerated sense I had that life and people outside the Unification Church were all "fallen" and terribly degraded.

Maybe I did get home just in time to help save my siblings' lives. However, it was not healthy for me personally to extend the addiction-related savior complex into my future life. Unfortunately, it would be more than a decade after I left the Unification Church before I would begin to be educated about the psychological disease of "co-dependency" (and another decade after that before I would be diagnosed with it). Religious indoctrination can play a role in "codependency" (which can involve an unhealthy self-righteousness, along with fear-based compulsions to control others). I would be in my late fifties, after a lifelong series of challenging relationships with addictive partners, before I would be diagnosed with the PTSD (Post Traumatic Stress Disorder) that had begun when my alcoholic father drove on the wrong side of the road, with me in the passenger seat (saving my own six-year-old life by continually repeating, "Daddy, you're on the wrong side of the road!").

If I had learned the Serenity Prayer sooner, maybe my life would have been easier, more my own. (Not because of my siblings, who were always my own, but because of the way codependence played into the mating game throughout my life).

"God grant me the Serenity

to accept the things I cannot change,

the courage to change the things I can,

and the wisdom to know the difference."

Niebuhr

Tug of War

After Christmas, I started getting phone calls from the D.C. Center. Some brother called me all the time, my mother says (but I apparently paid him so little mind that I do not even remember). It must have been whoever was my team captain for production and\or sales at the grain-arium factory, because everything was hierarchical. If I left, under him, it would have been according to Principle (based on "the way God's energy flows") for me to go back through him, or his higher center (or "central figure"). After leaving the Mobile Fundraising Team I had somehow gotten beyond letting anyone (that I had met in recent months) in the Unification Church make an imprint on my psyche. After Rex, in the MFT, I no longer saw them all as innocent. And the ones that I did see as innocent, I felt sorry for.

I still did not blame any of this, however, on the "True Parents" ("Father and Mother" Moon). They had their mission to change an imperfect world, with the help of imperfect people (and probably, I had started allowing myself to think, were imperfect too). Maybe, I imagined, I would be able to fulfill the vow I had made (to help with that mission) in other ways (by being "True" in service to God's universal family, as well as my own) during the course of my life. ("This I pledge and swear" was the often repeated end of the oath.)

Although I do not recall the arguments I had with the "brother" who was trying to convince me to come back, my mother, who is eighty-seven at this writing but still quite sharp, remembers one thing she overheard me telling him.

"I am not under Satanic attack in my mother's house," Mama Sue was happy to hear me say. "Actually, I was under Satanic attack much more there than I am here," she says I told him.

I was in a restful place, but I was also in Limbo (a state of mind in-between two worlds). I spent time going through the things still in the suitcase I had carried on my journey, writing to some of my old friends from the Unification Church who had sent me cards at various times, with return addresses. The UC kept track of its members and was generally good at forwarding mail within the organization (and returning mail when someone was no longer with them). Also, some friends had sent cards with their parents' addresses. I cherished those connections (and had not yet reconnected with my old school friends, or made new ones).

One day Mama Sue came home on her lunch hour and took me over to the local branch of the University, not far from where we lived. The semester had already started. She took me right into the registrar's office and convinced them to let me sign up for a few classes, as a "temporary student", without having to go through much of an admissions process.

Even the few college courses I took during the Winter session did not get me out of my room for long, however. I hibernated with my "World Governments" and "Philosophy 101" books. I had not read anything except the Divine Principle and related speeches, etc. for so long that I struggled to get my brain to work outside that system of thought at first. I also had difficulty concentrating. I had to read and reread one paragraph at a time, until I could grasp what the author was trying to communicate. My mind kept wanting to return to the Divine Principle as a sort of window to see the world through. So I ended up comparing everything to the Divine Principle (even in some of the papers I wrote, which the professors did not seem to mind, though their comments were elliptical). When I finally got my brain working well enough to read and think outside the Unification Church box, I made an interesting observation. I decided that, although the Unification Church was taking a right-wing, politically anti-Communist stance, the organization was (for its lower ranking members, at least), philosophically and practically, communist. "Communism", however, as it was being practiced in totalitarian regimes such as China and the

U.S.S.R., was a different story. Sharing-the-wealth (an idea Jesus himself put forth, before Marx or Moon) is not easy. Power and wealth get too heavily concentrated at the top in some of the most originally well-intentioned human organizations and societies. (And in Rev. Moon's case, this was obviously happening.)

Studying government and philosophy in my own room at my mother's house, I was forming my own beliefs. I cut pictures out of magazines I found around the house and made collages on file-folders that Mama Sue had a box full of. I cut the folders in half, pasted pictures of artwork and things I was interested in on them, and added my own drawings and writing around the edges. After punching holes in the sides, I tied them together and gave my booklet a title: "A New Woman's New Life Plan". Some of the pictures I chose were reflective of my Moonie experience, like an exercise program I had found in a women's magazine which included a yoga "sunrise salute" I had learned in the One World Crusade. (Oriental philosophies and practices were beginning to make their way into American popular culture through various avenues.)

The word "BELIEVE" was the title of a page of my New Life Plan. (*Now I can see that, although this was one of the pretty words from my idealistic youth which I did not intend to give up, like Love and Peace, I would not have needed to remind myself to "BELIEVE" if I had not been struggling with more DOUBT than I could handle at the time. "BELIEVE" was a seawall I built to hold back a tidal wave of DOUBT, and it would take the sands of time to wear that down.*) I intended to keep what I considered to be the "positive" aspects of the Divine Principle. If God had intended to "express unconditional love by creating the human family", for example, I did not want to miss out on that. I intended to love and serve my own natural family, work at loving and serving the wider human-family, and to have a family of my own. I made goals, lists. By the age of thirty, I wanted to have at least two children. I also intended to get my degree, maybe to teach, and certainly to write.

I wanted to write this book, but what was being sought for publication about the Moonies and other "cults" at that time was not my style. I wasn't even sure Rev. Moon was not the messiah. (I was sure that *I* was not the messiah, and I had given up the job of being one of a full-time army of assistants to someone who thought he was supposed to save the world). My mother (who would have made a good diplomat had she not been a journalist) tried publishing a book entitled "How I Got my Daughter out of the Moonies". Her book, however, was not sensationalistic enough to sell during an era when there were stories in the news about parents having their young-adult children kidnapped away from cults and "deprogrammed" by psychiatrists. And Mama Sue had gotten me out by simply being my friend.

I started my book in a journal (and would do that over and over again for many years) but would not be able to get very far with it until Rev. Moon died, in 2012, and I finished Book I of this version that year. Book II would not be written until now- while I am isolated, in the spring of 2020, during the novel corona-virus pandemic). In the early years it was difficult to separate myself from my character, the girl that I was. The writing flowed more easily when I let myself use the third person, although I have found myself writing in the first person toward the end. I am writing from the person that I am now. (But I am getting ahead of my *former* self).

In 1975, while living in my mother's house, my "deprogramming" began its natural and very gradual process. I continued college and got a part-time job, at a Head Start pre-school. I also made friends with the guitar-picking pre-K teacher I worked with. Natasha was a singer-songwriter I liked harmonizing with, both at work and socially, outside work. So I was getting my bohemian side back. A free-thinker, my new friend would put me in check (with affection, humor, compassion, laughter, and song) when my deeply indoctrinated mind went dark with fear. Once, when Natasha and I had been friends for several years, I had heard on the news that the Russians were charging into Afghanistan. I was sure it was the beginning of WWIII (and the biblical Battle of Armageddon). All of us sinners were doomed. I went to Natasha's apartment near the University and sat down at her little green table by the flower-curtained window.

When I told her what I was thinking, "Tash" shook her head back and forth. With a gentle smile she said, "Arti Rose, you're crazy. And your hair's not even parted straight."

I laughed, went to an antique mirror she had hanging on a wall with her magical watercolor paintings, and fixed my hair (which had grown out long and wild). She picked up her guitar and sang a new song she had written. I quickly learned the chorus and harmonized with her (feeling sane and happy in the world again).

I also renewed my friendship with another bohemian influence, my old college roommate "Sunshine", who had majored in Art and been admitted into a masters program at State U. She had hooked-up with her favorite male professor from that program, a flamboyant red-haired artist from Manhattan, NY who talked to me about the importance of the Self ("with a Capital S").

This philosophy of self-love sounded very Satanic to me at the time. Rev. Moon had defined goodness as a willingness to sacrifice the self for others, and evil as willing to sacrifice others for the self. I still think this is a genius way of explaining the difference between right and wrong. However, like anything else, it can be taken to extremes. (*A decade would pass before I would read "Women Who Love Too Much" by Robin Norwood, and other books about "Codependency"- a psychological disorder that can only be cured by learning to focus lovingly on the self as a personal priority, thereby healing our own wounded inner child*).

At the time, with Sunshine and her sophisticated boyfriend visiting me at Mama Sue's, I was guarded. However happy I was to be reunited with my old friend, I was somewhat wary of Sunshine. She had gotten me into trouble that I would never have been brave enough to get into without her. She would prove to be more grown up now, however, maybe more Vera Montgomery than "Sunshine" (or at least evolving toward a balance).

So, I did have a few friends, some new acquaintances, and a loving family. However, when I sometimes found myself alone in my mother's house, I felt a deep emotional ache (a veritable abyss with a psychologically agonizing gravitational pull). At the time, I could only interpret that ache as loneliness for someone else, a mate. All three of my family members (and most people in the "real world", it seemed) were playing the mating game. Saturday nights alone were hard, and I wanted to play too. So, I was in trouble (and so was the "someone else" I started aiming the arrow of my longing toward).

I started daydreaming about Danny. Real life trouble started, however, when Danny came down. Settled in my own room, I had made a mission of going through things (and there were things that reminded me of Danny).

Still intending to return to the Unificationist mission at some point, I had mentioned to Mama Sue that I would like a trunk. I had outgrown the 14"x21" hard-shell beige Samsonite she had loaned me when I'd left town with the One World Crusade. When I had left the UC, and settled in at her house, Mama Sue took me to an Army-Navy store where I found a red trunk (aluminum over cardboard, but what mattered, now that I was decorating my room at her house, was that it was my favorite color). For a while I was determined to fit every personal thing I owned in that 15"-by-30" trunk. I busied myself sorting things out (what to keep and what to get rid of), even cutting photographic negatives so that I only kept the best ones (which was, at that time, a printer's nightmare- some are yet unprinted).

Going through the old suitcase, looking at momentos, I found myself gazing most longingly at pictures of Danny, and there was even a Valentine card he had sent me when I was in the MFT. He had left the Family not long after the Shomans sent me away. The card was sent from his parents' home in a different state. I discovered it in time to send him a Valentines Day greeting card from my mother's home, (a year later than the one from Danny).

Meanwhile, I also answered other cards and letters, from my less romantic friends in the movement, brothers and sisters of the heart. Sirman, for one, sent me a nice note. Shortly after Art and Audra sent me to the MFT, they sent Sirman to study at the UC's new seminary. *(And I would more recently learn, in the twenty-first century, that Sirman became a full-fledged minister, had an arranged, interracial marriage and "blessed family" in the Unification Church, and posted some of his beautiful sermons on Facebook. But I am getting way ahead of myself).* Most cards and notes were from friends still dedicated to the mission (and assuming I was, as well).

In 1975, besides cards and letters and phone calls, all kinds of people from the Unification Church were calling me and sometimes showing up at my mother's house, sometimes just being friendly but usually trying to get me to come back into the fold. One who shocked me with a call was Art Shoman. *(In those days there was no caller i.d. or voicemail; we usually answered the phone whenever it rang.)* He kept insisting, from the beginning of the call, that he only wanted to know how I was doing. He did not seem intent on pressuring me to come back. So I settled down on the floor in the hallway upstairs and vented raw emotion to him over the phone. I mostly talked about recent experiences in MFT and the D.C. Church. I never mentioned Danny, or the sexual-petting drama that had happened while I was living in the Shoman family's apartment (and resulted in me being transferred to a different "mission"). He never mentioned that either, nor did he apologize for anything. Perhaps wanting some mending, via remorse, to take place between us, I offered up my own apology.

"I'm sorry I was such an emotional basket-case at times," I said.

There was silence. Then my mind searched for a different time (other than the time he had supposedly sought to soothe me with touch, and crossed a line). A different subject.

"That workshop you had about the challenges of racial unity," I said. "It was a good idea, and I about blew it by getting so emotional. I was the only one there from the Deep South, and I probably should have kept my mouth shut. I never really knew black people other than our maids, before I joined The Family. But when you asked if anybody had any relevant stories to tell, I figured you expected me to say something. So I talked about my awkward attempt at being friends with a black girl I'd worked with at Sears. When you stopped me, told me to sit down, and said I sounded like I felt guilty, it was like some dam broke. I couldn't stop crying, and I felt like I had ruined the workshop. Nobody had much to say after that. Remember?"

Art Shoman laughed a little. "I miss your crying," was all he said on the subject of my emotional drama, and all he said that felt really personal. Then he took on a serious tone, intentional and heartfelt, but abstracted. He was sending me love, with and from that force we had learned to draw on (bigger than ourselves). "You don't have anything to apologize for," he said. "You take good care of yourself now. Best wishes with your education and all of your future endeavors; I have no doubt that whatever you do will be wonderful. Please tell your mother I said hello and best wishes to your family."

I also got a letter from Audra, which she signed for both she and Art. It too was warm but somehow impersonal. The most personal thing she said was that she wished they could have protected me. But I felt that the word "you" was meant for all of she and Art's "spiritual children" who no longer lived with them, not just me personally.

Except for a few spelling errors, it could almost have served as a form letter. P.R. (public relations, and what we called informally in the school system, "covering your ass"). As I had written to them about some of the problems I had while serving in the MFT, Audra's letter seemed to be referring to bad things that happened *after* I left their Center (without acknowledging what happened in her own apartment, right before I was sent away). I kept no copy of the letter but think I had relayed the worst incident in my experience on the Mobile Fundraising Team (an event that had marked the beginning-of-the-end of my willingness to serve with that branch of the UC, and the beginning of a feeling that I just wanted to go back to the last place that felt like *home*- though Audra was not about to invite me back there).

There was a sister who asked me (as Team Mother), if she could stay back at the campgrounds for the day when she was not feeling well. I told the male Team Leader, who was our driver, that the young woman needed a day off. But he insisted that she come with us to sell our flowers. During that day she left the shopping-center parking-lot where she was dropped off, caught a ride, and was assaulted by a trucker.

Audra's responding letter said that bad things happening in the organization were due to immaturity on the part of leadership by people who did not understand the Divine Principle. I think she was referring to male leaders who got out of bounds at times when women should have been in charge, especially in regards to other women. (The Divine Principle teaching recognizes a female aspect of God, equal to the male.) "Art & Audra" was how she signed the letter, with both names in her handwriting. I appreciated the gesture but felt that if he had any part in it, Art could have signed his own name.

Art's call to my mother's house helped some, as his voice was warm and seemingly from-the-heart. But I communicated in a much more personally revealing way than either of them (still not talking, however, about what had happened to separate us). I guess Art and Audra, like many leaders, had learned to radiate a detached warmth. And maybe they did care about me, in a way. At least we ended things between us by wishing each other well (and I still wish them, and their family, well).

"To you and yours too," I said at the end of my conversation with Art, feeling flushed with emotion but not crying. I put the phone back on its hook, on that little stand with the giant phone book, in the hall outside my bedroom (where the suitcase I'd packed three years earlier, when I left with Art Shoman's One World Crusade team, was returned to Mama Sue's house- as was I. Hopefully, no-harm-done).

Gabe called too. He had left the Unification Church and returned to San Francisco. Things had gone downhill for him after Beth left his northern Center for a different mission. I got a nervous feeling in my stomach talking with him, like maybe he was looking for a woman. I had too much pride to be Gabe's second pick, especially when I knew I had been Danny's first pick. I rattled on and on about my new life, telling Gabe that Danny and I were still in touch (since we had at least exchanged cards). When I told him I was back in college, he asked what I wanted to do if I got a degree.

"Maybe be an English teacher," I said.

"An English teacher…" he said musingly, as if he himself was entertaining the idea.

Gabe had always liked to read, I remembered. When my feelings for him were still new and tender, Gabe had once made a point of letting me know that both he and Beth were "more well-read" than me (though it had been him who'd insisted I had more important things to do than going back to college, in the fall of '72). I had told him that I was more of a writer than a reader, when I had the free time. It had been an emotional issue between us then, since he, as Center director, seemed to be in a position to do either at his leisure. He had been at the door of the women's room then, reminding me that the others were downstairs in study groups, when I'd argued for that private time to write in my journal.

There were so many emotionally-charged memories between us. On the phone with Gabe, my pride kept trying to tap it all down, but my heart let little bits of love bubble up here and there. He sounded lonely. I had the feeling Gabe was a bit lost when he called me during that first year after leaving the Family. I did not hear from Gabe personally again, nor did I hear *of* him (other than little stories from my brother about the trip out West they'd taken that previous fall, after Gabe left the Church) for years. (It was Beth who brought news of Gabe in the later '70s after she had visited his family, a wife and four daughters, in San Francisco. Beth was still in the UC when she visited, nervously near time for "the blessing" of a Moon arranged marriage. I never heard from either of them since.)

Still going through my suitcase, after leaving the Unification Church in early 1975, I had found addresses for a few friends that I thought I wanted to stay in touch with at the time (whether I went back to the mission or not). I had sent Fanny a card, because I had her home address from when she wrote to me after staying with her mother and siblings when her father died. She was still loosely affiliated with the Church and somehow managed to get a mission involving a visit to the Center near me, so that she could come to see me. (Her hierarchical connection would probably still have been through the Mobile Fundraising Team, under direction of the national church and Mr. Nolan who had given me a plane ticket home for Christmas). I was glad to see Fanny, who brought me an unexpected gift. She presented me with the freshly dry-cleaned, full-length, camel-colored dress-coat she had borrowed from me.

"Fanny; you could have kept it," I said. She was all smiles and hugs and insisted I have it. I traded coats with her, giving her the more casual, shorter navy car-coat I had originally picked out for all the girls in our MFT group when I was "Team Mother". Franny, forever the sport, seemed as happy to get her old coat back as I was mine. I returned Fanny's smiles and hugs and mostly enjoyed her visit at my mother's house. We moved about on the main floor, from the living room to the kitchen, from the back balcony to the front porch, drinking ginseng tea and talking casually, reminiscing.

We'd had a special bond within a strange, changing family-of-sorts, clinging to each other as we had moved around like migrants or gypsies. However, despite our bond (or maybe because of it), I felt increasingly drained as Fanny and I interacted at my mother's home. Though I felt no less affection for Fanny, I remember also feeling strangely relieved when she left. On some level, I think I was just emotionally exhausted. With all the calls I had been getting from the D.C. Center, I was feeling defensive toward Unification Church members and did not make an effort to maintain a friendship with Fanny after that. Looking back, though, I think she really may have *wanted* to visit because she just genuinely loved me and missed me as a friend (even *if* her way of getting her plane ticket involved a mission to draw me back into the organization, or at least do some good damage-control PR for the church). I think she was a bit lost at the time, in limbo, not really wanting to go back to either the UC or her physical family. She wrote me a letter later that year, saying she was getting married to her old high-school sweetheart (though I knew that had not been an ideal relationship for her). I wondered if I should have helped her more.

Mama Sue Cronkite had met and liked Fanny (and probably could have helped her get back in school and/or get a job, do something toward her own independence). While Fanny visited, my mother was in and out during her lunch hour break from *The News*. She fed Fanny and I tuna-salad sandwiches and slices of her homemade butternut cake, at the little table in her kitchen. She liked Fanny enough that she would have let her move in with us, if I had asked (the way she had let my brother and sister and I move our friends in, off-and-on, since the divorce, until her home felt like a commune at times). At that time, however, I mostly wanted to be alone in my own room, upstairs. There were any number of people that I might cross paths with, in my mother's big, old house, when I went to the kitchen, downstairs, or passed through the living room to leave the house for school or work. In fact, there was one young man (whose name I do not even remember, as I avoided him as best I could) who used my mother's home as a halfway house when he left the Unification Church. Apparently, he had met her after I left town with a travelling branch of the church.. When Mama Sue missed me, she would take food to the Center where I had lived, and show them how to cook it. So she was a friend to the local UC, without being a member. She became known as a sympathetic and accessible adult. As a public figure of sorts, she was that anyway. Sue Cronkite's name was printed with the newspaper's list of editors, daily, and she was listed in the phonebook (which then included addresses).

This one particular (and peculiar) young man who came to Mama Sue's house, with sleeping bag and duffel bag in tow, was on his way to his mother's home (a day's bus ride south of us) but took his time with us before leaving. We were neutral territory. We did not speak for or against Rev. Moon or his Church. We were willing to listen to struggling souls. I, however, found the conversation with him to be quite draining. My tired brain must not have let him make much of an imprint, as I would not have remembered him well enough to include him here if my mother had not brought him up.

At this writing, over coffee with my visiting mother in the winter of 2022, she reminded me of a young man who wandered into our home nearly half-a-century ago and basked in our Southern hospitality for a bit. His hair was dark and his eyes were strange- barely focusing as he rattled on and followed us around the house, venting his confusion and asking if there was anything he could do to help. Mama Sue was not interested in training him to be a member of our household. He was in-between, and she wanted to help him find his way home. Like me, he had nothing against the Unification Church but no longer wanted to be a part of the particular Crusade he had been participating in. As for going home, something was holding him back. When he finally asked Mama Sue to take him to the bus stop, to travel to his mother's place, he asked for a ride to the police station first. When my mother asked him why, he said that he needed to report a "missing person".

"Who?" Sue Cronkite asked.

"My father," the young man said. "He left my mother and I, when I was six-years-old."

This young man told my mother that he had been filing a "missing person report" in every town he visited during his travels. (Mama Sue could not control the sudden surge of emotion that brought tears to her eyes, both then and now.)

I have often heard it remarked that people who follow cult leaders are looking for fathers. Maybe we all are (even our fathers themselves, who often seem at-a-loss, somehow, and have turned to various father-gods, as well as mother-gods, since the beginning of human history).

I had an encounter with my own father-wound soon after coming home for Christmas in 1974. My stepfather, the "Daddy Dick" of this story, died. I traveled south to his funeral, with my mother and sister. We sat in back of the church. His five daughters (the eldest being around my mother's age) and their families filed in and were seated in front with his widow (a woman closer to his age, who he had married soon after the divorce in 1972). As soon as I saw my stepsisters the tears started coming, sometimes convulsively, and continued throughout the event. It was like I could not turn off the tap (just choked it back to a trickle at times). There was the sense that I belonged but did not belong. His daughters were not my sisters, but they were, but they weren't. He was my dad, but he wasn't, but he was. I had lost someone who never really belonged to me. And I certainly had not belonged to him. The year after I turned eighteen, I'd had my last name changed back to my father's name (not as a tribute to my own- who had allowed my stepfather to adopt me- but as a tribute to truth. With adoption, my birth certificate had been a lie).

So there was no wonder a spiritual leader who was called "True Father" had appealed to me. And there was a tug-of-war going on inside me, as well as in my life.

Becky Farriday was the next Unification Church member that I remember visiting us at Mama Sue's house, in 1975, after I left the movement. Like Fanny, Becky was essentially a genuine person, but her visit felt different. She was clearly on a mission. I was her mission. I had lived in the same house as her, in Washington, D.C. We had gotten along okay. I respected her and liked her, but (like the older stepsisters I had grown up being familially associated with) we had not really been close enough friends for me to want to continue being connected with her. She was older than me and had kept her distance. We had never shared a room or snuggled up next to each other in sleeping bags. Becky had been the house mother at the grain-arium factory (and my most recent female "higher center", in Divine Principle terms). She was always busy with her "Blessed Family" (a husband and two small children), not-to-mention the herd of young Moonies that occupied all but one room of their house (a UC "Center"). On some level I knew that Mr. Nolan had given me to her for spiritual nurturing after my bad experience in the MFT. She was a gentler leader than I had known there, but Becky had clearly had not been up for the job. She had been motherly enough to see that I needed mothering (I had seen that look of concern and guilt whenever we'd bumped into each other), but she had clearly been too drained to pay me much attention. Now Mr. Nolan had apparently given her yet another mission. She flew down and visited both Mama Sue and I at home. We had tea in the living room.

Becky immediately complimented my "new look", while her expression said she was actually shocked. I had unselfconsciously picked what I thought was the most cheerful looking item in my little closet full of hand-me-downs. The shirt I wore for Becky's visit did not look like a hand-me-down, but it was. I didn't have many new things but certainly did not want to wear my old clothes, some of which I had already gotten rid of. (The only really new thing I owned was a blue-grey London Fog rain-cape my mother had given me for Christmas- perfect for wearing to the bus stop once I'd started going to college classes and working part-time.) I had not yet done much shopping for myself, but Mama Sue and Sissy had generously given me some of their stylish cast-offs. This meant that my blouse was a too-bright one they'd had second thoughts about wearing, my jeans were last year's style and too short for me, and my peacock-feather earrings didn't exactly match everything (but filled in that space between my ears and the shoulder-length I was trying to grow my hair to). The day Becky came, I wore a shockingly colorful polyester blouse, with large, exotic pink flowers on a turquoise background. My hair had grown out some, and I had rolled it. I may have even had on make-up. (It wasn't the real me, yet, but I didn't look like a Moonie missionary anymore.)

Becky, as usual, looked like a plain-Jane Moonie housemother (in other words, like a nun on her day-off from wearing a habit). Becky was soft-spoken and sincere, as her eyes met mine. "I know from experience," she said, that us sisters need to take a break from the mission sometimes, because it is essentially Father's mission and it can be very masculine. It feels good to get some new clothes, and have our hair done on occasion. But when there is a commitment, as I believe there has been in your case, a lengthy separation from the Church Family can be tragic," Becky said to me, in pure Moonie talk, as if my mother (who did not speak that language but clearly understood it at this point) was not there.

Mama Sue and I began making our case for my new life, as gently-but-firmly as we could.

Becky paused to pull something from her heart. She used her right hand in a gesture that went to her heart, then opened out toward me. "I feel like this is...a *divorce*," she said, squeezing her eyebrows together, frowning and shaking her head slightly from side-to-side, as if in puzzlement and disbelief that I showed no interest in returning to the situation I had left.

I felt detached. Here was this person I had lived in the same house with, but never really gotten to know, and she looked like she was on the verge of tears.

"I still feel like part of the Family," I said, "but in a different way. It's like I have a different mission. I want to serve God as an artistic person. I want to work from my own creative inspiration, my own gifts. Plus I feel that my family needs me here. I have younger siblings. And I have a job, working with little children."

"So you're doing what you want to do?"

"For now, yes," I said.

"Well, I just hope that you will continue to pray, and make sure you are doing what *God* wants you to do," she said. "And know that you are always welcome to come back. That is what I am really here to tell you, and I just wanted to say it in person," Becky said, glancing at Mama Sue, and then back at me.

I thanked her. Mama Sue politely offered more tea, which Becky declined as she rose. I responded to Becky's offer of a hug as Mama Sue opened the front door. And Becky flew back to her family, and The Family, in Washington, D.C.

It was just weird to me. I did not really doubt Becky's sincerity, but whatever she felt did not reach my heart. I don't think I was capable, at that age, of fully appreciating the fact that she went out of her way to reach out to me, leaving her own babies at home. I knew from working with pre-school children that some mothers felt guilty when they dropped them off, and some kids cried. I had not yet been a mother, so I did not understand that it is a twenty-four-hour a day job, and a priority that (for a true mother) never ends. I did get an inkling that Becky, and maybe the UC (probably Mr. Nolan, who had put me in her care) wanted me (and/or my journalist mother) to know that I was important to them. However, if I was so important, why had I felt so unimportant when I was *there?*

Shortly after that I got a beautiful, silk-screened painting in the mail, rolled up in a cardboard tube. It was signed, only with two tiny initials, by the lovely sister who had taken me out for a cucumber sandwich in D.C. (and taken me with her on a lobbying mission at the Capitol, which frankly I had liked far less). There was a sky-blue background with a rainbow and a white dove carrying an olive branch over a blue-green ocean with childlike renderings of small fish. In black ink calligraphy (centered over sky and sea) was written a verse:

"But ask the beasts and they will teach you,

or the birds of the air and they will tell you,

or the plants of the earth and they will teach you,

and the fish of the sea will declare to you:

'Who among all these does not know that

the hand of the Lord has done this?'

Job 12: 7,8."

I was thrilled to have it, but I did not trust the motive behind the gift. I felt that Becky must have told the sister who sent the painting that I wanted my mission to be of an artistic nature. They were trying to make the point that there were people in the UC doing artistic things. That was how I interpreted the gift. They had an agenda. I appreciated the gift but wanted friends with no agenda. Still, she had given me an olive branch. There was land, and I had found it. The Unification Church had been an ark for me, in the turbulent waters of my time. But I had no desire to get back on board. And I was increasingly less tolerant of those who tried to sway me that way. (Though it would be years before the force of that tide completely stopped breaching the shores of my mind, occasionally tugging at my insides, with or without Unification Church members in my life.)

There is no discounting that my mother was in The News business. There was a notice in the newspaper about me coming home (not written by her, but by one of her coworkers) soon after I enrolled at the University winter semester of 1975. It had my senior picture from a local high school. Home-girl was back, attending college, working with children at a day care center- just the facts, no doubt relayed by my mother, with a photo shared from her wallet. A few of my old friends from high school saw it and got in touch with me (but some, who probably also saw it, kept their distance).

A year later, there was a more in depth story, as the editor of the religion section of *The News* called me for an interview. There was little of the Moonie missionary left of me by then, but I did take *her* (the best of my old Moonie self) to one of the churches that called me after the article was published.

Though the headline of the article was something about a "Disillusioned Moonie", it was well-balanced. Yes I had come home exhausted and angry about some things, but I did not blame Rev. Moon personally. Still, readers took what they wanted to take from it. By the time I started getting phone calls about the article, I had already learned to sense who wanted a negative, sensationalistic story. (My mother had even turned down the infamous Helen Gurley Brown, of Cosmopolitan *magazine, who was hoping for some wild kidnapping story about how she got her daughter out). Worse than the publishers who wanted a quick fortune from a cult-thriller, I was surrounded by Bible-belt preachers who wanted a come-back-to-Jesus story.*

I took the one invitation from a church that seemed simply to want me to contribute to the education of their young. And I took the best of the missionary persona I had actually carried my truest heart and most sincerely truth-seeking mind inside of. I also took my mother, Sue Cronkite, with me, and she sat and watched and listened, proud as the day I was born.

What Mama Sue said afterwards was, "I guess you really did learn something."

I had put on my plaid kilt with a white blouse, stood at a blackboard in the youth fellowship hall of a large and well-established Baptist Church in the most prestigious neighborhood in the largest city in my state, and taught the Divine Principle to the teens and young adults in their "World Religions" study series. Afterwards I got a letter from their youth pastor, a mature gentleman not unlike President Jimmy Carter (who taught Baptist Sunday School his whole adult life). The pastor complimented me on the "poise" with which I gave my knowledgeable presentation (which had biblical references throughout). He also expressed hope that I would return, which I did not. By then I was more likely to be fishing with Danny in some mountain lake, early Sunday mornings.

"happily ever after"

In 1975, Danny Hart was the most important visitor I got, from my Moonie days. He had also freed himself from the hierarchy of the UC in 1974. Danny was a different story. Although I was consciously looking for friends with no agenda, at that point, I can't say that Danny had none. He, naturally, had Mother Nature's agenda (where I was concerned). But, so did I. I was a lonely misfit in a sexually oriented world. And we had become increasingly romantic pen pals, and our phone calls (sweet but short, with our parents complaining of long-distance charges) were getting steamy. There was something in the air. I was listening to the love songs coming from Sissy's radio, in the room next to mine.

I no longer believed that my sexuality had anything to do with the devil, or that I had "original sin" *(although I would be haunted by the archetype of Eve and her mythological Fall throughout most of my life, suffering the serpentine seductions of romantic vs. religious notions for decades to come).*

After I'd answered an old valentine Danny had sent to me from his parents' home (after he had left the Church, and before I had), we exchanged letters. Mine were longish and flowery friendship remembrances, with little poems and quotes from popular songs (and repressed romantic undertones, like someone from a different time-somehow both a hippy and a Victorian lady). His were personal news updates, on nice masculine stationary, earth-toned with matching envelopes. He never wrote more than a few, polite pages, and only on one side. But the message was between the lines: we still wanted each other. During spring break from his community college classes, Danny came down. He brought a dozen "sweetheart roses" (white, etched with deep red) and a rose-quartz "friendship ring" (which was also my birthstone and fit the same finger where he would later place a diamond engagement ring, followed by a band of gold). His hair had grown out some, and he wore tight jeans and boots, and a leather jacket. He looked sexy. He brought his guitar too, and that book entitled "Hits of the '70s". My family welcomed him, took him into our roomy old three-story house (if you counted the basement, where my brother had an apartment that opened above ground on the back side of the hill). So, I was in trouble before I could blink (much less think). But isn't that how life usually starts?

As natural as it may have been, the mating dance that happened between Danny and me, that year when we were both twenty-one, was not smooth or elegant. It was quite rough. One day I was praying and singing and sprinkling holy salt around my siblings' beds, another I was having sex with Danny on whatever bed we happened to find ourselves anywhere near when the mood struck us and nobody else was around. Not that I had not tried to keep him at bay for a while.

Danny's moving down was based more on an agreement between he and my brother than Danny and I. After visiting me that spring of 1975, and making friends with my brother, Danny started making his own connections and made his own way down. With Danny's knowledge of electronics, Davie easily got him a job with our old friend Will's dad, who was expanding beyond TVs and needed a repairman. And Davie had a fold-out couch Danny could flop on in the basement, until he got his own apartment.

Meanwhile, I stayed upstairs with my mother and sister. And, though Danny kept a respectful distance from our private spaces, he wasted no time making his moves when we were out in that sporty little car of his. Driving back and forth to work, he had spotted enough cheap motels to get ideas about where he would take me. But I wasn't even sure I wanted him kissing me, with his blue eyes blurred from smoking pot. I kept telling him, when he would start to kiss me, that we needed to have a serious talk before we went any further. Then after one of our evenings out for dinner and a movie, he got me into a motel room. His angle was that we could have that private talk I had been wanting, for as long as I wanted, without anyone interrupting us.

I pictured one of those little tables near the front window, drapes drawn, with two chairs (hopefully comfortable). But there was nothing to sit on, in the cheap place he took me to, other than a queen-sized bed. And he was bigger than me.

I'm not saying Danny raped me. We were already physically affectionate, and we were both more than ready for the sex. But I was not ready for Danny. With no-holes-barred, his shenanigans outside the Unification Church were more than I could control. Not that it should have been my job, as it had been as his "spiritual mother", but my journals from *after* we'd left the Church have lists of what I thought

401

Danny "must" do and not do. Not that he was anything more than entertained by the fervent counseling that my pretty face offered him. In reality, when he got in trouble with the law that same first year, it took my mother and her lawyer cousin and her friend the judge and Danny's parents flying down with their money to get him out- of jail, no less. That was after he picked up a hitch-hiker who also happened to be an undercover narcotics agent, and sold him some pot.

The law took his sporty Toyota Celica, but his parents bought him a brand new (but cheap, four-cylinder) Chevy Vega and rented him an apartment near his work. They furnished the place too, set him up for basic housekeeping. There was a brand new set of queen-sized box-springs and mattress, propped on a bare-bones metal frame. There was an earthtone upholstered couch with modern lines, surrounded by a blocky coffee-table and matching, vinyl woodprint covered press-board end-tables. The dishes were modern, brown earthenware. And the pots and pans were sturdy stainless steel. There were even big, wood-framed nature prints (one an autumn country scene, and the other a stormy seascape), fit for motel décor. Danny would add a hardwood hutch when he found one, with a shelf for his electronics books and a sort-of desk for sorting his mail and paying bills. A friend who knew I loved red would give us her mom's old formica and chrome table, 1950s diner style. And we would play house, shacking up when we pleased, 1970s America style.

Looking back, that stormy seascape, given to him by his parents, would be the most telling of Danny's first furnishings. Despite disagreements about how Danny's lifestyle, and ours together, should proceed, I would manage to get an engagement ring (of chunky gold, with a small but prominently displayed diamond, of Danny's private picking) for my next birthday after he got his apartment. We would be engaged for several turbulent years before marrying. I kept my room at Mama Sue's house (near downtown and the university) and visited Danny midweek and on weekends. At first he would pick me up, for a date, but end up keeping me until I had a class that I was not willing to skip (or drop). His apartment was in the suburbs near where I had gone to high school, so I knew my way around to do the shopping or take his clothes to a laundromat while he worked. Then I could take his car back to his shop and watch the register while he ran errands. Eventually he bought a used van and started letting me drive his little car.

My mother had introduced me to Planned Parenthood (which had been in The News, when it opened up in the Universitiy campus area that previous year) not long after Danny came down. The pill was still relatively new, but could easily be gotten for free by low-income students. So I managed my reproductive life long enough to get an education (if not a degree). I continued my studies in the Humanities for several years, and worked my way up to a paid position on the college newspaper staff (but participated less, and dropped classes more often, when Danny rented a house on the outskirts and I started spending more time at his place).

For a long time, I carried things back and forth in a cardboard box. When I got mad at Danny, which was often, I could easily gather my things and return to my room at my mother's house. But, eventually, I moved in with Danny and married him. With time alone while Danny was at work, I started working on this book (*personal project of a lifetime, when there is such a thing as "spare time", which was far from plentiful during the working years- especially those spent as a single mother*). Danny's shenanigans did not end, though there were lulls that made me think they might. (And it was nearly a decade into the marriage, which had come after nearly a half-decade of being "engaged" to him, before I would stop trying.) Ultimately, my efforts at shaping (trying to control) the young man I had chosen as a mate only served to help him bloom into a flaming "asshole" (like my temperamental stepfather had been, and like the MFT team-captain I had hated). And when I felt trapped, I managed some shenanigans of my own.

So it was not all roses and rings. But is it ever? And had I married within Rev. Moon's church, would it have been any better? Maybe; maybe not- from the variety of stories I have heard about "blessed marriages". I do not personally know any "ideal families" (and have heard too many stories about Rev. Moon's assortment of children to believe his was more ideal than most). All humans struggle with immaturity in love, it seems (as does the human race itself). Adam and Eve have still not evolved enough to deserve each other, to grow up in time for reproduction to be emotionally painless for all involved. And yet we try.

So Danny and I tried. And I would never say that we failed. We had two beautiful and bright children (a son and a daughter), and we made a home for them. We did not stay together forever, "in sickness and health, till death do us part". So we succeeded in some ways, and failed in others. Hopefully we have forgiven each other our trespasses. Maybe we learned some things along the way.

I certainly have learned more than I have sometimes wanted to know. I have followed the light, sometimes lingering too long as the sun was setting, sometimes struggling to find my way in darkness, sometimes revolving around a brighter orb until I became a mere reflection. I ultimately had to find my own light again, to shine from within.

In my youth I hoped to write a book that would have a heroic and romantically satisfying ending, inspiring the next generation. At this point, however, I have lived alone for over a decade-and-a-half. But maybe there is something heroic, even romantic, about female independence. Taking an early morning walk on the beach recently, I saw a new version of an old fairy-tale phrase on the back of another woman's t-shirt. It read, "And she lived happily ever after."

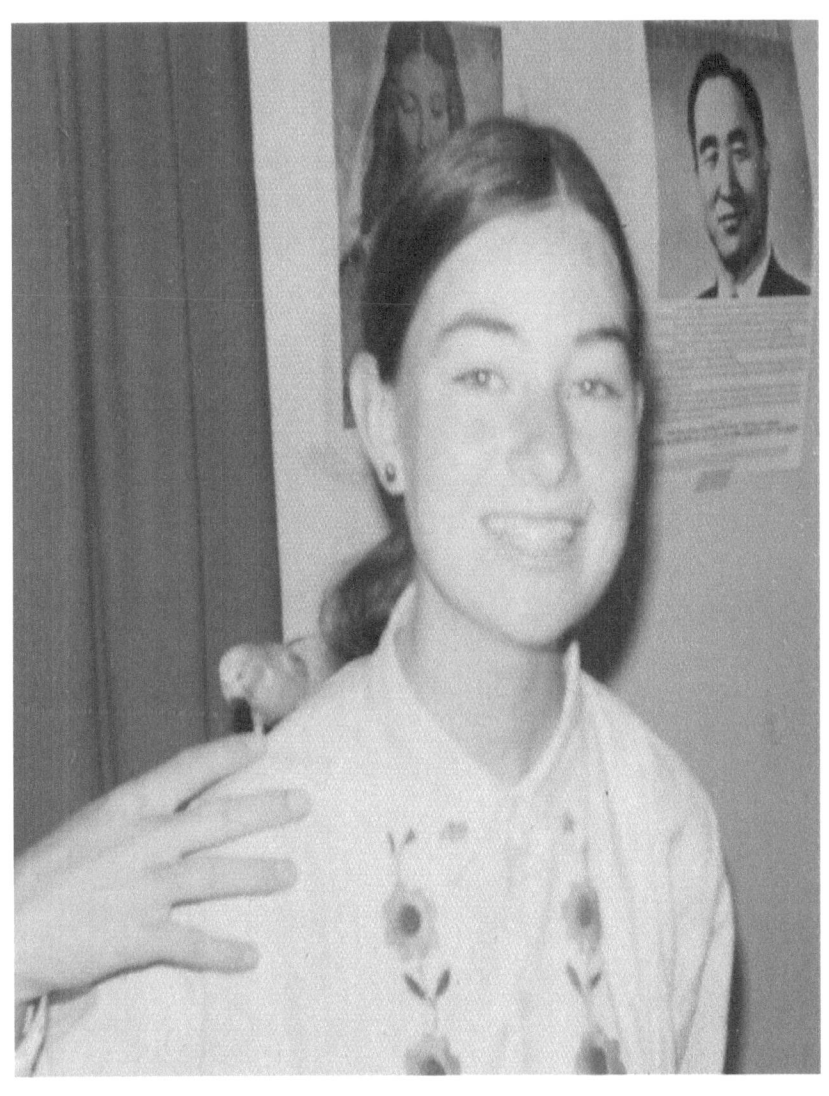

Author in UC Center in 1973. Poster of Rev. Moon on wall.

Author with her mother, Sue Cronkite, in Washington, DC 1974.

The author lives in the Tampa Bay Area, near her children and grandchildren. She is recently retired from working in supportive services for the public school system for nearly three decades. As a young adult she studied English and Journalism, worked for two college newspapers, won an award for a short story, and published poetry in literary arts anthologies. While raising her children and working, she continued to write in journals, as a personal outlet. During the pandemic lock-down, and with her subsequent retirement, she found time to take her writing to a different level. This is the first book she has offered for publication.